A DIFFERENT KIND OF WOMAN . . .

She waited a moment before speaking. "I . . . want to thank you for saving my life. I know you have found me . . . irritating. Not exactly irritating. Disturbing. No, that's not a good word . . ."

"Carsie." He set his hands gently on her shoulder and turned her toward him. "There is no need to thank me for anything. As for irritating, oh yes, you've been that. Disturbing?" He fell silent. Moments passed.

"Yes, you have disturbed me, Miss Carson Rose Summers," he went on. "Miss drum-banging champion of women. You aren't like other women."

"You've told me that before, and—"

"Don't talk, or I'll never get this out." He drew her close to him and his gaze penetrated right to her soul. "You aren't like any other woman I've ever known. Right now I want to kiss you as you've never been kissed before. And I don't know how you've managed to make me feel like this . . ."

She was melting under his touch, struggling to keep herself from falling into the sheltering embrace of his arms, the protective armor of his chest.

"Now, unless you have strong opposition, I'm going to kiss you." He bent his head, hesitated a fraction of a moment, then caught her lips in his.

He was right. She had never been kissed like this before . . .

Other Zebra books by Garda Parker

ARIZONA TEMPTATION
OUT OF THE BLUE (To Love Again)
TEMPTATION'S FLAME
LOVE AT LAST (To Love Again)
SCARLET LADY
BLUE MOUNTAIN MAGIC
CONSENTING HEARTS (To Love Again)

THE
BARTERED
BRIDEGROOM
GARDA PARKER

ZEBRA BOOKS
KENSINGTON PUBLISHING CORP.

ZEBRA BOOKS are published by

Kensington Publishing Corp.
850 Third Avenue
New York, NY 10022

Zebra and the Z logo Reg. U.S. Pat. & TM Off. The Lovegram
logo is a trademark of Kensington Publishing Corp.

First Printing: December, 1995

Printed in the United States of America

To
Amelia May
You can do anything you want to!
Love, Grandma

With thanks to
JeanPaul Janeck, Director
The National Circus Project

Prologue

The Journal of Carson Rose Summers

23 May 1866

I am utterly outraged! How can this be happening? I, as leader of the St. Joseph League of Liberated Ladies, am mortified.

My dearest friend, Sophie Baker, has gone off to that wild place, Montana, with a group of unscrupulous men engaged in the distasteful and ruinous practice of bride-selling to Western gold miners.

How could Sophie have succumbed to the lies so sweetly woven by those shysters? And after all the times we talked about it. Marriage! What is that? Just another way for men to keep women in bondage, own them, make chattel of them.

What kind of a friend was I to have been unable to stop her from leaving? I can't let Sophie be alone, no matter how strongly she feels about what she did. She might be killed—or worse. I simply have to do something about it now, that's all there is to it.

Perhaps taking on the challenge of Sophie's rescue will be the very thing to make me feel satisfied at last. It seems that no matter how hard I work, I feel *un*satisfied, as if something is missing. And I can't stop my thoughts.

There's only one thing for me to do. I'm going to that godforsaken place they call Virginia City.

One

Clint Bonner had been hoodwinked.

He shook his head and leaned over the top corral rail of the St. Joseph Westward Freight Yard. Four women clustered on the wood platform unpacking and repacking their belongings, discarding nothing that he could see. Three of them were clad in what he could only describe as city evening attire, even though it was barely noon. The fourth woman hung back, her plain blue dress a calm contrast to the splash of the other bright costumes.

The day was already hellfire hot and the low wind hung thick with the opposing smells of their exotic spiced perfume and the earthiness of the Missouri River. He drew a threadbare bandanna from his back pocket and swiped it across his moist brow and the back of his neck under his long hair.

When Miss Phoebe Goodnight of Goodnight's Good Times Emporium contacted him by letter regarding the moving of her business to Virginia City in Montana Territory, Clint had just naturally thought he'd be transporting ladies' dry goods. She'd written that her agent would meet him at the freight yard to discuss arrangements. There was no agent that Clint could see. What's more, the three new drivers who'd hired on with him a week ago were nowhere in sight either.

He scrutinized the women through sun-squinted eyes.

Those goods were far from dry. And they were far from ladies.

He pushed away from the rail and strode toward the far end of the corral where a peddler's wagon waited under a shed roof. Woo, the Chinese merchant, had been honest about the value of this wagon. The axles and box were every bit as strong as any Clint had driven or repaired during his circus days. At least he'd made a wise deal when he'd acquired this wagon.

But the Chinese merchant had driven a hard bargain. Mr. Woo had come to him to arrange safe transport to Virginia City for his wife and her wagon of Oriental wares. Clint had hedged since Mrs. Woo would be traveling alone. He much preferred to have only men with him on the trail. If the presence of women was unavoidable, he preferred them married and traveling with their husbands. A single woman could complicate matters. Besides, it was his opinion that whenever a man included a woman in his business he was surely asking for trouble. Big trouble.

Mr. Woo had been mighty persuasive, however. The stipulation was that Clint take Mrs. Woo on ahead along with some additional crates of goods in this wagon. He'd assured Clint that when be arrived later in Virginia City to meet his wife that if all of his belongings—including his wife—were safe, there'd be a considerable cash bonus in the deal for Clint.

Clint held more than vague suspicion about the contents of those additional crates. Opium. Public battles raged over its use in medicine and in Chinese joss houses, and its power of seductive addiction in less spiritual hands. He dismissed it. It was none of his business what his customers carried. He needed the money and he'd bartered the acquisition of the peddler's wagon from Mr. Woo in exchange for transporting his wife and his trade goods. And Clint needed that promised bonus.

If it hadn't been for this, this act of deception that somehow someone had managed to sidetrack him with, he'd be feeling mighty self-satisfied this morning. Bonner Overland Freight Company enjoyed a fine reputation. But he was ready to make this his last trip. He meant to set up his own business in the burgeoning gold-rich Virginia City, and in addition to the consignment freights, he was transporting his own goods, some dry and some not so dry.

He expected this trip to go smoothly—no jinxes, no trouble. Just get there and stop. He was simply going to have to explain to those females clustered on the freight platform that there'd been some mistake and they'd have to make other arrangements. As soon as his drivers showed up, he was going to pull this train out and on its way, and the wagons could begin none too soon to suit him.

He lifted the tarpaulin and checked the security of his own supplies, then concentrated on tightening the ropes and securing the canvas and wood flaps around the wagon.

"Got room on this train for one more, son?" an aged voice crackled from behind him.

" 'Fraid not, old timer," Clint said into the canvas. He hauled a rope up tight and wound it around a wood support. "You'll have to catch the next one." The last thing he needed on this train was an old man to tend to.

"Don't want the next one. Want this one."

"Sorry, no room."

"Make room. Think you're gonna need me . . . Clint."

Clint went still. *Jake.* He whirled around. A leathery-faced old man with a battered top hat crunched over shoulder-length silver hair leaned against the shed post. An unlit corncob pipe bobbled between his teeth.

"Jake Storms."

The old man spat into the dirt. "Last I checked. When'd you get so unfriendly?"

"Jake, you are a sight!" Clint clapped him on the shoulder.

Jake winced under the impact. "So they tell me. You're

lookin' pretty much a sight yourself, son. Hear tell you've got yourself a mighty fine freight business going now."

"Yep, but this is my last run. I'm stopping in Virginia City for good. Making enough with this one to do something I've always wanted to do."

"Still dreamin' of ownin' an opera house."

Clint grinned. "You remember."

"Hard to forget with all that pipe dreamin' out loud you did. Figured there wasn't enough money to be made in the world, let alone the circus, that would build such a thing."

"There wasn't, not in the circus anyway. But there is now. I'm going to do it this time."

"Well, then, it's a darned good thing I'm going with you to keep you out of trouble on the way." Jake hauled a canvas bag out from behind a barrel and proceeded to open the back of Clint's wagon and heave it in. He winced again and reached around and rubbed the small of his back.

"Look, Jake, not that I wouldn't like to have you along, but this cargo is going to be burr enough to me. And I got myself stuck with some shyster's idea of a joke, only the two-bit thimblerigger's too cowardly to show himself." He indicated in the direction of the platform. The women were gone. Clint frowned and turned back to Jake. "Thought you said you were settling down in Chicago some years ago. What happened to that?"

"Changed my mind. That ain't a crime, you know." Jake's gimlet eyes narrowed. "Like I said, you need me. I'm goin' to Montana with you. And I won't hear naught agin the idea."

"No you're not. Don't even think about it. I'd never be able to take it if you got hurt, or worse, while you were with me."

"Well, now, them are mighty kind words. But you ain't got no choice in the matter. I'm here, I'm going, and that's that. Don't talk back to your elders, boy."

Clint tabled the argument for the moment to savor the

reunion with his old friend from circus days. He cocked
his head toward the old man. "What are you doing in St.
Joseph anyway?"

"Don't tell me you didn't notice there was a circus in
town."

"I noticed."

"But you didn't come over." Jake shifted the pipe to the
opposite corner of his mouth and whacked the top of his
hat to keep an errant gust of wind from sweeping it away.

Clint shook his head. "Sure didn't. I'm through with that
life. 'Course if I'd known you were there, I might have.
Would have been worth watching you in action again. Pretty
good job recognizing me after all these years. How'd you
know it was me, Jake? I've changed."

"Knew it the minute I saw you ride in. I taught you how
to straddle a horse, remember?"

Clint remembered, all right. Jake had been a wagon master, trapper, barkeep, you name it, and the best and most
foul-mouthed bullwhacker and circus roustabout anywhere.
Clint had loved the old crank as a boy longed to love his
father. Perhaps he had loved him in place of a father since
he'd never met his own. He looked down and rubbed the
toe of his boot in the sand.

Jake grinned and motioned Clint toward the freight wagons at the far end of the yard. "Come on, got some fellas
I want you to meet."

Before Clint could protest, Jake grabbed him by the arm
and dragged him toward the wagons. He banged on the first
wagon box he came to. The canvas moved, and two women
clambered out and jumped to the ground. Clint shoved his
hat to the back of his head, and took in the curvaceous
figures in front of him. A distinct rustle of skirts and petticoats from behind enticed him around to face two more.
There they were, the four women he'd seen on the freight
platform and one he hadn't seen. The women blatantly as-

sessed Clint, boots to hat. He felt the heat of a flush creep up his already warm neck.

"These here are pals of mine." Jake's eyes twinkled when he said that. "From Goodnight's Good Times Emporium."

Clint turned back to Jake and tugged his hat forward to shade his eyes. "Of all the low-down—"

The oldest of the women stepped forward and draped her arm around Jake's neck, pressing her ample bosom against his chest.

"This here's Miss Phoebe Goodnight herself," Jake said quickly, "proprietor of the place."

"I'm pleased to meet you at last, Major Bonner," Miss Goodnight addressed him with the correct rank of wagon train boss. "Jakey's told us so much about you," she added suggestively in her whiskey and smoke voice.

Clint duly noted that Miss Phoebe was a handsome buxom woman with a mane of thick dark red hair coiled loosely around her heavily made-up face. "How I wish old Jakey here had told me as much about you," he said with exaggerated courtesy. Honey could be no sweeter than his voice at that moment. "Happy to make your acquaintance." He turned toward the fidgeting old man. "Jakey, could I have a word with you?"

"Where's your manners, boy?" Jake's grin twitched. "You haven't been properly introduced to the others. Now this here's Miss Hannah Holmes."

A woman of dubious age whose *cafe au lait* skin suggested Negro blood nodded to Clint. He touched the brim of his hat, and the smile she gave him held warmth without suggestion.

"And this here's a real French *madam-oy-zell.* Lola LaRue."

"*Oui,* Meester Cleent." The black-haired woman dipped a low curtsy, letting her full rouged cleavage press against her black bodice. Her rose pink skirt billowed around her hips. "I am most thankful you have volunteered to transport us, amigo."

Clint gave her a sidelong glance. Interesting accent, he thought. French with a touch of Mexican wrapped around proper English.

The last woman held tightly to Miss Goodnight's arm. She was innocent-looking with a faraway gaze in her pale blue eyes. Clint wondered what she was doing with that group.

"This is Miss Libby Allen." Jake's introduction offered no answer. The young woman nodded silently.

"Miss Allen." Clint touched his hat again. She didn't look at him or speak.

"We ladies are on a goodwill mission in answer to a newspaper notice calling for teachers in the new Montana territorial capital."

Clint smiled wryly at the perceived inference in Miss Goodnight's announcement.

"Virginia City." Jake nodded his head in enthusiastic agreement.

"Yes, I know," Clint said.

Out of the corner of his eye he caught a slight movement. A weathered older woman, appearing not to be one of Miss Goodnight's group, stood by herself at the end of the line of wagons. At her feet lay a bundle of clothing and other belongings tightly wrapped with heavy rope. Clint's eyebrow went up in curiosity at the sight of three bullwhips leaning against the pile. Jake pulled him over and introduced her.

"And this here's Martha Casey. The best lady bullwhacker there is, and maybe the only. Why, she fought in the War dressed as a man. Nobody woulda ever known either, if she hadn't got shot up so bad."

Martha wore her gray hair chopped short. Her clothing suggested the war was not over for her. She still wore part of the Confederate uniform with a long full skirt wrapped loosely over the trousers. The glare she sent Clint from her glass-hard dark eyes made him uncomfortable. It seemed like minutes passed before she turned, gathered her whips, and started around one of the wagons.

Clint tipped his hat to the women then took Jake's arm and firmly drew him aside. "Now look, this isn't gonna work. I admit I was a little slow at first, but I've finally figured out you're the so-called agent Miss Goodnight wrote me about. It was a dirty trick what you did. You'll just have to tell them I'm not going to take them."

"Yep, you shore are takin' 'em," Jake argued. "And don't you worry none, I'll take responsibility for 'em."

"You? Just how in hell are you gonna do that? Looks like you can hardly walk upright. How'd you get dragged into this one, anyway?"

"I wasn't dragged. Just kinda happened natural-like, you could say. I allowed as how I wanted to move west and they allowed the same. They asked for my help. I promised 'em I'd find a way to get 'em there, and I found it. They're payin' me for my expertise you might say, something I sorely need."

"What do you sorely need? Expertise or money?"

Jake ignored Clint's barb. He walked along the sides of the wagons inspecting axles, checking wheels, looking over the way the goods were packed, tightening straps and ropes.

Clint followed him. He couldn't have him looking in Mrs. Woo's wagon. Jake would remind him about past incidents with opium and a few other "medicines" that traveled along with some circus troupes. He'd be madder than a stuck boar and Clint didn't want to experience that. Just as if he were a boy, he didn't want to do anything that would disappoint this cantankerous old man, one of his two greatest friends ever. Still, this trip was too important to him to let anything jinx it.

"Look, Jake, I'm mighty sorry about this, but I can't take

your friends on this trip. There'll be other trains along you can hook them up with."

"Why do you think you can't take them?" Jake asked without looking at him. "What's stopping you?"

"They'll attract the kind of attention I don't need."

"You got somethin' to hide? I'm sure you got some sense of why it might be tough as nails to get the fellas hooked up with another train."

"I do. And I've got the same problem with it."

"Well, I promised them, and I can't leave them here."

"Jake—"

"Never woulda asked, 'cept they're anxious and I promised I'd help. And of course because I felt p'tiklar close to you ever since that time back in New York when I—"

Clint raised a hand. "Oh no, not again. You reminded me for years how you saved my life the night of the blowdown. I thought I'd paid for that a hundred times and then some."

Jake bent down and winced. He rubbed his back where a falling timber had cracked against him as he'd blocked it from hitting Clint during an intense windstorm. He rose and anchored his hat.

Clint let out a capitulating sigh. "All right, you win," he said to Jake's back.

"Win what?" Jake said over his shoulder. "We been arguing over something?"

Clint waited a long moment before uttering the statement that he knew he'd regret later. "I'll take the women."

Jake turned around then. "Never any question about that. So what'd I win?"

"You are the most exasperating old coot . . ."

Jake grinned.

"I'll check the wagons," Clint told him. "I am the wagon major here, just in case you forgot."

"How could I forget a thing like that?"

Clint grinned back at him. "Don't you sound innocent as a babe?"

He set about then inspecting the wagons filled with miners' supplies and merchants' goods he'd been consigned to carry. Satisfied they were secure, he moved to the two belonging to Miss Goodnight and her party. He lifted the tarp off the back of the first one and peered into the gloom inside. Jake was at his back like a tick on a hound dog. A glimpse of highly polished wood caught Clint's eye. He lifted a quilt.

"Is that what I think it is?"

"Depends what you think it is," Jake said evenly.

Clint yanked the quilt away to reveal an ornate bathing tub. A mahogany cap and brass rail circled its rim. Filled with all manner of clothing, it was surrounded by trunks and a mound of quilts.

Clint grabbed Jake's arm and dragged him away from earshot of the women. "That bathing contraption has to go," he rasped. "It's bad enough you're forcing these pals of yours on me, but that thing has to go."

Jake scratched his head, setting his top hat to wobbling. He said nothing. Clint believed he'd just issued a decree that would be followed. Watching Jake's calm reaction, there was just an inkling of question in his own mind whether or not he'd achieved that.

They moved on. In the next wagon he discovered something worse. "A piano?" he whispered sharply.

Jake leaned around Clint, peered into the wagon, eased out, and nodded in agreement. " 'Pears like you still got a good eye, boy."

"Get that thing off. The unnecessary weight will slow our pace."

Jake scratched a wiry sideburn. "I'll have to take it up with the fellas," he said calmly. "There ought to be a vote, you know."

"Women can't vote," Clint averred. "Especially not on my wagon train."

Jake ignored him and went to the group of women. He circled them around as if arming them against a band of marauders. Clint heard the women loudly protest removal of the tub and piano. Jake calmed them and whispered something. Clint strained to hear. He couldn't make it out, but it sounded as if they were agreeing with Jake.

Jake walked slowly back and took Clint aside. "Look, boy," he whispered, "that pianny belongs to Libby Allen. The girl's got no family and no husband. She ain't, uh, capable of, uh, working for a living. She'll need that there pianny out there in Montana to give lessons to support herself. Be a shame to take her livelihood away from her, now wouldn't it? Her bein' all alone in the world and all."

Clint narrowed his eyes at the old thimblerigger standing in front of him. For once Jake had removed the top hat and twisted it 'round and 'round in his gnarled brown hands like a guilty child. Clint raised his eyes heavenward, knowing full well he'd regret it, and softened toward that appeal.

"All right," he whispered back, "the piano can stay. But the bathing contraption has to go." He jerked his head in the direction of the wagon holding the tub to underscore the decision.

Jake nodded. "Now listen, boy, I know jest what you mean about the weight and all, but Miss Goodnight's ladies believe that cleanliness is next to godliness. You know about that. Well, that bath thing is important to them." Jake winked. "You understand."

Clint squelched his urge to break into disdainful laughter. He saw the controlled seriousness in the old man's eyes and feigned total gullibility. Knowing he would for certain regret it later, he pretended to swallow the story. "Yeah, I understand all right."

He realized he'd just accepted Jake and his "fellas" and all their belongings as his responsibility. As always, he could not refuse Jake anything. Face it, he told himself, you're stuck with this lot. Might as well make the best of it. It wouldn't make a bit of difference once they were in Virginia City.

He surveyed the train. With more people and more weight than he'd expected, he'd have to consider a different route. That could mean a lot of things—Indians, high rivers, endless prairie, and . . . snow. Clint frowned into the sky, trying to read the signs.

The two set about organizing the wagons in just the manner they'd done dozens of times during their circus days together. As he walked beside Jake, Clint's head pounded with a myriad of thoughts of the past and the unknown of the future.

A pounding of a different sort and a sharp jab in the ribs from Jake's bony elbow brought him back to the moment. Jake pointed toward the far side of the wagon yard.

Clint peered between the wagons. A parade of sour-faced townswomen marched into the wagon yard bearing banners proclaiming them the LIBERATED LADIES LEAGUE and waving signs emblazoned ABOLISH PAY-FOR-BRIDES. Their leader, a tall woman in voluminous dark blue bloomers, vigorously banged a huge drum which was supported by leather straps over her shoulders and suspended in front of her like a water wheel. She crossed the wagon yard, and the other women followed her like a row of dutiful ducklings. A handful of men with puzzled looks on their faces gathered around the women. Others drew near the crowd, curious about the commotion.

The bloomered one stopped in front of Jake, who tipped his hat to her.

"Afternoon, miss," he said warmly, too warmly to suit Clint. "You sure are lookin' mighty—"

"Determined, Mr. Storms," the woman said with jutted chin. She nodded so vigorously that the huge bun of chestnut hair secured to the top of her head vibrated. "I'm determined, and this time you can't sway me from my mission."

Clint frowned and eyed Jake suspiciously. "If this is another one of your 'fellas,' I'm going to yank that stovepipe hat down over your face till the top of your head pokes through."

"She wanted to hook up with our train," Jake said quickly with a swift glance toward Clint, "but I told her there was no room. She even begged, but I held my ground, I did."

"*Our* train? Since when . . ."

The woman slipped out of the straps and dropped the drum on the ground. It landed with a thud and tinny clatter. She whirled around to her followers and pointed an accusing finger at Clint, shouting, "*This* is the kind of low-down cur who deals in female flesh. Let us vindicate our duped sisters drawn to the West by false promises of noble work as teachers and nurses and who now live a life in slavery to disgusting wretches of men. Let us drive this man and others like him out of our midst, and cleanse the world."

A swell of cheers from her followers filled the air. One of the men guffawed loudly and was roundly thumped on the chest by a particularly overbearing woman. No doubt his wife, Clint figured. Irked and embarrassed, he roughly pulled the rouser aside to a chorus of gasps from her compatriots. He turned her around and peered down into her face, almost nose to nose, and glared into her eyes.

"Lady," he began, then stepped back and blatantly assessed her bloomers and man's white shirt. "I take that back."

She jerked her head and started to speak. He clamped his hand over her mouth. Another gasp from her cadre.

"Not that it's any of your business," he said loudly enough for all to hear, "but I don't deal in female flesh. I don't know what you're talking about. Furthermore I don't want to know what you're talking about. I don't even want to hear you talk. I'm paid to deliver goods. Nobody asks me why I want the money, and I don't ask them why they want the goods."

The woman grabbed his hand with both hers, tore it from her mouth, and wrenched free of his grasp. "Goods! Did you hear that, ladies? He referred to these women as 'goods'!"

The townswomen shouted protests and surged toward Clint, who stepped back, hands out in self-defense. He sent a quizzical glance at Jake. Jake shrugged then burst out laughing.

Spurred by the displayed vote of confidence, the woman raised a finger high into the air and continued. "There is only one thing to do, ladies. I, Carson Rose Summers, avenger of women and writer for *Harper's Weekly*, will go to Virginia City with this wagon train, expose the shameful practice of selling brides, and stamp out its existence once and for all."

Hands on her shoulders, Clint twirled her around to face him once again. He stopped, surprised to realize how young she must be. She might have looked as old as her pinched-up followers with her tightly bunned hair, but her face was young, and her green eyes snapped with fire. He jerked his shoulders, remembering what she'd just publicly accused him of.

"You, Miss Whatever-you-said, are not welcome on this train."

"Afraid to take me along?" she challenged loudly.

"Afraid?" Clint sputtered. "Of what? The likes of you?"

"Aha!" Carson Rose Summers countered, and strained over her shoulder toward the crowd. "He's not afraid to manhandle me in public, but he *is* afraid to allow me passage. It's clear I am a threat. He knows I can make him infamous across the land."

She wriggled out of his grasp and sat down on a freight wagon tongue. One of her followers rushed forward and tied her to it with a short length of rope. To his seething aggravation, Clint observed the wagon to which she was now firmly attached—his wagon, with Mr. Woo's opium crates packed inside.

With a defiant look on her face, she announced, "I shall sit here until you consent to my peaceable passage. If you don't, you shall be forced to drag me out of town trussed like a roast to a spit like part of your 'goods' with—I can assure you—the city constable and this group of citizens following. I shall swear I was kidnapped, my friends shall swear to my testimony, and you shall be arrested."

Straddled over the wagon tongue, she settled into her rope bonds, arms crossed over her chest. Clint bit back a retort he knew would only make this hellcat even more ferocious and bring the wrath of her league down upon him. He did not need any publicity of this sort, although since Jake and his fellas had arrived on the scene, he expected his heretofore clean reputation had a bit of stain on it already. He didn't want to call attention to the opium. And he wanted no more delays.

"Look, Miss . . . what did you say your name was?" He worked at sounding polite and calm.

"Summers," she said with the hint of victory in her tone, "Carson Rose Summers."

"Carson. Is that a girl's name?"

"Are you insulting my name now?"

"No, no," Clint said hastily. "Miss Summers, I do not engage in whatever you said, selling brides."

"Perhaps, then, you are more in the market of buying them."

"I wouldn't take a bride if I was given one!" He let out a long exasperated sigh.

"And just what do you call *them?*" She jerked her head to the side.

Clint turned to look over his shoulder at Miss Goodnight and her ladies, who'd gathered around Jake. Slowly he turned back to Carson Rose Summers. He leaned close to her face and whispered loudly, "Do they impress you as looking like brides?"

She whispered back just as loudly, "It's not me they have to impress!"

Clint threw his hands into the air in utter frustration. He paced back and forth in a short path in front of her, stomping up dust clouds with his boots. Then he slowed the pace. He turned toward the crowd and peered around him with a grin.

"Well, what the hell?" he said for all to hear. "What's one more?"

Carson Summers shifted in the ropes, which were loosening. "And just what are you implying by that . . . uh, implication . . . sir?"

"Yes, what are you implying, Major Bonner?" Phoebe Goodnight stepped to his side, her dark gaze direct and level with his. Her forces gathered behind her. Martha leaned against a wagon wheel and watched with a sullen expression. Mrs. Woo peeked shyly from behind her.

Clint breathed in sharply and let out a long weary sigh. "Please, Miss Goodnight, stay out of this. It doesn't concern you."

"On the contrary, Major Bonner, it does concern me. I will not have you including this . . . *person* . . . with my ladies. She is nothing like us. She is not acceptable to us."

"Well, I should say," Carson spluttered, ". . . or not. That's right. Isn't it?" She cocked her head toward her compatriots, who remained silent and had cleared back in order to give plenty of room to the imposing Phoebe Goodnight.

"I am implying," Clint began slowly through tense jaws, "and of course I could be wrong about this, but I am implying that you, Miss Summers, are a woman. Just one more of the several already booked on this train. Now, should you wish to deny the truth implied in my . . . implication, I would be most happy if you would have at it loud and clear."

"I most certainly do deny it, you insulting oaf!" she shouted.

"Aha!" Clint shouted back, towering over her. "Then I was right! You agree you are not a woman!"

"What?" Carson spluttered. "How dare you? Of course I don't agree with . . . uh, whatever it was you accused me of . . . uh, agreeing to."

"That you're not a woman," he breathed harshly.

"Exactly." Carson nodded her head vigorously, then stopped abruptly. "You tricked me!"

"Yeah, well, you tried to trick me."

"I did not. It's you who are the trickster, tricking innocent . . ." She looked over at Miss Goodnight then around her at the women who lounged against the wagons in suggestive poses eyeing the men in the crowd of townspeople. ". . . tricks." She shifted her weight on the wagon tongue and winced.

Clint noted she was without a traveling bag. This public display was probably all just a ruse to get herself free passage on a wagon train. He decided to take a different tack with her.

"Look, Miss, or whatever you prefer to call yourself, *if* you've got enough money to pay your passage, I might consider letting you go along like everyone else. But if you give me one minute's trouble, I swear I'll put you off the train and I won't care if it's in the middle of a nest of rattlesnakes or a band of murderous desperadoes and scalping Indians. You got that?"

Miss Goodnight planted her hands on her ample hips and glared first at Clint, then at the Summers woman. "Just a moment, Major Bonner. I and my ladies have something to say about this."

Carson moved uncomfortably on her perch and stared up at Clint. She shifted her gaze briefly to Miss Goodnight and the other women who glared at her, then toward the members of the Ladies League who stood with impervious chins in the air, then back to Clint.

"On the contrary, Miss Goodnight. While I know it isn't

exactly recognizable at the moment, *I* am the wagon major, this is *my* freight service, and *I* will take whatever goods *I* want to take and am paid for."

"Let me assure you, Major Bonner," Miss Goodnight countered, eyes blazing, "if you take this dried-up emasculating virgin in men's clothes"—she ignored the collective gasp from the ladies league—"on *our* train we shall be forced to make *your* life more miserable rather than the pleasant time-passing we could otherwise make it. Do *I* make myself clear?"

"Your wagon train?" Clint blustered. "And just what makes you think this is your train?"

"I do," Jake cut in.

Clint whirled on him. "And I call you my friend."

"They're set to pay you more money than you've ever seen, boy, to transport them to Virginia City. That's your grubstake. You need 'em."

"I have money," Carson Summers put in.

"She has money," Clint echoed, glaring at Jake, realizing a beat too late that he'd just defended the suffragist. No one was more surprised than he.

"You ain't seen it yet," Jake countered.

"I—I haven't seen theirs either," Clint faltered.

"I think you can see how much they're prepared to pay. And I can vouch for them."

"I won't ask just how you can."

"Go ahead, I got an answer." Jake held his ground.

"I'll just bet you have."

"No need to fight about this," Jake said, softening.

"That's right. We don't want this one with us." Hannah Holmes sashayed over, hands planted on her hips. She spoke barely above a whisper.

"Well, I'm going anyway," Carson Summers pledged.

Lola LaRue strolled past the gaping townsmen and leaned down into Carson's face, nose to nose. "And everyone weel theenk you're one of us." She let out a high tinkling laugh.

"Oh-h, they wouldn't," Carson Summers breathed.

"They would when we are through with you, beetch." Lola spun around and stuck out her chest, passing as close to the men as she could get without touching them. The women gasped loudly and clutched their own bosoms or glared at their grinning husbands.

"I . . . I can take care of myself," Carson Summers said with sudden timidity.

Clint thought he detected a hint of a chink in the armor of the suffragist. He couldn't let down the pressure now. "Fine. You can go if you really want to, but you'll have to ride in a wagon with one of Miss Goodnight's ladies."

Carson's league compatriots were visibly aghast at such a suggestion. Miss Goodnight's compatriots joined in vocal protestation.

That should do it, Clint thought with relief. He'd created a war between the two factions of women. Miss Carson Rose Summers would have to give in now and walk away quietly. Then maybe this train could get moving on about its business.

But, no. Bearing a look of triumph as one of the league ladies released her bonds, Carson Summers stood up and rubbed her wrists. "And which of you ladies shall I ride with?" She scanned their faces.

"Not with me," Phoebe said emphatically.

"Not with me and Hannah," Lola concurred.

"Got no wagon 'cept Jake's," Martha muttered and gathered up her bullwhips.

Mrs. Woo turned and scurried away in her tightly wound gray garment back to her own wagon.

"She can ride on our supply wagon, Miss Phoebe," the quiet Libby Allen said at last, "and I'll ride with her."

"Libby, you will ride with me," Phoebe said firmly.

"I'll be just fine with—Miss Summers, is it?"

"Yes," Carson said, rushing to Libby's side, "Carson Rose Summers. And thank you . . ."

"Libby Allen."

"Thank you for your generosity, Libby Allen." Carson held out her hand toward the girl, who did not raise hers but stood with a benign smile lighting her face. Carson dropped her hand. "Which one is it?"

"There," Jake pointed to the fourth wagon in line.

"Jakey!" Phoebe said with amazement.

Jake shrugged and popped his pipe back into his mouth.

Carson ran to the Goodnight supply wagon. Clint watched emotionless as she deftly climbed aboard, handling the reins like an old hand and waving to the crowd, who cheered her. The men laughed loudly. Two of the league ladies raced to the wagon and questioned the certainty of her actions. When she reassured them of her commitment and dedication, they each handed up a plump carpet bag to her. She stuffed them behind the driver's box.

Clint watched Jake lift Libby up beside Carson, without a show of strain, then stood back grinning like the clown he'd often played. He wondered if this was what he'd had in mind when he went into the freight-hauling service.

If that were so, it was sure sorry freight he was hauling—one cantankerous old circus thimblerigger with a bad back, a sullen bullwhacker who appeared half woman and half Confederate soldier, a buxom madame of a traveling whorehouse, two of her best employees displaying all their pulchritudinous assets, an innocent girl, a silent Chinese woman in a gaudily decorated wagon filled with Oriental trappings, a load of opium, a piano, a bathtub . . . and one chest-thumping, bun-haired, bloomer-wearing, man-hating suffragist with a savior mission.

A vague voice from his past in the circus echoed through his mind. "As goes opening night, so goes the rest of the run."

Two

Carson Rose Summers settled down in the wagon seat next to the young woman, thankful that the bloomers hid her quaking knees. She wrapped the reins around her hands in expert driving position.

But she was no expert. Knowing how to handle the ribbons came from childhood experience behind the family's old mule, Sally, and a plow. Little Rosie didn't have to drive Sally. The savvy mule knew exactly what to do, but holding the reins and pretending to drive her made Rosie feel powerful, in control like her brothers, if even for only a short time. No one would ever know she faked this little charade this afternoon. Once the drivers arrived and took over these wagons, no one would be the wiser.

She watched Clint Bonner through the swirling dust of the freight yard. He looked exactly like a copy of a picture that appeared in *Harper's Weekly* bearing the caption FRONTIER COWBOY. The same dark hair brushed Bonner's shoulders. He had the long, lanky build in rough pants, but she could tell his back was broader. The cowboy in the picture had a long-tailed mustache, but Bonner was clean-shaven. Their eyes were the same, sharp, seeming to envision something that less adventurous people couldn't even dream about. But the *Harper's Weekly* picture could never capture the ice blue of Clint Bonner's eyes.

He searched the sky with a concerned look as if help, or something, would come from above. Suddenly his searching gaze caught her scrutinizing one, and she was momentarily embarrassed. She held the gaze a moment before her nerve faded, then quickly jerked her head around and performed a settling-in ceremony on the hard bench seat. She wouldn't let Clint Bonner know how frightened she was inside. And she wouldn't let her league sisters know it either. They lingered in the freight yard to give her a proper send-off. And Carson Rose Summers meant to ride off in spectacular victory.

Clint caught the suffragist's victorious glare as she gathered up the reins and looped them around her hands. What happened to a girl that could make her turn into one of those banner-carrying, drum-banging, big-mouthed women? She even had a first name that was usually a last name. Carson. Had she made that up? Well, what did he care anyway? He wanted no trouble from her or from anybody else. He just wanted to get to Virginia City as fast as possible.

He searched for Jake and saw him talking to the women of the Ladies League who'd gathered outside the wagon yard. He could hear his friend regaling them with stories of his wild circus days. Naturally they appeared quite taken with him. Jake could be a charming old buzzard, that was for sure.

Clint scanned the sky again. Those were snow clouds building in the northwest. There seemed never to be a good time to travel this country. Spring was as unpredictable as autumn where snow was concerned. He wished it were closer to summer, but there was no pining over that now. These delays grated on his nerves, and he was all the more anxious to get started because of the sky signs.

Jake strode toward Clint. "We're ready," he announced, clamping his hat down hard on his head.

The action didn't help. The stovepipe perched on his silver hair at a precarious angle. Clint remembered how in the past he'd slyly watched, waiting for the hat to topple off Jake's head. It never had.

"Wonder where the drivers are," Clint said anxiously, scanning the yard.

"They ain't coming," Jake answered quickly.

Clint jerked around. "What do you mean they're not coming?"

"Didn't need 'em, so I fired 'em."

"Fired—? And just how do you think we're going to transport your precious cargo to Virginia City without experienced wagon drivers?"

"The fellas can drive."

Clint's exasperation went sky-high. "Your fellas? You mean your 'teacher' friends here? Crissakes, Jake, I need experienced drivers."

"Now, I won't have you cussin' in front of the ladies. And as for experience—"

"That isn't the kind of experience I had in mind and you know it!" Clint believed he would be taking a big chance traveling across the country with all these women in the first place. There was the added threat of what would surely be snow, or rainstorms at best, and now Jake had fired the drivers without consulting him and turned over the wagons to a troupe of city whores. He let out a sharp sigh. "I will not accept a bunch of women taking on men's work. They can't do it, and I'm not about to let them try."

Jake planted his boots firmly and stood his ground. "Them women can drive them freighters good as any man, and Martha's one of the best bullwhackers around. And with me as guide, nothin' can go wrong."

Clint shot his gaze heavenward. "Nothing can go wrong! You have a real short memory, my friend."

Jake leaned forward and squinted at him, looking as stern as he could. "And you worry a lot for a young'un, you know? You'll be old before your time, boy, if you don't calm down."

"I'll be dead before my time if I listen to you. Remember when you pushed me to do that high-wire act in Chicago? Almost lost my ability to use the experience these *fellas* of yours are clearly in the market for."

"Well, if you'da done it the way I told you, you never woulda slipped off."

"As I recall, you said something mighty vague about I had the feet of a fly and could just stick to the wire," Clint reminded him.

"See? Just shows how you never did pay no attention to what I told you. I said you had to *believe* it, not think it. Sure was pretty plain to me you didn't believe one iota."

"Yeah, well, after I landed with that wire halfway up my privates I almost believed my days in the circus and training animals were over. The only thing left for me was singing women's parts in the light opera."

"I have trouble graspin' here why you're complainin'. You ain't dead, are you?"

Clint shrugged surrender. "Got an answer for everything, don't you?"

Jake grinned. "Make it my business to, son." He stuffed his pipe in his vest pocket. "We best get these wagons situated if we're gonna roll out today. Looks like snow coming."

"For once, you're right." Clint shook his head and chuckled. "But I don't have to like it."

"You'll get over it." Jake started for a saddled horse.

Clint watched the women settling themselves in the drivers' boxes on every wagon, donning gloves and wrapping reins. "Women freight drivers," he muttered. "I'll need a passel of luck since I seem to have lost all common sense." He forced himself to take Jake's advice and remain calm, but the churning in the pit of his stomach told him this would be a trail journey like none other he'd experienced.

Carson Rose heard the entire exchange between Clint and Jake. Her hands perspired till the reins stuck to her palms. Godawmighty, now what was she going to do? She silently importuned Bonner to insist the men be rehired, but she knew that was futile action. Jake Storms had spoken, and no source in Bonner's sky was going to change that stubborn man's mind, she could tell that.

She turned to Libby Allen sitting beside her, silent and relaxed. "Are you a good driver?" Her strained voice carried a note of cheeriness she did not feel.

Libby gave a small laugh. "Oh, I don't think so, Miss Summers."

"Carsie. You can call me Carsie if you like. And don't be so modest," she urged. "I'm certain you're every bit as good as the others."

"Perhaps." Libby's quiet answer held a hint of acceptance.

"Then, here, I'll just turn these right over to you." Carsie shifted her hands and the reins toward Libby. "It is, after all, your wagon, and I apologize if I seemed aggressive by leaping aboard as I did. I didn't mean to just take over."

Libby stared straight ahead and chuckled lightly. "Oh, I thought you were quite thrilling. How I envied your bravery in the face of Mr. Bonner's sternness. You remind me of Miss Goodnight."

"I do?" Carsie tried to cover her dismay at the comparison, but knew she hadn't managed it well.

"Oh, yes, indeed. Miss Goodnight can handle any man."

"I don't doubt that," Carsie muttered.

"You shouldn't. Miss Goodnight can do anything she sets her mind to. Just like you can, I imagine. I was just so very excited when you said you wanted to ride with me."

Libby's voice conveyed sincerity that Carsie believed was honest. Was any woman this good through and through? She had her doubts, yet there was nothing but sheer happiness on the girl's face.

"Yes, well, thank you for your hospitality. I do appreciate it, honest I do. But you take the reins now. I . . . haven't had very much experience with this."

"Don't worry, I'll help you. I've traveled a great deal."

"Well, then, that settles it. I'm quite certain you're an expert driver. You look strong and sensible, with a good eye for direction."

Libby chuckled again. "Miss Summers . . . Carsie, I am

some of those things, and quite possibly I could be all of them." She sighed wistfully. "But I fear it takes eyesight to keep an eye on the direction as you say, and a great deal of strength to drive. Since I'm blind, we could end up in Deadwood Gulch instead of Virginia City and that would make a lot of people unhappy, including you, I imagine."

Carsie stopped cold at Libby's words. She dropped her hands in her lap.

"I sense I've shocked you," Libby said. "I feel it only proper that I should add one more thing in case you want to change your mind about riding with me."

"Oh, I wouldn't change my mind," Carsie said with shaky reassurance. Besides, where would she go? Not one other person on this train wanted her on her wagon. If there was the slightest doubt in her action, Clint Bonner would put her off and make her stay off this train and she wasn't about to do that. She *had* to go to Virginia City. That's all there was to it. There was nothing Libby could say that would make her even consider changing her mind.

"I'm pregnant."

Carsie blanched. "Godawmighty," she whispered.

"Excuse me?" Libby leaned toward her.

"Congratulations," Carsie said loudly, her nervousness overtaking her.

Libby jerked back. She lifted her chin. "I'm blind, Miss Summers, not deaf. There is no need to shout."

"I'm sorry. I'm just . . . I don't know quite what to say. You're pregnant."

"You're just happy for me, I know. You don't have to say anything more."

"Thank you for understanding," Carsie said, profoundly sorry she'd let out her unchecked reaction so quickly. "Will your husband be waiting for you in Virginia City?"

"I don't have a husband." Libby answered without a trace of emotion.

Carsie didn't move. She'd just blundered in again, and what was there to say now. "Oh," she managed.

"Now you know why I can't drive," Libby said simply. "I will need all my strength for the birth of my baby, which will surely happen as we travel."

"Of course," Carsie said dully. She glanced toward Libby, experiencing difficulty imagining how anyone in her plight could possess such good humor, could appear not the least bit daunted by what lay ahead. "Does Major Bonner have a town in mind? I mean, a place to stop when your time comes?"

"Oh, Major Bonner doesn't know about the baby. No one does. Except you now."

Carsie clutched the reins tighter. "Surely Miss Goodnight knows."

"No."

"Why not? You seem rather close to her."

"She'd think she failed me. She's so protective of me, of all of us. But it's not her fault. I went someplace where I shouldn't have gone."

Libby spoke calmly, without remorse, yet Carsie's insides churned. Her heart pounded. That someone could do something so unspeakable to an innocent blind girl . . .

"He . . . the man had no right to touch you unless you gave him the right."

"I did."

"Wh-what?" Carsie breathed.

"I wanted to know what it was like, what the others were doing. I forgot the part about getting with a baby. But it's all right, really. Now I'll have someone to love of my own. I've never had anybody."

Carsie wanted to rage against the injustice of it all. She looked at Libby. On the girl's face, in her voice was no hint of feeling violated, of having been done an injustice. Only a kind of thankfulness for the tiny life she was bringing into the world alone.

Libby turned toward her. "I feel very safe with you, Carsie, very fortunate that you are driving this wagon and I'm with you."

How Carsie wished she shared that sense of security. How she longed to possess real confidence and bravado, the extent to which she displayed them publicly. But no amount of wishing and longing would make them happen. The fear she believed she'd successfully held at bay for a very long time now gripped her.

Libby reached under the seat and extracted a bulging brocade pouch. Deftly pulling the top open, she rummaged around inside and produced a pair of dark leather gloves. "Here, you'll need these. Miss Goodnight's hands got all raw once when we were traveling, and she outfitted all of us with proper handwear."

"Thank you," Carsie said weakly and took the gloves. Her heart pounded in her ears.

"This is just going to be the most interesting trip ever, isn't it?" Libby settled back against the spring-supported wagon seat.

Carsie leaned forward. "*Interesting* won't be the word for it."

Jake swung up into his saddle and threw an arm in the air signaling the move out. Martha's whips cracked and shouts of "Get on there!" mingled with the grind of wagon wheels filled the air. A cheer went up from the crowd.

Carsie looked down at the four oxen nodding at the end of the reins. If only a little magic could turn them into Sally, her heart would settle. As her team pulled out to follow the others, the first yank of her arms away from her shoulders told her there was no magic.

Clint rode his rangy bay horse beside the wagons. He watched Martha on the other side, heard the loud crack of her long whip and the peculiar way she called the bulls.

The oxen responded to her as if they'd been born to the sound of her voice. Much as he hated to give in to the old coot, he conceded Jake was right, at least about Martha being an expert bullwhacker.

His gaze then shifted to light briefly on each of the other women as he rode past their wagons. They were not new to hard times; he could see it in their faces and the set of their bodies on the seats. They could handle this travel. And they could drive oxen teams. Jake had been right about them too.

He wasn't sure about the new one, though. Carson Something Summers. Most of these suffragists were all talk and no action that accomplished much, as far as he could tell. He sent a cursory glance toward her as he passed her wagon. The way her arms were jerking back and forth she'd have them dislodged from their shoulder sockets before the day was out. Who was she trying to fool? She didn't know one whit about driving a team. The oxen knew more than she did, and that was pretty lucky for her. Well, he wasn't about to help her. With any luck she'd give up and he could put her off near the next settlement.

He made a note to check on this wagon often, if only for Libby Allen's sake. The girl seemed so shy and fragile. She hadn't spoken a word to him. He watched her now. Libby was sure taking the ride well. She didn't seem the slightest bit worried about the fact that her driver didn't know anything about driving. She seemed relaxed, oblivious to what this woman named Carson was doing with those reins. He supposed he'd just have to keep an eye on them in spite of his intentions. Couldn't let anything happen to Libby Allen just because he'd let some harebrained woman talk herself onto the train.

Clint caught up with Jake. "Everything all right?"

Jake took his pipe out of his mouth and dropped it stem first into his shirt pocket. "Yep. I'm real surprised."

"Surprised? I thought you vouched for your fellas here that they could drive as good as any experienced drivers."

"Not them. I'm surprised about you."

"What about me?"

"You still ride a horse so light in the saddle it's possible the horse don't even know you're astride."

Clint grinned. "Don't know why you should be surprised. You taught me."

"Yep. Taught you to be just as good as me."

"And am I?"

"I'll let you know."

"I'll let you know if you were a good teacher or not."

Jake spat into the dust. "I been ridin' since I was strong enough to sit a horse, and that's a mite over seventy years, boy. You know I'm a good teacher."

Clint knew it, all right. The old man's lean frame belied his strength. He was good, and he knew himself well. There was nothing any young cowboy could do that Jake couldn't. But Jake had something those young cowboys hadn't—an intuition honed over years of living and working in circuses, and a philosophy about life that included "a reason for every reason," as he liked to say. Sometimes when Clint made quick and sound decisions based on intuition, he was struck by how much he'd absorbed over the course of his own life, as well as what he'd absorbed from Jake. He possessed what he thought was a good sense of his own honed philosophy. Most of the time. He'd surely been tested often enough.

Jake spat into the dust again, sharply reminding Clint of where they were at the moment.

"So you finally admit your age," he chided Jake. "What are you doing going to Virginia City anyway? You always talked about hanging up your gear and getting a cabin just outside of civilization somewhere, and staying put. From what I hear, Virginia City is nowhere near civilization."

"I ain't ready yet."

"Yeah, if you had that cabin, you'd probably never spend more than a night or two a year in it. You'd be worried there might be something worth seeing around the next bend or a great chance to go out with the next circus."

"Through with the circus." Jake reached around and gingerly rubbed his back.

Clint caught the movement. "Never thought I'd see the day you'd say something like that."

"You're seein' it."

"What's the matter with your back? You get hurt?"

"Long story."

"Long trip."

"I'll tell you sometime." Jake pulled his horse around and went back to where Martha walked beside the teams.

Clint rode ahead watching the sky and worrying about when and where he would settle them in for the night. He wished he knew this trail better. Maybe if he put Jake's *believe it* system to work, he could keep his mind focused on Virginia City and somehow they'd just get there. He was anxious to see the end of this trip. He knew it would be long. He hoped it would be eventless.

By the time they made camp that night, Clint figured they'd gone sixteen miles. It wasn't bad, considering they'd started late, and the drivers weren't seasoned freighters. He had to admit the women had done pretty well handling the teams this first day out. Even the drum-banger, he lamented silently. But his instincts told him they'd have to do a lot better or they'd be caught in a bad place when the snow came. And come it would. He could count on that.

How in hell had he got into this? It wasn't supposed to happen this way. This wasn't his plan. It was all so clear before—before Jake. Jake. If it hadn't been for Jake . . . He and Jake were going to have to talk. There was something about these women . . . all of them, the suffragist included.

Clint watched the women. They were silent, moving like

wooden dolls as they prepared a small supper. They were weary—he saw it in their faces and their bent backs and heavy arms. But he saw something else, too. Determination. For what? This new life they sought? Clint wondered, but didn't quite accept that idea. He'd expected them to give up and beg to be taken back to St. Joseph. But they hadn't. Not one had complained.

Where was the Summers woman? Clint noted she was not among the others around the campfire. Against his will he wondered about her, wondered if she had some other quest in mind when she'd forced herself on this train, something other than saving some nameless women from a fate about which she wouldn't have the slightest idea.

He went to her wagon. A low light glowed within the canvas walls. He banged on the wagon box. "Hey, bloomers!"

She moved the tent flap and peeked out, blinking her eyes to adjust them to the gloom.

"No supper?"

"I'm too tired to eat. Can't keep my eyes open."

Clint saw the stub of a pencil in her hand. "Not too tired to write, I see." Hastily she put the pencil back inside the wagon. "Now let me guess what a woman such as yourself could be writing. A scathing article on Clint Bonner, the flesh peddler? Or perhaps a secret diary?" Carsie pulled back. "Don't worry," he mocked, "I don't care anything about what's written in a woman's diary. But I'd keep it away from Jake, if I was you. Has to know everything everybody's up to. Won't rest till he does."

"Contrary to your own personally valued opinion, Major Bonner," she sniffed, "you are not the most scintillating subject on the face of the earth. There are many more important subjects one can cover in the course of recording . . . records."

"Really?"

"Oh, and aren't you surprised?"

Clint let out an exasperated sigh. "Look, ma'am, all I'm saying is that I don't want you writing things that aren't true."

"Don't ma'am me, Major Bonner. And just what thing might I write that might not be true in your opinion?"

"Understand this, *ma'am,* I will not take that kind of uppity tone from a snip in man's pants. And I will not stand for you making accusations about me that . . . uh, accuse me of things you know nothing about."

Carson jutted her chin and tilted her head back. She gave him a slitty-eyed glare that almost unnerved him. "And I do not have to take that kind of smug tone of voice from a man who's transporting females across this country for the purposes of money-making matrimonials."

"I'm not doing that—whatever it was you said!"

"Oh, really. Well, just what do you call it then? Are there not several women on this wagon train who are traveling without benefit of husbands?"

"Yes! You included, I might add."

Carson twitched her lips and ignored his barb. "And is it not conceivable that they will snare husbands when they arrive in Virginia City?"

"Yes. I don't deny that." Clint's voice went up a notch.

"And did they not pay you to transport them and their, ah, goods to Virginia City?"

"Yes."

"There. I rest my case."

"Rest what case about what?" Clint almost rose up on his toes to physically reach the escalation of his voice.

"You have just admitted to flesh-peddling, bride-selling. However you want to call it, you're doing it. I don't need to accuse you of any, ah, accusations. You, your very self, have admitted to your criminal . . . crime."

Clint whirled around in the dust, exasperated beyond the pale. He spun back to face her. "Where do you drum-bangers get this stuff? Don't you have more to do all day than to twist the truth into some perverted lie so you and your bloomer-wearing suffragists can have something to rail against?"

She sniffed. "It's clear you do not read the newspaper."

"Bah. Newspapers. Good for wrapping fish and lining animal cages."

"Cages? You would cage animals in cages? Aha!"

"Aha? What does aha mean?"

"If you would stoop so low as to cage animals, you have no compunction about caging these defenseless women, turning them over to men for money, men who will cage them in loveless marriages, turn them into sick mothers and overworked slaves."

Clint kicked the wagon wheel twice. "They are prostitutes! For God's sake, they've chosen to . . . to . . . prostitute." He hated this. He was starting to talk just like her.

Her eyes narrowed. "What were you going to say? They asked to enslave their bodies to men? Asked to work in those disgusting things they call cribs? Same as cages, you know. Did they want to do that? I don't think so, and I don't think they want to be sold to men either. And another thing . . ."

"Please. Don't give me another thing. I didn't say that. I merely said Miss Goodnight and her group chose to . . . decided to . . . that is, they want to do the work they do."

"They had no choice."

"Oh, and just what makes you an expert in the matter? What happened? Did you apply for the job and were rejected?"

She gripped the sides of the canvas. "Oh-h-h. You are the most despicable person I've ever had the displeasure of meeting."

"Yeah? Well, then, suppose you twist your bloomers around and face 'em back east and join 'em in St. Joseph. It wouldn't break my heart, Miss High-and-mighty."

"I doubt you have a heart, Major Bonner. And I further doubt you ever read books."

"Books?"

"Yes, books, Major Bonner," she replied with exasperating smugness. "You know, they have covers on the outside and writing on the inside?"

"I know what they are, madam. Just what do books have to do with whatever it is we're talking about?"

"One can learn something from reading books."

"Oh, can one?"

"Indeed. And plays. I suppose you've never attended the theater."

"The theater. You mean like a show?"

"If you must call it that."

"Well, then, Miss Smart Bloomers, not only have I seen a show, I've been in one. So there."

That caught her off guard. "You . . . you've been in a play? Acted?"

"I most certainly have."

She shifted her head sideways and stared at him with skepticism. "Just what play did you . . . play in?"

"Only the greatest show on earth."

She gave a light laugh. "And just what would you consider that to be?"

"The circus, of course."

She swallowed. "The . . . circus?"

"Yes. You know, the circus? With trapeze artists and wild animals?"

She tilted her head back and laughed out loud. "And what were you, the clown?"

He squared his shoulders. "Yes, when I had to be. And I was proud of it. I did a lot of things. I also tamed wild animals."

"Well, that is disgusting. Wild animals should be just that, wild. Leave them where they belong. I read something in the newspaper once about a man who owned an elephant.

He dragged the poor creature to taverns all over the East. And then somebody shot the poor innocent thing when it got loose in his garden. Then they skinned her and stuffed her and put her bones in a museum. What about her family? Her feelings?"

"Animals don't have feelings, at least not feelings like you're trying to say. Anyway, in the circus we treated them like royalty."

She sighed. "Major Bonner, I know you'll find this difficult to believe, but the circus can hardly be compared to the great literature of the world. Literature teaches lessons about life."

"Well, so does the circus. Ever seen one?"

"Never."

"I see you've led a rather unprivileged life."

"Just what do you mean by that?"

"Deprived of seeing a circus. Only the greatest thrills in the world. You missed all that. Darned shame."

She tilted her head in curiosity. "What do you mean by a thrill?"

"Aha!"

"What do you mean by that aha?"

"You don't know what a thrill is."

"I've . . . heard the word."

"Yes, but have you ever felt the word?"

"I . . . I'm not sure what you . . ." She felt a flush of warmth spread over her face.

"Of course you're not. You probably never will be sure."

"I will, too. If I ever want to, that is. Be sure, I mean."

"How? You're too busy demonstrating against everything a man stands for."

"Well, what about what a woman stands for?"

"What about it?" Clint stepped closer to her and lowered his voice with reverence. "I've seen women in circuses who could do everything from being shot out of a cannon to sticking their heads in the mouths of lions."

Carson Rose Summers was speechless for an all-too-brief moment. "Why . . . why in the world would women do a ludicrous thing like either of those? Were they forced?"

Clint shook his head in exasperation. "Because they could. They wanted to, and they did. Because that's what makes the circus the stupendous thing that it is. There's no life like it."

"Well, if there's no life like it, why aren't you in that life anymore?"

He stepped back silently. "That's my business."

"I see."

"I doubt that."

"I'm smarter than you think."

"If you're so smart, you'll eat regular meals, you'll work along with the rest of us to keep this train moving and do your share, and you'll go to bed early and get up early. You understand that?"

Carson Summers arched her back and leaned farther out of the wagon. "I'm smart enough to know how to take care of myself, Major Bonner. And I'll do my part of the work to keep things, ah . . . working."

Clint leaned forward, almost nose to nose with her now. "You don't know the first thing about what you should be doing. You're too busy lurking in the lantern light in this wagon scribbling untrue stories about me."

"Godawmighty," she muttered. "You are insufferable."

"Well, you're a suffragist, aren't you? Start suffering. I'm smart enough to know how to help you do that. And I will."

"Ah!" She slammed down the canvas flap. "Thanks for the warning."

Clint sent another warning through the canvas. "Listen, sister, it's not good for you to go without supper. You need your strength for the hard day ahead. I don't want to have to take up the slack when you faint away from hunger."

"Don't waste your time worrying about me, Major Bonner," her voice filtered through the canvas. "I'll make up for it at breakfast. I love a big breakfast. Good night, Major Bonner. Oh," she added with sweet sarcasm, "and thank you so much for your sincere concern regarding my welfare. And I'll thank you not to refer to me as 'sister.' That term is reserved for those who truly understand its meaning."

Clint watched the lantern light through the canvas move and fade. He stared at the darkened spot for seconds longer than he wished to, then stomped away knowing nothing more than he had before, and wondering what it was he thought he needed to learn about that bloomered woman anyway.

Three

Carsie stretched out on the quilts as best she could, given the cramped quarters of the wagon. She ran her fingers over the printing on the cover of her notebook. She opened it and held it close to the low lamp light, and carefully turned the pages until she came to the entries for the last week.

The Journal of Carson Rose Summers

7 May 1866

I was a reluctant bride, a child tricked into it by my father. He'd actually received money from the man he'd picked for my husband! I vowed at that moment that I'd never be so easily duped by a man again, no matter who he was. I suppose I should have sounded sorrier when I told Sophie the lie that my husband was killed in a gambling dispute a few months later. But I wasn't sorry then and I'm not now.

Sophie said I sounded cold-hearted. Perhaps I have grown to be so. I wasn't before I was married. I dreamed once of love, of being in the arms of one man, the man I loved and who loved me. I even dreamed about the private things between a man and a woman. But he ripped those dreams to shreds in one night and every night that followed until there were none left and my heart had turned to stone. Now

I'm grown up. I take care of myself. And I'd rather
be cold than to be made a lifelong prisoner to a man's
whims.

Carsie lifted her eyes and gazed off into a space long
since past. After one year of teaching and seeing how the
mothers of her pupils were downtrodden by too many children and difficult husbands, she grew exhausted in her attempts to help them help themselves. It was as if they didn't
want to be helped.

It was then she realized they believed there was no other
way for them, just as her own mother had believed. Their
mothers and their mothers' mothers had all lived the same
life as they were living now. The only alternative was to be
a spinster like herself, and they made it clear that was not
an acceptable fate.

Carsie had not even winced under those barbs. She believed the life she led was much more honest than theirs.
Except for the fact that she had no children. She would like
to have had children.

She had come to a significant personal choice. She simply had to take up the cause for women's rights. She had
to help those women if they couldn't help themselves, and
help the future generations of women learn to be responsible for their own fate.

She'd wormed her way onto a newspaper as a writer. Carsie smiled now remembering. She flipped back the pages
to the months of spring a year earlier and read a particular
journal entry that saddened her first, and satisfied her next.

20 April 1865
    The sting of the death of President Lincoln still
smarts in every corner of my heart and the hearts of
so many. What will happen to this country? What shall
the poor Negro do? To be a woman is difficult
enough. To be a Negro woman—I can't fathom how

despicable their lives must be. And now with Mr. Lincoln gone, who will champion those people?

I must continue my work in the cause for women, all women. The editor enjoys the publicity my writings generate, yet he pays me paltry sums far below that of male writers. It's the war. They write endless stories of the terrible war and of what the men went through. What about the women?

Carsie thought of those months now. She turned the pages forward to winter and the following spring.

30 March 1866

I've managed. It's been difficult. I've lived frugally, using much of what little money I earn to buy my own little house. I own it and the bank president is not too happy about it. He told me it was the bank's policy not to lend money to unmarried women. He was, however, most eager to lend it to me from his own personal reserves and offered to make a very generous plan to pay it back. Back is the correct word, for he would have required me to lie on my back for him. He was most embarrassed when I threatened to write about his exploits in a certain part of town known only to philanderers. Interesting how quickly the bank's policy toward unmarried women changed in a trice.

If it hadn't been for Sophie sharing the house with me and paying what little she can, I never could have gone on. Sophie is a big help and a good friend. She sews my bloomers and shirtwaists. I do so enjoy the freedom of bloomers. And I do not sew. I still cannot . . .

The papers have been full of those expeditions to the Northwest. Women being transported to become wives of who knows what kind of man out there? It's nothing more than a new way of promoting prostitution. In the East there is a shortage of men due to the war. And those who would transport them bemoan the shortage of women in the West. Get them together, that's what they say. They make it sound so absolutely sensible when it is insanity.

The new ladies league is growing in number daily. They look to me to be their guide. It is a huge responsibility, but one I relish. They've been talking about this disgusting practice of bride-selling. I have my calling now. I shall write about this new enslavement of women. I shall help them find the courage to break those bonds. I shall become a hero to all women!

Carsie sighed as she read now. *And maybe I'll even be a hero to myself.* She recalled now how her father would warn her about thinking too much. It would get her into trouble, he'd said, just as reading would do. He had beaten her, taken her books away from her, but he could never beat away her thoughts. She turned the journal pages to the entry of the day before.

27 May 1866

One of my league sisters informed me that, even as we were speaking, a wagon train carrying women to Virginia City, no doubt to become brides, was loading in the freight yard preparing to move out. I can only respond one way—I must go with them.

Carsie picked up her pencil.

28 May 1866

Well, I've done it. I write now from inside a musty-smelling wagon somewhere on the road to Virginia City. I'm on my way to Sophie and hope that I am in time to save her from a fate worse than death. It was difficult today, sitting on the hard wagon seat for so many hours. My shoulders and back ache and are stiff. I felt sick to my stomach so often. But I shan't give in to the pains of the flesh.

I admire Libby Allen. She does not complain and I know it must be terribly difficult for her in her condition. Blind and pregnant and barely a woman. Can she be searching for a husband as well? What is she doing with those other women? She seems to not be like them at all. Yet, she cares about them and they care about her.

I hope for her sake and mine that I will feel stronger tomorrow. I am nervous, I am frightened to death if the truth be told. But I shan't tell a soul.

Carsie slept fitfully in the wagon she shared with Libby. Three days and nights on the road had done nothing to ease her anxiety. She couldn't seem to fall into a rhythm of ease, such as it was, as the others did. Even though there was an overriding sense of them all being in the ordeal together, still she felt the outsider, the one who didn't fit in. Even Mrs. Woo, while remaining silent day and night, fell into the rhythm of the trail.

But not Carsie. The implausible circumstances into which she had placed herself, the completely new sensations she'd experienced since marching into the wagon yard, all succeeded in bombarding her weakened defenses and exhausting her mind and body with the endeavor to sleep.

This night was worse than ever. All day she'd nodded at the ends of the reins, worked hard to keep her eyes open. Now, when it was time to sleep, that blessed relief eluded her. Everything around her conspired against her to keep her awake. The oxen shook their heads, setting their chains to rattling. The horses tied to the wagons stomped and whickered. Carsie was certain their inability to stay quiet would alert nearby Indians or desperadoes to their where-abouts and vulnerability. Unless, of course, the incessant loud chirping of what suggested the presence of a thousand crickets didn't mask the sounds of their sleeping wagon train.

And then a drizzle of rain pelted the canvas, at first in sporadic drops and then in a drumming rhythm that pushed her down to a level of disturbing sleep.

Carsie's dream-filled mind whirled with a myriad of thoughts. Sophie's face tumbled about, fading in and out in a sea of scruffy miners' faces. Miss Goodnight lounged against the cloud-streaked moon. Jake stretched out on a floating bedroll, the other ladies of the Good Times Empo-rium ministering to him. Martha kept watch over them all with her arsenal of whips.

And Clint Bonner stood at the top of a butte, lean as a pine, hair blowing in the wind, hands on his hips, ordering her to haul that wagon up the hillside faster. He reached behind him and pulled Sophie out from a hiding place. Car-sie strained on a thick rope that burned her hands as she dragged the heavy wagon behind her, straining to get to her friend.

Carsie bolted upright, perspiring and gasping for breath in the close air. The wind had picked up and the wagon canvas, now smelling sour from its drenching, breathed in and out like a blacksmith's bellows. Her head throbbed from the emotional and physical strain of the day, her shoulders had stiffened, and her back ached. She dropped back down onto her blankets, but sleep still eluded her.

Libby, on the other hand, slept like the baby she was carrying, seemingly without a care. Carsie envied her. She must trust everything and everyone to get her through safely. How could she be so innocent, so naive about peo-ple? Had she been so sheltered all her life? Carsie caught a glimpse of her swelling belly as Libby stirred. The girl couldn't have been all that sheltered. Pregnant, no husband visible or implied. Wasn't that enough to shatter trust?

Carsie felt no concept of time, no sense of how long she lay awake, commanding sleep without success. The rain let up, but not before a stream of water found its way down the corner near her head and spread over her pillow. Quickly she pulled her journal out from under the pillow and moved it to an oilcloth pouch that held matches and candles. She stuffed a blanket against the running water to absorb the flow.

The rain stopped almost as abruptly as it had begun. She crawled to the opening, pulled the flap aside, and peered out into the darkness. Something moved. Something rustled. Carsie's heart seemed to stop beating for an instant before thrumming loudly in her ears. She waited. All was quiet. Then twigs crackled, something scraped along a stone, and then a match flared. She jumped, cringing behind the dank canvas. A flame caught and a low campfire began to glow. She saw a dark hunkered figure silhouetted in the glow. Who? The figure stood and came nearer. Fear slammed against her nerves and she rocked involuntarily.

"I'm not going to kill you—yet," came Clint Bonner's voice in a husky whisper.

Carsie shuddered violently and fell back against a trunk. Anger boiled and replaced her fear as she scrambled back to her knees and stuck her head out of the flap.

"Have you no decent sense of . . . of decency, Major? Surely you know how frightening it is to be out here in this . . . frightful place, enough to keep from . . . frightening the daylights out of a sleeping traveler."

"You weren't sleeping," came the whispered retort.

"How . . . how would you know? Have you been spying on me again?"

"Me spy on you! That's a good one. I have no interest in spying on the likes of you, even though I know that no doubt disappoints you, Miss Summers."

"You must think me dumb as a doorknob," she rasped. "How else would you know I wasn't sleeping if you hadn't spied upon me while I was in the midst of . . . not sleeping?"

"Because you were loud enough to wake the bones of dead buffalo, that's how," he cracked at the top of a whisper.

"Loud? Me? How can you say such a thing? Between the animals and those confounded crickets and then the rain, an earthquake could not have been heard."

"Well, I heard you thrashing around in that wagon. Must be you have a guilty conscience."

"What has my guilty conscience have to do with anything? I mean, that is, if I had a guilty conscience and should feel, ah, guilt, that is."

"Because you won't admit you're curious about me and are compelled to write reams about my perceived activities."

"You!" Carsie's knees ached from kneeling for so long. She grasped the wet canvas and leaned out over the wagon box. "Even if you'd spoken one crumb of truth in that last statement, it is not I who should feel guilt, Major Bonner. Oh, no, it is you, and I mean to get to the heart of this matter, no matter how high I have to go."

Clint stared at her long and hard. "If I knew what you're talking about, I'd have an answer. In any case, what I do is none of your business. You're sticking your nosy nose into my private business, and that's why you feel guilty."

"See? You admit it."

"Admit what?"

"That you have private business."

"Everyone has private business."

They stared at each other for a long moment through the low glow of the firelight.

"Everyone else is sleeping," he said matter-of-factly.

"Even Miss Goodnight and her ladies?"

"Yes."

"Did you see them sleeping?"

"Yes," he answered with heightened exasperation.

"There, that proves it."

"Proves what now?"

"That you were spying on me."

"What the—"

"You couldn't know Miss Goodnight and her ladies were sleeping if you hadn't spied on them while they were . . . ah, sleeping, so therefore you couldn't know I was not sleeping if you hadn't spied on me while I was not sleeping. You, Major Bonner, are a Peeping Tom . . . peeper."

"I'm a peeper?"

"There, you do admit it. I suppose there is something to be said for that."

"I didn't admit to anything." Clint stomped away from her, then stomped back. "What in the hell am I doing arguing with you in the middle of the night?"

"Exactly."

"What?"

"You are doing exactly that, arguing with me in the middle of the night, so why do you have to ask?"

"I can't stand this."

Carsie leaned far over the wagon box and flung a hoarse whisper at him. "Then don't do it!"

She lost her balance, tipped out in a somersault, and landed on her bottom in the mud. The wetness seeped through her white cotton nightgown. Her hair fell over her eyes and she brushed it away, too late realizing her hands were covered with mud. "Now look what you've done!"

"What *I've* done? Bloomers, you did that all by yourself. And from the looks of how smoothly you executed the tumble, I'd say you had a lot of practice. Are you sure you've never seen a circus?" He bent over to stifle his laughter.

Carsie sputtered and blew a lock of hair up off her forehead. "The least you could do is help a lady to her feet."

Clint looked over his shoulder. "Really? Is Miss Goodnight awake?"

"Oh!" Carsie slapped the mud with both hands. "You are despicable enough to . . . ah, despise." Her fingers folded over oozes of mud, and the cool dampness calmed her temper. "But, of course," she began sweetly, "I know you're completely correct, Major Bonner. This whole unfortunate episode is my fault because I was curious enough to peer out of the wagon wondering if a desperado might be about to catch you unawares. But then, I should have realized that you are too aware to be caught . . . unawares. Isn't that right, Major Bonner?"

Clint stopped laughing and looked down at her through the flickering light. She did look miserable. It was, after all, her first wagon trip, her first trek west, and it was an arduous trip for anyone, let alone a tenderfoot woman. He was used to hard living, hard driving. Circus life had seasoned him. And she had assessed it right. He was too smart to let anyone, well, outsmart him. He had to be. These people were in his charge. It was his duty to protect them from all danger, from surprise attacks. Just this once he supposed he could swallow his pride and help this burr under his saddle up out of the cold night mud.

"Well, Miss Summers, I'm glad you see things more clearly. I accept your apology. Let me help you up." He leaned down to catch her by the arms.

The cold splatter hit his face so fast and so hard it shocked and caught him off-balance. He fell back into the mud.

"Apology?" Carson Summers leapt to her feet. She wiped the mud off her hands by sliding them down the wet wagon canvas. "I have nothing to apologize to you for, you insufferable baboon. You are the one who owes me an apology. And unless it is immediately forthcoming, I shall be forced to . . . use force."

Clint, still in a state of shock, could only stare at her

slack-jawed and feel water penetrating his pants and shirt. When his amazement at her quick response subsided, he found his voice.

"Just because I tripped backward so as to save you from getting hurt, you have to misunderstand as usual."

"I knocked you over with nothing more than a handful of mud, and you know it. That, Major Bonner, is the force of a woman's power."

"Mud?"

"If need be. Any common substance used correctly can bring about uncommon results in the hands of the right person. I intend to arm the women of this continent with all the mud they need."

Clint laughed. "Well, your mud-slinging hasn't stopped me. Just what other kind of force do you think you could possibly use that would repel me? Other than the sheer force of your abrasive personality, of course." He pushed to his feet and turned to leave, then quickly turned back. "And don't call me a baboon."

"Ooooh," she sputtered, "you are . . . so very annoying."

"I know. I'm good at it, too, aren't I?" He grinned.

"I warn you, Major Bonner, don't make me any more exasperated with you than I already am."

"Why? What show of strength can I expect if I do?"

"This!" Carsie ran at him and, with her bare feet, kicked mud up on his shirt.

"Stop that!" He held up his hands in defense. "Now look what you did. This was a clean shirt. I only have two!"

"Now you only have one." She stomped back toward her wagon, shooting up splatters of mud as she went.

"I wouldn't get into that wagon, if I were you."

"Well, you're not me," she flung at him, "and I feel most thankful for that."

"Fine, suit yourself."

"Fine, I will." She strained to clamber up the side of the wagon, then hiked one leg over the box and inside.

"But there's all manner of insects and leeches that live in the dirt and mud and get caught between your toes. Once you get 'em in your blankets, there's no telling how you'll ever get 'em out, and—"

Carsie shrieked. She backed out of the wagon, dropped down into the mud, and hopped around. "Get them! Get them! Help me, you've got to help me!"

Clint took his own sweet time brushing himself off while she hopped around trying to keep her feet out of mud.

"Not that I have to help you, you being a free-spirited woman and all, but what was it you wanted me to do?"

Carsie swept hair out of her face, leaving a dark wet streak behind. "Help me, you fool!"

"Well, now, I was just about to. Then you had to go and call me a name again. I don't guess I can help you unless I get an apology first."

"I will not apologize to you. Not ever."

"Well, then, as I see it, I have to let you get out of this yourself. It's the best way for you to learn, anyway."

"Learn what?"

"Not to believe every cock-and-bull story somebody tells you."

Carsie stopped hopping. "You mean, you mean there are no insects and leeches? You lied to me?" Exasperated as much with herself now as she was with him, she started up the side of the wagon once more. She lifted one leg over and straddled the edge of the wagon box, dropping her foot into the blankets inside.

"I may be a lot of things, Miss Summers, but I am not a baboon and I am not a liar."

"Godawmighty," she swore.

"Wait a minute." Clint took a cloth from his wagon and came over to her. "Here. Twist around here and let me wipe your feet."

"Don't you dare touch my feet," she gritted, without turning around.

"What are you worried about? That I might get a glimpse of your ankles and your reputation would be ruined forever? Give me your foot." He reached out and caught one and enveloped it in the cloth, then started wiping.

She started to yank her foot away, but stopped mid-yank. "I'm not worried about ruining my reputation. I care nothing about that."

"Why? Because it's already sullied with your suffragizing or whatever you call it?"

She looked over her shoulder. "I call it, Major Bonner, advancing the rights of women. We are no longer willing to be merely the possessions of men, to do with what they will, to be at their beck and call, to be at the mercy of their every whim, to—"

"You're on a wagon box, Miss Summers, not a speech box." He released her foot. "Give me your other foot."

She complied, quickly exacerbating the persistent thought at how wonderful his hands felt. There was something about this impersonal yet somehow very intimate act of his wiping her feet that was making her insides turn to jelly.

"You really don't care, do you?" Clint rubbed the bottom of her foot. She pulled it back and he grabbed it again, knowing he'd tickled her and she didn't want to admit it.

"Not about a glimpse of my ankle," she retorted.

"I mean about your reputation."

"Oh. It's not important. I don't have time to indulge in such frivolity as worrying about what people think of me."

"But don't you want them to think highly of you? Think you're a lady of good breeding?"

"I'm not a lady of good breeding," she muttered.

"What?"

"All I want them to think about is advancement of the rights of women."

"What has happened to you to make you hate men so much?"

"Godawmighty. You're just like all the other men."

He set her foot on the wagon box ledge. "I am not. Just like you, I'm different from every other person."

"Not in your thinking. You think that just because I and women like me want to help other women out of the mire of too much childbearing, too much work, and too little education that it's because we hate men. While there are some men who deserve hating, Major Bonner, I can assure you our reasons go much more deeply and are much more personal than simply fighting against all men. Although I fear we are forced to do that as well. Not that the whole population of men needs to be fought. What I mean is, we stronger women must fight the war for our weaker sisters."

"Then you don't hate men." He made it sound as if he hadn't understood her words.

Carsie climbed over the ledge and sat down in the blankets, leaving the canvas flap open. She reached for some cotton stockings and her boots. "I don't hate all men, no. But some . . ."

"Then you like men."

"I like them, yes, I mean, not the way . . . ah, some other women seem to like men, I mean . . ."

"Like Miss Goodnight's ladies is what you mean." Clint started back to the campfire.

"Yes. No. I mean, I didn't mean it like that exactly." She wrapped a shawl around her shoulders and climbed back out of the wagon. Stiffly she walked toward the campfire. Her body aches had turned to downright pain.

"Coffee, miss?"

Carsie jumped. "Oh, Mr. Storms, I didn't see you there. I thought you must be sleeping."

"Pretty hard to sleep with all this noise going on," Jake said with an edge in his voice.

"I know exactly what you mean. The animals, and the rain, and those crickets. Why, I could not catch a moment's sleep—"

" 'Twasn't any of that would keep me awake. Them's a

lullaby mostly. It was that arguing and stomping around out here that kept me up. Figured I might just as well get the coffee going."

"I—I'm sorry. I didn't realize how loudly we were talking. I'm sorry for disturbing your sleep."

"It's done now. Clint get your feet cleaned up?"

Regardless of her declaration regarding her reputation, Carsie suddenly felt very embarrassed. "Oh, dear, you saw that?"

"Couldn't help it, what with the fire and night sky clearing the moon. Them ankles of yours just gleamed like belly skin on a trout."

"Oh dear."

Clint held out a tin mug. "None of this is what kept you up, and you know it, you old faker. Stop making her feel any worse than she already does."

Jake chuckled and filled it with coffee. "All right. I was just funnin' with her. Sorry, miss." He poured a mug for Carsie and handed it to her.

She accepted it gratefully. "I forgive you, Mr. Storms. You are a true gentlemen to recognize how you may have injured my feelings, but more, to have had the courage and decency to offer an apology."

Clint shook his head. "When you taste that coffee you'll think he's trying to poison you, not apologize." He slogged over to the fire to pour another shot of the thick coffee for himself. "What's going on with you?" he pressed the old man.

"Just a mite uneasy is all."

Carsie watched Jake's controlled movements as he replaced the coffeepot over the fire and lowered his body to a log. In the firelight, without his hat and with his hair pulled back, she thought he had an interesting face, one that had been quite handsome in a craggy sort of way once upon a time. She wondered about him and recalled Clint's words about everyone having private business.

"About what?"

"You notice we haven't seen any other parties along here? Seems unusual to me."

"I noticed," Clint replied. "Makes me wonder about the quiet."

"Heard the stories back in St. Joseph about the numbers moving out over this road, and about the Indian raids, and the other unspeakables traveling just as fast as the good folks. Where are they all?"

Carsie instantly wanted to burst in with questions about Jake's references to raids, but she thought it best just to listen to their conversation. Perhaps they'd forgotten she was even in their presence. That would be a typical thing for men to do.

"Not even government wagons," Clint said. "Last trip out I passed them thick as city traffic at times, loaded with arms for the militia."

Carsie could not hold back a question. "Militia? For what? You mean the war has progressed into the West?"

Neither of the men gave her the irritated look she knew her outburst would have elicited in other gatherings where men and women were together. A thought trickled into her mind that maybe these two weren't all that typical.

"Of sorts," Clint said. "They meant to wipe out the Indians."

"And they did not succeed, did they?" Carsie asked quietly.

"No," Clint replied. "And I believe they never will, no matter how much blood is spilled."

Carsie's stomach churned and then growled. The idea of Indian raids and advancing militia, and the killing of any people, sickened her. And she hadn't been eating enough and she knew it. She would give half her supply of pencils and paper for some fruit and potatoes, and something other than the thing they called hard tack and that greasy ham.

Jake rose and went to a wagon. He returned with a cup,

a spoon, and a loosely wrapped package. "Here, miss, try some crackers and molasses. That ought to cut down on your stomach complaining. Don't eat enough to keep a bird alive, I noticed."

Carsie managed a smile and took the offering gladly. "Thank you, Mr. Storms. You're very kind."

"Think nothin' of it, ma'am, but you'd best be thinkin' a mite more about keepin' up your strength. You're the only driver on that wagon."

"You're right, of course." She smeared some molasses on a cracker and consumed it heartily, then prepared another.

"Is the girl all right?" Clint asked. "Don't see a whole lot of her."

Carsie didn't want to give Libby's secret away. It was up to her to tell the gathering she was pregnant. Soon, she would not be able to keep it from them. Even in these few days together, Libby's growing body was starting to give her away.

"Yes, just scared I think," Carsie told him. Libby was the least frightened of all, she'd figured, as they rode together. For Libby the whole experience was a wonderful adventure, not a challenge to survival.

"Anything we can do to help her?"

"I don't think so," Carsie said. *At least not yet,* she added silently. Major Bonner had offered the assistance in a manner that gave no hint of sarcasm, she noted a moment later. Could it be that there was a shred of decency in him somewhere? "May I prepare some of those crackers for you both?" she asked.

"I wouldn't mind," Jake said.

"Thanks," Clint added.

"Never did like to get his hands sticky." Jake grinned through the fire's glow.

"Oh, and you do?" Clint chided.

"Never minded much."

"Comes from smearing that stuff all over your face."

Carsie handed first Jake and then Clint a cracker smeared with molasses. "Smearing something on your face?" She gave Jake an inquisitive stare.

Jake stuck the whole cracker in his mouth, chewed, and swallowed before answering. "Unlike the biggest mouth present, I was a sad-faced circus clown now and again."

Carsie's surprise burst out of her. "You were a performer in the circus, too?"

"At times."

"Best in the business," Clint averred.

"Naw," Jake countered. "Dan Rice. Now there was the best in the business."

"Dan Rice?" Carsie prepared the last of the crackers and set them over the spread paper wrapping. "Oh, yes. I read something about him once. I thought he was in politics."

"He thought he was, too," Jake said, chuckling. "Ran for president once."

"No."

"Yep. Probably coulda won if the women coulda voted. He was quite the gentlemen with the ladies."

"I think, Mr. Storms, that women, if they could vote, would consider issues other than the charm of a contender when using something as powerful as a vote."

"Now see what you've done," Clint said, and drained his mug.

"I ain't done a thing, boy. I agree with the lady. Sometimes it 'pears like government would run as good as a circus if the women could have a say."

"Why, Mr. Storms, I had no idea you were of an enlightened mind."

"If you mean light-headed, you got that right." Clint chuckled. "He's let all that perfume from Miss Goodnight and her ladies muddle his brain."

"Really, Major Bonner," Carsie sniffed, "I don't see how

you can say such a cruel thing about this fine man. And you, his friend."

"Yeah," Jake put in. "Sounds mighty ungrateful to the man who saved your sorry hindquarters more times than he can count."

"He certainly owes you an apology, but I fear it won't be forthcoming, Mr. Storms." She raised her chin, glancing at Clint before giving Jake a knowledgeable nod.

Rain came out of the sky then as if the gods had tipped over a cistern. Carsie rose quickly and handed over her tin mug to Jake, then turned and made for her wagon.

"Now see?" Clint called behind her. "That's what women like you do best, isn't it? Throw some comment out like that, then run away before a man has a chance to defend himself."

Carsie climbed up on her wagon and turned back to him. "Thank you, Major Bonner. I knew you'd apologize sooner or later. Good night."

Four

On a bitter cold morning a week later Clint roused the travelers before sunup. The rain had started not long after midnight and, while not a raging storm, had kept up a steady soaking for hours with no sign of letting up. Before nightfall he meant to get them past a particularly treacherous crossing along a bend in the Big Blue River where past experience had taught him what a foot-thick coat of mud could do to animals and wagons.

Among the silent travelers there wasn't inclination for anything but coffee, which Jake had started in the middle of the night. Huddled under a tarpaulin, donned in clothing for rain protection, not one of the women complained about the coffee's bitter thickness. Not even the suffragist. Clint noticed she took a heftier share of their dwindling sugar supply this morning, probably to cut the brutal strength of Jake's coffee. He'd have to speak to her about that. She had to learn about rationing provisions later on the road, especially if weather and Indians prevented them from keeping what was left or obtaining more.

He drew up the wide collar of his oilskin coat and wrapped it closely around his neck. There was nothing he hated more than rain pouring down the back of his neck and running cold down his spine.

He shivered as a memory chilled his mind. Once, while in a circus show in Chicago, the rain and wind had been strong and relentless for the three days the circus had

camped there. The main tent's rigging had repeatedly threatened to let go. Every few hours he worked on the ties and
anchors until his hands were raw.

Jake, being the lightest, had climbed along the rigging
halfway to the top where a tear was rapidly turning into a
huge rip. He managed to sew the rent canvas with strong
twine, but the paraffin and kerosene-coated fabric was difficult to cling to and he lost his grip and started to slide.
Clint looked up in time to see his descent and threw his
body against a guide pole to hold that part of the structure
as taut as he could. The agile Jake slid along it like an
acrobat, the breadth and weight of his body sending ahead
of him a wave of water that had caught in the depression
made by the dipping canvas. Strained as he was against the
pole, Clint's shirt and jacket pulled away from his neck and
shoulders and made a perfect sluice to catch the water. The
shock and force of it sent him to his knees and Jake sailed
down, skimming right over him. Clint's body had broken
Jake's fall.

When Jake came out of the daze of his impact with Clint
and the ground and saw Clint rolling to his feet and looking
like a drowned rat, he'd laughed till his tears had mingled
with the rain pelting his face. Clint hadn't laughed. When
he'd seen Jake lose his grip high up on the tent top and
start an uncontrolled descent, he'd panicked. His mind had
rushed with the thought that he'd lose his friend in the flash
of a lightning bolt. And Clint couldn't take any more losses
through death.

Now on the trail, that thought came back to him as he
caught glimpses through the driving rain of Jake working
around camp, hitching the teams, corralling the horses and
mule that had kept up their stubborn attempts to return to
St. Joseph, checking the wagons, hauling water from the
clear-running creek for the drinking barrels. He'd felt the
loss of Jake's friendship when they'd parted years ago. But

at least in that loss he'd left Jake alive. If only he could have done that for Mattie.

Tears filled his eyes instantly. They burned with the years of being held back. The memory of her had come unbidden, against his will. Why now, after all these years? He scraped the back of his hand across his eyes and swallowed back the emotion.

When he'd heard Jake's voice behind him in the St. Joseph freight yard a few days before, he'd felt a kind of rebirth. Jake was one of a kind. A man his age didn't have this kind of energy, usually. But then Clint had always known Jake was unusual. He'd walked most of the last two days, either with or across the teams from Martha. Clint calculated that was about thirty miles. But he was up and moving in the morning before anyone else, Clint included. He wondered if Jake ever slept. Martha was the same way.

Jake slogged through mud to Clint, carrying a tin mug of steaming coffee. "Think I'll ride out ahead this mornin'," he announced quietly, tipping a broad-brimmed oilskin-covered hat so the rain poured out the front of it. He never let his stovepipe hat get wetter than need be.

"You saw it, too," Clint replied, coiling a length of rope.

"Yep. Been watchin' that campfire keeping distance ahead of us for the last couple nights." Jake dropped down to sit on a molasses keg.

"Could be soldiers."

"Or Indians."

"I don't worry about them."

"Or renegades of either kind."

"Maybe."

"Figure it's worth lookin' into."

"Don't pull any of your wild stunts," Clint admonished. "If they look tough, you get back here and let me take care of them. You've got no cheering crowds here to appreciate your antics."

"Yes, Daddy," Jake said like a little boy.

Clint ignored the jab and set the coiled rope over a folded sheet of canvas. He leaned against the trunk of a dead tree. "We should be pretty near to Virginville by tomorrow's nightfall. Figure we can afford to stay an extra day there."

"What do you wanta stop for?"

"Rest, for one thing."

"The fellas haven't complained, have they? They're pushin' along good as any freight drivers you ever seen, ain't they?"

Clint grinned. "You're just trying to get me to say you were right when you tricked me into taking them."

"Well, I was, wasn't I? No trick to it. And no need to stop on their account. They ain't a bit taxed."

"All right. I need to stop for a day. The animals need a rest. They finally stopped trying to turn around and head back to St. Joe."

" 'Bout time, too. I'm sick of changin' their minds every time they get ornery."

Clint understood that. "Virginville's a good place to stop. And we need to pick up more provisions." Virginville, the largest place between St. Joe and Denver on this road, lay on the east bank of the Big Blue. "That suit you?"

Jake drained his coffee mug. "Just so long as you know it ain't me nor Martha nor Miz Goodnight's ladies forcin' you to stop."

"I admitted I was the one who wanted to stop, didn't I?"

"Yep. Good thing Miss Summers didn't hear you. She'd never let you forget sayin' that." Jake grinned and turned up his coat collar against the rain.

"And I'll bet you can't wait to go and tattle on me. Give her one more thing to use for ammunition."

"Me?" Jake asked with innocence any non-circus performer would have believed. "Long as we're goin' near a town, the fellas might like to have the chance to go in and see other people."

"You just better make damned sure they don't go setting

up shop while we're there," Clint said. "I don't want any drunken cowboys or married men with mad wives coming to camp with blood in their eyes."

"They got more class than that."

"You best be right about that."

Clint found himself wondering if a particular spicy little lady named Margarita he'd kept company with on his last trip might still be working at the Blue Door. He and probably everyone on this wagon train could be just as ornery as the animals once they pulled away again from a place that afforded them comfort and socializing. But every now and then it was necessary to make this kind of stop.

"Guess I'll get on with it and see who's up ahead." Jake stood and stretched the kinks out of his back.

"Think you can find us all right?"

"I got a sixth sense like a homing pigeon. I'll find you. Maybe get some other hunting in while I'm at it. Got a hankerin' for a prairie chicken dinner."

Clint pushed the wagon train forward, stopping three times to assist Mrs. Woo in controlling her team and getting her wagon over the deepest ruts. He kept wondering when the suffragist was going to break down and say she couldn't go on, then beg to turn back. But that hadn't happened so far.

He rode past her wagon. She sat on the box alone. Libby must have stayed inside this morning. Carson's eyes were fixed on the road ahead, the reins wrapped tightly around her gloved hands. The wind and rain plastered her hair over her face and she shook her head to free it from her eyes. She'd crack sometime. Maybe at Virginville she'd get off and never come back to the train. That would be just fine with him. He was sure sick of watching her scratch away on her writing pads every time they stopped.

Although, he had to admit now, he had enjoyed the verbal

sparring with her the other night. And she'd listened atten-
tively when he and Jake had talked about the militia and
the Indians. And she'd asked intelligent questions. He hadn't
thought of her as a flighty-brained woman then. Come to
think of it, he hadn't once thought of her as a flighty-
brained woman. He began to mull the import of that thought
when Miss Goodnight called to him as he passed her
wagon.

"Why is it we haven't caught a glimpse of Jake all this
time?" she shouted over the din of pouring rain and churning wheels.

"He's probably trying to stay out of sight and out of the
rain. Don't worry about him. He's a wily old goat."

"Shouldn't you try to find him?"

"He'll find us."

By midafternoon the rain stopped. Clint scanned the horizon, the craggy hills around them, but there was no sign
of Jake nor of whoever it was had been making camp ahead
of them every night. He drew the wagons to a stop along
the river to give the women a chance to stretch their legs
and give their arms a rest. He was just coming out of a
clump of trees where he'd taken the moment to relieve his
bladder, when Miss Goodnight strode toward him.

"We insist upon stopping right here and now and waiting
for Jake."

Clint slicked his wet hair back. "No need for that, and
no time. We have to make Virginville by tomorrow night."

The other women slowly gathered around Phoebe.
"We've decided that we're staying right here until Jake
shows up," Hannah said.

"Well, now, ma'am, I don't think that's a good thing for
you to do."

"We're going to do it, meester," Lola said, her hands
planted firmly on her hips. "You can't make us move."

Clint thought a long minute. "You're right about that. I

can't make you move. But I'm going, and Mrs. Woo is going to go, too. What about you, Miss Summers?"

Carsie approached the group, Libby Allen's arm linked through hers. "I'm anxious to press on to Virginia City," she said, and suffered the glares of the other women. "But I don't want to put another life into jeopardy. If it's necessary to stop here and wait for Mr. Storms to arrive, then I'm in agreement."

The others gave Carsie the slightest hint of appreciation.

Clint called over their heads to the bullwhacker, who stood apart from them. "What about you, Martha?"

Martha said nothing, just picked up a whip and started toward the head of the team.

"She's ready to move out." Clint snatched up his hat from a tree limb and jammed it on his head.

"Well, we're not." Phoebe folded her arms across her chest.

"Fine. You stay here. But those are my animals and I'm unhitching them and taking them with me. You can stay right here and wait for Jake while who knows what unspeakable humanity roaming around out here finds you first."

Clint saw the fury in their eyes as they listened to him and then loudly vocalized their opposition. Silently he ignored their protests. He knew Jake would catch up with them, or send up a signal it he was in trouble. He hoped he would, anyway. What if he'd fallen and was unconscious in the brush somewhere, or down at the bottom of a ravine? No, that couldn't happen. Clint's mind started to assume some of the fear he sensed in Miss Goodnight and the other women.

He shook his head then thought of something that brightened his outlook. "What you all seem to have forgotten is that Jake went out ahead of us this morning. We'll come upon him waiting for us soon."

The women fell silent then, giving Clint a collective cold

shoulder. They turned and went back to their wagons. He smiled in wry amusement. Now he knew what a Mormon man must feel like when all his wives are mad at him at one time.

"All right then. Wagons roll!" Clint let out a breath, relieving his tension. He gestured toward the west and strode to his horse. He wished he'd caught even a glimpse of Jake on the road ahead of them. That would sure have made him feel a lot better. He hoped to hell he was right about Jake, and that the old buzzard hadn't got himself into something bad.

The rains stopped. Twilight came with no sign of Jake. Clint drew the wagons to camp on a high, partially dry spot along the river. He kindled a cookfire, and then he and Martha set about unhitching the teams and getting them to water before settling them down for the night.

The women were bone-deep weary. The road had been treacherous owing to ruts made by hundreds of wagons and animals that had gone before, and from the driving rains. The oxen had stumbled often and Martha cracked them back into position and pushed them on. Stopping for evening camp was a relief to everyone, including Clint.

Silently the women climbed down from wagon boxes and opened canvas flaps to let air circulate among their belongings. Clint saw the exhaustion in their faces, the blank eyes and the drooping jaws. Yet each to a one approached him to inquire of Jake's whereabouts. Mrs. Woo held back, a silent wraithlike being in gray cotton standing behind them, but he sensed she understood whom the others were asking about. When they returned to their evening chores, so did she. If Jake didn't show up by dawn, Clint knew he could suffer some sharp tongue-lashings from this pack, who would have regained strength from their rest. Beyond that, he was getting worried about Jake himself. Maybe he should have gone out to check on that campfire himself instead of letting the old man go.

Once bedding had been draped over ropes strung between trees, a pot of beans and a skillet of ham set to simmer and sizzle over the cookfire, and the last of the milk which had gone sour mixed with flour to make biscuits, the women set about spreading wintergreen liniment liberally over one another's arms and shoulders. Martha silently declined their offer to rub some on what they all assumed must be her aching shoulders. Instead she grabbed an extra tin of it to use on sore oxen feet.

Carsie watched Clint, wondering what pushed him as hard as he pushed them toward Virginia City. She answered herself. No doubt it was the handsome proceeds he would receive from women-hungry miners upon arrival. She frowned. How much money would change hands? How much had a man paid for Sophie?

Clint Bonner was an enigma, she thought quite suddenly as she observed him leaning over the beans and adding a dollop of molasses to the pot, then tasting to test. He moved the big cast-iron three-legged spider away from the intensity of the fire to lessen the chance of the ham being burned, then carefully turned each piece. After preparing a pot of coffee and placing it over the fire, he set about with a large square of toweling to wipe off the plates and utensils that had become mud-caked during the journey when the box that contained them had fallen open.

Yes, Clint Bonner was definitely an enigma. Here he was engaging in bride-selling, and yet without visible sign of irritation, he also tended to the evening meal with care she had never seen in any man. In her father's house, and later in her husband's, it was always expected that cooking and cleaning were women's work. Her work. Her mother had long before been worked into an early grave.

Did Clint perform these chores as a ruse, knowing she would write them in her journal and even in an article for publication? That would make him look like something other than what she wanted to portray him and his kind as

in her writing. He confused her, confounded the very image
he was trying to depict.

Later, after they'd all eaten in relative silence and retired
to their bedding, Clint walked to the edge of the river. With
every muscle in her body aching, Carsie laboriously walked
over to where he stood peering off into the distance.

"Any sign of Jake?"

He turned quickly, clearly startled by her approach. He
turned back. "There will be."

"You're worried about him, aren't you?" she asked softly.

He walked away from her toward a leafless tree with
branches that reached into the gathering gloom of night.
"Nobody's ever worried about Jake." His voice contradicted
his words. "Just when you think there's not one trace of a
chance he'll come back from somewhere or something, he
pops up like toadstool in the morning mist. No sense worrying."

Carsie took a couple of steps toward him and stopped. "I
know exactly what you mean." She tried to sound hopeful.
"I had a friend like that. She'd disappear, then show up again
just like that with an explanation that sounded so logical and
simple, as if I was supposed to read her mind and see into
a crystal ball to know where she was and that she was just
fine. But I was never like that. I always worried. I still worry.
Like you're worrying. Oh, but you're not worrying, you said.
That's right. I was just sort of worried that you might be
worrying and I thought if I told you about my friend then
you would see that it's fruitless to worry, and—"

"What happened to your friend? Is she back in St.
Joseph?"

Clint did not look up at her, but he sounded as if he
really cared. Dare she tell him the truth? "She . . . she left
town. Again."

"Well, it sounds as if she has a wandering spirit. I know
how that feels."

"It was more than that," Carsie returned quickly. "She

answered an ad in the newspaper. And she believed what they told her and then she just disappeared one night."

"What kind of ad?"

Carsie took in a deep breath. "For women to go west to become brides for miners and other . . . Westerners."

Clint remained silent for a long time. Then, "Now I really do understand."

She waited in the gloom—for what, she didn't know exactly. Then she shivered and became angry with herself for telling him. "I would certainly suppose you would understand. Since you, yourself, are one of those very perpetrators . . . who perpetrate the duping of innocent young girls."

He pushed himself away from the tree. "Here we go again. It's impossible for you to have a conversation without bringing up your damned ideas of what my business is with these women, isn't it? All you're looking for is somebody to blame for your friend going off in search of a better life."

"What? I'm not blaming you for Sophie's going off. She left before I even knew you existed. Yet now that I do know you exist, I'm not so certain you couldn't be to blame. I mean, you're not exactly without intelligence, although the way you use it might be called into question. Maybe you did have a hand in it. Maybe the man who took Sophie away was a friend of yours, or someone who worked with you in that circus, someone who wouldn't be above transporting—"

"Now just a dadblamed minute here. You've got no call insulting circus people."

"Aha!"

Clint kicked a rock into the river. "Now what the hell does that aha mean this time?"

"So, you admit it was a circus person who took her away."

"I admit nothing of the sort. I have no idea who took her away. Maybe nobody did. Maybe she went willingly."

"Willingly? Godawmighty, why would any woman go off willingly to some promised marriage with some . . . some person of questionable background, and for money as well?"

"Speaking of intelligence and the lack of real use of it, you are a classic example. Did it ever occur to you that some women actually *want* to be married? Or, even though this might shock you, some women quite cheerfully accept payment for such an arrangement?"

"For heaven's sake, why would you even think Sophie would be so desperate as to actually accept money from someone to get her out of St. Joseph and into the unknown with people—a man—she doesn't even know?"

"Perhaps it was the only way."

"To do what?"

"To get away from you!"

"What?" Carsie turned around and kicked a rock into the river. "How can you even suggest such a thing, that my dearest friend would actually ask to go with some unscrupulous man into the terror of the unknown just to . . . just to get away from me? That's the most ridiculous and despicable thing I've ever heard from anyone so despicable and ridiculous in my life. Now, listen to me, Major Clint Bonner . . ."

He stepped very close to her and peered down at her with his nose almost brushing hers. "No," he said. "I am not going to listen to you one minute more." Then he stalked away from her.

Carsie was speechless and instantly rueful. For a fleeting moment she could still feel the heat emanating from him.

Below the river edge and just inside the circle of light emanating from the glow of the cookfire, he turned back. "Where did Sophie go, do you know?"

She swallowed her pride and barely concealed the fear she suddenly felt. "Virginia City," she rasped.

He stood still for a moment. "I see." He headed toward the fire, then turned back once more.

The wagons rolled at first light with Martha in command and Clint riding far ahead to figure the best place to cross the river and head toward the northwest. He'd saddled up in the dark and left camp just as the women were stirring. The last thing he wanted to hear was all those women blaming him for the fact that Jake had not come back. Where was the old buzzard anyway? If he was dead somewhere, Clint would never hear the end of it from them. And he'd never forgive himself.

He kept his distance where he could see the river's bend in front of him and the wagon train behind him. He could see Mrs. Woo's wagon wobbling back and forth, could keep track of his own wagon hitched to a team Martha kept loosely tethered between Phoebe Goodnight's and Lola LaRue's. And see Miss Carson Rose Summers driving a team, her bright yellow bonnet glinting with sunlight.

Damn, where was Jake? If the weather stayed good, they'd make it easily to camp near Virginville. That was it. Maybe Jake was already in Virginville. Maybe he'd lost whoever was ahead of them and just took it upon himself to head for a town. Or . . . maybe whoever it was found him first and . . . No. Jake was in Virginville. That was it.

Though swollen from the heavy rains, the Big Blue offered the wagon train an easy crossing in belly-deep water for the animals, who seemed more interested in drinking and soaking their feet and knees than hauling the wagons across. Martha had a time of it keeping them moving and wouldn't have been as successful without Clint riding herd on all of them and Hannah Holmes wading in and leading animals toward the bank. Clint was mightily impressed with the way those two women, all of them for that matter, concentrated and worked hard to get everyone and everything across the river.

Clint urged them onward without a stop. They ate their noonday meal from the drivers' boxes. He was anxious to get to Virginville early enough to get into town and search the saloons and dancehalls for Jake. Margarita only briefly lit up in his mind. Jake had better be wetting his whistle in one of those places because he'd need his strength for the argument he was going to be in with Clint and with the rest of the women once they knew he was all right.

Dusk was starting to roll in when Clint spotted a campfire in the distance. Beyond he caught a glimpse of the settlement that was Virginville. He signaled Martha to hold the train near a clump of cottonwoods while he rode on ahead to see who had built the fire. The women climbed off the wagons and slumped into the shade of the trees while the animals pulled up tufts of sparse grass.

Clint rode to the crest of a hill, dismounted, lifted his rifle off his saddle, and crouched behind a spread of boulders and rocks. He took off his hat, slung the rifle over his back, and crept up the smooth side of a boulder, losing footing, climbing again, scraping his chin, hitting his elbow, bruising his fingers in his attempt to get a good hold. He had to get a clear look at the camp below him. With great exertion he reached the top of the boulder and hung on to some thin roots. He lifted his head carefully to peer over the sharp ridge.

"If you ain't the worst tracker I ever seen in all my born days, then I don't know who is."

The voice from behind him jolted Clint. Losing his footing and his precarious handholds, he slipped away and skidded down the boulders and rocks. His rifle scraped off his shoulder and banged against his temple. His shirt hiked up and his back scraped along sharp stone ridges. He hit his nose on a curve of the boulder and somersaulted over to land at the scuff-booted feet of Jake.

"Good thing I ain't no Sioux hunting party, n'er a trigger-happy bunch of soldier boys, or you'd be deader'n a balloon on a hot day's all I got to say." Jake shook his head and the stovepipe hat wobbled with each word.

Clint scrambled to his feet, wiping flowing blood away from his mouth and spitting dirt and stones. "Where in the name of Beelzebub have you been, you old buzzard?"

"Would you just listen to this cussin'? You'd think I was lost or something."

"Well, weren't you?" Clint snatched a bandanna from his back pocket and wiped his eyes.

"Hardly that. I seen you every foot of the way. Heard you kickin' stones in the river, too. You shore wasn't careful who you let hear where you was settin' up."

"Why didn't you let me know where you were? If you were trying to hide out from those women for a while, I'd have kept your secret. Though you would have had to pay me back in spades, friend."

"Hide out from the fellas? Now why would I want to go and do that?"

"I can name a hundred reasons. Being with that bunch is worse than having a hundred wives."

"You'd be lucky to have any one of them as a wife."

"Careful."

"All right. Maybe not the drum-banger."

"What'd you find out anyway? Who had the campfire ahead of us all this time?"

A voice came from beyond the boulder. "None other than he who suffers the lack of appreciation by the unbathed masses who have, fortunately, the price of a ticket."

Clint spun around, then back to Jake. "No-o-o."

"Yep."

"Harry? That you? Come on out, you old hamfatter."

A diminutive man with a head of full black hair and a

smile bright enough to light the darkest night strode out
into the clearing. "Hamfatter, is it? I can see you've been
away from the genuine life of the theater for far too long
a time." He ran forward and leapt with easy agility into
Clint's arms.

"Harry Hardin," Clint puffed. "You've put on some
weight. It's a sure bet Dinwoody couldn't lift you to balance
on his head cane anymore."

"Perhaps not. The halcyon days of Dr. Dinwoody and his
Daring Dwarf are long past like grains of sand on an errant
wind, my friend, and this dwarf is on the road to greatness
himself." Harry gave Clint a big kiss on the cheek and
dropped to the ground before his friend could dump him
there.

Clint wiped away the wet kiss with his gritty bandanna.
"I don't believe it. You've left the circus, too?"

"As sure as that certain twinkle in the eye of Bertie the
Bearded Lady whenever The Five Flying Fredericos passed
by her in their latest costumes. Or lack of costumes, I
should say. Something about their brevity making the gentlemen slip through the air, as I recall. Slipping costumes
being something Bertie prayed for since her throne sat ad-
jacent to their high swings. Ah well. But this rambling recollection serves only to deter me on my road to fame and
glory."

Clint grinned. "You're on the road to Virginville."

"Just another name for glory." Harry grinned back.

"You two gonna stand here and jaw all day, or we gonna
get back to the wagon train?" Jake swatted a swarm of
gnats away from his ears.

"Yes, dear compatriots, you must be on your pilgrim way,
and I . . ." Harry lifted his eyes and swept his outstretched
hand across the darkening heavens. "I must find my way
to the galaxy that begs a brighter star, that splendid stage
with a discerning audience that yearns for the sartorial ser-
endipity of an actor of my depth and breadth, talents which

I was given as gifts to make up for a distinct lack of height which a creator with a rather warped sense of humor deemed to bestow upon me at the momentous moment of my birth. I seek the repast of life, I yearn to assuage the hollowness in my spirit, I—"

"Wish to be invited to a meal as usual, you shyster," Clint broke in.

"Ah, but you always were a rather astute young man for a horse-riding clown." Harry threw back his head and laughed the rich laugh Clint remembered from the old days. "Let me gather my valuables and accept your warm invitation to dine."

"What valuables? You never owned anything worth a sou except for that Shakespeare book."

"That, my poor misguided friend, is the bible upon which I base the deportment of my life. Sir William speaks with a velvet tongue that carries messages from the gods. And I modestly confess that I have been touched by these gods and can make the greatest truths apparent to all who hear me speak."

Clint nodded throughout Harry's speech, his bottom lip quivering in amusement. "Un-hunh, and mules can fly."

"Truly? Then I take it Dan Rice has put together a new circus."

"And everyone in it has to be six feet tall or he won't take them."

Harry pointed an admonishing finger up at Clint. "You always were a cruel boy, Bonner, but I shall forgive you since, as my dearest friend Jake here has informed me, you harbor a wagon train peopled with ladies of the most pulchritudinous variety. To redeem yourself, you must lead me to them forthwith. I shall be ready in a trice."

"I only understand what he's sayin' half the time." Jake motioned for Clint to follow him down the other side of the rocks.

When Clint could see down to the camp Jake and Harry

had built, he stopped short. "Whatever made me think I was going to get my wagon train across this wild country without calling attention to it?"

Five

Seated at the back of the wagon, her face to the west, Carsie took out her journal intending to make a long-over-due entry. But the spectacular setting sun captured her attention for several moments and became more important to experience than the recollection of the strenuous days of travel. Clouds streaked the gray-blue sky in dusty purple against deep red orange and gold, painting a stunning celestial landscape.

Absorbing the moments, Carsie thought this surely must be one reason why people were drawn to the West. Their quest couldn't be all for gold or other riches. Surely deeper human reasons caused people to change the course of their lives.

Twice she had torn herself away from the life she'd been living. She'd run away from her father and brother after her husband died. She'd run for survival and never looked back. Now she was running again, this time toward something, she told herself with resolution. Running to save her friend from what was surely a fate worse than death. That was altruistic, wasn't it? Selfless? That's what she'd thought she'd been doing, or hoped she was doing with her work in St. Joseph. But something always seemed to be missing within that fulfillment of her personal pledge. She hadn't felt well, *satisfied,* she supposed.

Libby came around the wagon and interrupted her reverie. "I feel the roll of wagon wheels coming near."

Carsie quickly jumped down from the back of the wagon. She knew she could trust Libby to feel something before any of them could see whatever it was.

"Who can it be?" Libby stood close enough so that Carsie could feel the brush of her arm lightly along hers. "Jake and Major Bonner were on horseback."

"You're right. We'd better warn the others."

Carsie took Libby's arm and went to Phoebe's wagon. Miss Goodnight looked up from spreading several pieces of wet laundry over a rope as they approached.

"Miss Goodnight, Libby senses wagons approaching," Carsie told her. It was the first time she'd actually addressed the woman face to face.

Phoebe wiped her damp hands on an apron she'd thrown over her green cotton skirt. The homely act struck Carsie in a way she wouldn't have thought could happen a few weeks ago; that the proprietor of a whorehouse would perform household chores and wear an apron seemed incongruous.

Phoebe stood still a long moment, contemplating. "Martha?" she called toward the corral they'd constructed of ropes and heavy brush. Martha emerged from the back, muddy and carrying a pitchfork. "Miss Summers and Libby have reported wagons coming near. What do you suggest?"

Martha came toward them in long strides. Some days back she'd shed the skirt she'd worn the first day Carsie had seen her in the freight yard and wore her uniform trousers and a collarless shirt and suspenders. Her heavy boots made deep impressions in the soaked soil.

"Which direction?" It was the first time Carsie could remember hearing Martha speak. Hers was a deep voice, strong as any man's.

"That way." Libby pointed toward a rise in a southwesterly direction.

The crack of gunfire broke the escalating tension. Two shots, then three more.

"Get the rifles," Martha commanded. "Then go where I tell you. I'll get the others placed."

Phoebe went to a wagon, calling out to Lola and Hannah as she went. They came around and she handed them each a rifle, and brought two more.

"I can't shoot a rifle," Libby said quietly. A small sob caught in her throat.

"Don't want you to anyway," Martha returned. "Your job is at the front line. You'll have the first response when I tell you."

"Yes, ma'am."

Carsie thought Libby was going to salute Martha, but she didn't.

"Me," a timid voice came from behind.

Carsie turned around to find Mrs. Woo standing very still, her eyes downcast. It was the first time the woman had spoken.

Martha nodded and motioned Mrs. Woo toward her own wagon. "You're going to help Libby," she told her. Mrs. Woo looked up at the woman in man's clothing with a blank stare. Martha made hand gestures indicating Libby. Mrs. Woo registered comprehension and motioned for Martha to follow her. She opened the back of her wagon and Carsie could see her making hand gestures and talking to Martha in Chinese.

A short while later, cradling a rifle she had only moments before been instructed on how to operate, Carsie crouched behind some scrub trees and thick brush. Several feet to her left around the semicircle line of defense that Martha had arranged, Libby and Mrs. Woo stood at either side of a contraption Carsie had only read about in books. A catapult with a great springing mechanism at one end and a leather and rope-laced scoop on the other, the machine looked capable of war action. Carsie wondered what other out-of-the-ordinary goods Mrs. Woo could be transporting. The two women had amassed a great many small rocks. A pile stood behind them and the scoop was full, held back by a heavy rock.

Lola crouched a few feet to Carsie's right, a rifle positioned on a steadying rock while she took sight and aim. Beyond her waited Miss Goodnight and Hannah with brush and logs piled taller than they, rifles at their feet.

All eyes were trained on Martha, who stood poised below on a ledge with a vantage point for sight around the river bend, a rifle in her hands, another not far behind her.

The sound of wheels and horses' hooves on the still-wet ground grew louder as they drew near. Martha leaned forward, her alert mind focused and sharp eyes trained in the direction of the approaching group. Carsie's heart pounded. She glanced around at the others. More than one wiped a damp palm over clothing. Miss Goodnight repeatedly swept hair from her face. Lola couldn't seem to hold suspended for more than a few seconds at a time, and even then she trembled visibly.

Libby and Mrs. Woo stood stock-still. Carsie was certain she saw the hints of satisfied smiles on their faces. She sensed that here were two people, though physically and socially rendered incapable of useful work, shackled by blindness and cultural molding, both accidents of birth, who felt empowered in this one isolated moment, self-armed with more than the weapons of war. These two were contributing equals, and they reveled more in these moments than any others she'd seen in the women's rights marches in which she'd participated.

We're all in this together, she thought. None of the times she'd marched down the street with primly dressed upright townswomen had Carsie felt an intrinsic part of them, a real member of a sisterhood. Somehow she'd always felt apart from them, a foster child taken in and used to do the most backbreaking of the work that needed to be done.

Yes, she believed in the rights of women. Yes, she rallied other women to action and led them on demonstrations. In those moments it seemed as if they were together for the same reason, yet Carsie never truly felt a total honesty from most of the other women. She sensed some of them just wanted a reason to show their husbands what they might be capable of if the men strayed from the straight and narrow. At the end of the march they would all go back to their cozy homes and their husbands and children, while she went back to the place she alternately lived in alone or shared with Sophie whenever her friend was there.

Right now, on this rocky hillside in the middle of an untamed land, participating in a tiny civil war of sorts, defending a little settlement on wheels alongside a troop of seasoned women commanded by a female with real war experience, Carsie felt a kinship, completely at one with them, connected by a strong thread of common purpose. This was more than a demonstration of underlying strength. This was an actual stance. They were banding together for a common cause they all believed in. This was action, not talk.

Martha's arm went up toward her troops.

Carsie's blood surged. Her heart raced. She raised her rifle.

Phoebe and Hannah rolled the brush down the hillside, then snatched up rifles and began to fire.

Lola fired shots.

Her rifle at her feet, Martha suddenly turned toward them and waved her arms wildly.

Mrs. Woo nodded her head in acceptance of a command and shouted in high-pitched Chinese. Together she and Libby rolled the huge stone away from their cannon. The scoop snapped up and catapulted the arsenal of rocks over the hillside. As if one mind was in control, their flurry of gunfire and employment of makeshift war weapons commenced.

Carsie snapped the heavy rifle to her shoulder. She clamped one eye shut and peered down the sight with the other. The swaying horizon in her one squinting eye made her dizzy and nauseous. Then she caught a glimpse of what looked to be the crown of a hat wobbling in her vision. With every ounce of courage and strength she could muster, she squeezed the trigger. The shot exploded, propelling her backward to sprawl on the ground. The rifle skidded away from her.

She struggled to her feet. What was that new sound? Shouts. She was certain she was hearing shouts. Was everyone all right? Wiping dirt from her eyes, she located the fallen rifle, picked it up, and crawled back to her position. Dust from the earth and brush and stones mingled with smoke from the gunfire and swirled in the air. Her eyes felt gritty, and they watered. She tried to see, but couldn't get a clear picture of what was going on around her. She could hear sounds of feet scrambling, Martha shouting, horses squealing, women's voices blending with men's. And Clint Bonner swearing a blue streak.

Clint?

Carsie crawled to where Phoebe had been positioned, but she wasn't there. The melee quieted suddenly. Then Clint's voice rose clearly into the settling dust.

"What in the hell did you think you were doing? You almost killed us!"

Carsie leaned around her shelter of rocks and saw him, hatless, blood running down his face from a cut on his head. Beyond him she saw something that astounded her. Two white horses, smudged all over with dirt, pawed the ground in their silver decorated harnesses. Bells sewn along the leather straps jangled loudly. Behind them was a long wooden wagon, painted red with gaudily drawn figures of an open-jawed lion and a black-booted man wielding a whip, and a woman seated on a swing wearing a white costume that resembled a corset. Thickly coiled ropes held down valises and boxes piled atop the wagon.

"Most fun I've had since that night in Chicago when the

constable arrested us for disorderly conduct in church! What a night, eh, Clint?"

The unrecognizable voice came from inside the red wagon. Then the curtained front flap snapped open and a man, barely half Clint's height, stepped out and easily alit to the ground. Carsie watched in mesmerized fascination. He wore the perfect costume of a rodeo performer she'd seen in a picture in *Harper's* once, from an oversized white hat to leather chaps, right down to perfectly tooled leather boots and spurs.

"And just what have we here?" The diminutive man perused the women who slowly advanced on the wagon. "A gathering of comely pulchritude such as I haven't seen since Boston. Dear friends," he admonished Clint and Jake, "how have you kept this secret?"

"As if anything could be kept a secret with this lot," Clint muttered.

"And one of you better own up to shootin' through my best hat," Jake called out, fingering the hole in his stovepipe. Martha inched her way down the hillside toward him. "Martha, was that you?"

Carsie's heart pounded. She'd never touched a gun in her life until a few minutes ago. The reality of those moments slowly crept into comprehension. The first time she'd fired a gun she'd almost killed someone. A friend, or someone she was coming to think of as a friend. She stood slowly, her knees wobbled.

"Mr. Storms, it wasn't Martha," she called out with a wavering voice. "I shot you, or I mean I fired at you . . . what I mean is . . . I did it."

Jake's jaw dropped.

Clint snapped his gaze in her direction. "Bloomers? You plugged Jake's hat?" His stern face shattered into a wide grin, and a hearty laugh erupted from him.

"Well, now, I'm glad you find this so dadblamed amusin'." Jake glared at Clint then back at Carsie. "She prack'ly blew my head off. Never mind my best hat is ruint."

"Say now," the little man said, moving in front of Jake and Clint, "you certainly have an array, haven't you?" He doffed the big white hat and held out his hand toward Carsie, who'd started down the hillside. "Harry Hardin, miss, at your service."

Carsie took his outstretched hand and he assisted her the rest of the way down.

"Thank you, Mr. Hardin." She couldn't help but stare at him.

"Fascinated already, I see," Harry said, kissing the back of her hand.

"Oh," Carsie faltered. "I'm sorry. It's just that I've never seen—"

"Such a perfect specimen of a man such as I, correct? Well, big things come in small packages, somebody told me once. I can't remember who it was, unless it was Madame Celeste the fortune-teller the night we were on the trapeze swing and—"

"Hardin!" Jake belted. "There's ladies present!"

Harry didn't skip a beat. "Let me inform you that the great Napoleon had naught but a scant few inches on me, Miss—?"

"Summers, Carson Rose Summers. I know it's not polite to stare, Mr. Hardin. It's just that I've never seen . . ." She walked slowly around him. "I've never seen such a full head of perfectly black hair on a man before. It's positively luxurious."

Harry shrugged and beamed. "It's hereditary. I rather like your bloomers, too."

"Really?"

"Yes, indeed. The fit is perfectly tailored, allowing freedom of movement yet portraying a decidedly feminine element."

Carsie smiled warmly, still staring at Harry's head.

Harry ran a hand through his hair. "Feel free to indulge in experiencing the pure texture of it if you wish."

Carsie's cheeks warmed. "You wouldn't mind?"

"Not in the least." He inclined his head toward her.

Timidly at first, Carsie touched the top of his head. She lifted his hair, let it fall back.

"It's quite wonderful," she exclaimed, "and so clean."

"Come, come, ladies." Harry motioned the others with both hands. "Don't hold back. I invite you to partake along with Miss Summers."

Lola and Hannah went quickly to him and plunged their hands into his hair. Harry turned his head one way and then the other, behaving like a cat reveling in the stroking of its fur.

"If we could dispense with this tonsorial assessment, could we get back to the business at hand?" Clint slapped dirt off his shirt and pants. "That is, if you don't mind, King Harry."

Harry brushed his hand through the air. "Do what you must, do what you must. Just pretend I'm not here."

"Of course," Clint growled, snatching up the reins to the white horses, "just like the next Sioux hunting party will do when they see this team and that wagon."

Jake led his and Clint's horses to camp while Martha took over the handling of the circus wagon and team. Phoebe, Hannah, and Lola exclaimed over the wonderful murals painted all over it, discovering details and pointing them out.

Carsie scanned the hillside. "Where's Libby? And Mrs. Woo?"

"I saw Mrs. Woo dragging some contraption back to her wagon," Jake answered. "That one of them catapult rigs? I figured as much."

"Libby, where's Libby?" Carsie squinted her eyes and peered into the gathering twilight. She attempted to climb the rocky face, but her feet slipped. How was it she'd scaled it so easily when Martha had lined them up in defense? Was it true what she'd read, that people have heroic strength when their lives are threatened?

"Where was she earlier?" Clint started up the rocks.

"There." Carsie pointed to where Libby and Mrs. Woo had been stationed.

A small cry echoed from the ravine at the other side of the hill.

Phoebe ran to the hillside and attempted to climb up. "She's fallen, I just know it. She must be frightened out of her wits."

Harry rushed over. "Where was she? I can get there faster than any of you. She'll see me coming and she'll wait."

Carsie directed him. "She's blind."

Clint took a step back. "She's . . . *blind?*"

Harry was off at a clipped pace, scaling the rocky-faced hillside as easily as an antelope.

"You didn't know that?" Carsie stared up at him in shock.

"No, I didn't know that."

"Well, you're not very observant, are you?"

Clint frowned. Silently he started up the hillside after Harry. Still shaking, Carsie followed him.

"You mind explaining just what took place back there?" Clint kept purposeful long strides ahead of her.

"We were defending life and limb and property," she said resolutely, her lungs working hard for breath.

"By almost killing the very one who owns that property?"

"You don't own the lives and limbs in question. We didn't know who was approaching. After all, you and Jake went off on horseback. How were we to know you'd come back with a wagon? How were we to know it wasn't a band of thieving desperadoes bent on . . . thieving and doing other . . . desperate things?" Carsie slipped on a rock, twisted her ankle, held her pain silently, and righted herself. She limped along behind him.

"So what did you plan to do? Question the dead bodies later?" Clint trudged faster.

"Nobody's dead, in case you hadn't noticed."

"Thanks only to the fact that you can't shoot straight."

"I'd never shot off a gun before."

"I suppose I should take solace in that. You almost blew the head off my best friend."

"But I didn't."

"Only by pure dumb luck."

Carsie groaned and snatched up a small tree limb that lay along the rocks. "Can't you forget this? It's over. What about poor Libby? For all you know, she could be hurt, she could be in pain and bleeding with the loss of . . ." She bit her tongue, thankful she'd caught herself in time to protect Libby's secret. Although it would be soon enough that Libby's secret would reveal itself on its own, even sooner if Libby had been severely hurt.

Clint stopped and turned around. "The loss, did you say? Of what? Why are you limping?"

Carsie ignored his first question. "I tripped and turned my ankle back there. Don't worry, I didn't expect you to notice or to care, for that matter."

"You are the most exasperating female I've ever met. I suppose now I'll have to carry you."

"Don't you even think of touching me," she shouted.

"Touching you?" he shouted back. "I wouldn't dream of it. I think of you only as a sack of cornmeal." He went to grab her behind the knees, intent on throwing her over her shoulder.

"Stop arguing and get over here!" Harry's voice echoed up from the ravine.

Clint scrambled over the rocks toward it, Carsie dragging along close behind him. They found Harry down the hillside only a few feet from the edge of a deep ravine with Libby clinging to his back. He was trying to work his way toward the top. Clint met them halfway down and lifted Libby, bearing her the rest of the way up. Gently, he set her down next to Carsie. Harry scrambled up behind them.

"I was so frightened at first," Libby told Carsie. "But then Mr. Hardin—"

"Harry, remember?" Harry cut in.

"Yes, Harry," Libby said shyly, "Harry talked very soothingly to me. His voice was so kind yet so forceful. I calmed immediately. He said he would save me and I believed he would. And he did."

"Thank God," Carsie whispered. She looked back down into the ravine and realized that Harry had prevented Libby from plunging to certain death with only moments to spare.

"She'll be fine," Harry said. "A little banged up, but nothing that can't be fixed." He helped her to her feet, and they started back to camp.

"Thanks, friend," Clint said, grabbing Harry's hand and sending him in front of him. "No doubt she was crazy with fear."

"She's quite courageous, actually," Harry said. "When she fell, she had the wherewithal to protect the baby."

"Yeah, that was pretty courageous— The. what?"

Harry stopped and turned around. "The baby, of course."

Clint stopped dead and swallowed hard. "Baby?"

"I can see you've been away from civilization so long you've forgotten how civilization comes about. Babies. Pregnancy. Miss Allen is pregnant—with a baby, of course. Do you recall any of this now?"

Clint stood there dumbfounded for a long moment. "Why should I be remotely surprised? The first time I stood in the St. Joe freight yard I should have known what I was getting into."

It was an animated group that sat around the campfire that night. Excitement ran through them over Libby's pregnancy and the events of the day. Harry and Jake produced

four prairie chickens they'd bagged before the women's warfare had ended their hunting. Hannah contributed biscuits
baked in a specially made Dutch oven she drew with great
effort from her wagon.

"These biscuits are the best I've ever tasted," Clint
praised. "Where you been keeping that oven?" He gave her
a teasing smile.

She raised wide brown eyes toward him, and Carsie knew
with that look she must have melted many a heart of the
visitors to Goodnight's Good Times Emporium. She felt a
bit embarrassed to even think such a thing. All of Miss
Goodnight's ladies had worked in her establishment. They
knew men intimately. And not just one man. Several.

Carsie had believed that women of easy virtue, women
who would go so far as to . . . do *that* for money, were of
the lowest sort. Yet these women puzzled her. They worked
hard around the camp every evening after driving wagons
all day. They never complained about the work or the
weather or unforgiving terrain over which they bumped and
jolted atop their wagons. And they'd all stood together this
afternoon to defend themselves as a group, herself included,
without thought for anything but the defense of the community they'd unwittingly formed together.

Carsie made a mental note to get to know each one of
these . . . ladies much more than she'd allowed herself up
to now.

"I'm sorry for keeping the oven a secret, Mr. Bonner."
Hannah's voice was as soft and smoky as her skin.

"You probably feared for its safe passage." Clint smiled
wider.

Hannah relaxed her tense shoulders. "Yes, I thought it
might suffer the fate intended for the piano and bathing
tub."

"You have a piano?" Harry piped up.

"Indeed." Phoebe broke off a chicken leg and licked the

juices from her fingers. "And Libby can make it sound as if it played only for the gods."

"Ah, Miss Libby." Harry rose and went to where she sat on a log with Carsie. "Might you favor us with a short concert this evening?"

"Oh, I don't think so," Libby answered without raising her eyes from her plate. "Mr. Bonner . . . that is, well, the piano must stay hidden."

"Why? Are there roving packs of wild piano thieves on the loose?"

Carsie giggled and quickly clamped a hand over her mouth.

Harry dropped down to sit at Libby's feet. "Note that the Dutch oven came out of hiding with rather palatable consequences. Even the otherwise stern taskmaster, Clint Bonner, has admitted the delicious outcome. And surely on a lovely night such as this, those piano perpetrators are safely ensconced in one of Virginville's many entertainment establishments, no doubt perusing some other person's piano with malice aforethought and liberty in mind, therefore being totally unaware of the one that sits out here waiting for the magic touch of the fair Miss Libby's fingers to bring it joyfully to life."

Libby sat mesmerized as Harry spun his tale, and for a moment Carsie was in the trance with her.

"Where did you learn to speak so prettily?" Libby asked, and promptly blushed enough to rival the fire's glow.

" 'Tis a gift, fair lady. Honed by many years of oratorical browbeating by Sir Marion Fosdick, the greatest teacher of drama in the Northern Hemisphere. And he told that to everyone within hearing of cannons."

"You took acting lessons?" Carsie became more interested than ever in the latest member of their wagon train.

"Stylistic stage presence as defined by Sir Marion."

"Now don't you go encouragin' him, Miz Summers." Jake scraped the juices from his place with a biscuit. "I knowed him to jump up on the back of an elephant and start spoutin' that Romeo dude's love talk."

"Ooo, Mee-shure Hardeen," Lola LaRue gushed, "I would dearly adore to hear you act."

"You don't know what you're asking." Clint grabbed another biscuit. "Once he turns on that stage charm, it's like opening a cistern with a broken spigot. You can't dam it up and all you can do is stand there useless until it runs empty."

"Sounds beautiful to me," Phoebe put in. "We don't often get to hear poetic words from so eloquent a man."

There was a long pause. Carsie thought Miss Goodnight sounded rather wistful. Could it be that she had not wanted to be a part of the professional business she now owned? Was she ever married? Did she have children? Carsie's mind was now flowing with questions like the cistern Clint had just described.

"I shall ignore Bonner's cutting remark," Harry said with great dramatic flair, "and favor the discerning Miss Goodnight with a rendition of Mr. Shakespeare's sonnets some evening soon if I should be so fortunate as to be among this fair gathering in the near future. But for now, I would importune Miss Libby to favor us with one composition." He reached over and took her hand, pressing it to his lips.

"It's probably way out of tune," Libby whispered. She fidgeted with her plate and fork. "And I—"

"Cannot refuse such a request," Clint finished. "Let me make the piano available for you."

All eyes save Harry's shifted to Clint immediately. This was a surprising concession, he knew. He went to the wagon which held the piano, loosened the ropes, and lifted the flap.

A nagging thought had been creeping in and out of his mind the last couple of nights as he lay in his bedroll, most often wide awake. It came to him sharply now as he set about uncovering the instrument and its stool. He, and maybe no man, ever had complete control over his own life, let alone a wagon train he thought belonged to him. And more, no man had real control over another, or over a woman, though he wondered why men liked to think they did. He realized he'd been wondering about just that for most of his life.

"Splendid!" Standing up, Harry took Libby's plate from her lap and handed it to Carsie. He took Libby's hand and slowly urged her to come forward.

With Harry's assistance, Libby climbed into the wagon. She felt along the piano until she came to the middle and, reaching behind her to locate the stool, sat down and lifted the lid that covered the keyboard. Carefully she located middle C and poised her fingers over the keys. When they depressed and moved, the sweet melody and sensitive playing rendered almost unnoticeable the flat notes from the out-of-tune instrument.

Clint allowed himself the peaceful moments to read the faces of those gathered around the campfire. Harry stood next to the wagon, an enraptured gaze lighting his countenance. To a one, including Martha, Libby's dulcet playing lifted the weariness in body and mind from the battering of travel, and transported them above the rolling land which had exhausted them for weeks. Even the oxen quieted in their corral, and the horses cocked one back foot and seemed to sway dreamily at their tethers.

Suddenly Clint wished he could hold this gentle night in his hands forever.

The Journal of Carson Rose Summers

20 July 1866
Today was filled with the most exciting adventure! Just when it appeared we women alone might be attacked by unknown assailants, we rallied under

Martha's expert command and defended ourselves as well as any men. It was exhilarating!

Even when our presumed attackers turned out to be Major Bonner, Mr. Storms, and a friend, a Mr. Harry Hardin, also a circus performer, we still felt victorious. I know that. And unless those men are more thick-headed than I suspect, they know it, too. No actual battles fought, no wars won, and yet I could feel among us all that something had changed for us.

I am weary to the core. How Libby has managed to stay alert every day is something I do not comprehend. She has such a sunny outlook on everything. I know it's getting very hard for her. The baby has grown quickly. She finds it difficult to sit for long periods and that's all we do during the day, sit on our hard wagon. And yet this evening she sat upon a piano stool in the middle of this vast country and with her extraordinary gift managed to soothe us all. Immediately I felt my own shoulders settle and the knots in them and the constant pain in my neck release. My mind emptied of all save the melody of "Auralea."

I felt something more when Libby ceased playing and no one spoke, something such as I've never experienced inside myself. I struggle to define it now. It was as if I was somehow connected to everyone in our gathering. Even with the withdrawn Mrs. Woo.

But perhaps not to Clint Bonner. He and I are more opposite than any of the others on this wagon train. Yet even he seemed entranced by Libby's music. He puzzles me. I catch him looking at me at times, and then he looks away quickly. I wonder what he sees, or does he see nothing? It disturbs me. Why, I can't say. I suppose I wouldn't be so disturbed if I didn't see him looking at me. I should stop looking at him, then I wouldn't see him looking at me.

I want to know about these people, about all of

them. How is it that I've sensed something new in me? I have always much preferred staying separate from other people. And I would never have consorted with women of the profession of Miss Goodnight and her friends. And now . . .

I must close my eyes. Tomorrow we go into Virginville. I wonder why anyone would name a town that. I am looking forward to seeing a settlement of people once more. And how I would love a real bath.

Six

The burgeoning settlement of Virginville was an oft-used stopping point for coaches on the Overland Stage Line. Beyond it lay the Mormon Crossing on the Oregon Trail. And so on this morning when Clint Bonner's wagon train rolled into town, like every other morning the town teemed with wagon trains of Western travelers buying supplies and taking needed rest from their journey. Townspeople, which seemed to be mostly men, were out in throngs.

Clint and Jake meandered past what were obviously Virginville's quickly constructed establishments. Miss Goodnight with Hannah and Lola had stopped into a restaurant for a town-made breakfast. Ahead of Clint and Jake, Harry escorted Carsie and Libby.

Carsie walked gingerly among rutted tracks deep with dirt and animal droppings along what the inhabitants enjoyed calling the streets of Virginville. Libby walked between Carsie and Harry, chatting excitedly.

"Do you think I might find baby napery here in the mercantile? I have a little money saved and I brought it with me this morning. The baby will need some gowns and so many things. Oh, isn't this place wonderful? So noisy, just like St. Joseph, isn't it? I love the noise."

Carsie considered Libby's comparison. Wood-framed buildings lined Virginville's three streets in such a manner as to resemble rows of dilapidated crates and boxes leaning against each other. She thought of how she and Sophie sometimes tilted a set of dominoes in the shape of the first letter of their first names. They would laugh gleefully when they touched one on the end and the entire letter would collapse in the same pattern. The buildings along streets of Virginville looked like leaning dominoes, as if a strong gust of wind at one end would set them all a-tumble in succession.

"Yes, you're quite right," Harry said to Libby. "While this seems to be a frontier town of the first water, it does seem to be a thriving community."

Carsie leaned around Libby and stared at him. In her opinion, Libby's blindness should not mean they must lie to her about her surroundings. Harry gave her an admonishing stare back.

"And what do the people look like?" Libby pressed. "Are they dressed smartly, and do the ladies carry parasols to protect them against this beastly sun?"

A man staggered toward them, obviously drunk even so early in the morning. His ragged and filthy clothes clung to his portly body. He swerved toward them and was met by a woman wearing what Carsie could only describe as a nightgown, who steered him down a narrow side street toward a row of shabby houses.

Harry deftly maneuvered the two women around them without so much as a brush from the foul man. "Yes, indeed," he told Libby. "They are all dressed in a manner which speaks quite accurately of their stations. Except for the parasols. I daresay these ladies are quite accustomed to the weather and cohabit with it rather well."

Carsie raised her eyes heavenward. She'd never believed in telling children outlandish stories. The truth of any matter was much better for them, in her opinion, so they wouldn't grow up with an unrealistic view. And it was much more important to be honest with adults, regardless of their situation. Here was Harry creating a false visual landscape for the blind Libby, painting a vivid watercolor of a landscape more accurately created with a dull knife against red-brown stone by an untrained hand.

Music, if it could be called that, same from inside a saloon. A tinny piano, sounding for all the world as if it were being pounded by fists, gave off a raucous dance tune. Carsie noted there were more saloons than any other kind of establishment.

"My, that piano is in dire need of tuning," Libby observed. "But isn't it a lively tune for the morning? Is someone giving lessons?"

"I'm not quite certain," Harry replied. "I'll take a closer look and let you know."

Carsie could not allow this line of conversation to continue. "No, Libby, no one is giving lessons, at least not music lessons. That's a saloon."

"Oh, my, a saloon open so early in the morning."

Harry gave Carsie a feigned look of disgust at her remark.

A rather portly woman scurried past, dodging a pair of soldiers who were not above leering at her. She swatted at a swarm of gnats that hovered around her head. The soldiers turned their attention then upon Carsie, who burned under their scrutiny.

One of them stopped squarely in front of her and stared openly at her bloomers. "You a female under them britches?"

Carsie sidestepped around him and got to Libby's side. Harry stood with a smile of amusement playing at the corners of his mouth.

"Of all the effrontery," Carsie breathed.

"Yeah," the soldier returned. "The front doesn't do much for you, but the back, now that's something else. That does a lot for you."

"Oh-h." Carsie took Libby's arm and urged her forward away from the offending soldiers.

"How nice of that man to compliment you," Libby said.

"And he doesn't even know you. They're so friendly in Virginville. Why do they call it that, I wonder?"

Harry took Libby's arm and gently steered her along the crude walkway past the open doors of three parlor houses where working women lounged in brief costumes. "Some reasons for things never reveal themselves. Such is the mystery of life."

Two painted women in bosom-exposing bodices sashayed toward the soldiers. Carsie flushed at their obvious intent. "Now that is simply too much—"

"You would be quite taken with the soldiers in their smart uniforms, Libby," Harry interrupted, giving Carsie another admonishing glance. "The ladies do give them the eye."

"How romantic," Libby breathed. "Soldiers and ladies. It's just like a book Miss Phoebe read to me last year. The soldiers were so dashing and smart, and the ladies fluttered their fans and dropped their eyes ever so flirtatiously. Is that what they're doing?"

"Oh, they're fluttering all right." Carsie gave Harry another stare, willing him to be honest with Libby, rather than filling her head with a lot of romantic fantasy.

A particularly tall woman, suddenly distracted, disengaged herself from the circled arm of a soldier and stepped toward them, hips swaying, her smile a wide gash of red in her powdered face. She bent down toward Harry. "Well, now, what have we here? Good morning, handsome little man."

Her heavy bosom strained against her bodice, which was just about eye level to Harry. Carsie was outraged to see that he hadn't the decency to avert his eyes. And so early in the morning, too. Why, the sun had hardly made it into the midmorning sky. Couldn't men control themselves enough to curtail their wanton desires to an appropriate time of day and place, such as at night in the dark behind closed doors?

"And a gracious good day to you, ah, madam," Harry greeted her, doffing his hat.

The woman gave the once-over to Carsie and Libby, and returned to Harry. "I see you've already busied yourself this morning. Couldn't I lure you away to . . . shall we say, more interesting pursuits?" She lowered her voice to a seductive growl. "I can promise to show you the experience of a lifetime."

"I beg your pardon, miss, or, madam." Carsie made a small stamp in the dirt sidewalk. "This gentleman is already occupied, as you've duly noted. Not that we are, that is, we don't pretend to offer him the—what did you call it?—the experience of a lifetime. But we—"

Libby surprised her by uncustomarily pushing toward the woman. "Just what is it you want with our friend? As I understand it, you have plenty of soldiers to take up your time."

The painted woman eyed Libby's plain brown muslin dress and swollen belly. "A girl can have a soldier any day, honey. Plenty more arrive when the others are used up. But a man like your friend here . . . well, let's just say my mother always taught me that big things come in small packages."

"Oh my." Carsie let it out long and slow.

"We could have had the some mother," Harry muttered. Linking his arms through Libby's and Carsie's, he drew them away. "Ah, the mercantile, and just in time." He directed Libby through the door and ushered Carsie in behind her.

The shop door closed with a jangle of chimes suspended overhead.

Outside the mercantile door Jake spat a stream of tobacco juice into the muddy street. "Well, that was sure fun to watch, wasn't it?"

"Best fun I've had in a long, long time," Clint agreed with a laugh.

"That Summers girl's gettin' an eyeful I bet she's never seen in all her born days." Jake chuckled.

"Let alone had the experience."

"Never saw a spinster couldn't benefit from an experience or two."

"Why, you old rogue." Clint gave Jake's stovepipe hat a tap on the top.

Jake scraped it off his head and reshaped it. He ran a finger over the spot where Carsie's bullet had injured it and Martha had deftly repaired it. "Now, don't go gettin' the wrong idea. I was just thinkin' that little gal could use some good kissin' for one thing. That would change her outlook."

From the street window Clint saw Harry conducting Libby and Carsie around the mercantile. "And just who did you have in mind to do that deed? You?"

"Me? Not hardly. I figured you to be the right one."

Clint coughed. "Well, you figured that one wrong, pard."

"What's the matter, boy? Lost your nerve?"

"Nerve's got nothing to do with it. I just don't see it as my job to do anything about Bloomers's outlook."

"Way I see it is you're scared."

"Scared of what?"

"Scared she'd slap your grinnin' face, that's what. And there would go the old Bonner reputation for makin' a woman swoon with just one kiss. Or was that story all made up?"

Clint fidgeted with his belt and then his hat. "You know how those things go. Doesn't take much to get a story like that started."

"Could be. But I tell you, them women talked about you for months after you left the circus back East. Never thought I hear the end of it. They was prack'ly useless. Me, I figured you was all talk. They tried to convince me, but I says I never saw anything would prove Clint Bonner was no great kisser."

"All right, all right, what are you trying to do here? If

you think I'm going to tell you who and when—well, I'm not, you old coot."

"Nope." Jake eyed him cagily. "I just figured nobody could be as colossal as what they said you was, is all. Seemed more'n any man could do."

Clint grinned. "Some of us have more talent than others."

"So I heard. Now, if I was to see you catch that Summers gal one of these times and plant a good one on her, *and* if she was t'faint dead away . . . well, then, I reckon I might begin to believe all them stories about you. She ain't no usual one what would just go to quakin' from good kissin'. Those others ain't no test. Now she's a real test."

"I know what you're up to now." Clint nodded to underscore his suspicious words.

"What?"

"Don't sound so innocent."

"I don't hafta sound innocent. I am."

"Admit it. You're trying to get me to kiss Bloomers."

"What would make you say that?"

"I know you. I know you're trying to goad me into it. Well, you can't do it. I'm not going to kiss her."

"Scared, aren't you?"

"Scared? Of what?"

"That she's the one woman who'll end your streak of female conquests."

"My streak of what?"

"Well, it's just a lucky streak is all, if you ask me."

"Luck had nothing to do with it." Clint smiled smugly.

"Couldn't prove it by me. I never saw nothin' said that. Like I said, if you was to kiss that suffragist and she was t'swoon, well, then, I might b'lieve them stories. I dare you to do it."

Clint stared through the mercantile window. Carson Summers was examining a bolt of dull gray cloth. Not far from her was a display of frilly women's nightclothes, but she didn't seem to notice them. Maybe Jake was right about spinsters and the right kind of experience. What if he did kiss her and she didn't go all weak in the knees like so many girls used to do when he first learned about kissing? Worse, what if she didn't like it? Nah. All women liked kissing, didn't they?

He had to admit he'd been out of kissing practice over the last few months. That was because he'd been single-minded about getting his freight business going. He was going to make this work, and he'd have to avoid getting distracted by women if he was going to succeed and make the money he needed. At least he knew that. He was getting too old to just wander the country.

All his life he'd wanted something permanent, someplace permanent to call home, something to call his own that he cared for and could watch grow, knowing it was his and his alone. He'd never had any money to speak of. Life had been a constant series of trades and barters. Cut and carry firewood for food. Muck out horse stalls for a bed. Fix a wagon wheel for a ride to another town. Flatter a woman for a night of pleasure that would erase his sense of emptiness.

That was changing now and would change permanently in Virginia City. He was determined to make it happen. The moment he'd discovered what he wanted, he'd known how to go about getting it. The whole incident had been like a burst of flash powder in the hands of a magician. And he meant to hold that remaining glimmer of his idea and realize his dream.

Still, what if he had lost his touch? When he was ready again for the diversion that women provided, would he still be able to make them weak with desire?

Jake was right, in his conniving way. The suffragist would be a good test of his masculine powers.

Clint grabbed the door handle. "All right, you old wizard, you just better keep your eyes fixed on me and Bloomers day in and day out, because one of these days it's going to happen. I'm going to kiss her so she can make no mistake she's been kissed by the master. And you just better be awake to witness it."

Jake grinned and spat the remaining tobacco juice. "Count on it!" He pushed past Clint, opened the door to the mercantile, and strode in.

Clint paused, a feeling of the breaking of dawn sweeping over him. "That was a stupid thing," he muttered. "Smart for Jake. Stupid for me. What is happening to me?" He followed Jake into the shop.

"My name's Anne." A young shop clerk approached Carsie. "Can I help you find something?"

"I'll take two yards of this." Carsie patted a bolt of gunmetal gray cloth.

The delicate skin between the girl's eyes pleated into a small frown. "Are you certain I can't show you some of that fine calico over there? It's just come in from the East, and all the ladies in town are quite taken with it." The girl picked up another bolt and fingered a corner of the fine white fabric. "Or this lovely cotton lawn."

Carsie eyed the girl's yellow frock, which was fussily decorated with a pleated bodice edged in wide lace. Her dark hair was pulled back from her face and caught in a yellow ribbon at the nape of her neck, allowing rich brown curls to cascade down her back. Carsie caught a wistful breath from escaping, then squared her shoulders.

"I'm not the sort of woman who wears calico. Or cotton lawn."

The girl colored becomingly. "Yes, I see. Do you always wear pants?"

Carsie lifted her chin. "These are not pants as you know them for men. This is a garment of freedom designed by Miss Amelia Bloomer, a courageous woman who has seen the plight of women and sought to make them free."

"Free? We are free. What does she mean by that?"

"My dear girl. Have you not seen your mothers, your sisters all around you who are caught in bonds . . . bonding them to men?"

"My mother's dead and I don't have any sisters."

Carsie sighed. "I mean your mothers and sisters in the greater sense, the worldly sense. We're all mothers and sisters of all other women."

The girl tilted her head with incomprehension then moved toward a display of women's nightclothes.

"Aren't these new gowns pretty?" She leaned toward Carsie and shifted her eyes around them as if being certain no one was within earshot. "And if you'd like to see some of the latest in undergarments," she whispered, "I can take you to the back and show them to you. I have a tiny room to myself. Father never comes back there."

Carsie exhaled a futile breath. "No, thank you."

"They're the latest from New York and Paris," the girl rushed on as if she hadn't heard Carsie's refusal, "and they're positively scandalous! They're called lingerie. I saw them in a catalog. 'Ladies intimate apparel,' that's what it said under the pictures. Father says he would never have such shameful things in his store, but I ordered them secretly and he doesn't know I have them. I've sold two already. And I'm wearing some right now and no one can tell."

"Did you say Paris?" a low voice came from behind Carsie.

She turned around. Hannah Holmes stood near the table bearing the bolts of cloth.

Anne blushed deeply as she took in Hannah's shimmering purple moire dress with its wide low neckline. Carsie supposed the girl thought the dress entirely inappropriate for morning wear, and probably suspected what Hannah's profession might be. She also knew Hannah had no other clothes in which to go to town. None of them had wanted to wear the filthy torn things they'd been traveling in.

The girl glanced around the room quickly. "I'm afraid I can't show them to you. Now, where did my father get to now?" She started to walk away.

Carsie caught her arm. "You were just about to show them to me. Why don't you just show them to Miss Holmes instead?"

Anne pulled her arm free. "Because I can't," she said through gritted teeth. "My father would tan my hide if I did."

"Wouldn't he have disapproved as much of your showing the undergarments to me?"

"No, of course not." Anne bit her lip. "Well, yes, because of what they are, and well, I guess he'd wonder what your kind would want with them. But he'd be madder if I . . ." Her gaze glanced off Hannah's face.

"I'm sorry. I'm quite busy now with other customers. Good day." Anne quickly walked away.

"Now just a minute . . ." Carsie started after her but was detained by Hannah's hand on her arm.

"Don't bother with her. She can't show me the undergarments." Hannah stepped toward a table spread with gloves.

"But why not? You're a customer as much as I am or anybody else in here."

"I'm a different sort of customer." Hannah examined a pair of eggshell-hued lace gloves.

"How? I don't understand."

Hannah turned around and faced her, her mouth set in a hard line. "Because of . . . of the color of my skin and what I do with men." Tears briefly wet her dark eyes and were gone instantly. "It's always been that way. Just forget about it, will you?"

Carsie watched Hannah's shoulders slump slightly then square again. She knew Hannah felt powerless, doubly so since she was a woman with dark skin. She wished with all her heart that women everywhere could find the way to make their own power, to take their lives and the futures of their daughters into their own hands. Even the clerk, Anne, without realizing it was perpetuating her own powerlessness.

And all of this over so female an issue as undergarments.

Carsie saw Anne talking to two young female customers. Buoyed by the wings of an idea, she linked her arm through Hannah's and drew her with resolute steps toward them.

"Excuse me, miss," she said loud enough so that if the proprietor of the mercantile were paying attention, he could hear her speaking to his daughter quite clearly. "We're ready now to view those lovely new underthings from Paris you were telling us about moments ago."

Anne blanched. The other two women blinked their eyes.

"Shh, please keep your voice down," Anne admonished, casting a quick and guilty glance toward her father.

"Yes, indeed. Paris." Carsie leaned toward the two with an air of complicity, and gushed. "They're the latest, you know, and positively scandalous. We're just thrilled, aren't we, Hannah? Miss Anne here," Carrie rushed on, "is wearing some of those nouveau underfashions."

"Oh my stars," breathed the younger woman.

With much surreptitious glancing around them, they checked Anne over as if trying to see through her dress. Anne squirmed under the scrutiny, keeping one eye on her father.

The older of the two women caught the hand of another female customer passing by them. "Mary, you must listen to this. It's wonderful."

"Oh, dear," Anne wailed low. "What shall I do now?"

Carsie leaned close to Anne's ear. "Become the most-sought-after store clerk in the territory. You have the power to bring these women some excitement and beauty into their lives. Offer them what no one else can. You and your undergarments will make more money for this mercantile than any other commodity in it."

Anne stared at Carsie, as if hearing brand new words. Then her lip quivered. "But my father, what will he say? What will all the town ladies say? They'll be shocked. No one will like me." Anne wrung her hands as the three young women now became four, chattering among themselves.

Hannah stepped forward, bolstered by Carsie's staunch presence beside her. "You will make it a careful secret that only these few will know about. They'll adore the secret and adore what you're going to provide for them. Then they will let a friend or two in on their delicious secret," Hannah said with an air of knowing.

"Swearing them to further secrecy, of course," Carsie interjected.

"Of course," Hannah concurred.

"Then what?" Anne asked in a tiny curious voice.

Carsie lifted her chin victoriously. "And then you may just have started your own business. A rather lucrative one, I might add."

"She's right, honey," Hannah added in her smoky voice. "But you'd better get started. Your father is casting a wondering eye over in this direction."

Anne stared at Hannah and Carsie, then a smile tipped the corners of her lips. She stepped into the middle of the group of women, who'd now grown to five.

"All right, ladies," she said firmly but quietly. "You must keep your voices down. Spread out and do not call attention to yourselves. When the moments are just right, I shall take you—two at a time, please—to the place where I keep the . . . merchandise. You may make your purchases privately. And you must promise to tell no one about this. It must be our secret."

The women nodded in enthusiastic agreement, whispering among themselves to decide who would be first into the hallowed sanctuary that held scandalous fantasy. Anne cast a watchful glance around before easing toward the back of the store. The first two women followed her through a curtained opening.

Carsie smiled at Hannah, who let a self-satisfied smile cross her face. She held out her right hand and Carsie grasped it warmly.

"Never thought I'd be working with a woman like you." Hannah slowly dropped Carsie's hand. Carsie opened her mouth to say something, but didn't. "And you never thought you'd be working with a woman like me," Hannah said for her. "I know." She turned and walked toward another counter.

Sometime later, Anne quietly approached Carsie. "Thank you for urging me on. Those women were so appreciative of what I did for them, even though Father won't be, of course."

Carsie patted her shoulder. "You're feeling pretty good, aren't you?"

"Yes, I am. Now, you can come back now and choose something for yourself. I'm sorry my selection has dwindled, but I'm certain you'll find something that will suit your fancy."

Carsie felt her cheeks warm. "Oh, no . . . no, I don't think so."

"Oh, please. I want you to choose anything you like, as a way of thanking you."

"No need to thank me. We woman must help each other."

"And you did help me—you and the other . . . lady." She looked over her shoulder to where Hannah stood examining some gloves. "What made her be so nice to me? I wasn't very nice to her."

Carsie smiled. "Something all of us have to learn is not to judge one another."

Anne looked down at her fidgeting hand. "I will apologize to her." She walked to the other side of the mercantile to where Libby had joined Hannah.

Grateful Anne had ceased to urge her to select an under-garment, Carsie strolled around, impressed by the surprising array of goods. She purchased several tins of oysters, and one of peaches to make a special cobbler for dessert that evening. Fresh baked bread and jars of preserves were en-ticing, and Carsie chose one of each. Her funds were rapidly dwindling, but she couldn't resist buying the treats to share with the others. Delighted to find a shelf containing books, she ran her finger over the titles on the spines and knew she would leave the shop with a novel in hand.

Anne approached her just as she'd paid for her selections. "Can you step into the back room with me for a few min-utes? There is someone who is asking for your help."

Carsie wondered who that could be, and followed Anne to the back. Libby waited by an open box of exquisite cami-soles and chemisettes.

"Libby?"

"Oh, Carsie," Libby breathed. "Aren't these beautiful? Miss Hannah told me about them. Feel the tiny stitches, the delicate lace."

Carsie smiled. "You want to buy one of these?"

"Yes. I do." Libby was flushed and almost breathless from excitement. "I know I can't wear it now." She rubbed her abdomen, swollen with her growing baby. "And maybe I never will. But I just want to own something as fine as this, to know it's mine. Will you help me choose the right one?"

Carsie went to her side. "I . . . I don't think I'm a good judge of . . . that is, I've never . . ."

Ignoring Carsie's reservations, Libby exclaimed over each piece that Anne produced and described for her. At last she decided on a lavishly lace-trimmed chemisette in a pale tea color. Even the straps were made of lace.

"What do you think of this one, Carsie?" Libby held the delicate thing against her bosom.

Carsie sucked in her breath. "Oh, it is beautiful, Libby, and the color is perfect with your skin."

"I'll take it," Libby said proudly and gently handed the garment to Anne.

Anne wrapped it carefully in brown paper, loosely tying it with twine. She escorted Libby out of the back room to the cash drawer to settle the purchase.

Carsie started to follow them, then paused and turned back. She let her eyes travel over the delicate, shocking garments spread in lazy disarray over large folds of brown paper. They seemed to vibrate with life. Carsie blinked. *Lingerie,* that's what Anne called them. She edged closer for a better look.

She lifted a corset kind of thing in black with long lace garters and a tiny red satin bow at the dip where the fabric would cover a woman's breasts. Timidly she walked toward a mirror. She stared at her reflection in her usual dark blue bloomers and muslin shirt, dark stockings, and boots long in need of repair and cleaning. She'd pulled her hair back in a tight bun at the back of her head. No nonsense, that was Carson Rose Summers. She didn't need such an unnatural undergarment to prove she was female.

For the briefest of moments Carsie lifted the black lace corset and held it in front of her. The reflected image hung in her mind like a daguerreotype. A white flash of her naked breasts held aloft by the boning, her waist nipped in, her hips accentuated, the white expanse of her thighs decorated by the long lace garters which attached themselves to black—scandalous!—black stockings. She felt something new to her—positively gorgeous. The garment possessed magic. She didn't know how to react to this newfound sensation.

Carsie sucked in a sharp breath, clamped her eyes shut, and spun around quickly, intent on dropping the shocking garment on the table before she was burned forever by the heat it generated.

Hands grabbed her shoulders.

She gasped and snapped open her eyes.

Clint Bonner stood so close to her she could feel his hard thighs through the black undergarment she held pressed to her body. His heat penetrated her bloomers right through to her cotton drawers and made her skin tingle.

His grip lessened but he did not drop his hands from her shoulders. He lowered his head and silenced her astonished gasp as his lips caught hers and held them fast.

Seven

The noisy chatter of customers, the tinkling of the bells over the shop door, all sounds faded away, save for the steady tick-tock of a big wall clock that seemed to grow louder with every swing of its pendulum.

Clint's lips held hers. Somewhere in the back of Carsie's stunned mind she knew that all she had to do was slide her hands up to his chest, give a mighty push, and release the tender trap that held her fast. But there was a sweetness about the kiss that was more powerful than the sheer strength of either of them. Carsie didn't want to slide her hands up to his chest, at least not to push him away.

When he began to release her, it was a long, very slow disengagement as if he were reluctant to leave her mouth. Almost cell by cell his lips released hers. He held on to her. His hands relaxed on her shoulders.

The moistness of her lips still clinging to his, Clint slowly lifted his away. He didn't feel eager to release her. Yet something in his mind echoed over and over, reminding him this kiss was a dare between himself and Jake, a test of his proven masculine powers to verify they hadn't diminished. His legs suddenly weakened and he locked his knees against the possibility of his falling into an awkward heap at her feet. He hadn't felt that sort of sensation in a long time. Not since Mattie. And this was even more unsettling than he remembered. He sensed a momentary twinge of guilt.

With trickling recall, he remembered the notes he was

there to make. When he kissed her, had her knees buckled?
How could he tell? The bloomers were hiding them. Had
she swooned? He couldn't tell that either. When a woman
went all to jelly when he kissed her, usually her eyelashes
fluttered and her eyes rolled back. That wasn't happening.
At the moment she just stood there staring at him, all wide-
eyed with eyes as velvet brown as a doe's. Tendrils of hair
the color of polished cedar had escaped their neat bun trap
and now trailed freely around her face.

He emerged from his transfixed state with his mind clearing second by second. The woman he'd just kissed and
who'd left him dazed around the edges of his mind, this
velvet-eyed woman standing within his arms' grasp had
flung mud at him not too long ago. He knew what she was
capable of when provoked. And she must surely be provoked by what he'd just done. He'd kissed her, and kissed
her good. If she hadn't swooned, and he could see no in-
dication that she had or was about to, then she'd be madder
than a cat with a tail slammed in the screen door. Why
didn't she just swoon like any other woman? Why did he
have this overwhelming feeling that she was about to do
something, that something was about to happen to him?

With inching steps he backed away and dropped his hands
from her shoulders. He figured she was about to slug him
with some hidden weapon. If he couldn't make her swoon,
he was certainly going to make her miss connecting with
him. His eyes fell to the array of lacy women's garments.
The sight of them rocked his senses. He'd never seen anything like this. One of them had a perfect shape of its own,
as if a woman had just stepped out of it. As if Carson Rose
Summers had just stepped out of it.

He stepped back. She was holding a black lace thing in
front of her. He went stock-still. His mind played a trick
on him. She was the magician this time. He saw her with
her hair loose and flowing about her shoulders, her

breasts—he was certain she did have them—swelling above
the boned stays.

The boned stays. They were what she was going to use
to hit him.

Quickly he backed out through the curtained door.

Carsie watched Clint retreat and fade behind the curtains.
Reality was staring her in the face, yet she held on to the
sweetness of Clint's kiss. The sweetness. That was the
thought floating around in her mind. How could that be?
Her kissing experience had been minimal, to be certain.
Only her husband had taken the privilege. Oh, and one boy
when she was in the third grade. That one didn't count. It
had brushed by so fast on her cheek, she barely knew it
had happened. Her husband, on the other hand, had kissed
her with a demanding roughness that hurt and repelled her.
Beyond those experiences she had nothing else with which
to compare this moment. This was different. Clint's kiss had
gone on and on for hours so it seemed, and even as she
watched him back away from her, she could still feel his
lips on hers.

Her knees buckled without warning. She gripped the
black lace corselet as if it were the only thing that held her
upright. Her head filled with a ringing in her ears. Her eyes
glazed over, giving the room and its contents around her a
soft-edged glow.

Clint's kiss. He'd kissed her. His kiss.

It wasn't just *his* kiss. *She'd* kissed him back. She knew
it now. She hadn't pushed him away. She hadn't become
indignant. She hadn't gone all fluttery, at least not so much
that it showed. She'd kissed him back, and she'd fancied
the fullness of the moment and hadn't wanted it to end.

Around her the lacy undergarments, which had seemed
full of life only moments before, now lay in still disarray,
shocked into paralysis.

The curtains parted then, and Carsie sensed that Hannah
had entered the room.

"Here you are. I was wondering where you'd gotten to."

Carsie didn't respond.

Hannah stepped closer. "Are you going to purchase that?" She didn't hide the surprise in her voice.

Slowly Carsie suspended the corselet out in front of her. She stared at it, motionless.

"Are you feeling ill?" Hannah pressed. "What's the matter with you?"

Carsie lifted her eyes. "I've been kissed."

Hannah stared at her for a long moment. Then, "It's your imagination. Sometimes things like these have a way of taking our minds to a place we really want to go but aren't able to." She lifted the corselet from Carsie's hands and folded it as best she could.

"No, I've really been kissed."

Hannah glanced around the room and toward the rear entrance. She gave Carsie a skeptical sidelong look. "Who by? There's nobody here. Really, this has been a shocking day for you, seeing all these things you didn't know existed. You best come with me now. You'll feel a lot better after a cup of Jake's coffee."

"No," Carsie protested, "not yet. I want to hold on to this for a while. He was here."

Hannah slipped her arm around Carsie's shoulder. "I once heard of a kissing bandit. Who are you talking about? A kissing corset phantom?" She gave a soft laugh. "If you've been robbed by some swift-footed thief who steals kisses, then it's best to forget about it. It's just a kiss. You didn't lose anything of great importance, believe me."

"This was different," Carsie said dazedly.

"That's what they all say."

Struggling to collect herself, Carsie reached out and took Hannah's hand. "You go on ahead. Let me make myself neat and I'll be along."

Hannah turned to leave the room. "Don't be long," she called, then parted the curtains and returned to the store.

Smoothing her dress, Carsie glanced around her to be certain she had everything that was hers. Her eyes landed on the black lace corselet. How could such a thing, something made by human hands, possess such powerful magic?

Clint strode down the street knowing he would run into Jake coming out of one of the saloons or dancehalls. He wished he didn't have to talk to him so soon after . . . He was feeling something, shaken, he guessed he could say. That made no sense to him.

Sure as the sun burned hotter with the passing hours, Jake stepped into his path. "Well, now, are you having an interestin' day?"

"Passable. You?"

"Passable. Haven't seen anything too out of the way yet."

Clint nodded and started to move away.

"Wait a minute, boy." Jake blocked his path. "Have you done the deed?"

"What deed?"

"Now I know you didn't need to ask that question. Did you?"

After a long pause Clint gave a reluctant nod. He hadn't been ready to talk about it yet, and the inevitable had happened. He'd been forced to answer Jake.

Jake chuckled and righted his wobbling stovepipe hat. "What was that?"

Clint kicked a stone out of the way. "I kissed her."

"What'd you say? I couldn't hear you. All the noise in this place is deafening."

"I said I kissed her," Clint snapped.

"Kissed her, did you say?" Jake shouted.

Clint grabbed his shoulder and headed down the street toward the Blue Door Saloon. "Will you keep still?"

"About what? You kissin' somebody? That ain't news to the world, boy, and nothin' new to me."

At the saloon door, Clint stopped. The way he was feeling was sure news to him. He decided to keep that news to himself and tease Jake back. "You owe me, pal. I kissed the suffragist at the peril of losing the ability to ever physically kiss any woman again."

Jake burst out laughing. "Well, now, you make it sound as if you kissed a coyote smack dab on the mouth. Was it as bad as all that?"

Clint didn't say anything, just held his gaze on the open space over the batwings of the Blue Door. Jake squinted to see through the haze inside the saloon. "Her knees go all weak and soft?"

Clint caught sight of Margarita sashaying her provocative hips past a table of card players. "Sure."

"And she swooned?"

Clint pushed the doors open and started to go inside. "I'm as good as I always was."

Jake's gaze landed on Margarita and her swaying hips. "I mean the Summers girl. It don't count, you know."

Clint stopped. "What are you talking about?"

Jake pushed past him and stepped into the barroom. "I didn't see you kiss her, if you really did, so I got no proof. Got no proof she caved in, got no proof you kissed her. Got no proof you're as good as you always was."

"Why you old thimblerigger . . ."

Jake snapped his head toward Margarita, who was now advancing on them. "And this one's too easy. She definitely don't count."

Suppertime around camp that evening was lively. Everyone had a story to tell about the day spent in Virginville. Clint listened to their banter as he sat at a makeshift table by lantern light and made entries in what he referred to as his company book. He was glad to have the diversion. To have been so disturbed by such a thing as a chaste kiss with a spinster lady made him out of sorts with himself. Even as he entered the figures for the provisions they'd taken on while in Virginville, he could still see the picture in his mind of Carson Summers holding a black lace underthing between them while he surprised and kissed her.

"Mm-mm." Jake smacked his lips as he dropped down next to the stump Clint was using as a desk. "Can you smell that peach cobbler Miz Summers is bakin'? She sure surprised everybody with that. Has a lot of talents, don't she? Some, most of us don't even know about. Right?

Clint pretended he hadn't heard. He checked his receipts and made two more entries before closing his ledger. "Fair price on the corn and oats. Should do us for a while."

Jake chuckled. "Nice night, ain't it?" He scanned the darkening sky. A sprinkle of dim stars was just starting to dot through the purple and gray fingers of clouds.

"Sure is. We're making better time than I expected. Should make Fort Kearny in another couple of days, I think. Glad the rain let up. Don't know what we'll find when we reach the Platte River." Clint covered his ledger in oil cloth and placed it inside a small wooden locker. "Mrs. Woo's wagon is in need of some frame repair. Best we do it first thing tomorrow. Once we leave the Big Blue, we'll run out of hardwoods. Better take more on. We'll need it later."

Jake kneaded his thigh as if to ease out some soreness. "What's eatin' at you, boy?"

"Hunh? Nothing. Just concerned is all. I can't tell if Mrs. Woo is scared or not, but I want to prevent any big problems with her wagon. It's put together pretty good, I'd say. Mr. Woo is quite the craftsman."

"Mr. Woo is a thief and you know it. Mrs. Woo is just fine. I want to know what's going on with you."

"Nothing's going on with me. Quit badgering."

Harry strolled over. "Can anybody join this confabulation? Or are you deep into some philosophical musings, solving the plight of man?"

"Nothin' so lofty as that. We're a little closer to home trying to sort out the plight, as you say, of one man." Jake winked and jerked his head toward Clint.

"I see. And what could possibly be the matter this time?" Harry stroked his chin thoughtfully. "I recall that most of Clint's dilemmas had to do more often than not with a lady—correction, several ladies. They being the complex mortals they are, and men being possessed of simpler souls, I conclude that our boy here has got himself into a complicating situation."

Jake took out a brush from a canvas pack he carried and commenced to cleaning his hat with quick and sure strokes. "Not that he's admitted to."

"Well, now, that's the first step to solving a problem, admitting one has one. A problem."

"Says nothin's bothering him."

"Then something definitely is."

"It's what I figured. Won't say."

"He always was stubborn. It appears it's up to us to draw it out of him, release him from the questions that confound his mind. Assist him in securing answers with the use and benefit of our collective intelligence and understanding. Agreed?"

Jake didn't lift his eyes. He kept up the rhythmic brushing of his hat. "I don't have no notion what you just said, but in this case I know to agree with you."

"Good. Now, then, what sort of strategy do you think we should consider implementing in order to best assist our fellow chap?"

"Will you two stop talking about me as if I'm not sitting right here?" Clint slapped the top of his ledger pouch.

"Why, dear boy, whatever do you mean?" Harry blinked his eyelids rapidly, feigning innocence.

"You know exactly what I mean. You and Jake did that all the time when we traveled the circus routes."

Jake gave one last brush stroke to the top of his hat, then

replaced the brush in his pack. "Only did it because you needed it, son. If we went to talkin' straight to you, you went straight to daydreamin' so's you didn't hafta hear a word we was sayin'. Force of habit is all. Right, Harry?"

"Exactly right. We only wish to give you the benefit of our wisdom and experience now as we did then." Harry rose. "But if you don't wish to use that information, there's nothing we can do about it. Right, Jake?"

"Right. You know best, son." Jake pushed himself up and gave Harry a tap on the shoulder. "You notice how the fellas all seemed a mite lighter in spirit this evenin'? What say we see how supper's progressin', pard?"

"Capital idea." Harry linked his arm through Jake's and the two strode off toward the cookfire.

Clint watched them leave. Never had a man had two better friends. And never had two men had as loyal a friend as they had in Clint.

Jake was the savviest man Clint had ever known. Harry was the most intelligent man he'd ever known. Jake had an understanding of natural thought and intuition born of living day to day by his own wits. Harry could quote the bawdiest lines from classic literature to the Bible, and weave stories that would leave children spellbound.

But the greatest thing about them, Clint believed, was that they were always taking care of people, strays, orphans, misfits. They were the reason Clint ended up in the circus. He'd been a worthless weed as a kid. The orphanage had done him no good and he'd run away from it when he was twelve. Three years later Harry found him in a tavern dealing poker, cleaning spittoons, and being drunk from morning until night. Harry had surprised him with brute strength when he'd bodily dragged Clint off to the circus camp at the edge of town and right into the clutches of Jake Storms.

Harry and Jake wrangled him as if were a belligerent calf. They'd worked him until he was dead tired at night, then roused him out of bed before dawn and made him start all over again. Jake taught him to ride and to shoot. Harry taught him how to use his wits and charm, and how to overcome some of his fears by urging him to perform daredevil feats in front of enthralled crowds. His years in the circus taught him how to apply every bit of his body and mind to working and living and, as an added bonus, to orchestrate people for his own purposes. He never was certain in his own mind he was as good at that as Harry or Jake, but he'd always admired their expertise.

One thing he did know for certain—Clint Bonner would have been dead before he'd turned twenty-five if it hadn't been for the persuasive charm of Harry Hardin and the old-fashioned disciplinary measures of Jake Storms. And for the love among the three of them that they'd never voiced nor felt the need to. But there had come a time when they'd had to part. Clint had given in to his gnawing need to try a life on his own.

He sighed wistfully as he settled his gaze on the cookfire where Jake and Harry had joined the women. What a life he'd lived over the last decade. More than once he'd longed to run back to the safe haven of the circus and his two greatest friends. But he hadn't run away, and after awhile he couldn't run to Jake and Harry. Time and circumstance had prevented him, and paralyzing grief when Mattie died. His sweet, innocent wife. She'd died a violent death and he blamed himself.

If there was one thing he'd learned, it was that there was always something else at work around him, around people, and it was not a force for good. He wondered if Jake and Harry had ever had a longing in their hearts as deep and sometimes acute as his had been and, at times, still was. Everything seemed right with them. They trusted one another, but most of all they trusted themselves. Clint hadn't felt trust in himself since before Mattie died. That trust had been hard-won and it had been lost in one numbing moment.

He pressed his palms against his knees and stood up. The gathering around the cookfire seemed lively, and the aromas floating through the air enticed him to join the group.

Mrs. Woo had come out to be a part of the activity, forsaking her usual silent keeping to herself. She prepared her nightly pot of rice, only this time she'd made enough for everyone. She spoke in quiet Chinese, making barely perceptible gestures toward Carsie, letting her know that whatever she was cooking looked good.

Carsie bent over a steaming pot, stirring the contents with a long heavy spoon. She let the warm mist waft over her even warmer face. Out of the corner of her eye she could see Clint coming toward them. Her hands shook. She wished she'd learned how other women acted after such a surprising event as she'd experienced that morning. A kiss she hadn't an inkling would ever happen, yet at the moment of its impact she'd surprised herself even more by becoming thoroughly engaged in it.

She and Sophie had talked about such things only on rare occasions when Sophie, amid spates of giggles, had told her how she'd let this man or another kiss her, or actually how she'd maneuvered him to kiss her. Carsie had never understood that. Her brief marriage hadn't taught her anything about kissing such as this kiss was.

How was she supposed to think? Had she done something shameless to have caused Clint Bonner to think he could just walk up to her and kiss her? Was he wholly at fault because he had perpetrated a male act by just walking up to a woman and thinking he could kiss her if he felt like it?

Did he really feel like it, like kissing *her?* He'd never even called her by name. It was always just "Bloomers." He seemed to find her aggravating at best.

And what about herself? She stirred the pot more aggressively, sending a bigger puff of steam over her face. Whatever had possessed her to simply—or perhaps it was not so simply—kiss him. Yes, if the truth be known, she'd kissed Clint Bonner as if something else controlled her. How utterly disturbing.

Now how was she supposed to react? Coy and flirtatious? That could never be her style. Cool and indifferent? She could not do that given the state of her emotions. Angry and contentious? Not in front of other people, and . . . those were not among the emotions she'd been experiencing since the surprising act had occurred among the ladies intimate apparel.

Oh dear.

It must have been those things! How powerful they were to be the impetus of such a thing! Who ever would have thought? Of course that was it. Neither of them could be accused of consciously planning to engage in kissing in a public place.

Clint was coming closer. She didn't want to talk to him or even look at him. Carsie shifted her eyes around the camp. There would be no place to run except into the deepening darkness and she had no desire to do that. If only a bolt of lightning would come out of the sky to distract him.

"Look what I have found!" Lola fairly skipped toward the group holding her skirt gathered into a pouch. "Plums! Can you imagine? I have sampled and they are *très magnifico.*"

Plums were as good as lightning sometimes.

Lola leaned over the makeshift table they'd devised over rocks and tree stumps and spilled the contents of her skirt. A mass of reddish-purple plums tumbled over the boards. Hannah squealed like an excited child and immediately snatched one and took a large bite of the juicy globe.

Clint made a sharp detour toward the table. He'd been headed directly toward the cookfire where Bloomers was bending over a pot and stirring the contents with both hands clutching a spoon as if she were shifting boiling linens with a long stick. What in hell did he think he was going to say to her? Apologize? Say he was sorry? Funny thing . . . he didn't feel sorry, although he supposed he should. Kissing her had been the prize in a game between him and Jake. He did feel a bit sheepish about that now, although the idea of it being anything but a harmless lark hadn't crossed his mind at the time.

Miss Carson Rose Summers was not a woman a man could take liberties with—he knew that. He knew she'd been insulted by his bursting in and kissing her like that. He'd almost checked himself and not gone through with it. But there she was in the midst of such an array of lacy women's underthings as he'd never seen in his life. So many of them just lying around her looking inviting, as if they possessed personalities of their own. And worse, she was holding one in front of her body. In a flash he'd caught a glimpse of her in it, or at least of a feminine shape inside it that he later suspected he'd thought of as being hers, and his momentary reluctance dissolved. He'd just gone and done it, kissed her. And he'd forgotten all about Jake's dare.

Since he'd returned to camp, he'd been trying to come up with a comment to her that would minimize the impact of the whole event on himself. And he felt an obligation to ease any embarrassment she might be feeling by treating it as a mischievous act. That all seemed pretty flimsy, and he hadn't found any satisfactory words anyway.

The arrival of the voluptuous Lola and her plums was a perfect diversion.

Harry picked up a plum, polished it on his bright red vest, and took it to Libby. Clint watched as she ran her fingers over it and exclaimed over its ripeness. Harry described the colors in it as rivaling those of a perfect sunset. She bit into it and laughed gleefully as juice escaped her lips and Harry gently wiped it from her chin with his handkerchief.

Clint watched them and couldn't help but smile. There was such an easy camaraderie between Libby and Harry, such an easy acceptance of each other. There didn't appear to be any of the usual nervousness or game of cat-and-mouse between them. In fact, it seemed more that they were *friends,* real friends. Clint marveled at that, and he sensed something even deeper growing between them.

His gazed darted to Carsie before darting back to Libby and Harry enjoying the plum. She was watching them, too. A half-smile tilted a corner of her mouth. Somehow he knew she was thinking exactly what he was thinking as she watched them.

That was a disconcerting thought if there ever was one.

"What are you concocting there, Miz Summers?" Jake walked over to her, removed his hat, and bent over the steaming pot. "It smells heavenly."

"Thank you, Mr. Storms. It's oyster stew." Carsie lifted the big spoon, blew on the contents, and holding her open palm under the scoop, offered Jake a taste.

He took it carefully at first so as not to burn his mouth, then slurped the remainder, obviously savoring the flavor. "Mmm. Now this is a treat. Haven't had a good oyster stew since I was in Boston. But say, what's that other flavor in there?"

Carsie smiled at him. "It's nutmeg."

"Nutmeg? I didn't suppose that was for anything but cake or cookies."

"I've learned it is apparently for the bath as well."

Jake cocked his head toward her. "The bath, did you say, miss?"

"Yes. I was just so fascinated by that. I had wished aloud that I had some nutmeg for the stew, and didn't Miss Goodnight go directly to her wagon and produce some for me. She says she uses it in her bath because it . . . now what did she say? Oh yes, because it gives a decided spicy scent to the skin that is irresistible. I did wonder what couldn't resist it, but . . ." She flashed an embarrassed look at Jake. "Oh, dear, I guess she meant . . . that is."

Jake looked down and brushed dirt from his pants. "Well, I'm certain nutmeg makes this oyster stew irresistible. Good fortune you've made enough to feed a troupe of acrobats."

Carsie went back to vehemently stirring the stew. "Indeed. Yes. Good fortune."

For the first time since the commencement of the journey, the wagon train members sat around their roughly constructed dining table together as if at a family holiday gathering. They consumed bowls of Carsie's oyster stew, Hannah's sourdough biscuits, a treat of apple butter produced from Miss Goodnight's belongings, the other uses of which Carsie did not want even to speculate on. They topped off the meal with mugs of Jake's coffee laced with cocoa, and slices of Carsie's peach cobbler for dessert.

Banter was light with comments from the day spent in Virginville.

Miss Phoebe allowed as how she couldn't fathom how the town ever got that name, judging by all she'd observed.

Libby exclaimed over its cosmopolitan atmosphere, corroborated enthusiastically by Harry. The others looked a bit skeptical about that, but Carsie said nothing. Libby was so happy at the moment, Carsie didn't want to spoil it for her with so trivial a thing as a reality description of what that settlement looked like.

Hannah detailed the number and kind of goods to be found in the Virginville Mercantile, carefully omitting one special kind of apparel. She dreamed aloud about owning such a shop. She suggested that Carsie would make a first-rate business owner, and gave only cryptic responses when pressed for details. Carsie knew she was blushing over her praise and was grateful for the fire to hide her heightened color.

Lola told them she'd found a young girl selling blocks of fudge and she'd bought enough to serve them all a sweet dessert the next night.

Through it all, Mrs. Woo sat at an end corner of the table

lifting mounds of rice to her mouth with an exquisite pair of handpainted ivory chopsticks. When others laughed over a story, she showed the fleeting hint of a smile. She had the kind of still face that made people try to get her to smile. Usually she wore a mask of sadness and anger, and everyone smiled constantly at her as if their smiles would be infectious.

Jake shifted his pipe to the other side of his mouth and commented that it was in such towns as Virginville that strange events occurred at times simply because of the variety of inhabitants and—he shot a knowing glance at Clint—visitors just passing through.

Clint sat back and listened and watched, only once sending a silent admonishment toward Jake. He was enjoying this evening. He could remember only a few isolated moments in his life when he'd enjoyed a gathering such as this one so completely. Those times seemed a lifetime ago now.

His eyes drifted toward Carsie more often than he would have wished prior to this night. He couldn't read her. Maybe he'd made the whole thing up in his mind that she'd be upset, or insulted or hurt that he'd had the audacity to just walk up to her and kiss her like that. She seemed oblivious to the deed now and even, it seemed to him, hardly aware of his presence.

Maybe Jake was right. Maybe he had lost his touch with women. He'd have to see what he could do about that. But he would take no more dares from Jake.

The Journal of Carson Rose Summers

21 July 1865

Today we visited Virginville. ~~The settlement was an interesting place.~~ 🔲 \ 🔲 ~~Virginville is a town of people who~~ . . . To describe Virginville would be to

write about the people, and there were some
very interesting ones.

    I don't know why they call it Virginville.
I never got a bath.

We had a nice supper.

I'm very tired.

The stars are abundant this night. They keep me
from thinking clearly. To look up among them is to
feel very small as if one is but a mere piece
of stone and light. Yet down here passing
through this vast land a human is almost greater than
all life.

We are so few in numbers here in this country. I've
been told there are more buffalo than people the farther west we go.

I must remember to record the scenes and my impressions of the journey before I sleep. Sometimes I
am too tired or my eyes are too sore for me to take
a few moments to write. Tonight I am quite awake.
Very unusual.

Surprising things happen in Virginville all the time,
I suppose. Perhaps because it's set way out on the
very edges of the beginning of the Wild West, it is a
strange combination of civilization and untamed frontier. People come from the East and the West and pass
each other in Virginville. It's very possible that when
people from both sides of that line converge in one
place then—then the atmosphere is filled with whatever they're giving off, like mist off a lake on the first
crisp morning in August.

They exude a sense of freedom. And soldiers caught
up in the defense of home and hearth. Courage and
bravery walk hand in hand with freedom. It's the true
American spirit people talk about, I would guess.

And that is bound to rub off on anyone who visits.

That sense of freedom, and bravery, I think. Or is it foolhardiness? I do wonder, in any case.

Do people behave differently than they normally would under usual circumstances? Is it possible that simply by walking through that atmosphere and among those people that any self-respecting normal person might—do something they might not normally do in their normal everyday setting? I'm certain that's it. Even Miss Goodnight and Lola stepped into a restaurant for breakfast and tea. I'm certain they wouldn't do that in their normal life. Or the life they lead, that is. Which is normal for them, I think.

I feel as if I've begun the first school grade all over again. Strangely it's as if all of my intelligence, all that I thought I knew and understood, is being challenged to the point of being wiped clean like a school slate. I have believed that schooling is a powerful thing for people, especially women. To be educated, to *know,* is to be armed. That's what I thought. I still believe that, but I am beginning to understand that education isn't all there is to learning and to knowing. One has to live in one's life. One has to be aware of everyone around. One has to be aware of one's self and take personal assessment. That is something I have not learned from teachers. I think it's real, but I don't know how to go about learning that. I shall look for a book when we arrive in Virginia City. It is a city. Surely there is a library.

Virginia City. It will be as Virginville was. It will have a profound effect on all of us. I wonder how it has affected Sophie. These Western settlements do things to people, it seems.

It must be so. Lola bought fudge. Imagine. Buying fudge rather than making it. I know she would never do that under normal circumstances. It must be that the atmosphere in Virginville brings that out of someone. I wonder if anyone has ever done a study on just such a thing. Not the fudge, but the possibility that people walk into some places, some towns, some obscure location, and immediately behave differently than they would normally.

And I bought tins of oysters and made stew for all of us for supper tonight. Now, I never would have done such a thing normally. I've never cooked for more than two or three people at a time. And it tasted quite tasty. Mr. Storms said so.

The mercantile displayed several books for sale. I found one that caught my eye and on a whim—most unusual for me, purchased it. It is well used, I think, for its purple cloth binding revealed the worn spots of dozens of hands. There was a pressed flower inside that appears to have been red once. The book is *Shoulder-Straps, A Novel of New York and the Army,* by Mr. Henry Morford. Mr. Morford is a most prolific author. I strive to achieve his output of the written word, but I fall quite short. This novel was his most popular, I hear. Perhaps I shall learn more about the war from this book and understand conflict among people who are simply trying to carve out their own niche in their tiny corner of the world.

The usually reserved Hannah became quite verbal in the mercantile.

~~The mercantile. The mercantile was an interesting shop.~~

Hannah and I shall become friends. I know it. That may not be from the atmosphere surrounding Virginville, however. Together we were quite effective today, I think. It's quite possible we could do more to change the course of women's lives. I'll talk to her about it at my first opportunity.

Libby did something today I think was quite out of

the ordinary for her as well. She purchased something unusual for her. And she sought my advice which, although inadequate, I was quite happy to give. I'm certain that once again the atmosphere was at work at that moment. I have never been in the position to offer advice about such matters.

The mercantile atmosphere—of course that was it as well—and some very interesting ⬠ ⬚ ⬳ pieces of clothing. Underclothing. The young shop clerk named Anne called them ladies intimate apparel. This was a most surprising development for a place such as Virginville, I thought at first. Now in retrospect I might rethink my thinking. Anne saw these articles in a catalog. From New York and Paris. She was quite pleased with herself for having ordered them and spirited them into her own little office at the back of the mercantile without her father, the owner, suspecting a thing. I think she will have quite a private business going for herself now.

The apparel—lingerie she called it—was of French design and intended to ~~display~~ enhance the female figure. Some of it was without boning, so it could be quite comfortable underneath normal clothes. Libby chose a lacy chemisette. Anne told her she could wear it with a dress that was open at the bodice to let the lace appear. Libby was taken aback, but then was determined to have it.

I, myself, was caught up in the atmosphere of Virginville for a brief moment. There is a kind of magnetic strength in the air there, I believe. On a moment when I was quite alone I felt drawn to examine more closely some of the articles of apparel. They, too, seemed to have a power of their own. As I held one in front of me—I thought I should learn how other women utilized them, how they were designed to fit a human body—I felt something. Somehow different.

It was as if I were transported out of myself and into the mind and body of another. Sophie would probably say I was momentarily possessed by a passing spirit. I never agreed with her about such things. But there was no mistaking the brief but very strong sense of—escape, I shall call it for now—from myself to another.

What happened following that is something I'm not certain actually did happen. Was it in my imagination as I stood there transfixed by the exquisite lace I held against my body? Was Mr. Bonner's presence in the room a mere flash from the weariness of travel? A mind playing tricks?

Now in the clarity of the close of day, I think it must have been so. For Mr. Bonner to have ~~wanted~~ to have ~~thought me as desirable as the other women~~ Mr. Bonner surprised me with a kiss. In the day-to-day atmosphere of my normal life I'd have been outraged and delivered a resounding slap to the face of any man who took such liberties. This is why I know it had to be Virginville. I did not behave as I normally would. I did not slap him as propriety would expect me to. But then, I have never held much up for propriety. So perhaps that was not a factor. I simply did not behave as I normally would.

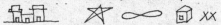

I kissed him back. I should not admit that to anyone. I wish I could admit it. I have had strong feelings since, feelings I don't understand. I have been kissed in the past. I have been married. I have cooperated in the marriage bed. Never did I experience the kind of ~~strange~~ disturbing feelings I have had from the moment ~~he kissed me~~ we kissed. Perhaps Sophie would be right. There is some kind of spirit at work in this atmosphere. I now find it difficult to look him in the eyes or converse with him. He avoided me at supper.

I wish I could go back to the way it was before the mercantile. I am feeling uncomfortable—with myself. Perhaps that will change once we are on the move again tomorrow.

How I wish I could talk to Sophie. No, I guess I wouldn't tell her anything about this. Sophie would be too bubble-headed to offer any real comprehension of what I'm feeling. I'm certain she doesn't truly understand the complexities of female and male relationships.

Perhaps I can talk to Libby about this tomorrow. No, perhaps not. She may be with child, but I sense it was not an act of love that brought her to this circumstance.

Perhaps I shall discuss the book I saw Miss Phoebe reading. I had no idea she was such an intellectual. She will have a view of ♡ ♡ things.

I must take to my bed. The day was most exhausting. And I never got the real bath I'd hoped to find in Virginville. Ah, well. I shall take a long bath in the river tomorrow—no matter how cold it is.

Eight

Daylight displayed its first glowing minutes above the hills in the eastern sky when Clint roused the band. After allowing time for a heartier breakfast than usual, he started them out on the road once more.

He'd mapped out the next leg of the journey figuring to take a cross road to the Nebraska and Laramie road along the Platte River, and wend their way toward Grand Island and on to Wyoming and the Bozeman Trail. This was where the country became wilder and harsher and populated with both white and Indian renegades. He knew they would all have to be more vigilant in their watch.

Jake rode up beside him. He yanked his ever-present pipe from his teeth and dropped it into his shirt pocket. Just as he'd often wondered and waited for the possible slipping of the stovepipe hat, Clint wondered why Jake had never suffered severe chest burns by dropping a lit pipe into his shirt.

"You worried about something?" Jake spat into the passing brush. "Seem pretty quiet this mornin'. Thinkin' about that bet we have and how you're gonna lose it, ain't you?" He chuckled triumphantly.

Clint gave him an exasperated glance. "I haven't given that bet you drummed up two minutes' worth of my time."

That wasn't exactly so. He had thought about it during the night when he'd awakened, and in retrospect, that had seemed to be pretty often. The whole idea had been childish. To catch the suffragist at a weak moment and just grab

and kiss her. Some dare. Some bet. Maybe a few years ago
he would have shared some lighthearted moments laughing
with Jake and talking about the escapade and the surprised
look on the duped woman's face.

What was happening to him? He must be getting old. It
wasn't very long ago that he would have relished those moments for a long time. Maybe it was because of the kind
of woman that Çarsie was. All serious and tough to prove
she was as good as any man. Why did she have to do that
anyway? What did she find so wrong with being a woman?

He should just let it all go. But he felt, well, disjointed
by the whole event. And kind of guilty. He realized he'd
made sport of Carsie and he didn't much like himself for
it.

"I'll just bet you haven't thought about it," Jake interrupted Clint's musings. He settled himself in the saddle and
scanned the panorama of scenery around them. "Never been
this far west. How do you know where you're going, boy?
Don't seem to be no markers." When Clint didn't answer,
he jerked his head around. "You do know where you're
going, don't you, boy?"

"Yes, I know where I'm going. Been this way before. So
have thousands of other people before us. You'll see signs
all along the way."

"Then why do you look worried?"

"Because I *have* been this way before. Desperadoes are
getting pretty thick out here now, I heard tell. And the Indians aren't taking all this emigration lying down."

"You mean we're going to run into tribes of 'em?"

"Maybe not whole tribes. But we're sure to run into
thieving parties of Pawnee and Cheyenne, and the Sioux
for certain. They've scared away the farmers who'd settled
along the Platte. You'll see by the deserted homesteads."

Jake craned back over his shoulder where the oxen plod-
ded along in lethargic clops pulling the wagons, Martha

along the side whistling and calling to the bulls. "What about the women? Will the Indians try to take them?"

"They'll want what we're hauling in the wagons. Hell, they might even want the wagons once they catch sight of Harry's and Mrs. Woo's. Never should have let those things go along. These women might be more trouble than the Indians would want." He gave a wry laugh. "Can't say as I'd blame them for leaving them right where they are. But they'd probably take one or two before they were through." Clint squinted toward the far horizon. "Wide open country, isn't it? Not a chimney as far as a man can see."

Jake squinted. "Why doesn't that strike me as such a good thing? A man can feel mighty alone out here. Kind of eerie."

"There're other ways to feel alone that don't have anything to do with wide open unpopulated land."

Jake gave a slight nod and the two fell silent for long stretch.

"Wouldn't mind having some pronghorn steak for supper." Clint's voice took on a lighter tone.

Jake grinned. "We've bagged some mighty ornery animals in our time with no notion of eating them, just showin' off to the paying customers. You point out them antelopes and you got yourself a dinner."

"Don't count your catch yet. Pronghorn are pretty bashful, and pretty wily."

"Well, I ain't bashful, but I am wily."

"That ought to provide the day's entertainments, you going after pronghorn."

"I had no notion of doin' it all myself, you know. Figured on a little help from you and Harry."

"I'm busy."

"Then if I get one, you don't get even a lick of it at supper."

"Two minutes ago you didn't even know there were any

pronghorn out here. I informed you. I get a good steak out of this." Clint laughed and rode out ahead.

Concerned about the purity of the water over the next several miles, and of the time when they could safely stop for the evening meal, Clint halted the train at a deserted farm house and urged a midday meal.

The women climbed down from the wagons and Harry assisted Libby to a clump of cottonwoods that provided some shade from the sun, which had grown beastly hot. The others led the horses and oxen to a slough for water. Before letting them drink, they were forced to scoop away frogs and a thick layer of insects.

Clint let the travelers rest and eat for an hour, allowing no cookfire. He watched the women stretch and rub out the soreness and cramping in their arms, shoulders, and backs. This was hard-driving, but nary a one complained. They surprised him with their stamina and prowess at the reins. Jake had been right. His fellas were as good as any freight drivers he'd hired in the past. And much as he'd hate to admit this to Jake, so far they were much better company.

His early judgment about the women had been dead wrong, and if the truth be known, that had shaken him. Usually he possessed a right sense about the men he hired to haul his freight. Except for the time when he'd had the consequential bad sense to hire Patch Wheelock. He shook his head to clear his mind of those memories.

They ate, took care of personal duties, then set about cleaning and replacing the remnants of the meal. Occasionally Clint caught Carsie's eye, but then averted his gaze as quickly as she did. Each occasion caught him off-guard and left him with a vaguely disconcerted sense. He didn't like it. He felt an unaccustomed weakness in his confidence and resolve, and it didn't set well with him.

Carsie wandered toward an outbuilding away from the others, leaned against a cottonwood, and ran her forearm across her moist brow. Not even a slight breeze stirred the hot air. From her fair distance she watched her traveling companions in the act of preparing to start out on the road again. Clint's gaze glanced off her and she averted her eyes. When she caught sight of him again, Jake was talking to him, grinning in her direction, and it appeared he was teasing Clint about something.

She frowned. Her lips parted slightly. Had Clint told Jake about their encounter in the mercantile? No. A gentleman wouldn't do such a thing. But then, she didn't suppose Clint Bonner was a gentleman. How embarrassing. She'd had great difficulty looking Clint in the eyes since that day. Now would she have the same difficulty with Jake? What a predicament for her, of all people, to be in.

Mosquitoes gathered in force and she was obliged to swat at them, defeating the whole means of cooling off in the shade. Somewhere something droned and buzzed loudly. An insect she couldn't identify. Overhead a half-dozen large black birds circled and dipped lazily against a white hot sky.

"Those vultures have a lot of patience, haven't they?" Hannah stepped into the shade and dropped down on the ground to lean her back against the tree.

"What are they waiting for?" Carsie squinted up at them, shading her eyes with her hand.

"Us, most likely."

Carsie grimaced and swatted at a swarm of aggressive mosquitoes. "They'll have to be quick about it if they're going to beat these hungry monsters." She gave an ironic laugh.

Hannah let out a tired sigh. "In the end it makes no difference what consumes you."

Carsie rolled her head to the side and looked down at Hannah for a long time before speaking. "You can't mean that."

"It's true."

"There are things worth dying for, and in my opinion, if

you want my opinion, being eaten by vultures or mosquitoes aren't two of them."

Hannah slapped a mosquito against her skirt and lazily flicked the dead insect away with a thumb and third finger. "What's worth dying for, in your opinion?"

Carsie closed her eyes deep in thought. What was worth dying for? Home? No. Not a house, anyway. She could always get another one. Just to be able to have a place to call one's own was more important. Family? Maybe, she thought darkly. For some people that would depend on what kind of family that was. She'd learned that the hard way. Children? If she'd had the fortune to have children, she knew she could die for them. But that hadn't happened and she believed it would never happen.

A way of life? Men had died in the war between North and South defending a way of life, and what had it got them? A country divided, Americans fighting Americans, the Negro further displaced in an unfriendly land, people distrustful of their own kind.

As far as Carsie could see, the only responsibility a woman alone could have was to herself. If every man, every woman took care of themselves first, then everything else would fall properly into place, wouldn't it? People couldn't own other people. So there was only one thing worth dying for.

"Freedom."

Hannah rolled her head and looked up at Carsie with soulful dark eyes. "And what, in your opinion—and I do want it—is freedom?"

"Being in control of your own self. Being true to your own good heart and strong mind."

Hannah turned back and gazed over the rolling land to the jutting snow-covered peaks of the mountain range beyond. "People won't let you be in control of your own self. No matter how good you are in your heart or how far you go. We'll go beyond those mountains over there. If we make it to Virginia City alive, what do you think we'll find when we roll into that place? Freedom? I don't think so. It's the capitol of the new territory. It's already corrupt. There'll be people there who'll control your freedom. And that's no freedom at all."

"There have to be laws to govern people. Without government, people would run wild."

"I know."

"And when people run wild, they infringe on other people's freedom."

"I know." With another sigh Hannah pushed to her feet. "So what is freedom? It's different for everybody. Nobody can say freedom is just one thing. It's not. So it's not always worth dying for, far as I can see. Yet, what's wrong with dying? Gets a body out of a world that's unkind to her most always." She started to slowly walk back to camp.

"Hannah?" Carsie stepped away from the tree. "Can we talk more about this? You sound so unhappy."

Hannah paused and looked up toward the sky and the circling vultures. The first breath of a cool breeze swept between the two women. She gave a brief glance over her shoulder. "Feel a storm brewin'. Don't you?" She turned back and headed to the wagons.

Carsie watched her walk away. Under the heavy clothes she could tell Hannah possessed a strong lean body. And she believed Hannah also possessed a strong mind. Carsie sensed an underlying flow of almost unlimited power in her. She could not comprehend what the life of a Negro woman was like, but she could feel deeply the instinctive connection between them, woman to woman. Where had Hannah come from? What had her life been like up to now? Why was she going to Virginia City? Would she be the same person there that she'd been in St. Joseph?

More than ever, Carsie wanted to be Hannah's friend. But Hannah might not let her be. While she might be attached to Miss Goodnight and the others, Hannah seemed an island unto herself.

Just the way Carsie had always believed herself to be.

Something rustled in the brush behind the building. A shiver ran over her arms and her back went rigid. She fixed her eyes upon the wagons. Clint was hunkered down next to Miss Goodnight's wagon applying grease to the rear axle. At that moment it seemed he was miles away. Slowly she moved her feet in his direction. She had to escape whatever was behind her, and she didn't want to look back and see the face of an Indian or a desperado. Or maybe a wild animal.

Whatever it was gave a loud snort, compelling Carsie to run with every ounce of energy she had. With both hands she held her bloomers out wide from her hips and ran with dogged determination right toward Clint. He looked up just as she was lifting her foot and planting it on his shoulder to propel herself right into the wagon.

He pitched forward into the dirt. "What the hell?"

Jake ran over. "What was that?"

Clint stood and wiped his hand over his eyes to get the dirt out of them. "Something in a flying clown suit, it looked like."

"What?" Jake spun around and peered up into the wagon.

Carsie peeked out from the flap opening. "There's . . . there's something . . . or someone lurking in the bushes behind the barn over there."

"What was it?" Jake squinted in the direction of her outstretched arm.

"I don't know. It . . . it snorted."

"Snorted?" Clint stared up at her.

She stared back. "Why do you have grease streaks on your face?"

"Could be a pronghorn," Jake said hopefully.

"I didn't apply the grease streaks myself." Clint continued to stare up at her.

"Then how . . . ?" Carsie's arms trembled as she braced herself against the seat back.

"I smell dinner," Jake said.

"When you used me for a springboard, they somehow got placed all over my face," Clint gritted out.

"I what?" Carsie leaned over to get a better look down the side of the wagon toward the wheel where Clint had been working.

"You used me as a springboard to propel yourself into the wagon. I suppose you're going to tell me that was not your intention."

"Of course it wasn't my intention. I did no such a thing. I wouldn't do that. I couldn't do that. Look how far down the ground is. I've never done such a thing in my life."

"You just did, and I no doubt have a footprint on my shoulder to prove it."

"Mr. Bonner," Carsie returned with an air of haughty denial, "if you have footprints on your shoulders, I can assure I am not the one who put them there."

"I'm going pronghorn hunting," Jake said, and started away.

"Just a minute!" Clint spun away from Carsie and grabbed Jake. "That is most likely not a self-respecting pronghorn hiding in back of the barn." He sent a sharp cursory glance over his shoulder toward Carsie, then brushed away dirt and debris from his shirt. He turned back to Jake. "If there's anything behind there at all."

"Wal, she was sure spooked." Jake jerked his head toward Carsie. His hat trembled.

"I wouldn't set store in that announcement."

Harry ran over to them. "Libby says she heard something prowling around out near that shed." He pointed. "And she thinks it went to that barn." He pointed directly at where Carsie and Hannah had been talking.

"See?" Carsie tried to get herself out of Phoebe's wagon and was having a devil of a time doing it. She couldn't remember how she'd managed to get up there. Somehow she must have used the wheel. When she tried to step down on it, her foot slipped. No. It couldn't have been that. "See? Libby heard it, too. Just like she heard you that day you met up with Mr. Hardin."

"And may I point out that event had potentially disastrous results?" Clint stepped toward her. "I suppose you'd like some help."

"No, I would not." She surveyed the wagon box, the tool-box, the tongue. "The results were not disastrous. We're all here, aren't we?"

"And while you two are spattin' at it," Jake said, righting his hat, "if there's a pronghorn out there, we're missin' out on dinner, and if it's a thievin' gang, they could ambush us, in which case we won't be needin' dinner. Either way I think it's in our best interest to investigate, don't you?"

"It's probably nothing," Clint sputtered.

"It's not nothing," Carsie countered, still searching for a way to get down from the wagon. "Nothings don't snort."

"That's a good one." Jake laughed and motioned Harry to go with him.

"You'd think so, wouldn't you?" Clint called after him. He watched his two friends walk away. "I suppose I better go cover their hides." He turned back to Carsie. "Get somebody to help you. Otherwise you'll be up there all day."

"Thank you very much for your concern," she muttered to his retreating back, believing he couldn't hear her.

"You're not welcome, I'm sure," he muttered back.

Jake, a rifle in hand, and Harry wielding a log as big as himself, positioned themselves at each end of the barn. Clint supposed Harry meant to club whatever it was before Jake plugged it. Spying a bucket, he turned it upside down, then stepped up onto it. He climbed to a window opening, then swung up to the edge of the roof where a hole could be seen. He reached for it, grasped it, and slithered his way toward the peak, then balanced on the rooftop.

Clint's belt scraped along the roof.

Jake's footsteps crackled in dry brush.

Harry sneezed as dust bubbled up around him.

If the three of them were trying a sneak attack, Clint figured whatever lurked on the other side of the barn was probably doubled over laughing.

"Now!" Jake yelled. He ran around the end of the barn and dropped to his belly, rifle sighted up.

Harry let out a high-pitched scream and advanced, club held high in the air.

Clint lost his grip and slid, back first, down the other side of the roof. He hit something on the way to the ground, rolled away into the brush and rocks, and came to his feet fast. He could hear Jake and Harry laughing. He came around from behind a rock and stopped. Jake, his rifle leveled, and Harry, the log balanced on his shoulder, guarded the intruder.

Clint laughed along with them. "A cow?"

"Pretty sure. 'Pears to be four under there steada one." Jake let out a spate of laughter.

"As I recall, however," Harry said, scratching his head, "arithmetic wasn't one of your strong points."

"You mean we did all this stalking on a cow?" Clint shook his head.

"Just like the old days, the terrific trio struck again." Harry dropped his log. "We certainly know how to call attention to the center ring, don't we?"

"A cow," Clint said dully.

"Yep," Jake concurred. "And Bossie here is just waitin' nice as you please to be milked. So we best get at it."

"Let somebody else milk her." Clint brushed dirt off his pants.

"You see anybody else here? I don't. See how her udder's all swelled up?"

"Looks pretty sore," Harry offered.

"I'm not going to stare at her, uh, udder." Clint started away.

"Now how'd you like it if you was all swelled up like that and nobody done anything to help you?"

"Who is all swelled up?" Phoebe came around the end of the barn.

"Time you kept still," Clint shot at Jake.

"What have we here?" Phoebe smiled widely and walked to the cow and stroked her nose.

"Clint thinks it's a cow," Harry said. "Of course he's been known to be wrong in the past. This time, however, we're inclined to believe him. Aren't we, Jake?"

Jake made a show of bending down and inspecting the animal's underparts. With one finger he ticked off the number of appendages. "One, two, three, four." He stood up. "Very inclined."

"Looks like she needs milking," Phoebe observed, pointing to the cow's heavy udder.

"That's been determined," Clint said.

"Well, then, let's get to it. Have we got a pail?" Phoebe peered into an opening in the barn.

"I'll get one." Clint sighed in the face of logic and went around to the front of the barn.

Carsie walked toward him. "I got off the wagon," she announced the obvious as she came near.

"Must be." Clint grabbed the bucket he'd used to get up on the roof.

"What did you find?" Following him around to the back of the barn, she stopped directly behind Clint and peered around his shoulder. "A cow?"

Harry scratched his head. "If my calculations are correct, that makes one more opinion. So it's my guess what we have here is a renegade cow. You, Jake?"

"I'd say."

"Give me that." Throwing an amused glance at the two jokers, Phoebe took the bucket from Clint's hands and shoved it under the cow. She hunkered down and leaned her shoulder into the cow's flank, took hold of two teats, and began a rhythmic squeeze and pull.

The cow danced her back legs. Phoebe cooed to her and kept milking, and soon the animal relaxed. Carsie went in search of sweet grass to feed her. Hannah and Lola, Libby between them, and Martha behind them, hurried over.

"Oh, eet's a cow!" Lola exclaimed.

"A cow?" Libby asked in wonder.

"Yes, a cow." Hannah took Libby's hand and drew it out to touch the cow's nose. "A pretty brown cow with big brown eyes and a white nose."

"Oh, it *is* a cow," Libby breathed, stepping closer and stroking the furry face.

"I guess that pretty much settles it, then," Harry opined. "Libby has given the final pronouncement. *This* fine specimen of bovine extraction is . . . a cow."

"I wanted a pronghorn," Jake said. "Guess we need this worse, though."

"We don't need it. It's just another flag to attract undesirables," Clint said. "I might as well ride on ahead and let everything and everybody out there know early we're coming. Get rid of any surprise attacks."

"It's a miracle," Libby said. "I've been so worried I wouldn't have enough of my own milk to feed the baby. I feel so fortunate to be given so many gifts."

Everyone fell silent then. Libby's words spoke the honest truth. They needed a cow for milk for her and the baby.

Jake laughed. "Never caught a cow before."

"Never was a reason to," Harry returned. He smiled warmly toward Libby. "Until now." He relieved Phoebe of her duties and kept up the rhythmic milking.

Clint knew he'd lost another battle and strode away before it was his turn to milk.

Days passed in endless driving. The air grew colder. Intermittently they passed houses, some inhabited, some abandoned. From those where people clung to a tenuous existence, they sometimes were received openly. Food and water were offered and gratefully accepted.

Libby's time was drawing near, Carsie believed. Libby spent much of her time inside the wagon, trying to stay warm and attempting to sleep. They'd tried their best to make more room inside the cramped wagon, but Libby said it wouldn't matter. She tried everything and still could not get comfortable. She didn't complain, but every now and then Carsie saw her rub her swollen belly and bite back the pain of a contraction.

The scenery rolled away ahead and around them. This country must go on forever, Carsie thought. Her arms and shoulders ached. Her hands were sore from gripping the reins all day and doing cooking and cleaning chores at night. Sometimes at the end of the day she would try to make entries in her journal. She'd had difficulty holding a pencil and keeping her eyes open. Her well-intentioned idea of keeping an extensive journal of the overland travel and the people often fell away as did so many other peripheral activities. All that was left was the survival. And the driving, the constant driving.

As they bounced and rolled ever forward amid the crack of Martha's whips and her air-piercing whistles, the grind of the wheels over grit and stones or the muffled turn of them through tall grass, Carsie's mind drifted to other destinations, other people. Some of those were behind her, others ahead. And one occasionally rode his horse beside her wagon.

She thought Clint wanted to speak to her, yet when they

camped at the end of the day, the activity of the evening meal and the preparations for night watch or bed consumed the hours they weren't traveling. Whenever she was near him, she felt a strong attraction toward him, and at the same time experienced her own resistance, though it had begun to weaken.

She tried to focus on Sophie, tried to will her mind and thoughts to travel to her friend, assuring her she'd arrive in Virginia City soon. But even Sophie and the hard driving didn't push the thought of Clint's fleeting kiss completely from her mind.

She was annoyed with herself. In the past she wouldn't have let such a trivial thing occupy so many of her thoughts. And it was trivial, of course. She knew she was supposed to feel insulted. Every lady at least pretended to be insulted or indignant over a man's taking liberties. Men were "supposed to" do that. At least that's what she'd heard among her lady friends in St. Joseph. None of them could ever answer her repeated question—why were men supposed to do that? The answer always was they were and they did. They were born with the urge.

"We're just a little over half way to Virginia City," Clint told the gathered travelers at an early evening meal. It had been a dull gray day, cold and damp, and the warmth of the fire had kept them all gathered closely, unwilling to move and clean away the dishes and utensils.

"Is that all?" Phoebe kneaded the muscles in her upper arms. "I could have sworn we'd been there and turned around and headed back without even knowing it."

"Amen." Hannah wrapped a shawl closer around her shoulders and sipped coffee.

Phoebe let Jake take over the muscle kneading. "But I'm not complaining, you understand. Merely observing."

Mrs. Woo, a worn Army blanket wrapped tightly around her thin body, silently consumed the contents of her rice bowl. The only sound from her was the clicking of her chopsticks.

Harry had hauled out of his wagon a low, lounge-like chair, had padded it with extra blankets, and had safely ensconced Libby in it with her supper plate and a glass of milk. The cow grazed nearby tethered to a tree, and in the roped corral the horses and oxen, satiated with water and grass, stood lazily flicking their tails.

Martha kept her distance and her guard, dividing her attention between the conversation around the campfire and the night sounds beyond its warmth.

Clint added a log to the fire. "You've noticed the change in temperature. We run into snow as we travel north, so be certain you have extra clothes available."

Lola moved closer to the fire. She stretched out a naked leg and fluttered her eyelashes toward Clint. "Eet's still summer yet, amigo. Hot nights. I dearly love a steamy night, *et vous?*"

Clint gave her a half smile.

Carsie swallowed hard. How did Lola do that so easily? The whole act occurred so subtly, she didn't understand the actual action. just the results. Clint's appreciative eye skipped fleetingly over the shapely white calf. Phoebe leaned forward and smoothed Lola's skirt down over her ankles. Carsie marveled at how the madame of a sporting house could urge propriety so easily.

"We'll be concerned with keeping warm and dry," Clint continued, glancing around them. His glance brushed over Carsie.

Harry tucked a blanket around Libby's feet. "Are you warm enough?" He hovered like a mother hen.

Libby smiled weakly. "I'm roasting, but thank you for your concern."

The others laughed lightly. Then all fell silent and stared into the moving flames. After a while, one by one they rose and performed cleaning tasks. Carsie noted how each one, herself included, had assumed certain camp chores which they performed automatically every day. Nothing was left undone. No one complained about working harder than anyone else.

She finished her work and wiped all the plates and utensils dry before replacing them in their box and hung the toweling over some bushes. Jake wouldn't let her touch his cast-iron spider. He wouldn't let anyone touch that, preferring to care for it himself at the end of the day, cleaning and greasing it in preparation for the next meal. Barely any meal passed without the use of that heavy three-legged frying pan.

Carsie went away from camp to take care of personals before heading off to bed. When she returned, she heard Jake teasing Clint.

"You're gonna have to do it again if you think any money's gonna change hands, boy."

"I'm not going to do it again. So you can keep your money." Clint set some brush on the fire. It crackled and sent a fountain of sparks into the blackening night air.

Jake scraped the bottom of his boots with a short stick. "Well, it finally happened. Never thought I'd see this day."

"What finally happened? And I know I'll regret letting myself ask that question."

"You're afraid of a woman. Nope, never thought I'd see the day, but it finally happened." Jake chuckled.

Carsie stopped in the middle of spreading her own towel on the bushes. Clint afraid of a woman? What was Jake talking about? Was Clint involved with one of Miss Phoebe's associates? She felt a pang of something stab at her chest. Jealousy? Hardly. She hadn't felt jealous of any other woman, ever. That was something she believed women should never do, envy each other. She stepped behind a clump of thin-trunked trees and listened more closely, feeling only slightly guilty about it.

"I'm not afraid, and you can just quit baiting me. I'm

too tired to put up with your jabs." Clint sounded annoyed yet not cutting.

"Well, then, I dare you to do it again. Prove you're not scared."

"I don't have to prove anything to you, you old buzzard." Clint poured two mugs of coffee and handed one to Jake.

Jake slurped the hot liquid. "Maybe not. I'm just helpin' you to prove it to yourself is all."

"You've always been very helpful." Clint's voice dripped with friendly sarcasm.

"It's my duty as your elder, boy. Why, I'd never forgive myself if I let your education slip."

"I'm a grown boy. Got all the education I want."

"But you've lost your nerve, son. Lost your sense of fun and sport."

Clint turned and looked at the old man. "You don't really think that, do you?"

"Makes me wonder sometimes, boy. Makes me wonder."

Clint turned back to the firelight. "Stealing a kiss from a woman just because you dare me to isn't exactly proof that I've still got nerve."

Stealing a kiss? Carsie clutched a tree trunk.

"Yes, but stealing a kiss from a certain woman. A man-hater. Now that's got some heft to it."

"You think she's a man-hater?"

"Hard to tell. I kinda like her. She doesn't seem like a man-hater exactly. Except for them bloomers."

Bloomers? Carsie dropped her hands to the voluminous folds at her hip. They were talking about her!

"Yeah, I guess that does kinda tell a lot, doesn't it?"

"Seems so. Is she a good kisser?"

Carsie's mouth opened slightly. This conversation had become personal, personal about her. She should leave, go to her wagon and go to bed, she knew it. It wasn't polite to listen to someone else's personal conversation. She started to leave, then stopped. Politeness be damned. Clint and Jake were discussing *her*.

"Now, Jake, I'm sure not going to tell you that."

"You've told me lotsa things in your time, boy. Told about all them women you kissed, all them women you—"

"I may have told you when, but I didn't tell you what it was like."

Jake drained his mug. "So I was right."

"About what?"

"You have lost your nerve. You didn't kiss her at all. Only way I'll believe you've still got it—and I bet the only way you can believe it, too—is if I see you kissin' the Summers girl and she goes all to jelly."

Carsie went rigid. Jake was goading Clint into kissing her, for some reason. Kissing her. Again.

"I don't need to kiss her. I'll kiss Lola. Will that suit you?"

"That's too easy. She'd more'n kiss you if you gave her half a chance."

Carsie clutched the tree trunk more tightly.

"Well, I'm not going to." Clint rose. "What in hell am I doing sitting around here talking to you about kissing women for? We both have better things to do."

"Sure thing. But I don't b'lieve you really did kiss the Summers girl, so the dare doesn't count."

Clint let out a long conceding sigh. "All right. If it will get you off my back about this, I'll do it again. But you better be watching closely. Then will you forget about it?"

Jake laughed. "So we got a bet goin' again, eh, boy?"

The two went off to the rest of the evening chores, leaving Carsie stunned and still standing in the clump of trees.

She leaned her head against the tree. It had all been a sport between Clint and Jake. Clint's surprising her with a kiss had all been because of a dare. She stood up straight. Once again she'd been right about men. Oh, she'd let herself slip a bit, allowed herself a momentary weakness to think about something so trivial and meaningless as a kiss by a brash man. Well, now that she was on to him, the last thing he would get to do was win a bet that concerned kissing her.

Nine

Clint pushed the train forward, urging as much distance as he could, within reason, out of human and animal. Whenever he rode past Carsie's wagon, he'd smile, tip his hat, and call out to ask how Libby was faring or how she herself was doing.

What was he doing now? Carsie wondered. One minute he would barely look at or talk to her and the next he was being friendly. She reacted as evenly as she possibly could, giving brief answers. But she couldn't deny the strange feelings inside that his presence provoked. Her hands perspired inside her gloves, and she was forced to slip them out and pass the palms over her bloomer legs to dry them. His smile was so engaging she almost gave one back, until the whole idea of his bet with Jake reminded her she owed him nothing more than a scowl.

Catching a glimpse of him galloping by to catch up with Jake, or easily swinging up onto Harry's wagon, set her stomach to fluttering. Fluttering. She would never have described herself, or her stomach, as a flutterer. Yet fluttering was exactly what she was doing.

In Wyoming they were joined by a train of twenty-eight teams, and twenty families with several children. The new travelers were a welcome sight and made Carsie feel less alone in the vast country. They traveled together for four days, and the exciting time passed quickly for all of them. In the evenings they gathered around the campfires while the men swapped stories. The wagon master was a crusty old Westerner with a yarn for every bend in the trail, and he loved to spin them. Clint seemed entranced by his every word.

And then Clint and Jake and Harry spun their own yarns about their years with the circus. The audience showed their appreciation by laughing and applauding at all the right pauses. Jake would regale them with tales of his derring-do, with Clint now and then refuting his embellishments with good-natured teasing, or Harry embellishing them further with his dramatic flair.

One evening, with much heavy-handed persuasion, Harry talked Clint into removing his boots and belt and shirt and performing with him several acrobatic feats and juggling tricks. Clint was admittedly out of practice for such antics, but after a few tries he fell into the old routines as if he'd never abandoned them. In the air between them passed a tin sauce pot, a ladle, canteen, and a child's long wooden whistle. The gathering cheered, and then hushed to a reverent awe when a hatchet was introduced to the juggled objects.

Carsie sat still, as entranced an observer as any of the children. She was as appreciative of their entertainment as were the rest of the weary travelers, who needed such extraordinary diversion. Watching Clint's face as he performed, as excited and concentrated as those of the children, and seeing his body clad only in worn blue denim pants that hugged the muscular contours of his long legs and slim hips, caused her fluttering to go deeper.

Libby loved talking with the children and telling stories to several of them when they stopped for camp at the end of the day. She had grown quite large, her swollen belly cumbersome, and she was weary from the jostling and lack of sleep. But when those children gathered around her, her whole demeanor changed. She became alive, her face radiant, her voice animated. When she spoke about her blindness openly and easily, the children asked rounds of questions with rapid-fire velocity. Their mothers admonished them for being impolite, but Libby told them she was not bothered by their questions and believed their natural curiosity about someone different than they should be addressed to allay any fears.

Carsie watched her, fascinated. Libby would make a wonderful mother, she thought. And it was clear the other women thought so, too. Libby asked them many questions and they gave her detailed answers. One woman gave Libby a package of baby clothes her last one had outgrown. She was determined, she said, to have no more babies. Seven were more than enough. Innocently Libby told her Mrs. Goodnight had a remedy to prevent pregnancy. The women within earshot pretended to be properly aghast, but after that incident Carsie noticed on several occasions that the worn-out mother watched Mrs. Goodnight from afar. She could tell she was working up her courage to go and speak to her.

Harry was a popular figure among the travelers. They were fascinated by the way he used his powerful diminutive body. The strength he displayed amazed them. And in typical showman fashion, he lapped up their admiration like a kitten with a saucer of cream.

The women often whispered among themselves while keeping wary eyes on Miss Goodnight, Hannah, and Lola. Mrs. Woo and Martha became the subjects of their reserved curiosity, and they gave only polite acknowledgment toward Carsie. It was then she understood the concept of a sideshow. From the way they observed with cursory, yet complete scrutiny, she knew they found this band of women peculiar at best. And who wouldn't? They were a strange mixture. A buxom, sporting house madam; her ladies, one an elegantly beautiful Negro, the other inappropriately dressed for travel who possessed an accent that alternated among French, English, and Spanish; a silent little Chinese

woman with clicking chopsticks and a gaudily painted
wagon; a whip-wielding mannish woman with chopped hair
wearing pieces of a military uniform; a suffragist in bloomers; and a blind and pregnant young woman who was friend
to all of them.

At Fort Laramie and the split-off to the Bozeman Trail,
the two wagon trains parted. The others were continuing on
the Oregon Trail to Salt Lake. It was an emotional goodbye.
Carsie caught sight of the woman with the seven children
hastily speaking with Phoebe at the back of the Goodnight
wagon. Phoebe handed her a small package. There was a
momentary stiffness in the woman's body, but then she
threw her arms around Phoebe, who hugged her warmly.

They traveled north along the Bozeman road and made
good time in Clint's estimation. Daily he watched the sky,
overcast most of the time with stark white borders around
gray thick clouds. The air held a decided chill.

Late one afternoon Jake rode up alongside him, a worried
look on his face. "You hear that?" A dull rumbling that
sounded like distant thunder reverberated around them. "Is
that a storm comin'?"

"I've been hearing it, but I don't think it's a storm." Clint
scanned the horizon.

"Sure is eerie."

"I'll go see how everybody's doing." Clint wheeled his
horse around and started back along the wagons.

Everyone had grown agitated, especially Martha, who
was jumpier than he'd seen her, ever more watchful around
her and over her shoulders. He came to Carsie's wagon.
She worked hard concentrating on her driving, and appeared
to have a difficult time holding her seat.

"Everything all right?" he called up to her.

"Libby's very upset about something. She thinks there's
going to be a terrible storm."

"I don't think so. Not yet anyway."

The rumbling stayed constant. Clint scanned the sky with

a questioning frown. While the clouds had built up thickly, they didn't look like active thunderheads.

Then the rumbling grew sharp and the air filled with a din that rivaled any circus tent full of spectators. Suddenly from over a rise behind them, a herd of cattle flowed down the hillside like a dark swarm of locusts. The roar was deafening. At least a dozen cowboys ran them, but it looked as if they were losing control.

Martha and Jake and Clint swung the wagons and animals out of harm's way, or so they thought. A group of the racing cattle strayed from the main herd and bore down on them with fiery-eyed speed. They were caught in a confusing frenzy of crazed cattle, shouting drovers, rolling wagons, and frightened teams.

Carsie's nerves went taut. She braced her feet against the wagon seat box and tried to hold her frantic team. Clint appeared to be everywhere at once. He whistled and rode hard at the herd, forcing some of the cattle to veer off. Spotting Martha trapped between Harry's wagon and the thundering herd, he leaned down and scooped her up. He deposited her on the Chinese wagon with Mrs. Woo, who was losing control of her team.

Carsie screamed. Her team pitched and snorted and side-stepped and she could not hold them to any path, nor did she have any idea how to go about it. Her fear for Libby's welfare mounted to hysteria. Clint rode his horse up to her wagon and stayed with her speed. He kicked his feet from the stirrups and hunched them under him, balancing in the saddle. He motioned to her, and somehow she managed to understand that he wanted her to move over on the wagon seat and make room for him. And then he sprung up and leaped from horse to wagon, slipping and hitting his head on the wagon box. Carsie screamed again.

Clint righted himself and grabbed for the reins. They were so tightly woven around her hands he could not free them. He wrapped his hands over hers and together they gained control of her team, slowing them and guiding them away from the herd of cattle which thundered around and finally ahead of them over the next rise.

Martha and Jake rounded up every wagon and brought them to a halt. They made a check of all the oxen and horses, and noted they'd lost the cow. He went to each woman, assessing any wounds and damage to the wagons. Harry scrambled into the back of Carsie's wagon to see if Libby was all right.

Numb, Carsie sat with her hands still wrapped in the reins. Clint slowly lifted his hands away. Sweeping off his hat, he wiped his brow with a shirtsleeve. He sat very still then, not moving from Carsie's side.

"Are you all right?" he asked at length, stilling his own pounding pulse. When she didn't respond, he touched her arm gently. "Carsie?"

She moved when he said her name and nodded her head like a wooden puppet. "Libby," she said weakly.

"I'll see." Clint twisted around to peer into the wagon. "Libby?"

"She's fine," Harry called back. "Pretty shaken up, but says she's all right. I'll know better when she can get up."

Clint turned back to Carsie. "Did you hear that?"

She nodded again.

"Let's get you down from here." He took her hands and tried to loosen them off the reins, but her grip was rigid, almost paralyzed. Carefully he peeled each finger away, rubbed the stiffness out of them, then lifted her down to Jake's waiting arms.

Clint ordered the wagons to a protected spot, stopping where they were to camp for the rest of the night. He knew they could all use the time to recoup some strength after their harrowing experience.

They had finished the evening meal, and most of the weary band had retired when Clint heard a horse and rider nearing camp. He and Jake were immediately at the ready, rifles in hand.

"Peace, pards," the rider called out as he dismounted. His leather chaps flapped as he strode toward them. He regarded Mrs. Woo and Carsie, who were replacing the last of the supper utensils, with a warm greeting. "Evenin' ladies." He doffed his dusty low-crowned hat and smacked it against his thigh. "Sorry about that scare we gave you today. Didn't spy you till we was hittin' the rise. Everybody all right?"

Clint nodded, lowering his firearm. "Shook up is all."

"Well, I shore am grateful for that." The cowboy stuck out his thick right hand. "Name's Pardee, Miles Pardee."

Clint grasped the proffered hand. "Clint Bonner, and this here's Jake Storms."

Mrs. Woo silently retreated to her wagon. Carsie slipped out of their sight, but Clint knew she stayed within hearing distance.

"Can you use some coffee?" Jake started for the cook-fire.

"Only if it's thick and black."

"That's the only thing it is," Clint said. "Jake here doesn't know the difference between coffee and mud."

"Sounds right to me. My cook doesn't know the difference between coffee and coyote piss." He followed Jake to the fire and dropped down on a log. "Where you headed?"

Clint grabbed a mug of coffee and stood with his foot braced on the log. "We're bound for Virginia City in Montana territory. You?"

"Place up north on the Yellowstone River," Pardee answered. "Rich Frenchman there thinks he wants to run a ranch. Bought this herd from a *compadre* of his down in Texas."

"I know the place. Frenchman's Bluff, they call it."

"That's the one. Probably a pretty close name." Pardee laughed.

Clint had plans to stop a few miles southwest of that ranch. There was a stagecoach stop there, with a hotel and restaurant he regarded as excellent in its offerings. Since it was situated more than three-quarters of the way to Virginia City, he figured it would be a good place to rest and a welcome change from their grueling journey.

Jake sat down on a molasses keg. "Say, Pardee, you no doubt got a stray cow in with all them you're runnin'. See if you can cull her out and send her back to us, would ya?"

Pardee laughed. "Don't count on that. Even if we was to spot her, she'd probably be pretty stubborn about leavin' that bunch. It's a good-lookin' herd. Been good water all along and pretty good grass, too."

Lola, clad in a green satin dress suitable for a night in an opera house, sashayed over to the fire, a glass of amber liquid in her hand. Clint figured she'd found a case of the whiskey he had tucked into the back corner of his wagon. He frowned and wondered if she'd spotted the boxes containing the opium. He made a mental note to secure those items more carefully.

She leveled a glittering gaze on Pardee and launched into her intriguing accent. *"Bone swahr, amigo."*

Pardee doffed his hat as his gaze raked over her. "Well, now, good evenin' . . . ma'am."

"And eet's a warm one, too." Lola made a flourish of retrieving a brightly painted Chinese fan from her skirt pocket, flicked it open, and fanned her face provocatively.

"Didn't think so till now." A corner of Pardee's mouth tipped up. "Where you been hidin' this lovely thing?"

Jake's back arched. "Miss LaRue keeps to herself, studyin' mostly. Better turn in now," he said directly to her.

Pardee shot him an amused glance before returning his gaze to settle on Lola, who made no move to retreat.

"Studying? What would this lovely lady want to burden her mind with studying for?"

"She's a teacher."

Pardee's eyes glittered. "And a right fine one I'll bet."

Clint threw the remains of his coffee into the fire. The hiss of steam punctuated the heavy moment. "Well, time to turn in. We've an early morning and a long trail. Thanks for checkin' on us, Pardee. We're just fine."

Pardee stood and set his mug down on the log. "Well, I'm sure glad for that. I'll be headin' back now." He donned his hat and took a step away from the fire before turning back and giving Lola a sweeping gaze. "We'll be traveling along with you a spell."

Clint exchanged knowing glances with Jake. "Best you keep your distance. Our people and animals were mighty spooked today."

"I am sorry about that. Got a couple of rowdies what need settlin' in the blood. I'll control 'em. Thanks for the coffee." Pardee tipped his hat toward Lola. "Mighty fine to make your acquaintance, ma'am. You sure do brighten the end of a hard day."

"Adios, miss-shure. Until we meet again." Lola fluttered her fan and took a long sip from her glass, never taking her eyes off Pardee.

He strode out of the fire's ring of light and disappeared into the darkness. They heard him whip his horse into a run.

"I don't like it." Clint grabbed up the mug Pardee had left on the log.

Jake nodded. "Next time, you stay outta sight," he said to Lola.

Lola pouted. "I was just being neighborly."

"Well, don't be anymore." Jake went off toward Phoebe's wagon, Lola sashaying behind him.

Clint sensed trouble brewing. Keeping the lid on things wasn't going to be easy now that Pardee had seen Lola. No doubt he was already spreading the word among the drovers. They'd be traveling in close proximity with the herd until they reached the stagecoach stop, and that was a good

five days hence. He dropped down onto the log and stared
into the fire's dying embers.

The next night after supper, Carsie wrapped a woolen
shawl around her shoulders and stood a few yards away
from camp. The others sat around the fire discussing the
events of the last couple of days. Clint had warned them
all about staying out of sight if the drovers visited their
camp, and Jake concurred. All of them agreed, except for
Lola, who allowed as how she could use a little excitement.
Clint told her that kind of excitement was dangerous and
something they could do without.

Carsie stood under the night sky and let her thoughts
drift to the entry she knew she would make in her journal
later. Her mind reeled with staggering impressions. So
many animals herded together, the scraping of so many feet,
so large a living mass moving constantly in all directions,
and yet always together toward the same place—seeming
like the masses who emigrated to the West for gold and
land and freedom.

By no means had she forgotten her mission, her reasons
for forcing her way onto this wagon train. Yet she felt almost
guilty for thinking about herself, allowing her own hopes
and dreams to be so brilliant in her mind. She hadn't forgotten Sophie. It was just that now St. Joseph seemed as
far behind her as Virginia City was ahead of her. And out
here in the middle of this vast country a woman's mind
could travel to rolling plains of its own, could picture deep
dreams more clearly. Her own had been taking shape and
she'd been almost fearful of allowing them clarity.

Now as she lingered under the great sky, the evening
breeze rendered the night song of the herdsmen almost tender as a lullaby, the chirp of the everlasting crickets a chorus. Millions of twinkling stars along with a silver moon
gave a certain light that left her with an almost impercep-

tible urge to meditate, to engage in deeper introspection. Old fears slipped away and were replaced by new ones of a much more basic nature. Old dreams seemed frivolous in retrospection, and new ones, while seeming to require the wisdom of the ages and the strength of Atlas, nevertheless seemed more possible to achieve. It was as if she'd shed a mantle of her preconceived self and donned an armor that would see her through any battle no matter how fierce.

A cloud crawled over the moon with slender dark fingers. Carsie shivered. She drew her shawl up over her head and returned to her wagon.

Clint's concerns about the nearness of the drovers were not unfounded. During the day several of them made rides back to the wagon train "just to be neighborly." They were a loud, hard-drinking lot who eyed the women, were very curious about what the freighters contained, and teased Harry unmercifully. Clint drove them off without use of a firearm as often as they appeared, and spoke to Pardee repeatedly, warning him to keep them away from his train. He and Jake and Martha and Harry took turns on the night watch.

They were three days from the place where the herd would leave them to travel north when the first confrontation occurred.

Unable to sleep, Carsie thought of spending a few minutes with Harry, who was on night watch. He'd become a friend to both Libby and herself, and she wanted to know more about him. He wasn't at his post. She waited a few minutes, then looked around for him, being careful not to wander too far away from camp. She thought she heard voices. Perhaps Harry was with Jake or Clint. She shouldn't bother them. She started to turn back when she distinctly heard Harry's voice.

"All right. I like good fun just like everybody else, but enough is enough."

Slowly she walked through the trees and thick brush toward the sound. At the edge of the clearing she saw a terrifying scene. Five drunken drovers had Harry entrapped in a blanket and were making a game of pitching him up and down in it. He was trying to be good-natured, to joke them out of it, but they wouldn't stop. The game was getting rougher by the moment and she could see in Harry's face that he knew he was in greater danger than he could handle.

But what could she do to help? She had no weapon. Where was Clint? Or Jake? The drovers might kill him. She froze with immobilizing fear.

Suddenly she remembered the night Lola had stepped into the group and totally distracted Mr. Pardee from his conversation with Clint and Jake. It looked easy. All Lola had done was talk about the weather and Pardee had lost all concentration on his conversation.

Boldly, Carsie stepped into the clearing.

"Good evening, gentlemen. Do you think it might rain?"

All activity stopped.

That had been easy.

The blanket fell from their hands and Harry landed with a heavy thud that dazed him. Carsie's palms sweated. She started for Harry, but one of the drovers grabbed her.

"Well, now, lookee what we got here, boys. A girl in boys pants. Might be interestin' to find out just what's under 'em."

"Take your hands off me, sir." Carsie struggled against him.

The man laughed. "Sir! Ha! Did you hear that one? Ain't she polite? Now s'posin' you just say please."

Harry groaned and fainted. Carsie tried to get away, but the man's arm only gripped her more tightly.

"Oh, all right then," she said with as much polite courtesy as she could muster given the situation, "will you take your hands off me . . . please?"

The man laughed and she saw yellowed teeth and smelled his acrid breath. He wore a filthy black patch over one eye.

Her stomach churned. He was moving his hand over her hip and starting to fumble with her waistband.

"No, thank you," he mimicked her politeness. "But I would be pleased to take these pants right off you." He tore at her bloomers and brutally whipped them down over her hips, exposing white cotton drawers. "Now, boys, what do you think? Is she all woman under those things, or might she be a he disguisin' a little bitty thing?"

She sucked in her breath and would have screamed if not for the smelly hand that clamped over her mouth. Her head swam and her heart pounded so hard she thought it might give out and she'd die on the spot. He pulled her back against him.

Another one advanced upon her. "Let's find out. The runt was gettin' to be no fun anymore."

He grabbed at her shirt and ripped it open. He reached for her camisole. She clamped her eyes shut, desperately willing the nightmare to be over. This had to be a nightmare. In a blinding flash the memory of her husband and brief marriage returned. She was about to be raped. What her husband had done to her was the same thing. He'd said it was his right. When the last nightmare was over, he was dead and she was holding a pair of bloody scissors.

She wrenched hard, trying to get away from the one who held her. The other one grabbed her feet and a third joined in and tore her bloomers away. She couldn't breathe. She was choking. Just like before. And just like before, her stomach churned harder. She vomited.

The one holding her swore and dropped her. She gagged and choked and vomited some more. The other two laughed harder and tore at her clothes.

The one with the patch raised his open palm. "I'll teach you. You're gonna lick my palm clean before I—" A shot cracked through the air and something else cracked in sickening echo. The man screamed and fell to the ground, clutching his shoulder. The others flattened.

"Get away from her!"

Carsie's mind cleared enough to recognize a chance to move. She crawled toward Harry, who had come around and was struggling to get up. She peered around to see who had shouted.

Clint jumped down from a tree branch and stepped into the clearing, rifle leveled at the drovers, fire in his eye. "Get out of here before I lose control and kill you."

The others ran. The one with the patch struggled to his feet, clutching his bleeding arm. "Bonner," he spat.

Clint blanched at the sound of his voice. Wheelock. There was no mistaking the hatred in his tone. He lifted the rifle level with Wheelock's heart. "Go on back to camp. Tell Pardee I'll see him tomorrow."

"You'll see me again, Bonner. Make no mistake." Wheelock spun around and disappeared through the trees.

Clint dropped his rifle and ran to Carsie and Harry. "What the hell happened?"

"They jumped me on my watch." Harry rubbed his head where a goose egg had formed. "Figured I was good for a game of dwarf pitching."

Clint sucked in his bottom lip, then released it with a hard breath. "It's my fault. I should have stayed with you. I knew they were going to be trouble." Clint took a look at Harry's head and used his bandanna to wipe away the blood that trickled down his temple. "I'm sorry, my friend."

"Apology accepted." Harry stood up. "But I'll thank you not to let it happen again." He gave Clint a friendly push. "I must say, Miss Carson Rose, you have a way with diversionary tactics. Dropped me like a hot potato the minute they saw you."

"Yeah," Clint said, irritation heavy in his voice, "just what in hell did you think you were doing?"

"Saving Harry, of course." Carsie tried to stand up. Her knees buckled and she fell against Clint.

He caught her. "Yeah? Well, don't try that again. You

almost got yourself worse than killed in the process." He held her at arm's length. "What's that smell? You roll in a dead animal or something?"

Harry grabbed Clint's bandanna. "You've got some compassion, haven't you? She's been sick to her stomach. You would be, too, if you had that scum looming over you with evil on his mind." He wiped Carsie's face.

Clint softened. He saw Carsie's disarray fully. With shaking hands he pulled her shirt back around her and then retrieved her bloomers. He started to redress her. "I know about that scum."

Embarrassment showing, Carsie lifted her bloomers out of his hands. "I . . . can do that. Thank you." She pulled them against her, trying to cover her embarrassment and her drawers, which were stained with dirt. She shivered.

Clint took off his shirt and draped it around her shoulders.

"You know him?" Harry walked to the edge of the clearing and retrieved Carsie's shawl.

"I did. You did, too, if you think about it. Never thought I'd see him again. But then, I've thought that twice in the past." Clint relayed the story of when he'd known Jim Wheelock.

Wheelock had been nothing but bad company during all the years they'd worked together in the circus. He courted death, always taking hazardous chances, risking life and limb and not always his own. He often put other people in danger. But mostly he would single out Clint as the target for his malicious deeds.

Clint was the taller, the handsomer, the smoothly successful one with the ladies. Women avoided the stubby-trunked and unkempt Wheelock. He reacted by being more aggressive with them and more aggressive in his attempts to discredit Clint, make him look the coward. He'd begun to go so far as to put Clint in a position of possible severe injury or even death.

One afternoon when Clint had gone to feed one of the lions, he noticed fresh marks along the top and bottom of the cage bars. He'd gone back and put the meat away that he'd intended to feed the animals, and told Jake he thought there was damage to the lion's cage.

He returned to inspect it. Jake sent Wheelock to help him. Carrying a length of heavy chain with which he hoped to secure the top bars, Clint had climbed to the top and was hanging over the edge when Wheelock arrived. He had an insane sneer on his face and started to climb to the top with a hatchet in his hand. In that flash of an instant Clint knew Wheelock had severed the bars enough to cause them to break apart with the movement of the big cat. He had most likely hoped that when Clint appeared at feeding time the lion would sense freedom and maim or kill Clint on his way out. Wheelock hadn't been far off in his assessment of that event happening.

Clint started to push himself back to scramble to the end. He saw the bars start to give way. If that lion escaped, he could do real damage to innocent people. The way Wheelock was bent on coming after him, those hacked bars could break. Clint scrambled over the cage roof and came around behind Wheelock. He dropped the chain down upon his head. The glancing blow made Wheelock lose his grip. One of the bars split apart. It sprung out, catching Wheelock in the face and piercing his eye. He screamed, and the lion lunged and raked his mighty paw down Wheelock's face and chest and below, ripping him open.

Jake and several of the others had run to the cage. They pulled Wheelock away and caught the lion before he could do more. Wheelock had been taken to a hospital and never returned. The circus had pulled out without him.

Clint hadn't seen him again until three years ago back East when Wheelock had appeared in the wagon yard. He was pathetic, scarred all over his face and wearing an eye patch. He seemed subdued. He claimed he was penniless and couldn't work in the circus anymore. He'd blamed that on Clint. Told Clint no one would hire him because of his looks and scars. It was his idea that since it was Clint's fault he was like this, Clint owed him a job. And Clint had given in, figuring even Wheelock deserved a second chance. He himself been given a second chance when Jake had saved him.

And so he'd hired Wheelock to work for his freight service. The other drivers called him Patch. He was constantly drunk and surly. And soon several accidents occurred, with one of the drivers being severely hurt. Clint had given Wheelock a month's wages and put him off the train in a hell town along the trail, believing he'd never see him again.

"Just shows you how wrong you can be about things and about people," Harry said when Clint finished his story.

"I know. And it's not over."

Carsie shivered as she walked between them back to camp.

"Don't try any heroics again," Clint told her firmly. "Especially where he's concerned."

"I won't," she said. "Thank you for saving me . . . Clint."

Clint looked away, feeling embarrassment of his own and covering it with a quick remark he regretted instantly. "Think nothing of it. Don't forget I have to have my quota of brides when we get to Virginia City."

Carsie let out a long breath. "Thank you for reminding me."

The Journal of Carson Rose Summers

6 August 1866

As we traveled yesterday, we came upon a deserted farmhouse. There seemed to be an abundance of good hay in the barn. There were about a half-dozen chick-

ens picking and clucking about the yard. A lone cat
sat in a window. The house seemed in quite fine condition, except that everything movable, even to the
window sashes, had been moved. There were no
graves. It was as if the people had lived there almost
moments before and like grains of sand had been
borne away on a savage wind. It made a rather powerful scene that stays with me even now.

Libby kept asking why the people didn't take the
cat with them, and she fretted so at our water stop
that Harry took Jake's horse and rode back to the
house to get it. The cat did not scare and run off, but
fairly leapt into Harry's arms as if she knew he'd come
back to rescue her. While he was at it, Harry bagged
three of the barnyard chickens and eight eggs. Libby
squealed with delight when he returned and presented
his spoils to her. And Harry's face lit up as if a queen
had just benighted him.

I am no judge of such things, but I do suspect that
Harry has feelings for Libby that go beyond one per-
son caring for another in need. But more, I think
Libby has found her soul mate in Harry.

I don't know how it happened. Libby did not flirt
with Harry. And Harry has been nothing but the gentlemen to her. So how did it happen? I wish I knew,
I wish I understood. I sense that this is true love. But
when did it come? It seems that if indeed it has, it
came upon soft, gentle footfalls, catching the two unawares and cloaking them in a mantle so warm and
cloud-like it had embraced them both before they even
knew it.

But they must have known it. One doesn't fall
asleep one night and wake up the next morning in
love with the right man who is in love with you. Nothing is that wonderful. Then how? And how does anyone know it is the right love with the right person?

Or if she finds the right person, how does a woman know how to attract him? After what I went through two days ago, I know that simply walking up close to the fire and talking about the weather didn't bring me anything but a nightmare.

How I wish someone could help me, show me, tell me how. But why do I want to know how anyway? Have I lost sight of my mission, my life's work?

How do I know what is my life's work? I could be wrong about that. As wrong as I think I've been about Clint Bonner.

Ten

Maybe it was the spectacular lightning that had been slicing the sky since dusk and making the air heavy with the impending power of a storm. Maybe it was the sense that there were still a few more days that the massive herd would be traveling with the wagon train, and the drovers were all fired up for action. Maybe it was the tenseness among the women and the wariness of Harry and Jake. And maybe it was all those things combined that made the night before they were due to reach the ranch feel charged with high emotion and a feral sense of the hunter and the hunted.

Clint sat by a dying fire, unable to sleep, anxious for their departure at dawn and permanent separation from Pardee's company. From their camp over a gentle rise he could hear the escalating voices of the drovers as their consumption of liquor increased. He tapped his foot impatiently, and drew his rifle closer to him.

Carsie wandered out under the sky. It was thrilling, the white hot lightning against the black velvet night. The crickets sang in rhythm, it seemed, or maybe it was in fear. What was it about lightning that elicited fear and fascination at the same time?

She watched Clint from afar as he poked at the dying fire, then wandered a few feet from her wagon and peered out into the dark expanse. She felt edgy. The sounds emanating from the drovers' camp were disturbing. They were drunk; that was easy to tell. Yet she was disturbed this night

by more than their drunken sounds and the memory of her
encounter with them. She had so many questions speeding
around in her mind, and no answers caught up with them.
She longed to talk to another woman about them.

She heard something and whirled around. Miss Goodnight was passing by, lantern in hand to light the way. A
determined look was etched on her face in the sallow glow
of the lantern light. Her steps were resolute. It looked as if
she was headed toward Clint and the campfire.

"Miss Goodnight?"

"Oh, dear, Carson Rose, you startled me." Phoebe
clasped her shawl around her throat against the chilling air.

"I'm sorry." Her mind spinning, stiffly Carsie walked toward her, trying her darnedest to look nonchalant. No one
had called her Carson Rose except for her mother when she
was a child. "Do you have a moment?"

"I . . . well, I must speak to Major Bonner."

"It won't take long, I promise."

Phoebe set her lantern on the ground. "All right. Is there
something I can help you with? Or I mean—"

"Yes, actually I think you can help me, or perhaps answer
a question for me."

"I'll certainly try."

Carsie swallowed. "How does . . . that is when . . . ?"

Phoebe inclined her head. "Are you having female problems? Don't be embarrassed. Just spit it out and we'll know
what we're looking at here."

"Yes, ma'am." Carsie entwined her fingers and looked
down at them. "I think Libby and Harry are in love," she
blurted, "and I was just wondering how that happened. I
mean, I didn't see her flirt with him. So how . . . And how
does one know how to flirt anyway? I mean, what do you
do to get a man to notice you?" She jerked her chin up
quickly. "Oh, I didn't mean that exactly. I mean, you certainly know how to get a man to notice you. Oh, I didn't
mean that exactly. I just meant that you're so, you're very,

you're . . ." She sucked in her breath and willed back angry tears.

"Obvious is what I am." Phoebe laughed lightly. "Honey, I may bring 'em in with what I got but what I got I ain't giving to them. Never have, never will. Unless of course I deem the circumstances to be dire."

"Oh, dear, I didn't mean to imply . . . that is . . ."

"I know you didn't. Now, it appears to me you could use some mothering, and if there's anything I'm good at it's mothering motherless girls. Suppose you just tell me what you want or . . . or who you want. Is it Major Bonner?"

Carsie lost her breath for a moment. "Oh my, no. I didn't mean to imply . . . I was just wondering. I was married once." Where had that come from?

"So was I. Not once. What has that got to do with anything? Unless, of course, you're still married. Do you want to know how to seduce your husband?"

"Seduce? Oh no. I can't anyway. He's dead."

"I'm sorry."

"I'm not."

"I see."

"I mean, if I was married, I must have known how to do that, flirt or whatever, but I don't think I did. Shouldn't I? I mean, if I was married . . ."

Phoebe shook her head and wrapped her arm around Carsie's shoulders. "Marriage doesn't teach you anything about that most of the time, unless you have a most incredible man. I've met a few, but I taught them more than they taught me. Now don't be embarrassed about such talk. I think you have to know these things at the outset, so you can be certain to attract the right moth to your flame. Do you understand? Of course, if you're not careful you can attract a whole passel of moths and find yourself swattin' 'em away all evening. But you have to see past the swarm to that special one."

"H-how?"

"Well, honey, only your heart can tell you who's the right

one. Nobody else can, because somebody else's idea of the right man most of the time is the wrong one for you. You have to trust your feminine intuition on this one."

"I don't have that, I think. That intuition."

"Yes, you do. It's our gift. If you ponder on this often, you will understand your gift." She gave Carsie's shoulders a small squeeze. "Now, I want to check on Libby and be off about my business. We can talk again tomorrow if you'd like."

Carsie stepped away and faced her full on. "I would like that very much. Thank you, Miss Goodnight."

"I should think that since we've shared such intimate talk you might call me Phoebe." She turned, picked up her lantern, and headed toward the campfire.

Clint poked at the fire he'd decided to stoke up again. It might be best to keep a bright light in their midst. Phoebe Goodnight joined him before long.

"Good evening, Phoebe."

"I won't mince words here, Major Bonner. There is bound to be trouble tonight. Sure as I'm standing here, there is bound to be trouble."

"I know. Keep everyone out of sight and we'll handle them if . . . when they start coming."

"I have a suggestion, Major. I've talked to my ladies and we're all agreed."

"Agreed about what?"

"We can diffuse the powder keg that's building over the hill there. We have everything we need."

Clint narrowed his eyes. "Everything you need . . . for what?"

"To put their fires out. We'll construct a canvas shelter and call it the Traveling Good Times Emporium. We'll have music and dancing, and—"

"No." Clint rose sharply. "You will do no such thing.

You're asking for trouble you can't handle, we can't handle. Things will get very ugly before they get better."

"I assure you, Major, we've handled very similar situations in our time. We can handle almost anything that comes our way. We have to do something to ease the tension. You can trust us to do what is necessary to keep the others free from harm. In this instance, we are much better equipped than you are."

"I don't like it."

"That doesn't matter. We believe it to be necessary. And I believe you know we are right."

Clint stared into the fire. Then he nodded, reluctantly agreeing.

Jake and Harry and Clint hauled out tent canvas and raised it into a makeshift building. Hannah and Lola strung up quilts for a decoration, and lit lanterns shrouded in lace. A table was set up with some food. And then Phoebe, Lola, and Hannah went off to make themselves ready.

Carsie emerged from the wagon, where she'd been recording her thoughts in her journal. She saw Libby feeling her way alongside the wagon.

"Where are you off to?" The lilt in her voice faded when she saw the glowing tent off in the trees. "What is that? What's going on?"

"Oh, you must mean the tent," Libby replied.

"Yes, I guess so. When did that happen?"

"Just a few minutes ago."

"Why?"

"Miss Goodnight believes we will have trouble with Mr. Pardee's men. She says they've been drinking heavily and Harry heard them talking about coming over here. She plans to calm the drovers by opening a Good Times Emporium for the evening. I am going over to offer my services as pianist. Music quite often helps."

Carsie's mouth had dropped open at this news. "You can't mean they're going to . . . they wouldn't do . . . what it is they do . . . when they're . . . doing . . . working. Would they?"

"Well, of course they would. Oh, they're very good at making people feel good. Miss Hannah can sing like a nightingale. Before she came to Miss Goodnight, her master would get her to sing at his fancy dinners."

"Her master?"

"Oh yes. She was a slave, you know. Can you imagine something so reprehensible as people making slaves out of other people. Anyway, she escaped. Isn't that absolutely courageous?"

It was absolutely courageous, Carsie could agree on that. But what they were all doing tonight was not courageous. It was foolhardy for certain. These men would . . . She shuddered, remembering only a few nights before when they had attacked her and meant to rape her. Her stomach churned.

"They can't do that. You are not going in there in your condition. There's no telling what might happen. These men are crazy. I must stop them."

"You must *not* stop them, Carsie. You can trust Miss Goodnight's wisdom."

"I can't stand by and do nothing. Please, Libby, promise me you'll stay right here until I come back."

"Well, all right, but don't be long. Miss Goodnight is going to need me in the tent."

Carsie ran off in search of Phoebe. She found her outside her wagon placing a jeweled plume in her massive hair arrangement.

"Phoebe, you can't do this. Libby told me what you have in mind, and I beg you not to do this."

Phoebe continued the adornment of her hair. "Now, Carson, this is the best way to handle our little problem," she said with controlled calm, drawing out her words. "Three days hence we shall be nearing the hotel Major Bonner told us about and this business will be behind us and we'll all be safe. Women have great power."

"Not that kind of power. Why don't we all just gather up our rifles and fend them off? We can do it, just like the day we defended ourselves against . . . well, against Clint and Jake and Harry. I know that was much different, but we showed the kind of strength we had pulling ourselves together. Why can't we do that again?"

"This is a different kind of warfare and it requires a different kind of ammunition." Phoebe assessed her hair and makeup in a mirror she'd propped against a trunk. "It occurs to me that this is a most opportune moment for you to observe, to learn that art and those skills you seem to crave. Why don't you put on a skirt and come over and see how we handle men in this kind of situation?"

A pounding of horses' hooves broke into the night air. Phoebe gathered up her fan and shawl and started for the tent.

"Isn't there any other way?" Carsie called to her back.

Phoebe turned around. "No."

Carsie dropped her hands limply at her sides and watched Phoebe enter the glowing tent. Was Clint in there to protect them? And what about Jake and Harry? Surely Martha would not be in attendance. Nor Mrs. Woo. She would seek them out and among the three of them they would come up with a plan to protect and defend their friends.

Friends. The thought struck her like the flash of lightning slashing the sky. These people were her friends, her real friends. Even more so than Sophie had been. She knew it now.

She went in search of Martha and Mrs. Woo. They were not in camp. Could it be? Could they be there, ostensibly with the same thoughts as she'd had? To protect their friends?

Maybe it wouldn't hurt for her to at least keep a distance and observe the goings-on.

At the tent opening, Phoebe stood peering out into the night and the gathering storm. "I believe the thundering herd is approaching now."

Clint tensed and looked around.

"We're ready for them." Hannah stood near the piano.

Libby struck up a lively air, wincing at the out-of-tune notes.

Lola lounged on a makeshift divan. Phoebe went to the center of the room and struck a pose. Mrs. Woo stood at the food table ready to serve the things they'd put together quickly. Martha stood at the rear entrance to the tent, her rifle and whips set discreetly in a corner. Harry was outside the rear entrance, and Jake had positioned himself along the side.

The heavy beat of horses' hooves came to an abrupt halt outside the wooded area in which they'd set up the tent.

"What the hell is this?" Pardee's voice.

Libby stopped playing.

"Now just what do you suppose is goin' on in there?" Wheelock's voice.

"Why don't we have a little look-see?" One of the men whom Clint had seen the night he'd rescued Harry and Carsie.

The flap snapped open and Pardee strode in. Seven rowdy drovers, drunk and carrying liquor bottles, reeled in behind him. They stopped dead when they saw the setup, and Clint in the midst of it.

"Bonner. It figures." Patch Wheelock took a long swig from his bottle. "I told you I'd see you again. I just didn't figure it would be so soon. Bet you didn't either."

"Well, now, Bonner," Pardee began, and strode toward him, "were you fixin' to keep this little party a secret?"

Clint glared at Wheelock for a tense moment, then swaggered just a bit toward Pardee. For effect, he told himself. "As a matter of fact, we've been expecting you," he said evenly. "We were just beginning to think you weren't going to come."

Phoebe ambled toward them, fluttering her fan over her ample bosom. "Welcome, gentlemen. You've just entered the halls of Goodnight's Traveling Good Times Emporium. Come in, enjoy a little food, a little music and dancing. We're here to ease the burdens of your long drive."

"Well, now, madam, we don't have to be invited twice." Pardee turned back to the others. "All right, boys, you wanted a little entertainment and it looks like you got a lot just waitin' for ya'. Go to it!"

The drovers whooped and headed toward the women. Clint stepped forward and laid a hand on Pardee's shoulder. "Just don't let this little party get out of hand, Pardee. You hear me?"

Pardee shifted his shoulder out from under Clint's hand. "I hear you. And I don't take threats lightly. You've got a threat in your voice, Bonner."

"You bet I have. And I mean to make good on it if need be. Take care of it. You know what I'm talking about." Pardee grinned and headed toward Lola.

Carsie had had enough observing. She didn't want to see what would happen next, although her mind offered quick images. How could any woman allow such things to happen to her? Her mind and heart could not take another moment of the scene. She left her observation point at the tent and returned to her wagon.

For two days the wagon train had traveled north with Pardee and his herd. Clint had been thanking his lucky stars that they hadn't encountered Indians or renegades along the route, but he wondered now whether they might have been easier to handle. Miss Goodnight had been right. Her Good Times Emporium offered enough diversion to keep tempers even, tension to a minimum. Pardee had kept his word about controlling his drovers. Even the surly Patch, while a troublemaker every step of the way, seemed to be on a short rein.

Just one more day to the pass, and once they got through that, the herd would continue north and he'd turn the wagon train west toward Virginia City. Once through the pass and the snow, he could turn his face west to the goldfields and the wealth they produced to be enjoyed by those who were smart enough to get it.

Supper over, Clint knew the nightly revelry would begin. He would take up watch in the tent as he did every night. There was a time he enjoyed the free manner sporting women had about them. The laughter, the dancing, the talk, and more had entertained him as much as it had men for centuries. But these few nights had left him restless, angry, almost proprietary about Miss Goodnight and her women. They were his drivers, after all, responsible for his wagons. He had investment in them.

It was more than that and he knew it. And he knew Jake would tell him so one of these days. Reluctantly Clint rose and headed toward the Good Times tent to take up his watch.

The night before the train would begin to push through the pass, Libby sat huddled under blankets away from the campfire. The air was almost biting with cold, but she couldn't stand the heat of the fire on her skin nor its glare in her eyes. And the last place she could stand to be was in the Good Times tent.

She felt desperately ill. Her stomach ached and her head throbbed. Pains low in her back and pelvis came and went, now with some regularity.

It was too early for the baby to come. Libby panicked. She was desperate to protect that fragile life by keeping it inside her for as long as possible. She rocked back and forth under her blankets. *Please God, don't let my baby be born yet.*

At the cookfire before first light, Clint paced with a mug of Jake's coffee, strong enough this morning to move a wagon on its own. Snow was falling steadily. Martha was already hitching teams while Jake set out breakfast. It would be a miracle if they made it through the pass in this snow. But they could do it if they didn't delay, and with the herd pushing through ahead of them, they could have a clearer path. If the snow didn't come any harder. He never thought he'd be glad Pardee and his herd were with them.

Wrapped in woolen shawls draped over her head, Hannah hurried toward them. "Phoebe says we have to stay here today. Libby's going to have her baby." Her words made small puffs of frosty vapor in the air in front of her mouth.

Clint set his mouth in a firm line. "We're moving out. We have to keep ahead of this snow."

"But we can't leave," Hannah argued. "Libby's in labor. She shouldn't be moved, let alone knocked about in a rolling wagon. We have to wait out the birth."

"We are leaving. Babies are notorious for taking their time coming into the world. Maybe they're smarter than we know." He took a long swallow of the thick coffee. "By the time that baby is ready to be born, we'll be on the other side of the pass and out of danger. You tell everyone we're moving." He turned his back and headed for Martha.

Hannah stood motionless for a long moment. A cold wind whipped around her. She pulled her shawls closer, then turned and hurried back toward Libby's wagon.

Libby moaned. Her head rolled from side to side on the

blankets. Phoebe looked at her locket watch. Hannah held her hands.

"How is she?" Carsie whispered, crawling inside the wagon with an extra blanket from Martha.

"Bad off." Phoebe took the blanket and laid it aside. "Poor child. This one won't be easy."

Lola arrived with more toweling. "I put some water on the fire to heat. How is she?"

"Scared, I think," Carsie told her.

"I'm not scared!" Libby shouted. Hannah tried to calm her. "Please don't let my baby be born. Please. Not yet. Not till we get there. Just stop it, please, Miss Phoebe."

"Now, honey," Phoebe soothed, "you know when a baby wants to be born, there's just about nothing anybody can do except help it happen as easily as we can. It'll be fine, Libby honey, you just let go and let it happen."

"Moving isn't going to be good," Lola cautioned, all traces of any accent absent. "I've seen how it can affect a birthing mother."

"Shush." Phoebe raised a warning hand. "We'll do what we have to do."

"Clint says we're moving out," Hannah said then. "He's worried about weather."

"The weather will be nothing to face if things go wrong with this birth," Lola countered.

Phoebe blotted Libby's head with a handkerchief. "I wish he'd reconsider." Her voice carried an edge.

Hannah shook her head. "I tried to talk him out of it, but he wouldn't be persuaded." She packed a small opening in the canvas with a thick blanket to block out the wind. "He's never had a baby before. He doesn't know what it's like."

Carsie heard the words of the women, and memories of painful and fatal births back on the farm came thundering back into her mind. How her mother had suffered from too many births, and too many abuses at the hands of her father.

He'd offered no help, no compassion whatever when her mother labored for hours, sometimes days. And he said nothing when often a tiny still form, wet with her mother's desperate tears, was taken from her and buried in nothing but a piece of toweling.

Libby cried out, then stifled her scream. Carsie knew she didn't want to be a bother to anyone. But she knew how profoundly Libby wanted this child, how her love for the infant and her desperate desire to keep it transcended any pain she would endure over the next hours. Libby deserved to have those hours pass as mercifully as possible. She didn't deserve to be tossed about in a miserable rolling wagon, the weather be damned.

Carsie wrapped a blanket around her shoulders. "I'm going to go talk to Mr. Bonner. There must be something that will dissuade him from his bull-headed idea of moving out this morning."

She crawled out of the wagon and headed toward the morning fire. Jake was finishing the breakfast cooking and Clint was oiling a harness when she approached.

"Well, now, glad to see you people are finally getting out of bed. Breakfast has been ready 'most a half hour." Jake handed a plate to her.

"No, thank you. Mr. Bonner, you have to be reasonable about moving this morning. Libby is in labor and it's very hard on her. She can't be moved."

Clint rose and did not look at her. "We are moving. If we're caught in a storm in the pass, it will be worse than any labor. We could all freeze to death in there. Have you ever seen anyone freeze to death? I think you might choose birthing a baby over that."

Carsie's teeth chattered. She clamped them together for a moment, and then tried again. "Thank you for that chilling account, Mr. Bonner. But I'd like to point out that you have never had a baby, and perhaps you'd consider your frozen death option over that. Libby cannot be moved. If you push

like babies themselves last night." He gave a laugh rife with suggestive reference to Phoebe and the other women.

"Shut up, Pardee. We're moving out. The weather is turning bad."

Pardee helped himself to some coffee. "What's a little snow? I've got a herd through that pass before when the snow was chest high. It blows out fast as it blows in sometimes. But I know this bunch. They got a storm brewin' in them that only Miss Goodnight and the ladies can put out."

Clint ignored him. "Jake, clean up your kitchen and douse the fire. We're moving, we're *all* moving."

"Don't you dare douse that fire, Mr. Storms. We're staying," Carsie countered again. "And what's more, based on a unanimous vote, if you force us to go there will be no . . . no . . ." She turned around for assistance from the others.

Phoebe stepped to her side. "There will be no Goodnight's Good Times Emporium to accommodate our traveling companions."

"What?" Pardee stepped up to them. "You can't do that."

"We can do anything we want to." Hannah stepped to Carsie's other side.

"That's right," Carsie agreed.

Clint glared at her. "What have you done?"

"You can't do that," Pardee said again. "This is the best thing that's happened since we moved that herd out. Them are the hardest bunch of drovers I've ever had the misfortune to hire. Up to now I wasn't so sure I could get the herd there with most of 'em accounted for, the way they work. But the idea of them workin' all day to end up in that sportin' tent at night has 'em all rarin' to go."

"Well, we took that rarin' right out of 'em, didn't we, *Moo-shure* Pardee." Lola planted her hands on her hips and fixed a glittering stare on him.

"You bet you did, little lady. Took the piss and vinegar right out of 'em." Pardee laughed.

"Well, *moo-shure,* you best find a way to do that yourself, because we are feenished unless we stay right here and birth Libby's baby."

Pardee swung toward Clint. "Bonner, you tell 'em they can go have their baby so we can have that tent."

Clint stepped closer to Carsie. "What have you done to these women?" He gave Carsie a glare that would have melted the snow on the mountain peaks if he'd been close to them.

"I don't know what you mean."

"You do, too. I don't know how you managed it but you've turned these perfectly nice women into . . . women who . . ."

"Have the power to exercise their rights over themselves, Mr. Bonner? That's what you were going to say, wasn't it? And you'd be right."

The women nodded and murmured among themselves.

"Martha? You feel the same way?"

"I do." Her voice was strong and clear.

Clint studied their faces. Carsie had organized a revolt among them. She was playing out her drum-banging routine with a group of whores and a female bullwhacker who was tougher than any man he'd ever known. How had she managed such a feat?

The women gathered behind her announcing they would camp there until the baby was born, or no tent. Pardee moved in next to them in front of Clint and demanded that he stop the wagons to wait out the birth. He needed that tent. It was a standoff, and it was clear to Clint that the longer they stayed there arguing about it, the worse things were going to be with the weather, and the delay could be greater. He looked at Jake. Jake was staring at the women, obvious admiration on his face that made no sense to Clint whatsoever.

Realizing he was fighting a losing battle, Clint gave in, hoping at least that he could win the war. "All right. We'll wait until morning. But if that baby isn't born by then, we are *all* moving out. I hope you're hearing me. You will have much worse things to feel on your conscious if you don't. None of you understands the grave danger we're in."

Carsie spun around and raised a hand in the air, signaling another victory for women. They cheered as they headed back to where Libby lay in labor.

The birth was many hours long and arduous, and brave though Libby was, she cried out often with the pain. Carsie couldn't bear it. There were too many reminders of her mother and all the births at home. She ran way from the wagon and stood alone in a clearing away from the fire. All her display of independence and strength failed her at the moment of this birth, and she sobbed openly.

Clint followed Carsie—for her protection, he told himself. He watched her from beside a distant tree until she pulled herself together and turned to go back to camp. Seeing him watching her caused another flood of tears. Clint walked slowly to her, reached out, and put his arms around her. It was a reaction he did not think about. He just did it. For all her bravado, he knew now there was an equally strong compassion and sensitivity toward other people inside her. He held her without speaking until her crying subsided, then walked silently with her to the wagon.

A frail boy was born toward morning, his feeble cry penetrating the gray dawn. Libby held him to her breast, then looked up with grateful weary eyes at the equally weary women gathered around her. "He will be a great hero because of the valor you showed him, making sure he was born safe and healthy."

They all christened him with loving kisses on his head. Harry peeked inside the flap then.

"Everything all right?" His voice was shaky.

"Yes," Libby whispered. "Say hello to Master Harry Bonner Allen."

Eleven

On the last night, quaking in her boots, Carsie decided she would go to the tent and observe. It would make a good article for *Harper's,* she reasoned, a female eyewitness account of . . . she wasn't certain she wanted to know what this account might be. She headed for the tent, stopped abruptly, and turned to go back to her wagon. Maybe Libby had a skirt she could borrow.

Hesitantly, Carsie made her way toward the tent opening and peeked inside. Harry had taken Libby's place and was in there playing a lively tune on the piano. She stepped through the opening and into the tent.

The drovers were there, and Mr. Pardee. They were dancing with the women, even Mrs. Woo, who had painted her face with brilliant color. And they were loud and kept pawing over the women, who looked as if they were fending them off easily and with a smile no less. Carsie frowned. How could they do that? Mrs. Woo wasn't doing that. But Carsie noticed she'd stuck a long pin in her tightly coiled hair and even now her little hand was raising slowly toward it.

Was Clint here? She scanned the room. And then she saw him. His arm was draped around Hannah. A twinge of jealousy caught her off-balance, something she'd never felt before. She didn't know quite how to react to it exactly. Maybe if she watched for a while and then tried to emulate the Good Times women, she'd figure out how to get him to notice her. But why did she want that? Maybe she just meant to somehow get back at him just a little for making a game of her with Jake. Making a game of kissing her and then practically ignoring her afterward. But of course she'd wanted him to ignore her. Hadn't she?

"Hey! There's a new one!" a gravelly male voice shouted in her direction.

Carsie looked around behind her, then back. No one else was near her. He must have been referring to her! Two drovers, one big and burly with a long scruffy beard, and the other a short stub of a man with a withered arm, descended upon her.

"Let's dance, little lady, whaddaya say?" The burly one grabbed her around the waist and spirited her off her feet and around the room.

"Wait," she said, breathless from the surprise of his behavior, "I don't know how to dance."

"I don't care!" He dropped a big slobbering kiss on her.

She jerked away and tried to wipe the wetness off her face with her shirtsleeve. "I'll thank you not to do that again, sir."

"Then you won't be thankin' me at all, but I'll be more'n thankin' you before the night's over!" He laughed loudly and snatched her to his chest. "All you gotta do is feel the beat and feel me pushin' ya and you'll learn all the dancin' you're ever gonna need."

As he pushed his lower body into her and she kept an unnatural curl to her spine trying to keep hers away from his, she suddenly caught sight of Patch Wheelock. He watched her with a lascivious grin. He sauntered near her. Carsie's stomach knotted. She wrenched free of the burly man and spun around, crashing into the waiting arms of a drunken cowboy. She pushed away with all her strength, but he was too big and too drunk to let go. Surprisingly, Patch intervened and wrenched the man's arms free, drawing Carsie away.

Carsie smoothed her skirt. She did not look him in the face. Seeing that one blood-shot eye and remembering her last encounter with him would be her undoing. "Thank you for rescuing me. Now if you'll excuse me—"

"Can't do that." He swiped his arm across his forehead. "I think you can find a better way to thank me."

"Of course. Why don't you wait right here and I'll go and fix you a plate of food." Fear rising in her breast, she made a move to get away from him.

His hand shot out and clamped over her arm. "No whore cuts me off like that and does it again with the same face." He yanked on her arm and sent pain shooting into her shoulder.

"My turn." An even bigger man pushed between them and shoved Patch out of the way. "C'mere. You're a strange-lookin' one, but you must have somethin' different, hunh?"

Relieved for the interruption, Carsie seized upon it to sidestep way from Patch. "Yes, sir, I am very different. For one thing I'm not a . . . Let me tell you . . ."

"Don't tell me. I'd rather be surprised." He picked her up and whirled her around until her head spun. In her dizziness she thought she saw Patch storm outside the tent.

Phoebe strolled near and whispered in her ear. "Do something about that grimace. Here." She handed over her fan. "Look like you're having fun or they'll get suspicious."

Carsie nodded, took the fan, and let out with a tinkling laugh that sounded more like glass being crushed under boots. She tried to flutter the fan but it kept getting caught in the man's shirtsleeve.

Around his thick upper arm she peeked at what the others were doing. Lola was giggling as Pardee was slipping a garter off her leg. Another man was nuzzling her neck from behind. In the process she had slipped her hand around his waist where he had a knife sheathed. She slipped it out and tossed it toward the back. Martha was there in an instant and grabbed it up, then disappeared out back. Phoebe had a particularly burly man, drunker than a lord, dropping to his knees and begging her to dance. She smiled at him and said she was too warm and needed a drink. With that she snatched his bottle away from him, and while he wasn't looking, she tossed it out the back.

So that was it, Carsie thought. All she had to do was pretend she was having a good time. If anything went wrong, she'd throw something to Martha, who would take care of it.

She got caught up in the spirit of the revelers then and pretended to be as good a Good Times lady as she could, all the while trying to keep one step ahead of the drovers and one eye on Clint to see if he noticed her. When he did notice her, he frowned. But what was he doing dancing with Hannah anyway? Shouldn't she be doing . . . whatever her training had trained her to do?

Or was she going to do that with Clint?

Carsie stumbled then and the big man stepped on her foot. She kicked him in the shin.

"Ow!" He let go of her and tried to grab his leg. He was so drunk the action sent him keeling over into a heap at her feet.

Someone grabbed her from behind and spun her around. She faced Patch Wheelock once again.

"Well, now, seems you and me have got some unfinished business, haven't we?" He roughly propelled her around the room.

"I . . . the music isn't quite the beat you're using."

"I don't need it. I been waitin' for Dankers to let go of you so's I could get my chance. I know better'n to mess with him when he's drinkin'. He's a mean son of a bitch."

"Please don't swear. I don't like to hear it." Carsie knew that sounded feeble. Asking this lout politely not to swear was futile.

"You're going to hear a lot more of it and a lot I'll bet you never heard before this night is over," he growled. Then he added the threat, "I intend to finish what I started the other night, and I ain't waitin' any longer." He pushed her toward the tent's front opening.

"Oh, I don't think we should leave the party." Her voice was thin.

She resisted him hard, but he tightened his hold. He was strong, very strong, and he was pressing the air out of her. She was becoming light-headed. Would she faint? Would no one see her? Carsie panicked then. She tried to plant her feet solidly in the dirt and push at him, but he lifted and started to drag her.

Something stopped him. Carsie froze.

"Now, really, haven't I told you not to be in such a hurry all the time?" Phoebe Goodnight blocked the entrance, shaking her finger at Carsie.

Why was she admonishing her? She should be reprimanding this oaf Patch and rescuing her from his clutches. But no, she was making it easier—for him!

"Now, you just dance this gentleman right back over there and offer him some of our delicious refreshments," Phoebe continued. "He has to get his money's worth or our reputation will be at stake."

"I've had enough of that stuff," Patch muttered. "I'm ready to leave now." He clutched Carsie even tighter.

Carsie pleaded silently with Phoebe to do something about the predicament she was in. Did she actually expect her to go through with . . . what they were expected to go through with?

"Say, now." Hannah strolled up, shifting her hips provocatively. "You said you'd share everyone with me, and you haven't let me near this handsome man all night." She smiled up at him with a come-hither look on her face.

Carsie felt nothing but shock at this. How could anyone want such a disgusting human as Patch? And share him? She'd never said anything about sharing anybody with anybody.

"Back away, beetch." Lola stepped in and gave a hitch with her hip that knocked Carsie right out of his clutches. She grabbed Patch's arm and wrenched it away. "I saw heem first, and I fully intend to have heem before you ruin heem." She gazed up into his startled face, tapped his eye patch, and insinuated her body against his. *"Voo-lay voo, moo-shure.* What do you hide? A leetle dance weeth me will reveal all."

Carsie stepped back and stared open-mouthed. What could they all possibly see in a filthy one-eyed pig like Patch? She'd been forced to dance with him. She certainly hadn't chosen to. But here they all were fighting over him. She watched them maneuver him toward the middle of the room.

Patch let out a whoop. The others stepped back and glowered at him. Carsie thought they looked pretty mad. Well, why not? He had all of the women now except for her and Mrs. Woo. She hoped he wouldn't go in search of Libby. Martha was smart. She stayed hidden out back.

Not content with the three women he had, Patch snaked out an arm and caught Mrs. Woo off guard. She stumbled. Carsie went to assist her, but in the next moment she knew there was no need. Mrs. Woo whipped the long pin from her topknot and stabbed it into Patch's thigh.

"Yow!" he screamed.

The other women cooed over him as if he was a poor hurt puppy.

And then Clint was at her side. "You're leaving now."

So, he was finally paying attention to her now that all of the other women were occupied with someone else. Well, if she'd learned one thing from her visit to the tent tonight, she'd learned that a woman couldn't be too quick to just fall into a pair of male arms. She'd use her newfound knowledge right now.

"Thank you, but actually I'm not. Things are just starting to get lively and I—"

"They're starting to get mean. You're one of the problems, so you're going to disappear."

"I don't want—"

"I don't care what you want." He pushed her outside the tent.

Clint propelled Carsie forward. And she let him.

Clint felt a mixture of emotions regarding the women on his train as he observed them amid the revelry in the tent, new admiration for their strength and determination on the drive and regret that they had to resort to using themselves as bait to distract the drovers and dilute the tension that had surrounded them for the last few days. Strangely, he'd felt anger rise in his throat as he'd watched Patch advance on Carsie. Patch was no good through and through. Even the prowess of seasoned professional women like Lola and Hannah had been stretched to their limits. Carsie was no match for any of those men, but most especially Patch Wheelock.

They were almost to her wagon when he stopped outside the circle of light from the lantern that Harry had left for them. Libby was settling down for the night and Harry was saying his goodnights. And lingering rather a long time, Clint noted. Harry looked around, signaled to Clint, then went back toward the tent.

Clint stood next to Carsie without looking at her. "You took a big chance going into that tent tonight. You're lucky you weren't hurt. Why did you go over there anyway?"

She was silent a long time. "Everyone has been there every night," she said in a small voice. "I thought I should be, too. I'm a member of this party."

"Yes, you are. But you had no business being there."

"Libby's been there, even while she was pregnant."

"And she took a big chance. Harry didn't take his eyes off her for one minute."

"She said she had to be there. She could contribute the music that would have a calming effect."

Clint sighed. "I don't know about calming, but her music did add to the activities."

"See? I had to make a contribution, too."

"What did you think you were adding? You're not one of Miss Goodnight's ladies. You can't play the piano, far as I can see. You put yourself in a bad way in there. If it weren't for the others intervening, well, who knows what might have happened?"

Carsie went still. Then, "They did intervene, didn't they? I misunderstood at first. But you're right. They were protecting me, weren't they?"

"They know how to take care of their own." He moved one foot. "I didn't mean that to sound as if you were one of them, one of their profession. I just meant that—"

"I know what you meant." There was an excitement in her voice. "I am one of them. They might think of me as a . . . friend. Mightn't they?"

"Yeah, that is pretty surprising, isn't it?"

She turned toward him. "Now what do you mean by that?"

He turned toward her. "Just that you are difficult to be friends with. You're not the usual female. And you've won the prize for being the most exasperating one I've ever come in contact with."

He ran a hand through his hair. It was an act of frustration and for something to do with at least one of his hands. He was quite suddenly consumed with the intense desire to kiss her, and he knew that was a bad idea at best. A chilling wind swept through the air around them.

Carsie's excited voice transformed into frustration. "Haven't I worked just as hard as everybody else on this train? Haven't I kept my complaints to myself when my body and bones ached so much I thought I might die from the pain? Haven't I kept my opinions to myself about how I feel about what you're doing? Well, at least after the first hundred miles, anyway. I've kept mostly to myself. I've controlled myself, even when I discovered . . . things that upset me. Haven't I? I've done all that and more, and . . ."

Clint stared down at her. He saw her lips moving but he didn't hear her voice. He saw her tall frame which had become lean and hard from weeks on the road now concealed in a skirt. All he could think of was how he wanted to tear that skirt away and find . . . her bloomers still under there. The idea jolted him. He wanted Carson Summers to remain in bloomers! Did he think they made her look like less of a woman? Did he think they would make her less desirable to him? No. That wasn't exactly the answer. He knew it. Even wearing bloomers she attracted him. There was no answer for why that was so.

"You talk too much," he muttered. And then he had her in his arms and was kissing her and cutting off the next flow of words that were about to come out of her mouth.

At first she was startled into rigidity when he kissed her. Then she went all soft and yielding in his arms. He wrapped them closer around her and deepened the kiss.

Abruptly she pulled free and backed away from him. "Are you out there, Jake?" she called into the trees.

Stunned, Clint watched her peering around them. "What—why are you looking for Jake? I wasn't going to hurt you."

"Every hurt one inflicts is not physical. I just wanted to be certain you would win your bet this time, so I wouldn't have to wonder anymore how long I would be made sport of."

Her voice was thick. She knew. Somehow she knew about the bet he and Jake had made. She thought he had kissed her this time to fulfill Jake's dare. He hadn't. This time he just wanted to kiss her for some reason even he didn't quite understand.

"How did you know?"

"I heard you two talking about it."

"You never said anything."

"I couldn't. I was too mortified and I didn't want to be the one to make your game a bigger sport." She turned and started for the wagon. "Good night, Mr. Bonner. Thank you for escorting me to my wagon."

She disappeared inside before he could say another word to her.

"Damn!" He kicked a small rock, wanting to see it careen over other rocks taking the knocks he knew he should be taking. It didn't move. The pain shot up his foot and shin and made his knee tingle. "Damn."

Weary in mind and body, Carsie lay down in her blankets without undressing. But sleep wouldn't come. She tried to write in her journal. But words wouldn't come either.

No matter how hard she clamped her hands over her ears, she couldn't shut out the sound of mixed laughter as the women entertained all the men. Including Clint Bonner. She felt . . . something. Embarrassed yes, but more. All she'd thought and believed in was being man-handled and woman-proved. She knew now she'd been letting go of all she'd built up around her, but she was terrified of all that was coming in its place.

As the revelry died down, she finally fell into fitful sleep while her mind whirled in a strange dance amid a jumble of confused ideas. In her dreams she knocked on doors labeled NEED, WANT, SHOULD, SHOULDN'T, and suddenly found herself hanging over a ravine, a tangled mass of leering faces glowing at the bottom. Clint Bonner stood at the top, his hand outstretched.

She awoke in a sweat and sat upright. All was quiet around her except for the wind that knocked against the canvas flap of her wagon. She had to relieve herself, and the urgency was pressing her. She crawled out of the wagon, careful not to wake Libby and the baby, and headed toward the clump of trees not far from camp. The night had turned very cold, the wind biting and there was snow in the air. Snow! She shivered and wished she'd thought to grab her shawl.

She heard something and turned. Blackness engulfed her.

When Carsie awoke, she was not in her warm blankets in her wagon. She was on the hard ground and it was snowing so hard she couldn't see beyond a place where someone was building a fire. Where was she? She didn't remember the wagons pulling out or leaving camp. She pulled herself up and moved toward the man at the fire.

Her vision cleared enough for her to see that it was Patch Wheelock.

It was almost dawn before things finally calmed down and Pardee rounded up his drovers and forced them to go back to their camp. Clint sat hunkered down in front of a fire with a blanket draped over his shoulders. Damned snow was falling. God, how he hated snow.

Gunshots sliced his thoughts, followed by a thundering rush of cattle and horses.

Clint ran to find Jake and Harry and Martha struggling to keep their own animals together. When the sounds of the pounding herd faded away, they discovered the drovers had taken two of their freight wagons. Clint's jaw hardened when he realized one of them was the one that contained the opium. He started to ride out after them, but knew he hadn't a chance of catching up to them—not yet. He went back to camp to assess the damage.

"Clint, we have a problem." Harry caught up to him, Hannah close behind. "Libby says Carsie is missing."

"What do you mean missing? Are you sure she isn't just out to . . ."

Hannah's eyes filled. "We're sure."

Clint peered out over the terrain, which was slowly coming to life with first light. "Fan out and search these woods and the area as far as that tree stand out there to the north. It's cold. Maybe she stumbled and fell someplace. This damned snow—"

"I don't think she's out there." Tears fell down Hannah's face. "I remember how the one-eyed man said something about making her pay for snubbing him. I thought it was just a big-mouthed threat from a drunken drover, but now—"

"Patch Wheelock." Clint uttered the name as if it were the most abhorrent oath he could use. Silently he went to saddle his horse.

"Where is everyone?" Carsie asked to Patch's hunched back. "H-how did you . . . how did we get here? Where are we?"

Patch rose and swaggered over to where she huddled on the ground, pulling the filthy blanket he'd dropped over her more closely around her. He towered over her in a triumphant stance of one who has claimed the spoils of war.

"Well, now them friends of yours just pulled out real early. Didn't even know you wasn't with them. Be sundown tonight afore you come up missing. Looks like I saved you again. And now I've saved you for myself." He grinned.

Carsie looked away, repulsed by him and fearful of what he meant to do with her. She cowered under the blanket, felt herself folding into herself. The acrid smell of the blanket, stale sweat mixed with whiskey and tobacco filled her senses.

Her mind cleared instantly. She knew the kind of danger she was in and the fear of it slammed across her nerves. It would be better to be alone in the blizzard than to stay with him. Someone would surely come along and rescue her. But who? It was dark and she had no notion of where she was.

She'd have no notion of her whereabouts even in the daylight. Think. She tried to think. The wind whipped around her. Patch went back to tend the fire. Carsie made her move.

She pushed up and ran into the sparse trees. Branches whipped her face. The icy air stung her skin and made her eyes water. She heard footsteps behind her coming closer. Her feet were cold and wet. She tripped on a tree root and fell headlong into the cold wet earth.

Patch caught and fell upon her, flattening her to the ground. "Now that's not being very grateful to the man who saved your life. I'll just have to teach you how to say thank you properly, won't I?"

"You—you didn't save me. You kidnapped me." She pushed at him and kicked him.

He took out a length of leather strap, wrestled her arms behind her back, and bound them. "Them's just fancy words. Way I see it is you're lookin' to have a good time only you was too shy to say so. I'm gonna show you that good time." He dragged her to her feet. "Just keep walkin' or I'll drag you. It's up to you."

Near the fire and in the cold break of morning she could make out one of Clint's wagons. Patch pushed her to it and tied one of her arms to a wheel with a strip of rawhide. She shivered violently and he threw another blanket at her.

He went into the wagon and she heard him breaking open some of the crates. The wagon creaked as he thrashed about inside. Several minutes later he jumped out and came around to her, a whiskey bottle dangling from one hand. He swayed in front of her, obviously still drunk from the revelry of the night before.

"Looks like we got ourselves a cozy little situation here." He took a long swallow on the bottle, choked on the whiskey, and sent some of it flying to hit her in the face. She hunched her shoulder and wiped it off. He held the bottle out to her.

"Here, have a swig. That ought to warm you up. Loosen

you up, too. Or have you and Bonner been loosenin' up every night with that rich load he's carryin'?"

"I—I don't know—wh-what you're talking about."

"Sure you do. Your lover is carryin' some interestin' cargo here in this wagon. Good sippin' whiskey for one thing, and some real good medicine. Why do you s'pose he's carryin' opium?"

Carsie raised her eyes in shocked terror. "O-opium?"

"Don't play innocent." He kicked her foot and she drew it up under her. "Bonner. He hasn't changed a bit . . . Still workin' deals." He took another gulp of whiskey. "Still got all the women. Never did learn his lesson."

"Learn his lesson? About what?" Carsie thought if she got him to talk he'd keep drinking and pass out. She tried working at the leather strap that bound her. Her arm and shoulder were growing numb.

Patched laughed insanely. "I showed him. And I'll show him again. That big cat shoulda got him, made chewed meat out of him. This time I'll make meat out him."

"Are you—t-talking about when you were in the circus?"

"You know about that. He probably told you he beat me down. But he didn't. I came back every time, didn't I?"

"Tell me about the circus."

"I know what you're doin'." He swayed and caught hold of the wagon box.

"What do you mean what I'm doing?"

"You think if you get me to talk about me and Bonner in the circus, I'll forget why you came with me."

"I didn't . . ." Even in her feverish state Carsie knew she shouldn't antagonize him by arguing. She had to choose her words carefully. That hadn't been her style for a long time. She was used to just saying what she thought with great bravado. She'd felt safe doing it, and it kept many people away from her. This time she knew it would have the opposite effect.

"You played coy with me, didn't you? Not like those

other whores. No. They just sally right up to a man and let him know what they want him to do to them. But you had to play coy."

"I wasn't doing that. I'm not like them." Carsie felt guilty saying that. She didn't want it to sound like she had no respect for those women, her friends, even to the likes of Patch Wheelock. Somehow when the words came out of her mouth, she was instantly sorry.

"You made me look bad in front of Pardee and the boys. I don't take kindly to that."

"Oh, now I think you're exaggerating just a bit. I'm certain your friends didn't think a thing of it. They're probably laughing at me right now." She was grasping at straws and she knew it.

"They're not my friends," he said harshly. "And they better not be laughin' at you. Nobody laughs at my woman, not anymore."

His woman. Oh God, he was never going to let her go. She knew that now. Panic settled inside her and made her stomach churn.

"Do—do you have a, uh, lady friend?"

He let out a hard sigh. "Did once. Started playin' fast and loose with Bonner. I hated to do it, but I had to. I couldn't let her get away with that."

"Maybe she didn't mean to go so far. Maybe she just really cared for you and she didn't think you cared for her, so in order to make you care she, uh, flirted with—someone, so maybe you'd feel a little jealous and show her you cared, and—"

"Shut up your yammerin'!"

He cuffed her shoulder and sent a wave of pain over her.

"I only mean that—"

"You're all like that, you women. I ain't never puttin' up with that again. I gotta show you who's boss. You're gonna pay for what you did. Maybe then you'll learn your lesson like she had to."

Carsie swallowed back the bile that rose to her throat. Fear of a proportion she'd never known engulfed her. She worked to keep her head. "I understand. Where is she now?"

"Texas."

"Well, you probably should get right back there. She's probably waiting for you and wants to apologize. I'm sure you showed her who's boss. She's waiting, I just know it."

"You don't know nothin'," he muttered. "She's waitin' all right. In the cold hard ground. She's nothin' I want to see anymore. I told her. I told her I took that only once. She didn't listen. I made her listen. But she ain't listenin' to anybody anymore, 'specially Bonner."

"What—what do you mean?" Dread consumed Carsie now. She was afraid to hear the answer she already knew.

"You know what I mean. You're playin' coy again."

"No I'm not. I—I'm just, uh, interested in your, uh, story."

Patch hunkered down in front of her and peered into her face. She felt his breath and smelled the stench of him and she gagged, swallowing it all back as hard as she could.

"Interested? All right, I'll give you all the details. She's dead. The worms ate her. But I kept all her best parts."

Carsie could only stare at him in horror. Patch saw that and laughed maniacally. She looked away from him in disgust. He grabbed her chin and forced her to look at him.

"This part is even more interestin'. Before I killed her, I cut off her three best parts. I looked at 'em for a while afore I left her grave. Then I threw 'em to the wolves. That oughta teach her. She won't be able to use them where she's goin'." He dropped back onto the ground and started blubbering. "I told her she shouldn'ta done that but she wouldn't listen. She was just like my mother. My father showed her, too, afore he kicked the shit outta me. I fixed her a nice grave. She woulda liked that." He took another drink and swiped his filthy shirtsleeve across his eyes.

Carsie's teeth chattered. She broke out into a cold sweat. "You—you made a grave for your lady friend?"

"No, you stupid whore! For my mother! That bitch didn't deserve no real grave."

Carsie shrank back. Patch jumped up and took out a long knife from his belt. She shrieked as he leaned over her.

"Don't worry none. It ain't your time yet. You'll know when it is. That's what the preacher says. My father was a preacher. He says everybody knows when they're gonna die. My mother did. And *she* did, too." He reached over and sliced through the leather strap that bound her to the wagon wheel. Then he hauled her roughly to her feet, dragged her around behind it, tied her hands together, and shoved her into the wagon. She fell against some of the open crates and cut her forehead. Her own blood trickled into her eye. It was warm. The warmest thing she could think of.

"Where—where are you taking me?" she screeched.

"That don't matter to you either. Where we're goin' is just where we're goin'. It don't matter." He leaped up onto the wagon and beat the horses savagely into a screaming run.

Carsie fell back into the boxes and into unconsciousness.

The wagon train made camp after driving fewer hours than usual owing to the blinding snow and rain. Clint guided them to an area protected by high stone and trees. He was responsible for these people and he wouldn't leave them unguarded. Yet every hour they plunged ahead, he thought about Carsie in the hands of a madman. Would she be alive when they found her? Would they find her? He shook his head to rid his mind of that thought and tried to figure how Patch would travel.

When the group was settled into the evening meal, he went in search of Harry. His friend was as good at tracking as he was. On more than one occasion on a trek between cities they'd searched out stray circus animals, or tracked down an errant child who'd followed the circus. Together they could cover more ground, backtracking in search of Carsie. He instructed Jake and Martha to keep the wagon train where it was, not to move until they returned to camp with Carsie.

"Do you think you can find her?" Hannah asked with an uncharacteristically shaky voice. She'd brought two blankets from her wagon and had tied them into a secure bundle.

"We'll find her," Clint vowed, "no matter what it takes. And Wheelock'll wish he'd never been born." He took the blankets, then gazed off into the gathering gloom.

"How do you figure he's traveling?" Jake asked moments later as he handed up another rifle to Clint after he'd mounted his horse.

"He won't be on the road, that's for sure. And he won't come this way."

"He ain't smart enough to have much of a plan."

"I know. And once he finds out what's in that wagon, he'll be crazier than he already is. Carsie will be in more danger if . . ." He jerked his head around in search of Harry.

"She can take care of herself." Jake tried to sound reassuring. "If anything, she'll talk him to death."

"It's not talk Patch wants."

Harry rode up to them then. "I thought I saw a lone wagon back along the river, but this damned snow and rain . . ."

"Show me." Clint wheeled his horse around behind Harry's. The two started off.

It was just before dawn when Clint spotted a wagon near a clump of scrub brush. Harry followed him to a stand of rocks above the rough road. They dismounted and looked down. It was his wagon all right. The horses were tied and had not been unhitched from the wagon. With impatience they strained for food and water. That's what brought Patch

Wheelock from the wagon, whip in hand. He swore at the team and drew the whip across their faces. They squealed and strained to get away.

"Mean son of a bitch," Harry muttered.

Clint uttered low agreement. "Once those horses are loose, they're going to go wild. He won't be able to control them. If Carsie's in the wagon . . ."

Patch threw the whip up onto the wagon box and went around to the back and climbed inside. A faint moan and then a hoarse scream echoed around the rocks. The distinct sound of an open palm against bare flesh followed.

"She's in there," Harry whispered.

"And still alive." Clint didn't add the thought that slammed behind his words. *What kind of condition would they find her in?*

"Which way?" Harry moved around the rocks.

"I'll take the back of the wagon. You come in through the box. And be careful. Carsie could be—"

"Don't worry about me. Nimble on my little feet, you know. You get him. I'll get her."

Clint nodded and the two began the descent down the hill toward the wagon.

Carsie pulled herself tightly into a ball. She was cramped and her body screamed with pain. Would he never stop? The wagon lurched and the horses squealed again. Behind tightly clamped eyes she knew Patch was drinking whiskey. Then he'd come at her again. If only she could die in her mind. He was right. He'd said Clint and the others wouldn't know she was missing until it was too late to turn back. The snow had already begun. If they didn't make the pass before it came full force, they could be stranded there. It was better to sacrifice one person than endanger all of them.

It's over. It's all over. Sophie . . . How I wish I could have seen you once more. Why was I put here? What did I

accomplish? I hope some people will remember me with
kindness. If they remember me at all.

A small moan escaped her swollen lips. "Water," she
rasped.

Patch lurched. "What was that?"

Carsie worked at forming the word, the precious word.
"Water."

"Shut up. I can't hear." The wagon jerked again as the
horses grew agitated. "Goddam animals. Time I showed
'em who's boss."

Carsie forced her eyes open. Through the dim light she
saw him flail his way through cartons and the debris of
crates and bottles and . . . her clothes. He opened the back
flap and a blast of chilling air filled the cramped space.
She shuddered and tried to reach for something to pull over
her raw skin.

"Bastards!" Patch's voice cut through the canvas and as-
saulted her hearing.

He was probably going to whip the horses. Carsie didn't
think she could bear to hear their anguished cries again.
With great effort she pushed up to her knees. She grabbed
some of the pieces of her clothing and with trembling hands
tried to put them over her exposed body. She felt something
warm and sticky seep between her legs. She was bleeding
again. Maybe it was her body's way of cleansing itself of
the poison of Patch's invasion. Revulsion swept over her.

No. She would not cry anymore. She would not vomit
anymore. She would get out of the wagon, and this time
she would get away from him and hide so he could never
find her. Then she'd just lie down and . . . go to sleep.

The light beyond the flap grew brighter. Just a few inches
more . . .

"Get the hell back in there." Patch shoved her with both
hands. She fell back against the crates. Something cut into
the skin between her shoulders. "Looks like Bonner found

us." He snatched up a length of rope and wound it tightly around her wrists then lashed it to a wagon rib.

Carsie forced her lips open. "C-Clint." Hope swelled inside her.

"Yes, Clint." Patch sneered. "This time he won't win. And you'll get to watch it." He laughed derisively.

"C-Clint." In her exhausted mind Carsie thought all she had to do was get to the canvas opening. Clint would see her. Clint would save her.

"Save your breath, bitch. You're gonna need it later." Patch made a blowing sound and patted the front of his pants before dropping out of the wagon.

Carsie fell back against the crates as the wagon lurched forward.

Clint and Harry had scrambled back up the hill to their horses when they knew Patch had spotted them. In those precious moments the wagon gained a good start. The trees grew denser and Patch was forced to turn the team back onto the road. He whipped the horses along a ridge high over a ravine. That turn gave advantage to his pursuers.

Clint tailed the wagon, gaining on it. Closing in, he kicked off the stirrups and drew his feet up under him. With a powerful lunge he was up on the back of his horse and propelling himself onto the speeding wagon. He started around toward the front to get to Patch and control the team.

Then Harry seemed to come from out of nowhere. He dropped down from the trees and jumped onto the back of one of the horses. Patch used the whip over his back, taunting him. "Just like a little monkey!" he shouted. "I've seen little monkeys cut to ribbons when they got where they didn't belong!" He laughed maniacally and cracked his whip.

The whip shot out and landed a stinging lash over Harry's

shoulders. Undaunted, Harry continued to work at loosening the harnesses on the frantic team.

Knowing something awful was happening outside the wagon covering, Carsie tried to free herself. Her mind sharpened and overrode the pains of protest in her body. She would get out of these ropes or die trying. Suddenly the canvas flap tore open and a man burst inside the wagon.

Carsie clamped her eyes shut and screamed.

"Carsie, here!"

Clint! Forcing her eyes open, she burst into hysterical tears and jerked toward him. He pulled out a knife and sawed at the rope. He got through it then handed the knife to her to finish the work. Numbly she stared at it. Quickly he took her hands and closed them around the knife, then leaped up and lunged toward the front of the wagon.

Though weak and bouncing against the crates and hard wood as the wagon pitched violently, Carsie gathered enough strength to cut the rest of her bonds. Her hands were too cold to maneuver the knife enough to cut through the rest or to pull it out of the wagon rib. She was almost crazed as frustration and fear gripped her.

Clint grabbed Patch from the seat and pulled him into the rolling wagon. Carsie screamed. The two men struggled over and around her. Then Clint was down and Patch's fingers closed over a whiskey bottle. He raised it high and meant to smash it over Clint's face.

Harry came through the front opening then. He jumped inside just as Carsie plunged the knife into Patch's shoulder. Patch screamed and pulled back, dropping the bottle. Clint rose and slammed Patch unconscious. Harry grabbed the knife and cut Carsie free.

"We've got to get out of here now!" Harry yelled. "I cut the horses loose!"

Holding Carsie between them, Clint and Harry jumped from the wagon as it careened to edge of the ravine. They rolled into the brush and looked up in time to see the wagon pitch over into the ravine, taking Patch with it. In that moment Clint saw the load of opium that was going to bring him the kind of money he needed from Mr. Woo in Virginia City crash away from him. And in that moment he knew he didn't care.

Clint held Carsie, wrapped in blankets, against him on his horse as they headed back to camp. He whispered apologies every few moments if his horse misstepped and jostled them. He knew the pain that was coursing through her, knew what brutality and humiliation she'd suffered at the hands of Patch Wheelock. He was sorry he'd ever given the bastard a second chance. And he never should have allowed himself to get talked into that makeshift Good Times Emporium on the prairie. He should have known better. It was his fault Carsie was hurt and that they had all been in danger.

At camp the women took care of her like hens with a new chick. Mrs. Woo offered a tea made from her special herb supply. Hannah bathed her and treated her scrapes and cuts while Phoebe tended to the private wounds Patch had inflicted upon her. Libby held several folds of toweling and a basin of warm water. Lola made the trek often between the fire and the wagon to replenish the basin with clean water.

Satisfied that Carsie was being well taken care of, and leaving Martha guard, Clint took Jake and Harry to make a sneak attack on the drovers camp to retrieve their stolen wagons and horses.

Harry came upon a man on watch. He leaped into the air and landed on the man's back. Then with lightning speed he slammed him in the head with a small log, then hobbled him hand and foot like a thrown calf. Jake set up a stampede of the cattle. While the rest of the drovers went after them, Jake and Clint recouped their wagons and horses. Harry grinned when he spotted their stray cow and went on a small roundup of his own.

For the next five days the wagon train made its way over the most treacherous stretch of the journey. Intermittently they were pelted with icy rain and driving snow, which worsened at the mouth of the pass. Clint paused only briefly. Once they were through the pass, the rest of their journey into Virginia City would be relatively easy. There could be no stopping for very long from now on.

His band of weary travelers sensed the danger of what faced them, yet at the same time sensed that they were almost home. Home. Funny how he let that word creep into his mind now and then. He watched them all. Martha, with dogged determination to move ever forward. Harry, with boundless energy it seemed, and constant vigilance over Libby. Libby, obviously weakened and devoting all of her attention to her frail infant. Clint vowed to get them safely to Virginia City, where there would surely be a doctor for them.

Phoebe, Lola, and Hannah worked like the best team of drivers he'd ever hired. They did not complain, and became caretakers of everyone else at the end of every day. For Jake especially. His back had become noticeably worse, and he seemed to be aging right in front of Clint's eyes.

And then his thoughts settled on Carsie. She hadn't spoken much since her ordeal with Patch. He attempted to speak to her but she responded with nothing more than a nod of the head. The first couple of days after they'd pushed on, she had thanked him and Harry several times for saving her life. But in the ensuing chilling days and nights she had not spoken much at all to anyone, and had kept mostly to herself.

Twelve

Clint rode ahead of the others toward the river. The pause at the stagecoach stop would be sorely needed after these last few days. Drenching rain had slowed their progress for three days, but at least the snow had been passable. Everyone was cold and weary, yet anticipation that Virginia City would appear on the horizon ran through them like lightning in the night sky.

Day after tomorrow they would press on into Virginia City. He was ready to be there, now.

"A dry sheltered place is over that next hill," he told them at supper. "A hot meal there, and maybe even a real bed, will make us all feel better."

"Amen," Phoebe underscored.

"A meal cooked by somebody else," Hannah added.

"A bed, maybe with sheets." Lola sighed.

Carsie said nothing. Her hands seemed to work independently of her mind, Clint observed. She worked herself harder than ever, and she rarely spoke to anyone. He also observed how Hannah hovered a safe distance from her. She talked to her in low tones and short sentences every now and then, offering a smile, a light touch. He wondered about that, wondered how the friendship between women seemed to differ vastly from the friendship between himself and Jake and Harry. Most of the time, men didn't communicate much, in words or in actions. Women seemed to speak volumes of understanding between one another, even without words.

The next day presented a grueling sixteen miles through high winds, mud, and cold driving rain mixed with icy crystals at times. In the late afternoon the wagon train rounded a bend and the corral at a stagecoach stop came into view.

Clint's spirits sank. He kept his gaze fixed on the station. No matter how hard he concentrated, he couldn't make any sign of life flicker into hope. There were no coaches, no fresh horses in the corrals, no one working around the place. Now new worries crept into his mind. What scene inside the station awaited them when they pulled up?

He rode back to Martha and Jake. "Wait here. I want to ride ahead and see how things are."

Jake searched Clint's face. "By the look of your look, things ain't goin' to be good there."

Harry came up beside them then. "I'm going with you, Clint. You may need some help. I'll come back and get you," he said to Jake, "when it's safe to bring everyone down."

Clint and Harry reached the stagecoach station, their spirits dropping with each clop of hooves in the mud. Only the shell of a burned-out building remained. It had undergone total destruction at the hands of thieves or Indians or both, and no one and nothing was there waiting for them. Except for the remains of the man and woman who ran it. Vultures and other creatures had started the next degree of disintegration on the corpses.

Clint pulled out a bandanna and covered his nose and mouth, indicating for Harry to do the same thing. "We'll take care of these poor people and make the place presentable for the others. We're here. We might as well make the best of it."

Harry dismounted and took a small shovel from his pack. A look of sadness crossed his chiseled features. "It never ceases to amaze me how people treat people."

"I know."

Clint thought of Carsie then. He could only surmise what had happened while she was in Patch's hands. And now he felt at a loss for knowing how to treat her, and had succeeded only in cursory nods and abbreviated sentences. He simply didn't know what to say to her that would make her feel any better. To blithely go on as if nothing had happened seemed wrong to him. To speak of what may have happened, inflicting ongoing pain, seemed just as wrong. What was left? He wished right then that he had been smarter or more intuitive. But then, he'd never been very good at that. Mattie's death proved it.

Clint and Harry finished the grim job of burying the two people and cleaning up evidence of the carnage. At least there was still a part of the roof and walls still standing. They would provide some long-deserved sheltered rest for the wagon party that had performed so valiantly.

The rain let up, and only a drizzle fell with a soft lulling sound. By the time Harry had ridden out to bring the wagon train to the station, it had finally dissipated and a decided warmth was creeping into the air.

The sun tried a last warming gasp before giving in to twilight and darkness. Clint found some dry wood and Jake stoked a hot fire and set up the cooking contraption. Martha hauled her groaning bones and muscles around to secure a corral for the animals. Harry started supper.

Lola checked the bathtub as she did every evening before supper. Dipping into cold streams for weeks had done nothing for the aching bodies of the women. An idea came to her. Hurrying, she set about filling pots with water from the stream behind the station and putting them over the fire to heat.

"Ladies, there will be a real bath available in short order," she announced, "complete with hot water. Everyone decide in a democratic way who shall be first in line."

"And just how do you think you're going to arrange

that?" Jake did not conceal his amazement over her announcement. Imagine them bathing in the middle of the mud-rutted trail. And before supper, too!

"You can't move that thing off the wagon yourselves," Clint protested, knowing a split second later that his words had served only to present a challenge.

"You think so?" Hannah was already around the back of the wagon and considering a strategy for extracting the tub.

Behind Hannah, Phoebe surveyed the wagon interior. "Start moving things out of the way. I have an idea." She called over to Martha and asked that she start a fire behind and away from the building.

"Is it safe?" Martha asked Clint before piling the first kindling.

Knowing he'd lost the battle of the bathtub yet again, Clint considered the wisdom of building another fire. They were so close to their destination. The last thing he wanted to do was to call unnecessary attention to themselves. There was still danger lurking in the hills and trees around them. He watched the women. The urge to bathe in the tub ran through them like an epidemic. He gave his approval to Martha and picked the most secluded spot he could find for her to build a fire. That was necessary and so was the bathing ritual.

The women joined forces and descended upon the wagon like experienced thieves, moving away trunks and quilts and boxes and canvas bags to present a clear path for the removal of the object of their obsessed devotion. The bathtub.

Phoebe persuaded Jake and Harry to haul two long flat-sided logs she'd discovered. Clint joined with them to slide the tub off the wagon and down the logs and carry it to a grove of trees. They rigged up the canvas they'd used as the temporary Good Times Emporium in such a way as to construct a bathing room with the fire in it to warm the air.

Lola added heated water. Mrs. Woo offered herb-scented oil. Phoebe surrounded the tub with low candles set in cups of water. Hannah brought out a bottle of champagne she'd been saving for a personal celebration.

Libby stood near the entrance to the bathing room, cradling little Harry. "We've unanimously voted. Carsie is to have the first turn."

Carsie stopped at the edge of the grove clutching an armload of small branches she'd gathered for the fire. Her face was drawn. Her hair was matted around her head, dirty and stringy. Her hands, like those of all the women, were rough and scratched.

"No, no," she said, her voice weak. "You go ahead." She set down her collection of firewood on the gathering pile.

"We will. You first." Hannah stepped forward and ushered Carsie inside. "I am famous for my hair washing and head massage. And tonight I will do that for you."

Carsie stared at her as if she didn't understand what was happening. When she saw the tub sitting in a circle of candlelight giving off the feeling of being an altar of reverence, she fell into a trancelike state. "It's too beautiful. Too perfect. And I'm . . ."

". . . the perfect choice to take the first bath." Hannah drew her to a warm corner of the tent. "I've set out this basin of water and soap so you can remove the first layer. And here's one of my robes to put on when you get out of the tub." She handed Carsie a fold of satiny deep rose.

"I couldn't . . ." Carsie started to protest.

"Yes, you can," Hannah assured her.

Carsie turned her head slowly, appearing to be lost in a deep wood. "Don't leave," she whispered.

"Don't worry," Hannah whispered back. "I hope you don't want complete privacy. We're all in this together and we will all share in your enjoyment as well as our own."

Each of the women had scrubbed off the worst of the grime at the river. They gathered inside the tent, sipping champagne and getting fairly bubbly.

Slowly Carsie removed her filthy clothes. Mrs. Woo

scooped them up and scurried away with them. As she began to wash, she felt with each stroke of the soft soapy
cloth that she was stripping herself of everything painful
she'd known. Her washing gained strength. She scrubbed
so hard and so fast that her skin tingled. Hannah stopped
her and encouraged her to go to the tub.

A pile of toweling had been laid near the fire, and a
china plate with a round of French milled soap sat on a
small tree stump near the tub.

Naked, Carsie stepped hesitantly toward the tub. Hannah
took her hand and assisted her into it and handed her a
glass of champagne when she'd settled down under the
water. Steam from the scented bath water rose around her,
filling her senses and washing over her body in a baptism,
leaving a protective silken cloak over her ravaged skin.

Hannah rinsed Carsie's hair in a separate basin of water
and began to wash it. With luxurious foam covering her
head, Carsie gulped the first glass of champagne, then
sipped the second. Hannah massaged and drew her fingers
through the tangled strands. Carsie dropped her head back
against the curved tub rim while Hannah performed mir-
acles on her head and hair.

And then one tear escaped the corner of her eye. Then
another. And then warm salty emotion flooded her eyes and
fell down her cheeks. Sobs wracked her shoulders. Her
stomach clutched.

All of the women silently surrounded the tub. One patted
her arm. Another gently wiped the tears away as they fell
steadily. Mrs. Woo produced a paper fan and gently stirred
a fragrant steamy cloud into a mist around her. Hannah
stroked her temples. Libby brought her baby close and
crooned. Unabashedly then, Carsie let the painful memories
erupt into tears. They fell and mingled with the bath water,
turned to scented steam, and floated off into the night.

Little Harry let out a baby gurgle then. Carsie's tears
stopped as quickly as they had come. New life. Little Harry

represented the regeneration of life. He gurgled again. Carsie giggled and drained her glass. She giggled more. And then she burst out laughing.

And then they were all laughing and Libby was dancing, her baby gurgling happily in her arms. And Lola burst into song, in French so flawless they all were surprised.

Carsie reached for a towel, stood up, and stepped out of the tub. She wrapped herself in the warm cocoon and turned to face her friends. *Her friends.*

"Thank you," she said with genuine love. She didn't have to say more because real friends didn't need words in order to understand what she'd experienced and the purging she'd just been through.

The water was changed after each had their turn luxuriating in the tub. The others waited their turn or lingered afterward, lounging around the fire inside the tent, talking and enjoying one another's company and sharing in the soft pleasures.

Outside Clint and Harry and Jake hunkered down by the cooking fire stirring stew and making coffee and biscuits. Clint supposed he should allow the women this bit of luxury, chancy though it was. Then he realized he'd had no say in the matter whatsoever. Sometimes he still wondered when it was he'd lost control of this wagon train.

The three men eyed each other furtively as soap bubbles wafted through the rain-washed night. Feminine gleeful laughter mingled with the splashing water was matched in intensity by the early baying of coyotes against a rising pale yellow moon.

Another day of hard travel brought the wagon train across the river. They stopped on a bluff overlooking the descending road down into the valley that cradled Virginia City and its promise of a new beginning. They made camp for the night and the chatter around the supper fire was excited with anticipation of their arrival the next day.

As the others prepared to retire for the night, Carsie stood apart from them and leaned against a tree. She could see down into the valley but the night had engulfed the vague outline that defined Virginia City. From the beginning of her determination to get there, the focus had been on Sophie and finding her, saving her if she was still alive. Sophie was still on her mind, yet the idea of rescuing her friend from something she'd chosen to do didn't seem as all-consuming in Carsie's heart. Maybe Sophie hadn't been her sole motivation for going. Maybe she'd been running away from her own life.

Clint watched Carsie walk slowly away from camp. He kept a watchful eye on her as he had constantly since her ordeal with Patch Wheelock.

He wondered about her, wondered about all of them. This trip had been so much different from all the others. Or maybe he was different now than he'd been then. His feelings recalled those he'd experienced while traveling with the circus, first as a young boy and then as a man. They'd become a family, better than some families he knew. After a rocky start, they'd grown to care about one another. They moved like a community, working together to defend themselves and their property and their way of life.

Was Virginia City a beginning of something? Or was it the end of something? Or was it a little of both? And why did it bother him that there would be goodbyes? Surely they'd see one another again as they established themselves in Virginia City. Yet he knew it would all be different. They would not be united by a common bond. And the thought saddened him. What a confession to be making to himself. He'd miss this bunch of misfits. Miss their close association. Miss the things he could count on. A coming together at the end of the day. Living with one another's moods. Talking. Learning. Caring.

Virginia City represented a dichotomy of endings and beginnings.

Carsie disappeared into the shadows and he edged away from camp after her. He wasn't about to let her put herself in danger from attack again.

The air was chill, invigorating enough to keep sleepiness at bay. The moon was so brilliant and so big Carsie thought she could reach across the valley and touch it. Around their camp on the high rock ledges the coyotes engaged in their moon-inspired baying. When she'd heard them on other nights, she'd thought they sounded lonely. But on this night she felt the strength of their command of their territory in their voices, and the flicker of a sense of coming home in her heart.

"You shouldn't be out here alone," a low voice came from behind her.

Clint. A shiver went over her and she pulled her woolen shawl closer around her.

"I know." She turned to face him.

The moon bathed his face in an ethereal golden glow, lighting the shadows in the creases around his eyes and the crags in his chiseled features. *Lighting his handsomeness,* she thought. *Clint Bonner is a very handsome man.* She'd been nagged by the knowledge that she'd deemed him so from the beginning of their journey, but now she was freely admitting it to herself.

"Sometimes a man can have a sense of feeling safe from harm when we're out in the wide open country like this. It's as if no one or nothing could lurk anywhere in such a clean vast country that could hurt us. There's an overwhelming sense of freedom for a man like none other. But . . ." His voice trailed away, implying more, knowing he didn't have to say it.

"For a woman, too." Carsie didn't move. And she didn't feel the need to enlarge upon her spoken thought. One of the many things she'd learned on this journey was that the farther west one traveled, the fewer words one needed. So much was spoken in the air and the sky and from the land beneath their feet and churning wheels.

"Everyone is weary." He was making meaningless conversation and he knew it. "We'll all be glad to stop moving for a while and settle into town living."

She nodded slowly. "Yes. What will you do? Will you turn around and head back to St. Joseph?"

She watched his face change as wispy clouds passed over the moon. She shivered again. The effects of his nearness grew stronger each day. The feeling was new to her, strangely new and not altogether unpleasant. Unsettling. That was it. He unsettled her. Everything about this trip had unsettled her. From the first moment in the freight yard in St. Joseph until this moment overlooking their destination and the unknown of a new life.

"No. I mean, I'm not going back. I meant this to be my last trip. I'm selling the wagons, and I hope what I get is enough bankroll to set up a place of my own."

"What kind of place?"

He dropped his gaze and fixed it on the toe of his boot, which was making small trails in the dirt. "Something a woman like you will disapprove of. A saloon and opera house, and a gaming room in the back."

"I see. Won't the loss of the opium alter your plans?"

His eyes came up quickly. "You know about that."

She nodded. "In the wagon with Wheelock . . ."

"He didn't make you . . ." When she shook her head, he went on. "I can just imagine what he told you. But he was wrong. I know about the bad uses of opium, but there are good uses, too. It's used in laudanum, for one. I was carrying it for Mr. Woo. There's already a Chinese population in Virginia City. They use it in their religious ceremonies, in the joss houses, they call them."

"Oh," she said again. She believed him.

"He's not going to be happy about this. And he won't

pay me what we agreed to." He let out a sharp breath. "I mean my place to be clean, nothing questionable." He sounded determined to make her understand his intentions. "That is, the ladies there will entertain only. Downstairs . . . only."

"Miss Phoebe and the others will be working for you?"

"No. You've been wrong about me, about that from the beginning." His voice took on a hard edge. "Miss Phoebe will do whatever she planned to do on her own. So will the other ladies. Something tells me Libby's life is going to change drastically now that the two Harrys are a part of it." He chuckled lightly.

She turned around and gazed out over the valley again. "Yes. And isn't that something lovely? One never knows when love will somehow make itself known, I guess. That has always been a mystery to me."

He stepped closer to her and she felt his warmth spread over her back and shoulders. Yet she shivered once more.

"And to me. A mystery, an illusion."

"Yes," she whispered.

"And painful."

Painful. Carsie absorbed his word and the heaviness in it. Did men feel pain over love the way women did? She hadn't supposed so. "Painful," she whispered. "Have you . . . is there . . . someone?"

Clint swallowed. "My wife."

Carsie held inside the shock that rocked her. "You're . . . married? Is she waiting for you in Virginia City?" Her voice carried a lightness she did not feel.

Clint did not speak. The long moment hung heavily between them. When Carsie made a move to leave, he reached out and grasped her arm. He hadn't spoken about his wife to anyone, not even Jake and Harry. He'd locked the memories away, fiercely held them from his mind. But lately, thoughts of her came to him often, unbidden.

"Mattie's dead."

Carsie let out a breath. Pain crossed her face. "Oh, Clint. I'm so sorry. Had she been sick?"

He shook his head. "I've never told anyone . . . I don't talk about . . ."

Carsie placed her fingers on his lips. "You don't have to now. I had no right to ask."

He took her hand away and held it. "No. I want to tell you. I want you to know."

She nodded silently.

"Mattie was . . . having a baby. I was scared. We lived in a shack far out of a town. I didn't know how to help her. I went to get a doctor. It was a long way in the snow. I didn't know how to read the sky signs then. I just didn't know. I should have stayed with her. But I was afraid. I let her down. When I came back, she . . . and the baby . . ."

He didn't have to say anything more. Carsie understood completely. So much about him was much clearer to her now. The snow, Libby's pregnancy, his anxiety, even anger over them all stemmed from the loss of his wife and baby in a snowstorm, something he could not control. And now he wanted to be in control of everything and everybody.

Without a trace of apprehension, she stepped forward and took him into her arms. "I'm so sorry you've been hurt."

Stiffly, he let her hold him, then relaxed slightly as she rubbed his back and murmured comforting words. He slipped his arms around her waist. After a few quiet moments, he leaned back and studied her face.

"Are you feeling . . . well? I mean . . ."

She closed her eyes. "I know what you mean, and thank you for asking." When she opened her eyes, she caught a message of warmth and genuine caring in his. She could recognize such a message now. She'd learned so much about herself and about other people since she'd traveled.

Her nervousness returned. She broke the embrace and turned to gaze out over the valley. "Virginia City," she whispered. "I feel as if . . . that something will . . ." She shook her head.

He moved to stand next to her. "Wait," he said, tipping his head back, "let me savor the only moment since we met when you were at a loss for words."

She took his good-natured barb in the spirit in which it was given. "Well, it was my turn to surprise you, after all."

"Are we taking turns now?" He grew serious. "I hope you find your friend. And I hope she's well and happy."

Carsie sighed. "I do, too."

There was a long pause. "After you do find her, what will you do in Virginia City? Will you stay?"

Another long pause. "I don't know. I've never thought about myself beyond finding Sophie. Does anyone ever really go back after they've come out here?"

"They may go back to where they came from in body, but I think the spirit of this west never quite leaves them."

She waited several moments before speaking. "I . . . I want to thank you for transporting me here. For saving my life . . . I know you have found me irritating at best, but I never meant to . . . that is, I did mean to be irritating, in the beginning that is. Well, not exactly irritating. Disturbing. That's not a good word. I . . ."

"Carsie." He set his hands gently on her shoulders and turned her toward him. "There is no need to thank me for anything. I'm supposed to get my passengers safely to their destination."

"Of course," she said tightly. His warmth penetrated her shawl and shirt, and she could feel his handprints on her skin.

"As for irritating, oh yes, you've been that and more."

"Yes."

"Disturbing?" He fell silent. Moments passed. "You have disturbed me, I admit that."

She didn't say anything. His words seemed to imply more than one meaning. His eyes held a look she could not define. Perhaps it was the way the moonlight sought out the planes of his face that made it difficult for her to read his expression.

"You have disturbed me, Miss Carson Rose Summers. Miss drum-banging champion of women. You disturb me and I haven't known how to live with it, or even what it means. You aren't like other women."

"You've told me that before, and—"

"Don't talk or I'll never get this out." He drew her close to him and his gaze penetrated right to her soul. "You aren't like any other woman I've ever known. I'm glad, I think, but I don't know why. Right at this very moment I want to kiss you as you've never been kissed before. Want you to kiss me as I've never been kissed before. And I don't know how you've managed to make me feel like this."

She shifted her head from side to side. "Is Jake . . ."

He let out a harsh sigh and gently brought her face around to meet his gaze. "This has nothing to do with Jake and that stupid damned bet. I regret that ever happened and I hope you'll forgive me."

She was melting under his touch, struggling to hold herself together, keep herself from falling into the sheltering embrace of his arms, the protective armor of his chest. This was much different than comforting a friend. This kind of talk, this kind of touch, held no comfort. This unnerved her. This was purely sexual between a man and a woman, and she didn't know how to act.

"Now, unless you have strong opposition, I'm going to kiss you before I burst into fragments from the desire."

He bent his head, hesitated a fraction of a moment, then caught her lips in his. There hadn't been time for her to express any opposition. Not that she felt one drop of opposition to this. The rise of memories of violence were blown from her mind in the depth of the kiss. Clint's mouth communicated something that erased them in a blinding moment. His lips were soft, inviting, then strong, soul-stirring, demanding in a hypnotic way.

He was right. She had never been kissed like this. And she had never kissed back like this.

A piercing whoosh of something startled them. Clint jumped back and dragged Carsie with him to crouch into the protective darkness of the trees. The crack of a gun or an explosive reverberated in the air. And then overhead a shower of stars and balls exploded in a rainbow-colored canopy leaving silver tails to streak the night sky as they fell to earth.

"What the hell?" he whispered, his pulse pounding in his ears.

"I've never been kissed like that before," Carsie said as if her mind and voice were controlled by an outside force.

Again the whoosh of speed cut through the air followed by an explosion and a shower of brilliant stars.

"And I haven't kissed like that. But I wouldn't credit either one of us with those . . ." *Fireworks?* Maybe he should retract his last statement.

Voices several yards from them brought them to their feet. Carefully they came out of their shelter.

"Clint!" Jake called. "Come here and take a look at this."

Clint led Carsie through the filtered moonlit trees toward a small fire where the entire number in his wagon train had gathered overlooking the valley.

"Lookit this," Jake urged, pointing at an array of dark shapes spread out around them. "Better even than those fireworks in Chicago back in 'fifty-two, remember? Mrs. Woo brought 'em. Did you know she had 'em?"

"No I didn't and I'm sure glad Pardee and his men hadn't known about them either. What's going on?"

"Celebration, near as I can gather from Mrs. Woo. I guess since we all made it across alive, that's cause. And she's lettin' the good folks of Virginia City know we're a-comin'!"

"Yeah, well, I hope those good folks don't come looking for us to welcome us with loaded guns."

"I think they'd all be pretty scared. Ain't nothin' gonna touch us now. What a night!" Jake shifted his stovepipe hat and strolled over to where Martha stood watch.

Mrs. Woo's wraithlike silhouette against the firelight moved with the grace of a cat in the wild. He could see a low three-legged stand upon which she was securing a Roman candle angled toward the sky. She held a small torch at the low end, lit the fuse, and stepped back. Another whoosh, another explosion, and the sky lit up with reds and greens and golds.

"Ah-h-h!" came the collective appreciative sigh from behind him.

Mrs. Woo watched the faces of her traveling companions. When they expressed their appreciation, Clint saw a smile light her own. It was the first time he'd seen her truly smile with pleasure. She knew, he thought. She knew she was offering them something no one else could. This was her own unique contribution to what they'd all given to her. Safe passage and friendship.

Realizing Carsie had left his side, he turned to look for her. He saw her at the edge of the clearing. And he saw them all, standing, sitting on blankets, little Harry cradled in Harry's arms—the women had taken to calling him Big Harry, a sobriquet he reveled in—while he described the display to Libby. Hannah leaned against a tree trunk, pensive, an enigmatic smile on her face. Miss Phoebe and Lola clapped like gleeful children. Martha stood at the edge of the gathering ever watchful, yet caught up in the excitement of the moment.

Carsie stood a few feet away from the group, never taking her gaze away from the sky until the last glowing ash from each candle had fallen to earth. It was as if the heat in each fiery star illuminated the moments of a day then burned out, making room and time for the moments of tomorrow.

Tomorrow. What would tomorrow bring? Sophie? Happiness? Disappointment? She could feel nothing about that now. No emotion. A numbness had set in and settled deep in her bones and heart.

Tonight. She could still feel the moistness from Clint's kiss on her lips. Feel the strength of his arms around her. She knew she would dream about that kiss like a schoolgirl with her first love. She was no longer a schoolgirl, but she knew this was the first time she'd ever been in love. Yet she could not give in to the strength his arms seemed to offer. She would not. That strength, even that kiss, had been offered only in the magic of a moonlit night, underscored by the greater magic and surprise of fireworks.

She was still on her own and she knew she must be. Especially for tomorrow.

Tomorrow. Virginia City. All or nothing.

The Journal of Carson Rose Summers

11 September 1866

I wish the wheels would keep on turning and I never had to stop moving. But then, I would never see Sophie again. And sooner or later I would fall into the ocean.

Still, I wish I never had to stop moving.

Thirteen

Virginia City

November Freed sat in a wooden chair on his front porch. Just past dusk. His favorite time of the day. And this was his favorite place to be. His own front porch, sittin' and whittlin', as his father used to say.

Now he felt the years-worn back of the chair that had belonged to his father curve around his own weary back, and felt the memory of his father's huge mahogany brown hands guiding his own as he formed a chunk of wood into the shape pictured in his mind. Most often November liked to carve people, people with straight backs and eyes that could see more than just their own sweat and tears.

He propped his elbows on his knees and watched the display of explosive brilliant lights splash against the night sky. They looked to be sent from the hand of God, yet he knew there was an unnatural quality to the explosions. Not sent by God, but made by man. Must be fireworks, something he'd never seen, only heard about. Without too much concern, he wondered who was sending them and what they meant.

From his house at the end of town he could hear excited citizens of Virginia City screaming and gathering horses to light out toward the horizon to see what was going on. Fools, he thought at first. Although knowing what an explosive place Virginia City was right from its gold-crazed birth, he supposed on second thought they all had a right to get excited.

He set down his whittling pieces on the brand new porch floorboards and stretched his long legs out in front of him. A man hadn't a right to want more than what he had right now. Freedom and a place of his own. Wouldn't the old master fill his drawers if he saw his former field slave sittin' and whittlin' on his own front porch? And wouldn't his boots be filled next if he knew that same slave owned a right fine business? Owned it outright! November laughed out loud.

And best of all, he'd given himself a right proud name he could call his own, November Freed. Mama would have liked that. She told him his birthday fell in November sometime, she couldn't remember which day. And to be a freed man . . . he wanted everybody to know it. When they came into his place, they called, "Good morning, Mr. Freed." And it was Mr. Freed this and Mr. Freed that and thank you very much, Mr. Freed.

Yessir. A man hadn't the right to want more than November Freed had right now. There was nothing more to need in life. There was nothing more to want.

Except maybe a woman.

He hadn't let himself think about that, but the longing in his soul had gnawed at his gut with increasing intensity. The need was more than physical, the desire deeper than gut level. No one had a right to everything in life, he argued with himself, and he was right lucky to have all that he had.

November watched the last of the fireworks fade into the brightening stars. He stood and straightened his back, placed his father's chair near the door, and went into his own house to go to sleep in his own bed. Yes, indeedy, life was good.

* * *

"Virginia City has been touched by King Midas himself!" Harry exclaimed as he escorted Libby and Carsie along Wallace Street. Clint sauntered along behind them. Little Harry Bonner Allen slept peacefully, riding in a woolen sling Harry had devised and slung over his shoulder and across his stomach.

Carsie gave Harry an admonishing glance for filling Libby's head with embellished half-truths.

"Tell me all about it," Libby breathed.

"Across the street the Overland Stage has just rolled in and several well-dressed passengers are getting down," Harry told her, winking mischievously at Carsie. "There's a lovely hotel with a wide porch sporting several tables and chairs for guests. It's painted blue with pink trim. I've never seen such a hotel in my life."

It's a slapped-together building with falling boards and two benches, Carsie observed silently.

"I wonder if they have a public dining room." Clint stopped for a moment to watch the activity in front of the hotel, then resumed following the others. "I suppose I'm not dressed properly." He was momentarily detained at the door of a rowdy dancehall by two women in abbreviated brilliant yellow and red costumes, their hair adorned by matching feathers.

"In this place it would appear that being dressed in anything at all is probably as proper as it gets."

"You'd best get off your high horse, lady," Clint whispered at the back of Carsie's head. "You're a newcomer here. These people own this town."

Carsie pulled her shawl closer around her shoulders as a sharp moist breeze swirled around them. She scrutinized the faces of three properly dressed women as they walked toward them. Satisfied Sophie was not among them, she resumed walking.

"Everything we've heard is true," Harry rushed on. "There is great golden wealth in Alder Gulch. It's as if

Midas himself sifted the gravel through his fingers and let the gold dust drift over the citizens of Virginia City."

"You've got the gravel and dust right," Carsie muttered.

"It's a real boom town. The stories of it are legendary." Harry escorted the two past a particularly boisterous saloon, dodging a flying chair followed by an unwanted patron as both flew out the open door. "Ten thousand men. A handful of hearty women from every echelon of society."

"All of them tossed together in a land without law," Clint chimed in, "where gold can be had simply by breathing the air and wading the streams."

Harry shook his head dreamily. "Ah, yes, this is a magical place."

"And you two are spreading delusion." Carsie stopped in front of a bakery and read a sign in the window. "First building in Virginia City."

Harry chuckled. "If the proprietor is telling the truth, then this is the first time in history that Ceres beat Bacchus to a mining camp!"

"Proving once again the power of a woman." Carsie smiled with a look of friendly triumph.

"*Touché.*" Harry grinned and touched his wide-brimmed black hat, his first purchase upon arrival. "And the bank," he continued his description for Libby, "has brass hardware—or . . . could that be *gold?*" At Libby's delighted intake of breath, he continued. "In any case, the hardware on the door fairly glitters in the sunlight."

Little Harry let out a delicate baby's cough.

Carsie patted his head. "You can't fool all of the people . . ." She strolled a few steps ahead of them until she came to the office of *The Montana Post.* Shading her eyes with her hand, she peered through the grime-glazed window. "A real newspaper. Imagine that."

"I suppose it couldn't last," Clint said, drawing near.

"What?" Carsie wiped some of the grime away with her

handkerchief and tried to see more inside the newspaper office.

Harry stood next to him. "That civilization would manifest itself in the form of the Fourth Estate even in the golden kingdom of Virginia City."

"The people have a right to know," Carsie said.

"Why?" Clint asked.

Carsie spun around. "Because . . . of course."

"Exactly." Clint jerked his head to make his point.

"What does that mean?"

"Shall we find a place to eat?" Libby tugged Harry's arm. "I will soon have to feed little Harry."

"This looks passable." Harry motioned toward the entrance to the Wells Fargo Coffee House. "Shall we?"

"You go ahead," Carsie told them. "I have to find an inexpensive boardinghouse and start to make inquiries about a friend."

"Don't worry about that. Miss Phoebe is making business arrangements for a place for us to live right now. I'm certain she will find room for you, too, Carsie." Libby smiled and nodded as if the most natural thing in the world was for a bloomer-wearing angularly built spinster to move in with a group of flashy bawdy-house women.

"Oh, well, thank you, Libby . . ." Carsie could not think of a gracious way to decline the offer at the moment, deferring her final decision.

Clint held the door for Libby and Harry. "You'll think better on a full stomach. Sure you won't come with us?"

Carsie eyed him warily. She'd been positive Clint would have simply brought her to Virginia City, unloaded her few belongings, and then given her a cursory goodbye before strolling off to the nearest saloon. Yet here he was politely inviting her to dine with him. How was it that he had the knack for knocking her off-balance just at the moment when she felt certain of herself?

She'd watched him closely as they'd journeyed, intending

to write a scathing news article about him. At least that had
been her motive in the beginning. It was just that she hadn't
been prepared for her observance of him to become a con-
suming emotion.

As she caught and held his beckoning gaze, she became
filled with an unexplainable sense of longing, something
she'd never truly experienced before. Why hadn't she let
down her pride enough to confide more in Libby, or Miss
Phoebe? How she wished she could talk to a real friend
about something so personal and disturbing.

For his part, Clint was surprising himself at this moment.
A tall, rangy spinster had never been the object of his interest before now. He didn't like the feeling one bit. He'd
thought he would be rid of Miss Carson Summers once
they came to the end of their trail. Yet here he was walking
down the street with her, inviting her to join him in a restaurant. Strangely, this felt very comfortable to him. Easy.
Almost too easy. These kinds of feelings had been known
to get a man into trouble.

He watched Carsie's face change in the throes of making
a decision. The gnawing in his gut returned sharply. Over
the years he'd learned that his wanderlust would not satisfy
the hollow rumbling inside. He needed to stop moving. Now
he had plans to settle into the life of a prosperous business
owner. He flattened his palm over his stomach to quell the
escalating grind.

"I could eat a whole buffalo. After that I'd best get down
to business. Might as well join us." He touched Carsie's
elbow.

Her hand twitched as she touched the small pouch she
carried. "Actually, I really should get on with my search."

Clint realized she didn't have much money. "And you'll
need strength for that. How can you turn down a free
meal?"

"Free?" She lowered her face, flustered at his suggestion.

"Oh, no, thank you. I couldn't possibly accept your paying
for—"

"Me? I wouldn't dream of it." He ushered her inside the
dining room. "Harry's buying."

Wearily Carsie stepped off the wide front porch of the
last respectable boardinghouse in Virginia City. No vacancy,
and they didn't know Sophie Baker. She'd heard it from
every proprietor she'd spoken to.

She couldn't afford even one night in any of the hotels
if there had been a room available. Money for the residents
did not seem to be an object. Could it be that Harry was
right? Was everyone in Virginia City rich from the rewards
of their own personal gold mines?

She'd scanned the face of every woman she'd seen on the
streets, convinced Sophie was not among them. She didn't
even know why she'd expected to find her friend that easily,
or even in town. No doubt her lout of a husband held her
prisoner in some ramshackle godforsaken place next to an
ore sluice somewhere out in those menacing hills. Tomorrow she would have to start out there. How was she going
to do that? Walk? She had no means of transportation she
could call her own, and hiring a conveyance was out of the
question. For the first time, Carsie felt her energy and enthusiasm waning for Sophie's rescue. She was weary to the
core.

Even though she was certain evening must be upon the
gulch, daylight was still strong and the city did not show
signs of simmering down for the night. That was just as
well, for she had no place to sleep. She wondered if the
wagon she and Libby had traveled in would be available to
her. And safe. The thought of another encounter such as
she'd had with Patch Wheelock terrified her.

Maybe it wouldn't be so terrible to ask Miss Phoebe for
a place to stay, temporarily, just for one night. She could

simply make herself inconspicuous and go to bed. But what if they . . . needed the room. What would she do then? She couldn't stay there until they were . . . finished. And she could hardly sit in the parlor of a bawdy house looking as if she were hawking her own wares. And who would buy these wares anyway?

"Oh, dear," she breathed, placing the back of her hand against her warming cheek. "I can't believe I even thought that."

"Feeling all right?"

"Oh!" She whirled around. Clint had come up behind her and startled her.

He narrowed his gaze to concern. "Are you going to faint?"

Carsie gathered her senses. "Of course not. I don't faint, Mr. Bonner."

"Are we back to that? I thought we were on first names, especially since we shared such a personal experience back there on the trail."

Quickly she scanned the space around them, then whispered, "I'll thank you not to speak openly of that personal experience we . . . you . . . that is, I . . . experienced . . . so personally."

He leaned toward her with an air of complicity. "Don't worry, your reputation remains unsullied here in Virginia City."

"I have no reputation in Virginia City."

"Sh-h. I wouldn't admit such a thing out loud if I were you. You never know who might be listening in what corner."

"I would expect these people have more important things to occupy their minds with than the reputation of a stranger."

"It's been said that no one is a stranger in Virginia City. Gold makes friends and enemies of everyone here."

"Really."

"Really."

A couple of drunken rowdies staggered toward them, stopping and tipping battered hats in Carsie's direction. She stepped back, visibly shaken by the encounter. With good nature, Clint urged them on.

"You'd better let me escort you to wherever you're staying. It's clear your reputation is at stake if you stroll out on the streets nice as you please this time of night." He took her arm, intending to escort her.

Carsie pulled away from his grasp. "My reputation is not at stake. And it doesn't even seem to be night yet."

"It will be. Night, I mean. Twilight can be long and quite entrancing here. The colors can linger in the mountains till as late as ten. It does things to the mind. Not a fitting time for a woman to be out on the streets. At least not your kind of woman." Again he took her arm.

"Oh! Listen to you. You sound just like Harry and his silver tongue." She stared at him. "Just what do you mean, my kind of woman?"

"Miss Summers, you are a reasonably intelligent woman who has just traveled across this vast expanse of country with the finest whores in all of St. Joseph. I think you know the difference between you and them is as wide as the prairie."

"I thought we were on a first-name basis, Mr. Bonner. And we are all sisters, after all."

"I find it difficult to think of you as my sister, but if you wish . . . Come on, sister, off to your boardinghouse."

"I didn't mean you. And I—don't have a boardinghouse."

"Well, then, what hotel shall we invade?"

Carsie shook her head slowly.

"No boardinghouse? No hotel? Hm, ordinarily that would be a dilemma. But not for you. Miss Goodnight has just purchased a small establishment. She won't turn a fellow sister away." He urged her down the street with a firm hand.

"Oh, no, I couldn't . . ."

"Of course you could . . . *sister.*"

* * *

"I wish I could help, but every habitable room I have is taken." Phoebe Goodnight clucked her apology.

Carsie's shoulders sagged with a mixture of despair and relief.

"The house was supposed to be a refuge for missionaries and the clergy. The preacher and his wife gave it up and were ready to let it fall in on itself. They were practically out of town when I caught up with them. I guess Virginia City isn't ready for too much religion. They couldn't make a living and had to fend off inappropriate guests, as they called them. I aim to change all that."

"I have no doubt of your business savvy, Phoebe." Clint looked around the drab parlor. "You have a lot of work to do."

"That's true. Currently the rooms are quite small and will not accommodate more than one person, perhaps with a temporary guest." Phoebe offered that without any trace of double meaning. "I do have plans to enlarge the place. From what I hear, Virginia City offers great opportunities for anyone who has the stamina to put themselves into any venture. It there's one thing I have, it's stamina."

"I've no doubt you will make a success of anything you decide to do," Clint said.

"Have you tried the Virginia City Hotel?"

Carsie nodded. "I've been to every boardinghouse and hotel in the city. There is nothing available to me."

"What about your friend?" Phoebe asked. "Do you know where she is?"

"No, and I've asked every person I spoke to, but none of them could remember ever meeting Sophie. She probably lives out near a mine, but it's too late for me to start that search now." Carsie's voice was weak with fatigue. "Perhaps I might sleep in the wagon tonight and then begin my search for Sophie tomorrow."

"Oh, my dear, I sold my wagons. They went as fast as we could unload them right along with Clint's. One man bought the whole shebang. He sure seemed anxious to get to California. Martha went with him."

"Well, looks like there's only one thing left for you to do," Clint said, stroking his chin.

"What's that?" Carsie answered weakly.

"Spend the night with me."

"What?" That came with a sudden burst of strength.

"Now don't go thinking I have some romantic notion in mind."

"I wasn't thinking—"

"Frankly, I'm too tired for such antics, so don't expect anything from me."

"Expect? I expect nothing from you!" Carsie sputtered.

"Well, now, am I glad to hear that. Anyway, there's room at my place for you, at least for tonight."

"Your place?" Phoebe put in. "Have you found something already?"

"Sure have. I didn't know what I was going to do for certain. I lost part of my investment when that wagon went over the ravine with Patch Wheelock. I'm not too excited about having to explain that to Mr. Woo."

Carsie shuddered, remembering the incident. She also recalled Patch's words about the opium that was in the wagon. Clint didn't seem to be too worried by the loss of it, other than the money involved.

"How are you going to pay for it?" Phoebe asked.

"The fellow who bought the wagons? Turns out he owned a place the bank had foreclosed on. They'd been trying to force him out, but he'd stood his ground. I heard the whole thing and just traded the wagons and some cash for the building."

Phoebe smiled widely. "Now isn't that grand?"

"In a manner of speaking." Clint winked.

Carsie tipped her head toward him. "Are you saying you have rooms to let?"

"Could be."

"Oh, I see. For the right price, you mean."

"You have the right price."

"Mr. Bonner . . ."

"There you go again getting all formal on me and misinterpreting what I say."

"Well, then, just what did you mean?"

"Simply that tonight is on the house. You can stay in my place free of charge."

Carsie stepped back. "No, I couldn't accept your offer."

"Must be you have a lot of better ones I don't know about."

"It's not that."

Phoebe touched her arm. "Go on and go. If I had a room, I'd offer it to you without charge myself. Accept Clint's hospitality. That's what friends do for friends—help out in their time of need."

Friends. Carsie weighed the word.

Clint covered a yawn. "I'm ready to bed down for the night." He turned to leave. "If you want a place to stay, you'll have to come along now."

Carsie took one step toward him. "All right. Just for tonight. And I will pay you just as soon as I can."

"Fine. Whatever you say, only, could we please go now?"

"Come by and see us tomorrow," Phoebe told her. "Everyone has asked about you."

"They have?"

"Of course. Did you think they'd just walk away and forget you once they got here?"

Carsie managed a small smile.

"Leaving," Clint announced, his hand on the door handle.

Carsie turned and followed him out.

* * *

"This is your place?" Carsie stood beside Clint in front of a building half a block long.

They'd stopped by the freight office on the way and picked up her bag. Clint had carried it as if it were a pile of feathers. Might as well have been empty for as much as Carsie owned.

"Like Miss Phoebe said, it's grand, isn't it?" Clint stepped up on the boardwalk.

"That's what the sign says." Carsie noted the sagging roof line, the cracked porch pillars, chipped paint in the places where it had been painted with a haphazard hand, the lack of a front door, the broken window lights on the second floor, and the precariously swaying sign that proclaimed this building THE GRAND PALACE.

"It's had a lot of use. Nothing that can't be fixed."

"If you live long enough."

"Say now, for someone who's gone a-begging for shelter for the night, you're a bit free and easy with your criticism."

Carsie was immediately contrite. "I am sorry. It's just that . . . are you certain you've made a wise business deal? I mean, you've put everything you own in this place."

"That's right. That means I have no choice but to make it a success, and I will. Shall we?" He ushered her toward the door.

Inside, Carsie found Jake and Harry in what might have been called a tavern once upon a time, sitting around a table that looked to be the only one with all four legs. Broken furniture was everywhere. A clunky stove stood off in a corner, Jake's battered old coffeepot sitting on top.

"Howdy, Miss Carson." Jake pushed up from his chair. "Ain't this nice to have a guest on the first night we open."

"You're . . . open?" Carsie could not keep astonishment from her voice. "For what?"

"And what do you mean *we?*" Clint added.

Harry came over to her. "Glad to see you are intact with life and limb. Libby has been very concerned about you."

Carsie smiled. "Thank you. Where are they? How is little Harry?"

"They're fine. They're at Phoebe's right now. With any luck, I shall alter that living arrangement fairly soon."

"Harry . . . does that mean what I think it does?"

Clint pulled an extra chair to the table. "It means he has been tripped by the trap of love and is considering matrimony. Coffee?"

"Oh, Harry, I'm so happy for you both!" Carsie hugged Harry, who gave her a hearty embrace. "You are so perfect, all three of you. I can't tell you how much this means to me."

"Wait a minute." Harry raised both hands. "I wouldn't go that far."

"Damn." Clint poured coffee into two mugs. "Looks like I lost some of my goods."

Jake laughed.

"I don't find that humorous," Carsie said.

"Come on, that's a joke," Clint replied. He leaned over near Jake's ear. "She still thinks I'm in the bride-selling business."

"From what I can see, that would be a very lucrative business to be in." Harry motioned to Carsie toward a chair. "Have you looked around at the population of men here?"

"Not what I'm interested in." Clint set the mugs on the table, sliding one toward Carsie. "Now, Miss Summers here can shop to her heart's content and pick out that special one she just can't live without."

"Oh-h." Carsie fumed and sat down.

"You ought to stop teasin' like that, boy," Jake told him. "Picking a husband is a private thing for a lady."

"I am not here to pick a husband," Carsie said evenly.

"Too bad about that. No matter what I do, it looks as if I can't shake you." Clint made a loud slurping noise in his mug.

"I did not want to come here with *Mr.* Bonner." Carsie

directed her words to Harry and Jake. "It's just that I could not find a vacant room in the city. Can you imagine such a thing? I couldn't sleep in the streets and so I had to forfeit comfort and propriety for—"

"A grand palace." Clint waved his arm over their surroundings.

Carsie gave cursory inspection. "Indeed."

"If I were you, I wouldn't be so free as to criticize the only establishment in town that will take me in."

"Fortunately, I'm not you. You make that sound as if I am the unsavory person here."

"Have it as you please."

"Children, children," Jake cut in, "stop this bickerin'. Time you two shared your toys and got on together."

Harry laughed as Clint's mouth dropped open. "I'll have you know I *offered* her a room here. That's sharing. It's she who's got the nerve to criticize my place."

"Well, then, come along, Carsie." Harry stood and picked up her bag. He offered his arm. "I'll take you to the best room we have to offer."

"Thank you." Carsie stood and took Harry's arm and they started out of the parlor.

"Wait a minute here." Clint stood. "I own the place. The best room ought to be mine."

"It's only temporary," Harry shot over his shoulder.

"And what do you mean *we?*" Clint shouted toward Harry's retreating back.

"I really shouldn't be here, Harry." Carsie stepped into a room Harry had opened for her. When she looked around and saw the shabbiness and filth of it, she believed her own words.

"Nonsense. Of course you should." He struck a match and lit a glass lamp on a battered bureau, then bustled about making up the bed. "I've tried to make this room and one other as habitable as possible for one night. Sorry it's not better. The linens are clean at least. Got those from the laundry down the street. Guess who owns the place? The mysterious Mr. Woo. I'd like to know how he got out here so fast. He had a lot of things that belonged to this place, including the feathertick, which he boasted his staff had a secret way of thoroughly cleaning. I confess I wanted to believe him about that."

"I'm glad to hear that, too. Did the man who owned this place owe him money or something?"

"I wouldn't doubt it. Woo's a shyster. My guess is he stole all the stuff and cleaned it, knowing someday somebody was going to take this place again, or build another hotel and would need supplies. Wouldn't let go of any of them until I paid him."

"That's very generous of you."

"Not at all. Now, don't you worry. Tomorrow there will be a different light on everything. Perhaps you'll find your friend. I'm on a quest for other housing and I will keep an eye out for something for you, too. Meantime, you stay right here for as long as you want."

"Oh, but Clint—"

"Now don't worry about him. This is my place, too. And Jake's. And we want you to stay as long as you want to. Clint doesn't know we put up money at the bank for the place."

"But he made it sound as if he made a deal."

"Oh, he did. But since he, ah, lost Mr. Woo's wagon, he lost out on the bonus he'd expected. Not to mention Mr. Woo was pretty hopping mad about that. We had to pay him, too. He just shrugged. Seems he has plenty of other suppliers. Wait till you see what Mrs. Woo did the minute she found her husband's store."

Carsie smiled. "I hope she's happy at last."

Harry grinned. "She ought to be after she cleaned house. She shooed all Mr. Woo's painted lovelies right out of the place with a big broom, all the while chattering in Chinese while they protested all the way down to the Canary Cage. Then she set about rearranging all the wares. They were open for business an hour after she arrived. Mr. Woo just stood there stoic with his arms folded into his sleeves. Best show I've seen in a long time."

"I knew she could be strong if she wanted to." Carsie yawned.

"Now you get some sleep. Tomorrow is a new day in your new home. Everything will look much brighter. I'll take you to breakfast with Libby and the baby. There's a great little restaurant down the street. Partook of a buffalo steak that could have been prepared by the finest chef in the world, it was that tender. The potatoes were cloud-light, and the berry pie perfectly sweetened with a crust as flaky as new fallen snow. Man's a culinary genius."

"I'd really like that." She leaned over and kissed him on the cheek. "Thank you, Harry, for all your help. You've made me feel better already."

"It's only what you deserve, my friend. Good night." He stepped out of the room and quietly closed the door.

Carsie sank down on the bed. There was that word again. Friend. Funny, she'd never thought of men as friends. In fact, she'd always felt as if there was an invisible line that existed between men and women, and it was constant friction between the two that kept the line impenetrable. Wasn't that the correct order of things? She was of the mind that women had to be islands unto themselves. It was the only way to survive in this man's world. Women had to be in control of themselves.

She'd been in control of herself, or so she'd thought. Yet here she was relying on a man, correction, three men to give her shelter. How was it she'd given up so easily?

She sat in the yellow glow of the lamplight, too tired to undress and get into bed. Her weary mind suddenly clicked. She rummaged through her bag for her journal and a pencil.

The Journal of Carson Rose Summers

12 September 1866

Perhaps I am justifying my feelings when I write that I did not give up easily to men. On the contrary, I accepted their assistance and hospitality at a time when I sorely needed it. I would have been out on the streets in an unsavory city had it not been for—my friends.

Indeed, Harry and Jake are my friends. I rejoice in writing that! There is nothing adversarial about that. No underlying physical feelings that would erode a friendship. This is like having two very excellent women friends. What a revelation this is! Other women might be horrified at first to think of such a thing, but in the end if they could feel this friendship without apprehension, they would find that men can be helpful toward a woman when they want to, when there is not an unspoken "payment" for services rendered. How I love this feeling of having friends. Friends who are men.

And then there are Miss Phoebe and the other women. I find I am full of surprising responses. They are indeed my friends, but perhaps a more important element is that I, Carson Rose Summers, champion of women's rights in a man's world, I am their friend! Even Mrs. Woo and I are friends, even though we cannot converse due to the language. Of course I am a friend to Libby, and she to me. That is the normal order of things, two women in ordinary circumstances.

Ordinary circumstances. That is ludicrous to write. Not one of us is an ordinary person in ordinary circumstances.

And I must not forget Clint Bonner. Even though we cannot be in each other's company for more than ten minutes without the friction erupting into small volcanoes, nevertheless he saved my life and brought me to Virginia City safely. Why do I always feel jelly in my joints whenever I see him?

I suppose we can never be friends as I think of the others. The kiss changed all that. But I can't forget to think of him as I write about the culmination of our journey. But then I always think of him, and it becomes very annoying at times. I don't do it on purpose. It's just that ever since he kissed me—

I think I will never forget Clint Bonner as long as I live.

Fourteen

In the ensuing weeks, the air grew colder, and snows came in flurries then in large flakes then in huge dumping clouds. And through it all, Clint's Grand Palace was transformed into a structure worthy of the name.

The crumbling interior walls of the main structure and the two smaller buildings attached to it were rebuilt. The exterior walls of all three were shored up and repainted.

The new center roof peak was the topic of conversation around town for two days, for it was made of the most brilliant red, most ornate imported tile anyone had ever seen. It rivaled the sun in brilliance during the crackling cold of the day, and took on a blood-hued depth in the moonlight. But more than that was its shape. It sloped up to a peak upon which a giant whirligig of an acrobat on a trapeze flipped over and over propelled by the wind.

There were plenty of people to barter with to get the work done, and even though the days held a decidedly frigid edge, the workers swarmed over the buildings like bees working a hive. The Grand Palace grew to great proportion the way Virginia City had grown—almost overnight. When the construction was completed, the tall center structure stood out brilliantly like a polished diamond in a hod of coal.

Carsie had made herself as comfortable as possible in the room over the tavern Clint had offered her. She'd thought the arrangement would be temporary, but in the days that followed she was unable to secure lodging. Nor was she able to find Sophie.

She was relieved to discover at last several townswomen who spoke of acquaintance with Sophie. They told her it was not unusual for Sophie and her husband to leave for weeks at a time and then return. A couple of the women had offered Carsie a spare room in their homes but she declined, explaining that she did not wish to impose upon them. The truth was she preferred to live alone. And she was not ready to leave the Grand Palace. She could barely admit that to herself.

As she'd made her rounds through Virginia City on her search for lodging and for Sophie, her mode of dress brought her attention, some good, some questionable. Bloomers had never been seen in this town. Now that it was cold, she'd exchanged them for woolen skirts and heavy stockings and she was no longer looked upon as very unusual.

Several of the most respectable female citizens had asked her to tea on several occasions and listened to her thoughts on women's rights and tales of her exploits and those of other women engaged in that noble aim. Her fervor was contagious. With great exuberance they formed the Virginia City Women's League. Ideas began to flow, and they made plans to regulate the kind of business they would allow, to clean up their community and rid it of undesirable people and establishments. They elected Carsie president of the league and urged her to write pamphlets detailing their mission. Mrs. Dimsdale, wife of the newspaper owner, swore she would make her husband print them on his press.

Carsie managed to avoid contributing anything to the conversation the moment they began to discuss Miss Goodnight and the mysterious goings-on at the Grand Palace under the watchful eye of the equally mysterious Clint Bonner. Even those long-married women, while discrediting taverns and gambling dens, could not keep themselves from gushing over the handsome Clint Bonner and expressing their wonder about his private life.

She'd felt she had to distance herself from him in some fashion, believing her improper living arrangement would have less of an impact upon the ladies league. A great part of her didn't want to care about that. Miss Goodnight had told her that the most important judge of a woman was the woman's own heart. Carsie had been having difficulty even knowing what the truth of her own heart was. When the women questioned Carsie about Clint, she evaded answering by saying she never saw him. He worked constantly and she was either out of the building or fast asleep by the time his day ended.

She'd done her best to stay away from the construction at the Grand Palace, choosing to go up the outside back stairway to her room. In any case, no matter how often she declared it, she found it rather difficult to distance herself from Clint given the fact that she shared his roof and a wall between their rooms. The constant hammering and sawing late into the night made sleep difficult in addition to her own active mind. Not one night had passed without her knowing what time he retired. Once she heard his door close, her sleep became less disturbed, but it had nothing to do with the ceasing of hammering and sawing.

On the morning of the opening night celebration, Clint stood in the street letting horses and rigs funnel around him as he gazed up at the new sign emblazoned across the front of the building: THE CENTER RING.

"Yes, sir," a rich bass voice came from behind him, "you got yourself one fine-looking establishment here."

Clint turned and looked into the ebony eyes of November Freed, the proprietor of the city's lumber and hardware establishment. The Center Ring couldn't have magically appeared without the interest and diligence of Freed, who'd managed to find the most obscure pieces of equipment, trims, furniture, and the tiles for the spectacular roof, including the construction and mechanization of the whirligig. He clapped a hand on the big man's shoulder.

"Are you a gambling man, Mr. Freed?"

November chuckled. "Oh, no sir. Daddy always said, money was a tool. A man has to work for it then put it to work for him. Gambling isn't for the working man."

"Your daddy was a wise man. I never gamble with money myself. Much rather barter for what I want. And if that turns into gold, I figure I've done some good business."

"Until you run out of things to barter with."

"Ah, my friend, if you think about it, you'll know you can never run out of things to barter. Somebody else always wants what you have, and you can pretty much figure they've got something you want as well. You just have to make sure nobody just goes and takes it."

A rig driven by a young man with a wild streak and a frothing horse sped by them, narrowly missing their backsides.

"I'll say this, Mr. Bonner, if we don't get out of the street, there'll be a lot less of you to barter with in the future." November started for the front door of the Center Ring.

Clint followed him. "Couldn't have done this without you, Mr. Freed." He shook the big man's hand warmly. "You are a true artist, a craftsman, and a man with a clear vision. You could be a magician. That's all thinking, you know. A magician sees first what he wants to accomplish, then goes about making it happen for those who do not have his sharp eye. I am deeply indebted to you."

"I know you're good for it." November laughed.

Clint nodded. "I couldn't have done it without your sharp eye for credit as well, and your willingness to trust a stranger. I'll gamble I can pay you back everything I owe you within the year."

"Well, you go ahead and make that bet with somebody

else. Least I know one of you will pay me." He chuckled. "I'll be back in a few minutes with that light fixture you wanted for your office. I haven't had the chance to open the crate yet." November shook Clint's hand once more and headed toward his own place.

Clint had his hand on the brass door latch and was about to enter when Carsie and Hannah came toward him.

"Good morning, Clint," Hannah called. "And congratulations. Tonight's your big opening, isn't it?"

Carsie uttered a soft good morning, all she could manage above her quickening pulse. Clint removed his wide-brimmed black hat in greeting. His dazzling smile rivaled the impact of his new clothes. A fact blazed in her mind— he was decidedly handsome in a black frock coat and straight black trousers over perfect black boots. A silver and white striped vest stood out under the coat, cut perfectly to skim his white pleated-front shirt. He'd gone without the collar and left the top button open.

"I'm sorry if your sleep was disturbed, Carsie," he said. "The workmen were obliged to work through the night in order to be ready for today."

"Quite all right. The steady hammering into the night has become almost a lullaby. I shall probably miss it when I find a place of my own." So far that had been a futile mission. If a room was appropriate, it was not affordable given her lack of funds. If it was affordable for her pocketbook, it was not appropriate for her person. Nothing ever balanced out, and she had yet to find Sophie.

"I don't think it's going to get any better once you're open." Hannah tried to peer through the front windows, but white drapes covered the glass.

"With any luck." Clint winked and opened the door a crack. "If this place does the kind of business I'm hoping it will, nobody will be able to sleep. Would you like to come in and see it before the revelers turn it upside down tonight?"

"Oh, yes I would." Hannah was almost childlike in her excitement. She looked at Carsie. "You've probably seen it take shape right in front of your eyes. I must say, you've been diligent in keeping it to yourself."

"I haven't seen it, actually."

"Well, then"—he elevated his voice like a ringmaster—"you will be the first to attend the unveiling of the Grand Palace's Center Ring." He swept open the door and, with an expansive open-armed gesture, ushered them inside.

"Welcome, ladies and . . . no gentlemen!" Harry boomed from a high balcony overlooking the main room. "Welcome to the Center Ring and the greatest show in Virginia City. Make yourself comfortable."

Carsie sucked in her breath. Beside her Hannah was speechless. The place was spectacular. Everywhere were splashes of color. Reds, blues, greens, yellows covered walls and ceiling.

Harry pointed out the special features. "I want you to know that I hung upside down on scaffolding to stencil those sailing balloons over the ceiling. Felt like Michelangelo himself."

"I'm certain your ceiling rivals the Sistine Chapel," Carsie told him with a warm smile.

"The web of fancy iron grill below my masterpiece was designed and constructed by Mr. November Freed."

"He must have a very modern forge," Hannah said. She craned her neck to watch an array of trapeze bars and colorful banners sway in the soft breeze generated from wide-bladed fans. "What makes those fans work?"

"It's quite ingenious," Clint put in.

"I was quite fascinated with the clever mechanism," Harry said.

"I'll say. I couldn't keep him off the roof when it was being constructed. The fans are powered by a specially made windmill on the roof, conceived by Mr. November Freed."

"Imagine." Hannah walked around in a circle, her head dropped back as she scrutinized the fans.

"Ohh," Carsie breathed, "look at that." She went quickly to the bar and peered over the highly shined mahogany. On the back of the bar in front of a mirror stood a carving of a wild pony almost three feet in length. Intricate detail showed in the wavy thickness in the animal's mane and the free set of its massive tail as if carried by a strong wind.

"A work of art, is it not?" Harry walked behind the bar and stepped up on a specially designed platform. "Mr. November Freed is indeed an artist. He made a gift of this horse to Clint."

"I was honored by the gift," Clint said. "I've never had such a piece."

"Said it took him three years to complete," Harry went on. "When he first came west, he saw horses running free. I gather he was quite impressed, having never seen horses other than in harness."

Hannah stared at the carved horse, taking in every detail. "He has caught every ounce of freedom expressed by that animal," she said in hushed tones. "Right down to the eyes and flaring nostrils. That horse could breathe freedom."

"I've never seen anything like it," Carsie said.

"Who is this magical Mr. November Freed?" Hannah asked in awe.

Harry jumped down from the raised platform. "A wizard if there ever was one."

"He owns the lumber and hardware business on the other side of town," Clint said. "We couldn't have made this place happen if it weren't for November Freed. The roof tiles were the biggest surprise. I don't know how he did it, but they appeared as if he'd pulled them from thin air."

Hannah twirled slowly, taking in every detail. "He must be a very special man."

"Never met anyone like him, ever," Clint concurred.

"Children would love this place." Carsie wandered around the huge room.

Harry laughed. "Children? I doubt very much Clint had children in mind when he conceived this place. Right, Clint?"

"Right. I want free-spending grown men in here."

Carsie turned to face him. "And women?"

"Definitely women."

"Come along," Harry instructed, "you haven't seen the rest of the place."

Hannah and Carsie followed him, with Clint behind. Carsie felt his presence even when he kept silent and let Harry point out the features of the Center Ring. Tables spread around the room with heavy armed chairs awaiting customers. A raised dance floor displaying a rather fabulous piano on yet another raised platform. Brass and glass lighting fixtures hung from the ceiling below the fans.

Behind the main room was a room for card playing. Down a hallway was a sumptuous office for Clint, complete with an impressive desk over which was strewn building plans. Next was a room that seemed filled with a gleaming oblong pool table. Carsie remembered what an uproar the billiard parlors in St. Joseph caused. Apparently the game was addictive, for husbands were notoriously late for supper throughout the city once the game caught on.

Harry took them upstairs and they walked along the balcony that overlooked the circus atmosphere of the Center Ring. "We've only just begun to complete the second floor. The main thing was to get the first floor finished so the money could start coming in to help pay for all this. The workmen and Mr. Freed can wait only just so long to be paid."

"There will be plenty of room for overnight guests." Clint shoved open a couple of warped doors to show the ladies what was scheduled next for renovation.

At the end of the hallway Harry stopped outside two

doors. "And these rooms belong to Carsie and Clint," he told Hannah.

A smile played over Hannah's full mouth. "Really."

Carsie flushed. "Harry, you make it sound as if we are a . . . a couple. We're just two people with two rooms. Isn't that right?" She turned toward Clint.

"If you say so." There was a definite devilish gleam in his eyes.

"Now let me see." Harry propped an index finger against his chin. "Of course it's been quite a long time since I've been in school. And admittedly I've been away from arithmetic for quite some time as well. But I distinctly remember that two people, as you say, are . . . are . . . what is the word I'm looking for?"

"Couple."

"Hannah!"

"Well, he's right," Hannah said, holding back laughter. "Even with my meager schooling I know that a couple means two. Therefore, two people must mean a couple."

"Clint . . . Tell them they just twisting all this around. While we are two people . . . I mean two separate people . . . and while that could rightly mean in some places that two people are indeed a couple . . . that even though we are two . . ."

"Exactly." Harry nodded.

"A couple," Hannah concurred.

Carsie let out a frustrated sigh and set pleading eyes on Clint.

"I try never to argue with a lady," he said. "Only gets a man into trouble."

"Let me see your room, Carsie." Hannah went to the door and grasped the latch.

Carsie rushed over. "It . . . it just looks like every other room in the Grand Palace."

"Don't worry if it's untidy." Hannah lifted the latch and pushed the door wide. "Isn't this cozy?"

Carsie stepped into the room behind Hannah, then pushed her way by to get to the battered bureau on the other side. She wasn't fast enough. Clint was in the room with Harry at his side before she could get there.

"Well, now, look at that," Harry let out long and slow.

"That's exactly what I'm doing," Clint said in a faraway voice. The hint of a curious grin tilted one corner of his mouth.

Hannah breathed, "Oh my."

"Oh dear." Carsie was mortified.

Hanging from the wall on two wooden pegs like a painting displayed in a gallery was the black lace corselette she'd purchased in Virginville.

"Interesting decorating idea," Harry said.

"Why didn't we think of that?" Clint said.

Hannah sent an apologetic look to Carsie. "Why don't we move on?" She made a sweeping gesture behind the men and urged them out of the room.

Flustered, her cheeks burning with embarrassment, Carsie followed them and slammed the door. To have Clint see the undergarment like that, and in her room of all places! Now of course he would think she was just mooning after him, and being all dreamy over his kiss. He would just be incorrigible from now on, she knew it. He would never let her forget it. He would tell Jake for certain, and that awful mess about their bet and their kiss would come back to haunt her.

As if it didn't haunt her already without the kind of help Clint had just received.

"And here's Clint's room," Harry announced, obviously attempting to break the tension.

"No need to see that," Clint said quickly. All these rooms are alike. Now down here is the second-floor balcony. You really should see that. Spectacular scenery."

"Must be he didn't make his bed," Harry whispered loudly.

"We don't care about that," Hannah said, looking over her shoulder. "Do we, Carsie?"

"I don't care about anything," Carsie muttered.

Before Clint could stop him, Harry pushed open the door to his room and stepped inside, Hannah close behind.

"Well, now, look at *that*," Harry said, and stifled a chuckle.

"Oh my," Hannah breathed.

"What?" Carsie's curiosity was piqued.

"Nothing." Clint took her arm and drew her away from the door.

"Well, it must be something," Carsie said, carefully extracting her arm from his grip. She pushed inside.

Clint's room was in a state of rebuilding like the others on that floor. Carsie felt a bit guilty about stepping inside his private domain even though he was present, but the others had and they'd seen something that caught their curiosity. She swept her gaze around the room and didn't notice anything until she turned to leave. Then she saw them. Her mouth dropped open slowly.

She looked at Clint. He leaned against the door frame, a perturbed look on his face. She looked back into his room.

"Dolls?"

"Let's all go downstairs and have some coffee, what do you say?" Clint grabbed the door latch in effort to usher them out.

"Dolls?" Carsie said again.

Harry chuckled and drew Hannah out into the hallway. Her mouth tipped up with an amused unasked question. She turned toward Clint, who was fairly dragging Carsie out of his room.

"There is a perfectly logical explanation for this." Clint locked his door. "Which I do not care to discuss at this moment."

Carsie stared at him. "Dolls?"

With wide arms Clint herded them toward the stairway

as if he were sweeping out. It was very clear the discussion of the contents of his bedroom was closed for good.

Carsie knew that if the ladies at tea wondered about Clint's private life without knowing anything about him, they would truly be abuzz if they heard he was harboring two dolls, a cradle made especially for their size, and bits of clothing and a baby blanket. She would keep her knowledge to herself, of course, but she would also pursue why Clint Bonner would feel the need to keep dolls and doll clothes in his bedroom.

That evening at six-thirty the doors to the Center Ring were flung open by Jake in formal attire and a recently cleaned stovepipe hat. He'd forgone his corncob pipe for a brand new one with an ivory bowl, a gift from Clint.

The population of Virginia City was curious to a one, and so it was that the respectable folk mingled with whores and gamblers and even prospectors in from their claims who hadn't taken time for a bath. Music was provided by members of the town band, who were loud if not melodic.

Phoebe Goodnight had closed her establishment for two hours in order to urge attendance at Clint's opening and in order for her and her employees to attend. Harry escorted Libby and little Harry to the celebration. Carsie borrowed a dress from Libby. Hannah dressed Carsie's hair, the first time she'd ever experienced such a thing. She found it rather a pleasure to have it released from the daily prison of its tight bun and to feel soft coils at the back of her neck.

The Center Ring was adorned with festive decorations, some specially delivered by Mr. and Mrs. Woo. Mr. Woo's frown of admonition toward his wife for her open behavior with the women from the wagon train did not last long when, at the group's insistence, she gave him a frown of her own. They greeted her like the true friends they had become.

Clint presided over the gala like a ringmaster, directing patrons to the dance floor, the tables laden with food, the extensive bar stocked with the finest whiskey and its special taps for beer and root beer from the local brewery, and the card and billiard rooms. His excitement and enthusiasm rose above the revelry in the place, if that was possible.

Carsie approached Phoebe at a fraction of a moment when the handsome woman was not surrounded by admiring men. "Could I ask you a question of a rather, ah, personal nature?"

"Of course, dear. Are you still wondering about how to attract men? I'd say you were certainly attracting admiring glances this evening."

"Really?" Carsie scanned the room without really seeing. "No, it's not that. I have discovered . . . when I was in Clint's room . . ." She placed her cool hand over her burning cheek for a fleeting moment. "I mean that Harry, Hannah, and I were on a tour of the Grand Palace, and when Clint showed us his room . . . well, he didn't exactly show us his room, we more or less just pushed right in and I suppose none of us should have done that, but—"

"Carson, dear," Phoebe said, placing her hand on Carsie's arm, "the evening is rapidly dwindling while we stand here. What is it you're trying to say?"

Carsie cleared her through. "All right. We discovered something very strange . . . or maybe it's not strange at all, I just don't know."

"Out with it, then." Phoebe assured an approaching businessman that she would speak with him shortly.

Lola approached them. "Some party, eh?" Whenever she was in the company of her friends, she lost her carefully cultivated foreign accent. "How are you both doing?"

"Carson has a question about something strange she discovered in Clint's room."

"Clint's room? You've been to Clint's room? Well, now I am jealous."

Phoebe grew impatient with both women. "Carson, if you

want to discuss this with me, we must do it now. I have some pressing business."

"Yes, ma'am," Carsie said dutifully. She swallowed and took a deep breath. "When we were in Clint's room we saw some . . . dolls, and doll clothes and a doll cradle." She waited for the impact to stun Phoebe and Lola. It didn't.

"Hm," Lola said, her gaze drifting over the crowd to land on Clint. "Never would have figured him for one of those."

Carsie frowned. "One of those what?"

"For pity's sake." Phoebe's tone was decidedly exasperated with these two women. "Clint Bonner is hardly one of those."

"One of those *what?*" Carsie repeated.

"I'm not saying it can't happen," Phoebe said, shaking her head. "All I'm saying is Clint Bonner isn't . . ."

Carsie stamped her foot and shouted, "Isn't *what?*"

Phoebe and Lola snapped their heads around and said as one, "A man who likes dolls the same way he likes women."

The heavy pause among them was supported by the roar of the crowd as, atop the bar, Clint and Harry did their juggling act.

"You can't mean . . ." A whirlpool of pictures Carsie had never thought of in her life swirled around in her head.

"Sure do. Some men do." Lola adjusted her feathered headpiece.

Phoebe shifted her ample bosom inside her stiff bodice. "Not Clint Bonner, mark my words." She smiled a welcome to the man who appeared through the crowd. His arm circled her waist and they moved toward the dance floor.

"Probably not." Lola set her smoky sites on a particularly big man in a white collarless shirt and striped trousers, and sauntered off.

"Oh my." Carsie stood dumbfounded while the crowd pressed around her.

"Carsie? You all right?"

Carsie came out of her trance. Hannah peered into her face.

"Yes, yes, I am. Of course."

"You look stunned. Did something happen?"

Carsie sucked in her bottom lip, deciding whether she should ask Hannah. If there was anyone she knew she could trust, it was Hannah. "Remember earlier today when we were in Clint's room and we saw . . ."

Hannah tilted her head. "The dolls?"

Carsie nodded. "Lola says that some men—"

"Not Clint Bonner," Hannah said quickly.

"That's what Phoebe said."

"You can believe her." Hannah reached out and straightened the collar on Carsie's dress. "Isn't it a marvelous party?"

"I guess so." Carsie looked around again. "I hadn't noticed."

"Ha! How could you not notice? I can barely hear myself in here. It's incredible . . ." Her mobile face went still. Her eyes fastened on a space beyond Carsie's shoulder. "Who is *that?*"

Slowly Carsie turned toward the direction Hannah was concentrating on. A big man, broad shouldered and heads above every man in the crowd, stood several feet from them. His mahogany skin glowed in the light, his tightly curled black hair glistened. And his glittering dark gaze was fastened upon Hannah.

"I don't know," Carsie breathed, "but I have never seen such an intriguing-looking man."

"Nor have I." Hannah's voice was constricted. She stood frozen to the floor.

"He's looking right at you."

"Thank you," Hannah said dreamily. "I wasn't certain I was right about that."

And then the big man started toward them through the

crowd, which parted as if he were Moses and they were the Red Sea. His gaze never wavered from her face. Hannah's pulse quickened the closer he came, the larger he loomed in her vision. The roar of the crowd seemed to lower to a dull thrum, and Carsie and the people surrounding them faded to the back of her mind. And then he was in front of her, stopping a respectable distance away.

"Good evening, ma'am." The rich deep voice settled over her like warm syrup.

Hannah slowly lifted her hand, and her trembling fingers drummed lightly on the cameo locket at her throat. She could not take her eyes from his handsomely chiseled face. "Good evening," she whispered, barely forcing it past her lips.

"I wonder if you might favor me with a dance should this band play something softer than a march or a polka."

She couldn't speak for a moment, and then something settled her raging nerves, and she felt an unfamiliar sensation that all was right in her world. "I would enjoy . . . sharing a dance with you."

The big man smiled widely. "Then I think I'll persuade them to change their tune—immediately. Will you stay right here?"

Hannah nodded. "Yes."

He smiled again, turned, and headed for the bandstand. The music stopped abruptly, then began shortly thereafter in a hesitant, albeit lilting, waltz. He threaded his way back through the crowd and extended his hand.

"Thank you for waiting, ma'am. Would you tell me your name?"

"Hannah. Hannah Holmes."

"Hannah," he said musically. "Hannah." He led her toward the dance floor.

Hannah paused before stepping into his massive open arms. "And may I ask the same of you?"

"Yes, ma'am. Hannah." Smoothly he drew her into the

throng of dancers. "November Freed. And may I add, at
this moment the most fortunate November Freed who ever
lived."

"November Freed," Hannah whispered into his chest.
"The wizard."

Across his biceps she could see Carsie blending away
into the crowd. And then the crowd faded from her sight.

Carsie watched the beautiful couple glide away from her
toward the dance floor. They swayed to the music as if no
one else was in the room. She'd felt the power of lightning
flash between them and then settle to a steady fire. The
utterly romantic sense of it engulfed her, the sensation palpable.

Being in the presence of such a moment as this propitious
meeting between two people suddenly filled her with a profound sense of loneliness and longing. The gaiety in the
crowd was too much for her to experience any longer. She
turned quickly, pushed her way through the press of people,
and left the Center Ring.

In her room, Carsie moved slowly, methodically changing
into her nightclothes. She buttoned the neck of her white
cotton gown, and smoothed the long sleeves, ruffling the
cuffs.

She could smell smoke in her hair as she brushed it out
long and free. She tilted her head and let her hair fall over
her shoulder. For her to be as unencumbered from the con-
straints of society and her own self-imposed emotional exile
seemed an elusive and unattainable dream.

The room seemed to close in around her. She needed to
breathe fresh air, needed to gaze into the vast openness of
the Montana sky. She took a woolen robe from the end of
the bed and pulled it closely around her, then left her room
and stepped out onto the back landing.

Fifteen

The night was cold and clear, the stars big as fists and brilliant as polished diamonds. Carsie let out a long sigh and her breath instantly turned to white mist. She took some comfort in knowing there was something warm and alive inside her that she could see when she let it out. Music from the Center Ring floated out onto the sharp air. A breeze filtered through her hair, cleansing it of the smoky smell.

Another sound came to her. She listened carefully. Singing. A man singing. Where was it coming from? The voice grew louder as whoever it was came near the bottom of the stairway. She stepped back and saw him then.

Clint was climbing the stairs, humming and chuckling to himself. A bottle and glass clinked together like a faraway bell as he scuffed up stair by stair. And then he saw her.

"Carsie?"

She shivered and pulled her robe tighter. "Yes."

"What are you doing up here? You should be downstairs having a good time among all the revelers."

She watched him climb closer. "I . . . I wanted to get out of the crowd and breathe some fresh air. Isn't that where *you* should be? Amid the revelers? It's your big opening night."

"I've had opening nights before. Harry and Jake can take care of everything." He reached the landing and stood in front of her. "And I needed some fresh air as well."

She couldn't tell if he was drunk or not. He didn't seem to be, yet there was a look on his face, in his eyes, that hadn't been there earlier. It was almost smoldering and it unnerved her. Had something happened to him down in the bar?

"Champagne?" He held the bottle and glass out to her. She shook her head. He poured some into the glass. "First drink of the night. Imagine that. I own a saloon and couldn't even get one drink out of it. But that's all right. Just seemed best I take this particular bottle to bed with me. Better than a bedtime story for bringing on sleep. Sure you won't have some?" He held out the glass to her.

She started to shake her head, then held it still. She'd never drunk champagne before. Why not try it? She was only a few steps from her room so if it affected her badly she could just leave and not embarrass herself. And besides, Clint had just said it was better than a bedtime story for bringing on sleep. And she could certainly benefit from some sleep.

"I think I will have some champagne." She reached out slowly and accepted the glass.

Her first sip sent the bubbles up her nose and caused a light sneeze. The liquid was tart and left a dry but pleasant taste. She started to give him the glass then changed her mind. Instead she took another sip, then a good-sized third one. The effervescence seemed to go directly to her brain and open it wide. It was instantly a marvelous sensation. She drained the glass.

"That's what I like to see. Enjoyment of one of the earth's best products." Clint refilled the glass and drank it himself this time.

"It is quite lovely, isn't it? I never knew."

"Never? You've never tasted champagne?"

"Not until now."

"Well, then, you must take this bottle for yourself." He thrust it toward her.

She put up a hand. "No, I couldn't. I mean, I wouldn't dare . . ."

Clint refilled the glass and held it out to her. "See? There you go again putting all kinds of restrictions on something you want to do."

"But I don't want to do it . . . Well, maybe I do." She accepted the glass and drank. "Oh my, that certainly is wonderful." She held the glass high, and the moonlight made the bubbles sparkle. "Like drinking from a bottle full of stars," she whispered.

She felt his eyes on her, his gaze strong, and she was afraid to face him and interpret the meaning in them. She felt an escalating sensation that every inch of her skin was aware, alive with a kind of anticipation. What had caused such a swell of awareness? Was it the champagne? Was it the moonlight? The clear sharp air? The lively music from the Center Ring? All of them put together?

Or was it Clint's nearness that made all those things more powerful than they might have been without his presence?

Quite involuntarily she rocked onto her heels and back again.

"A bit tipsy are you?" Clint chuckled.

She took a breath. "Would the champagne do that so quickly?"

"It could."

She held the glass out to him to take. He refilled it in her hand. Then he lifted the bottle to his lips, tilted his head back, and emptied it.

"I think that's enough stars for you to drink for one night," he said, setting the bottle on the railing. "You're starting to get talkative again, and the last thing you need is something that loosens your tongue."

His good-natured barb didn't faze her. She felt her blood warm, felt her shoulders relax. "Do you really think so? I've heard the expression 'from wine comes truth' or some such. Do you think that means that champagne can loosen one's mind enough to make the tongue speak what the heart really means?"

It was Clint's turn to rock back on his heels. She'd stunned him with those words. He looked at her long and hard. Her hair glowed like a halo as the moon silhouetted her against the blackness beyond the landing. Her robe had fallen open and the whiteness of her nightgown rivaled the moon for light. He could see the darkness of her nipples through the thin fabric.

Embarrassed, he lowered his eyes. Could the champagne do that to him? Under ordinary circumstances the sight of a woman's breasts straining against a thin garment would cause his blood to heat and his pulse to race, and he would be in a position to simply reach out and take them into his hands. He had often enough. But not lately. Not for lack of opportunity. He found it strange to realize that it was his own lack of interest in the women that kept him from accepting the offer.

Now as his mind held the visage of Carsie in the moonlight, his blood did heat, his pulse did race, and he was clenching his fists to keep them busy.

"I don't think I can answer that," he said thickly.

Carsie drained the last of her champagne and turned toward him, pressing the glass into his hand.

Surprised, Clint took the glass with both hands for fear of dropping it. Carsie's eyes were heavy-lidded, her lips held a mysterious smile.

"Do you think . . ." She paused as if she'd forgotten for the moment what she'd meant to say. She took in a small sharp breath. "Do you think that on a night like this and with champagne like that, people might be compelled to do something they might not have realized they wanted to do until that combination occurred at one particular moment?"

He inclined his head toward her and frowned, studying her face. So she *was* tipsy. "I'm not certain I understand exactly what you mean. Maybe you should give me an example."

She smiled enigmatically then stepped close to him. Slipping her cool hands up his warm face, she drew his head down and kissed him—a long, slow, sensuous kiss.

He felt lightning-struck and could not move. Her soft lips held his prisoner. He could not have drawn away if he'd wanted to. He was a willing prisoner, and the idea of it overwhelmed him. This was the third time they'd kissed, yet each successive time felt like the first all over again. Such a sensation was new to him.

And the sensation fired him beyond reason.

He sent the glass sailing over the rail and gathered Carsie into his arms with a power and desire beyond any mere physical lust he'd ever felt for any woman in his past. This transcended the physical, this engulfed his mind and emotions, blending them into one explosive force.

His physical desires grew stronger. The burgeoning heat grew hard against his thigh. He pressed it into her soft belly. And then his mind jolted him out of the stupor of the kiss. Getting hold of himself he gently broke the bond of their lips, and started to step back.

"I—I apologize for my—unforgivable behavior. I—it could be the champagne, the moonlight . . . the excitement of the opening." *And the utter desirability of you in my mind.*

She wouldn't let him step away from her, but clutched the front of his shirt. "I won't forgive you."

He cursed himself silently. There was so much swirling around his mind, swirling around the two of them on the upstairs railing in the brilliant moonlight. He wanted her forgiveness, wanted it desperately. He'd try to figure out what that meant later.

"I won't forgive you because there is nothing to forgive." She was breathing hard, her breasts rising and falling against his chest. With a groan, he captured her lips again. When he broke away, he stepped back to look into her eyes.

Carsie met and held his gaze. Then taking him by the hand, she drew him through the open door to her room, and closed the door behind them. A lamp glowed on the bedside stand, casting golden light in an arc over the bed. She removed her robe and draped it over a chair. Then she stepped close behind him and slipped his jacket down over his massive shoulders and over his arms. Carefully she draped it over her robe.

He turned to face her. "Carsie," he began. As she started to unfasten his shirt buttons, he clasped her two hands and stopped her. "It is the champagne. And I can't let this happen no matter how much I want to. I hope I'm more of a gentleman than to—"

"Shh." She slipped out a hand and reached up to clasp his neck and draw his head down. She kissed him tenderly.

His spine seemed to melt and he curved his body into hers, gathering her tenderly into his arms. He kissed her sweetly, almost with reverence.

He released and unbuttoned the top of her gown. Trailing light kisses from the pulse in her throat down the tender skin between her breasts, he bent to grasp the bottom of the gown and raise it over her head. He dropped it over his coat. When he stepped back to look at her bathed in the golden glow of the lamp, he sucked in his breath. To think this glorious womanly form had been concealed under a shirt and bloomers for months.

She reached out and unbuckled his belt, then opened his trousers. He sat on the edge of the bed to remove his boots.

"Let me," she said. And then piece by piece she stripped him of his clothes.

He rose then, slightly embarrassed by his body's show of desire, which his mind was unable to control. And then she was in his arms, covering his chest with kisses, while

his hands began a slow exploration of her skin and contours.

When they lowered slowly to the bed, Carsie melted into
him, willing herself to be consumed by him, wanting to
consume the very essence of him. All defenses were cast
away as she yielded to him one moment and took from him
the next. All self-consciousness faded away as they reveled
in one another with kisses, touches, communion deep
within, mutual giving and demanding.

A new sensation overtook her. The surprise of it almost
stopped her, yet compelled her to go on. The fluttering deep
inside, the gathering momentum, the desire to hold back yet
break out at the same time was almost more than she could
take. She cried out as a tremendous release set her free from
the exquisite ache. And Clint followed in the expression of
his ecstasy and was filled with joy in the moment.

The lamp had long sputtered out and the sun was penetrating the lace curtains when Clint gently set Carsie out of
his arms and drew the quilt over her.

She stirred and lifted her head. "It's time, isn't it?"

"I'm afraid so." He dressed slowly.

"I wish—"

"Your honor is at stake right now. I have to get out of
here without being seen."

"I don't care about my honor."

"I do."

She watched him silently. He slipped on his coat, the last
of his garments, then came back to the bed.

"Thank you," she whispered.

Her words gave him pause. "Only the night has passed."
He leaned down and kissed her tenderly.

And then he was gone. Carsie dropped back onto the pillow and breathed in the scent and warmth of their lovemaking. She should have felt shocked at her behavior. She didn't.
She should have felt ashamed at her seduction of him. She
didn't. She should have felt like running away and hiding

someplace. She didn't, and wasn't about to either. She should not have been lying there in bed and thoroughly enjoying the memory of last night with Clint, their incredible love-making over and over. But she was, and she intended to hold on to the next few minutes to keep the memory close.

Lovemaking. It truly was making love, for her at least.

This was her truth with and without the champagne and the moonlight—she was completely in love with Clint Bonner.

What would she do about that? What could she do about it? She believed that one night of passion was all there would be with Clint. She'd known it the first moment it came to her in the moonlight that she wanted him, wanted to make love with him. He had plenty of women around him, and if he wanted one, all he had to do was beckon and any of them would go running. After all, it had taken a bet with Jake for him even to kiss her the first time. It wasn't because he'd wanted to. She couldn't forget that.

And she couldn't forget his feelings about his wife. She sensed that he would never get over them. His soul was tortured by her death, and that he hadn't been strong for her. She knew he might never let himself love again.

She was strong. She would keep her emotions and feelings in check, and she would get on with her reasons for coming out to Montana in the first place. Slowly she'd been shedding parts of herself with every roll of the wheels westward, and aside from a deep and abiding desire to find Sophie, it was as if she'd shrugged out of a cloak she'd constructed from fragments of her life and left it patch by patch on the westward trails.

Not that she'd given up her feelings about women's rights and freedoms. Not by a long shot. It was just that for once she was wondering about her own life and what she would do with it. St. Joseph seemed a world away, and little Rosie Summers a mere speck in the population, someone she'd met only once. She was without direction, without a burning desire for something to do with her life as before.

Once she found Sophie and rescued her, that would be the end of her mission. She'd have to move on or turn around and go back to St. Joseph. There was nothing for her to do in Virginia City, not really. She'd looked around. There were few females here who wanted to be liberated from their lives, in her estimation. Most of them were already liberated, freer than many women back in the States in many ways. The many layers inherent in Eastern society hadn't arrived in Montana yet. She liked thinking about that. Could it be that Montana might just be a new land where women had the opportunity to live complete and satisfying lives on equal footing with men? And was it possible that Montana men liked it that way?

She knew one thing for certain—she'd better find some work that paid so she could rent a room if one became available. She couldn't stay a guest of Clint's forever. It wouldn't look right to some of the townspeople. She'd said in a show of bravado she didn't care about that. He'd said he did. How strange it was that he cared about how the situation looked and she did not. In the West everything seemed reversed.

She sat up and slowly got out of the nest in the bedclothes. Time to move on. She felt so different this morning. She was a different person somehow. Now what would she do with this new person?

"Well, now, you're up early, aren't you?" Harry was just emerging from the kitchen with a coffeepot when Clint came through the back door into the Center Ring. Harry's eyes narrowed in scrutiny. "Or haven't you been to bed yet? To sleep."

"I'm up early," Clint muttered. He pulled out a chair and dropped down at a table, the only clean one in the place. "You got a lot of that coffee?"

"You know I have." Harry set the pot on the table and disappeared into the back, emerging a minute later with another mug. He poured for both of them and sat down.

Clint drank the steaming brew and barely felt the near scalding temperature on his swollen lips. "Jake didn't make this, did he?"

"No, I did. No need to worry about losing the inside of your stomach this morning. Very profitable opening, Clint, very profitable."

"I'm sure."

"We made almost enough to build another saloon."

"That's good."

Harry scraped his cup across the table. "And Jake ran off with Miss Phoebe and got married and they have twins already."

"That's nice."

Harry slammed his mug on the table.

Clint jumped and spilled some coffee down his shirtfront. "What the—? What are you trying to do, kill me?"

"How about you try to get into this world this morning? You seem to have taken leave of your senses. What's the matter?"

"Nothing's the matter. I'm just having trouble waking up is all. How'd we do last night?"

"We discussed that already."

"We did?"

"Yes. More to the point, how did you do last night?"

Clint gave him an exasperated look. "What kind of a question is that?"

"The usual question. And by that answer I'd say you spent the evening with a lady who's identity you'd rather keep secret."

Clint did not respond.

"All right," Harry pressed, "but you know we have ways of finding out who she is sooner or later. Now, let's see . . ."

"Never mind, Harry. You won't get it from me this time. I'm on to your wily ways. And where's your accomplice?"

"Jake's making breakfast. Said something about knowing you'd need a hearty one this morning." Harry chuckled.

"What did that old coot mean by that?" Clint drained the coffee mug and rubbed the space between his eyes.

A bang at the kitchen door heralded Jake's entrance carrying two plates of steaming food. He set them down in front of Harry and Clint, then returned to get one for himself. He plopped down at the table and surveyed the plates of ham and eggs and biscuits, then took a long swallow of coffee before he spoke.

"Never figured you'd get to Bloomers. How'd you ever break her down?"

Harry choked on a bite of ham.

Clint dropped his fork, picked it up again, and did not look Jake in the face. "What are you talking about?"

"He's in trouble," Jake commented, and poured more coffee.

"Bigger than usual." Harry broke into a biscuit.

"What do you two think you're doing?" Clint set his fork down.

"Nothing," Jake said.

"Nothing at all," Harry concurred.

"Yeah, well, I've seen your nothing jobs before. Now quit badgering me."

"Who's badgerin'?" Jake asked lightly. "I was just makin' a mere observation. That the right word, Harry? Observation?"

"Exactly correct, my friend. Observation. Now, let's see if my observation is as astute as yours. You have identified the lady in question and I am very impressed with your powers of discernment. But upon further scrutiny, I would say this is more than simply a man spending the night with a woman."

"You would?" Jake's head jutted forward as he studied Clint's face.

Clint clamped his lips together and frowned as menacingly as he could at the two people he counted as his greatest friends.

"Indeed," Harry concurred. "The great Bonner, the Casanova of our time, has fallen. No more can we hold him as the example of a man at the height of the chase, a man with the cunning mind of a wolf, a man with an appreciative eye for all the ladies. No, my friend, we will have to look elsewhere for guidance when it comes to understanding the wiles of women. Bonner has been trapped, and by a suffragist no less." Harry chuckled and poured another cup of coffee.

"Look who's pointing fingers," Clint said at last. "When are you going to do something permanent? You're with Libby and her baby every minute you haven't been here. You best get on with it. There are plenty of other men who are interested in her, you know. I've seen them."

Harry fidgeted in his chair. "I'm just watching over her. She's new here, and with the baby and all her other plans, well, she needs all the help she can get."

Jake laughed out loud. "You're bad as he is. You're as guilty as all get-out. You're in love with Libby, so why don't you quit your stallin' and do something about it?"

"Yeah," Clint underscored, grateful to have the attention focused on someone other than himself. "Why don't you declare yourself to Libby?"

Harry stared into his coffee mug. "Now what would a lovely young woman like Libby want with a dwarf former circus performer? She needs somebody who'll provide for her and her son, give her a farm or something, a nice house. Anyway, I'm a saloonkeeper now." He raised his eyes quickly to Clint's face. "And I'm glad of it, don't get me wrong. Thanks to you, I've got this place. Never figured I'd be doing such a thing and be happy at it."

Clint was instantly sorry he'd chided Harry. He'd always

looked up to Harry, thought of him as bigger than life, learned as much from him as he had from Jake. Harry was his friend and he loved him. He laid a hand on his friend's shoulder.

"You know Libby doesn't see you as anything but a big man, and it has nothing to do with your size."

"Oh, I don't know about that. Back on the road it was something else. We all needed each other to survive. Here in civilization it's another story."

"You don't give Libby enough credit," Jake said. "She's got a fine mind and can think for herself. And I've watched her smile whenever you show up. She's got it for you, too."

Harry stared at them both for a moment. "I know what you're up to. You're just trying to divert attention from Clint to me."

"And you're afraid of facing reality." Clint shoved his plate to the center of the table.

"Oh, I am, am I?"

"Yes, you are," Jake said, nodding vigorously. "Why don't you just go on over there and ask that pretty gal to marry you and get it done with?"

"Marry!" Harry slumped back in his chair. "She's not going to . . . I never figured I—"

"She will and you'd better start figuring." Clint rose, yawned, and stretched. "Guess I'd better get this day going. What a mess this place is."

"Got it covered," Jake said. "Hired me a bunch of boys to come in here and clean it up. Said I'd teach 'em how to juggle if they'd get it done in good season."

"Bartering. The best thing we ever learned in the circus." Clint started for the back door.

"Don't think you're getting away," Harry called after him. "We know you've got it for Carsie. Libby's going to be excited when I tell her."

"Don't you tell her a thing," Clint said over his shoulder, "unless it's the date of your own wedding."

"See you out at the place this morning?" Harry called back.

Clint stopped. "I'll be there, you thimblerigger."

"You love it and you know it. You'll bring everything with you?"

"I will. I want to get it out of my room anyway."

Jake scraped off the table with a rag. "Afraid Carsie's still wonderin' why you're playin' with dolls?"

"Harry," Clint said on an exasperated sigh, "see if you can barter this tough old rooster for something we can stand to live with. Preferably something that doesn't talk." He pushed through the back door and went outside.

Behind the building he paused in the brilliance of the rising sun. A revelation, that's what morning was every day the sun rose. A revelation. And that's what last night was, too.

He must have been losing parts of himself. Last night, last week, the last months. He felt as if he were skulking through a forest like some sneaky predator, keeping one watchful eye out for a trapper but the other eye always on his prize.

Love. He couldn't believe he was even thinking such a word let alone feeling such a powerful emotion again.

Love. *Would this be all right with you, Mattie? I'm sorry. I never meant for it to happen again.*

He stepped around the building and out onto the street. There she was ahead of him walking into the office of *The Montana Post.* Why? That woman was exasperating. She was always doing something that had him wondering about her. And after last night he would be worse at his wondering, he knew it.

He had to stop this and get on with business.

Sixteen

Hannah entered Freed's Store with Libby, a disturbing feeling of anticipation fluttering low in her breast. Harry and November sat in battered armchairs near the wood stove deep in conversation. She had no real business being in a lumber and hardware store. If Libby hadn't insisted, she probably never would have ventured into this one. On the other hand, she had been considering getting hooks and wire to hang some picture frames in her room. Somehow she'd always found an excuse to put off going to Freed's Store to get them.

The sight of November in a woolen shirt with the sleeves rolled over muscular forearms gave Hannah's pulse a jolt. It was at once a frightening and wondrous sensation. All her life she'd numbed her senses to men, suffering indignities at their hands, fighting to keep her pride even when the last ounce of it was threatened by both the white masters and the black men living with her in mutual hell.

Stunned once again by her reaction to November Freed, she tried to compose herself with the use of a steel will she'd cultivated all her life. Two weeks had passed since that evening in the Center Ring when their eyes had met through the sea of white faces and she'd felt magically drawn to him. The physical magnetism emanating between them surprised her. She'd never felt physical desire for any man.

Her mode of existence was to put her strong mind on

another plane and tolerate without feeling what was happening to the shell of her body. While working for Goodnight's Good Times Emporium had changed the outside of her relationship to men because of Phoebe's strict codes of customer conduct and cleanliness, inside Hannah felt cold, unloved, unloving. Her body had been her only value, it seemed, and it had been used from the time she was nine years old. The only life she'd ever known involved the use of her body by men. At least in Miss Phoebe's establishment she had a say over whom she would allow into her bedroom. Still, she'd shut her mind off, shut her feelings away with every encounter.

Since their arrival in Virginia City, she'd been thinking more and more about leaving the life and working at something else. For the first time she was beginning to feel as if she was in a place where the color of her skin would not find doors slammed in her face. Montana seemed the place where she could truly be free to be herself. Whoever that was.

She considered Lola, Phoebe, and Libby her friends, but they were part of the profession in their own ways and did not judge her. Carsie was the first woman on the outside, as they called a woman not in the business, with whom she truly felt an honest friendship forming woman to woman, human to human. For all the years she'd felt less than human, her new friendship with Carsie had been the beginning of a decided return of emotional sensation.

Maybe that was part of why everything was different from the moment her gaze had collided with November Freed's. And when she'd floated into his arms and they'd moved as one over the dance floor, the magic became complete, the attraction came full circle in emotional and spiritual completion. An avalanche of emotion had descended upon her so heavily she had difficulty breathing at times. She'd gone to the Center Ring one other evening in the last two weeks. November hadn't been there and she hadn't gone back.

Now as she stood inside his establishment and watched him rise slowly from his chair, his gaze fastened on her, every part of her trembled involuntarily.

Libby, her arm linked through Hannah's, leaned close. "Is something the matter?" she whispered.

"No, not at all," Hannah whispered back. It was a lie and she knew it. Everything was the matter, and Libby's acute senses had felt it all.

November and Harry walked toward them, both smiling. "Good morning," November greeted them in his rich voice.

"Good morning," Hannah returned shyly.

"Ah, now I understand," Libby whispered to her. She turned her head in the direction of the voice. "Good morning, Mr. Freed. Is Harry here?"

"Right here." Harry rushed over, lifted Libby's hand, and kissed the back of it.

"I missed you this morning," Libby said without a trace of guile in her voice.

"I missed you, too. I'm sorry, but I had to stay and clean up the mess our enthusiastic patrons made last evening. And I wanted to see November before he got too busy this morning."

"I know. I understand. I just wanted you to know that I missed you. And so did little Harry. I think he prefers the way you dress him." Libby laughed lightly. "His arms and legs move so fast I can hardly hold them still long enough to get his clothes on. Miss Phoebe is entertaining him this morning."

"I have a feeling it's the other way around," Hannah said, nervously focusing her attention on Libby and Harry. "I've seen the way she dotes on him like a grandmother."

"And how is it I haven't met your son, Harry?" November gave his new friend a good-natured push on the shoulder.

"He's not exactly—" Harry began.

"Well, we shall just have to remedy that, won't we?" Libby interrupted. "Harry's just been so busy these last weeks, and I have found so much work to do that I fear we haven't been very neighborly and thanked you properly for your generosity. You must come to Thanksgiving dinner, Mr. Freed."

"Well, now I'd certainly enjoy a meal prepared by a good woman's hand." November smiled warmly at Libby and Harry. "And will Miss Hannah be joining us?"

"Oh, I don't—" Hannah started.

"Of course she will," Harry cut in.

The bell over the door jangled.

"Good morning," Carsie called, stepping into the store.

Libby turned slightly at the sound of her footsteps. "Good morning, Carsie. You're out and about early."

"The morning was so crisp and glorious, I couldn't stay inside huddling near a stove for warmth." Carsie smiled widely and took in a deep breath. "Oh, Mr. Freed, I do love the aroma of new lumber and . . . what is that other spicy scent?"

November indicated the top of the stove where the largest tea kettle Hannah had ever seen, yet hadn't noticed at first, sat emitting curls of lazy steam.

"That's my mother's brew. She made a special tea during the winter months with herbs and spices to take the chill from weary bones and, as she liked to say, lift the spirits from the mud. Would you like some?"

"I would love some. Jake gave me a cup of his famous coffee this morning, and I'm afraid my stomach is rebelling."

November once again settled his warm gaze on Hannah. "Miss Hannah and Miss Libby? Can I prepare a cup of tea for you?"

"Oh my, yes," Libby said.

"Thank you," Hannah whispered.

Harry grabbed his coat. "I'll go over to the bakery and get a sweet to have with it. And then I'm afraid I'll have to leave this fair company."

"Shall I go now and get little Harry so we'll be ready to leave?" Libby asked.

"Not yet. But stay and chat awhile. I won't be long."

November took down some tin mugs from a wooden rack behind the stove. "I'm sorry I don't have proper china cups for you ladies. I promise to get some especially for you if you will honor me often by stopping in for tea."

"With such a gracious invitation as that, how could we not visit you?" Carsie said with great enthusiasm.

Hannah tilted her head and studied her friend. "What has made you so happy this morning? You seem different."

Carsie's hand shook as she accepted the mug of tea from November. "Do I?" Her voice was unnaturally high. "It's probably just that I . . . well, I feel full. Of ideas, that is. Yes, just full of ideas. I am determined to find work that will pay me a wage decent enough to afford me a place of my own to live."

November gestured toward the chairs near the stove and pulled up a couple of nail kegs for extra seating, then guided Libby to a seat. The four sat around the stove as if at a proper tea party.

"I thought you were busy with the ladies league," Libby said.

"I am. But I must work for wages. My savings will not take me through the end of the year. I've found nothing suitable. The city has almost doubled in population since we arrived. Everyone has their own work or someone to do it." Carsie breathed in the spicy aroma of tea and new lumber. "But I'm determined. I will find something, or create my own work somehow. I don't know what that could be."

"I've been feeling rather the same things," Hannah said, then bit her tongue for speaking so openly.

"But you have work and a place to live," Libby said innocently.

Hannah felt her face warm in the rush of embarrassment. She sipped at the tea and tried to shift the focus. "Mm, this is delicious. Your mother certainly created a special brew."

November set down his cup and picked up an iron poker. He opened the front of the stove and poked at the logs, sending up new flames. "I felt the same way," he said thoughtfully and with a slight air of mystery. "By the time I stopped traveling and settled here in Virginia City, I knew I wanted to do something I'd never done before. I wanted to be my own boss. I could never do that before. Now I am, and I'm the best boss I ever had. I treat myself like I'm the best worker I got. And I am." He laughed.

The others laughed along with him, completely at ease. Hannah surmised exactly what he meant. He'd been a slave and now he meant to serve no man except himself. She admired him for his conviction. Reluctantly she drew her gaze from his handsome face and turned her attention to Carsie.

"Do you know what you want to do? I think that, like Mr. Freed, a person must have it clear in her mind what it is she wants or wants to do."

"I suppose," Carsie said, sipping thoughtfully. "Or have a friend look right at you and tell you what it is they believe you can do. Sometimes a friend can understand that better than yourself."

Hannah stared at Carsie for a long time. "Then you'll be going over to *The Montana Post* this morning to ask for work."

Carsie stared back. "What?"

"Of course," Libby said excitedly. "Hannah, you are so smart. Carsie would be perfect to work for a newspaper."

"I take it you're a writer," November said, leaning forward in interest.

"She certainly is," Hannah responded. "Pages and pages flow from her pen. She records events and feelings. I wish I could do that. I'm afraid I don't have . . ." Her thoughts trailed away.

"Now would you listen to her?" Carsie said with good-natured exasperation. "Only probably the most perfect head for business sits on my dear friend's strong shoulders."

"Oh?" November turned his full attention on Hannah.

She moved nervously under his scrutiny. "Business? I don't know what you mean."

"I don't see how you can forget," Carsie said. "She sold almost the entire inventory of . . . certain ladies' apparel at a mercantile back in Virginville, just by talking about it."

"Yes, you did do that." Libby turned toward Hannah. "Why, if it hadn't been for you, I never would have purchased such a garment, and neither would all of those other ladies." She turned back toward November. "She charmed us all into buying them."

"I'm not surprised by that one whit. And now I am intrigued," November said, smiling. "What was it you so cleverly sold?"

Hannah fidgeted. "Just some things they all wanted anyway but were too timid to say so."

"True, but you helped them know that's what they wanted. You should have seen her, Mr. Freed." Carsie leaned toward him in earnest. "Just by being mysterious about the merchandise, she had customers clamoring for it and turned the shop girl into a first-rate sales clerk. Well, it was just thrilling to watch."

"I certainly wish I had seen her," November said dreamily, never taking his eyes off Hannah's face. "I'm certain it was thrilling."

"You could do the same thing in Virginia City." Carsie spoke as if a brilliant idea had just formed in her head.

"Of course she could." Libby slapped her knee in enthusiasm.

"I have no doubt she could sell sand in the desert," November said, his gaze still resting on Hannah's face.

Hannah caught the way Carsie was studying them both, caught the hint of a knowing smile playing on her lips. Thankfully the shop door burst open and Harry bustled in carrying paper-wrapped bundles.

"Hot from the oven," he called out. "I waited for the cinnamon raisin buns to finish, knowing you ladies would like them." He set his bundles on a keg. "What exciting news have I missed while I was waiting in the bakery?"

"Well, Carsie's going to go over to *The Montana Post* and ask for a job as a newspaper writer," Libby told him excitedly.

"It's about time," Harry said.

"What?" Carsie looked at him, puzzled.

"Perfect place for you." Harry cut the strings on his bundles and spread open the paper. The scent of cinnamon and cloves wafted out and mingled with that of November's tea.

"They may not need another writer," Carsie countered. "And they probably wouldn't hire a woman anyway."

November nodded. "No harm in trying. Things have been changing fast. You best take Miss Hannah with you," he advised Carsie. "It sounds as if she could talk the publisher into hiring you right off."

"Oh, now—" Hannah started.

"And Hannah's going into her own business selling ladies undergarments," Libby told Harry.

"What?" Hannah let out a surprised breath.

"Ah," November let out slowly, nodding his head with understanding.

Hannah felt the heat of a blush rising from her throat to spread over her face.

"Absolutely brilliant." Harry lifted a cinnamon bun and placed it carefully in Libby's free hand. "I know the perfect place for you to set up shop."

"Where?"

"At the east end of the Center Ring building."

November stood. "Right. There is enough space for two shops in that section. I stored some supplies in there, but what isn't used I can haul away. There's plenty for shelving, and whatever else goes into a ladies' . . . things shop." Nervously he scraped the tea kettle over the stove top.

"And it's quite possible to provide rooms upstairs," Harry said deliberately. "Private living quarters for the proprietors, don't you think, November?"

"Absolutely. We could make it very bright with more windows to catch the morning sun. There's a perfect spot for a veranda, and—"

"Wait just a minute," Hannah interrupted, flaring. "You're all doing my thinking for me. I'm perfectly capable of making decisions that affect my life. And I haven't made any yet that I remember hearing."

"Quite right," Carsie agreed. She reached out and touched her friend's arm. "Your friends are simply excited for you, for whatever you decide, and we just want you to know we'll pitch right in and help—if you want us to, that is."

The others nodded, murmuring agreement.

Hannah softened. She was always on the defensive and she knew it. Old habits had served her purposes in the past. She reminded herself this was no longer the past. "I'm sorry. I do appreciate your help, and when I decide what I'm going to do, you will all be the first to know."

The five enjoyed the treats from the bakery. Hannah, Libby, and Carsie asked many questions of November about Virginia City. He obliged them with the best information he had, which was pretty accurate since a great number of customers in and out that morning seemed comfortable enough to linger to exchange news and gossip.

"Is Clint pleased with the turnout at the Center Ring these last few nights?" Libby asked Harry.

Carsie straightened her shoulders at the mention of his name.

"Indeed he is. I think he may have been celebrating a bit too much himself. He seems a little distracted lately."

November chuckled. "Didn't stop by like he always does. Guess he had something on his mind."

"And somewhere to go," Harry added.

Carsie wondered what they both meant. Was he thinking about the hours they'd spent together on the grand opening of the Center Ring? Or had he put them out of his thoughts? He avoided her whenever she was in his establishment. She didn't stay long. Just enough time to observe, to write her thoughts, to describe the people. And she'd caught him watching her on more than one occasion, frowning most of the time. She couldn't keep from watching him.

His reputation among the unmarried women of Virginia City was one of legendary conquests. She knew some of it was wishful thinking on the part of the gossipers. She'd seen him in the company of Miss Goodnight or Hannah or Libby, but knew they were not his conquests, even if other people thought so. *Friendship* was the word that came often to her mind. Still, she rarely saw him during the day.

One thing was for certain. She no longer believed Clint had anything to do with bride-selling or dealing in the trade of women for money. And even though the ladies' league had been pressing her to write another leaflet for distribution, she'd found herself drawn more to write about what was unfolding before her. Virginia City was growing with the speed of spring hay, about to become the new territorial capital. There was even talk of the railroad coming through. Excitement was high. She wrote about how women had adapted to horrendous conditions by drawing from their own inner strengths. She wrote about men and women carving new lives in the West, emotionalizing the whys of what they did to build and to survive.

This was not what she had set out to do. Finding Sophie and freeing women from bondage to men, those had been her noble quests. She would not stop her search for Sophie. She believed even more deeply in personal rights and freedom for all women. But she'd been growing into a new understanding of people, regardless of their sex. People building a new civilization, a new country. People just being people together.

She'd sent one packet of articles to an editor at *Harper's Weekly,* the same one she'd promised to send scathing articles about bride-selling to. She hadn't sent what she'd promised. She was quite certain the editor would not print them or anything else she might choose to send. That spelled doom for her idea of becoming a famous champion of women. She knew that.

"Clint does spend a lot of time there." November's voice broke into Carsie's musings. "I'm just getting to know him, but I never would have figured him that way."

Where? What way? Carsie's mind insisted on answers. Did it have anything to do with the dolls in his room? She fidgeted for a more comfortable seat on the keg, but succeeded only in pressing its rim more deeply into her bottom. She had just about gathered enough courage to ask when Harry rose and broke the conversation.

"Well, I must be off myself." Harry lifted Libby's hand. "My dear, shall I take you back to Phoebe's to gather little Harry?"

Libby held out her cup. Harry took it and set it on the stove. She rose. "Yes, I'm certain he's getting hungry by now. Thank you so much, Mr. Freed, for the lovely tea party. Now, don't forget, you will come to Thanksgiving dinner." She held out her right hand to him.

November took her hand and shook it, then lifted it to kiss the back of it. "I'm honored, Miss Allen. I do hope you'll come back whenever you wish to set a spell. And bring your son."

"Oh my," Libby breathed. "You are so gallant. Isn't he gallant, Hannah?"

"Definitely gallant," Hannah murmured.

November cast his warm eyes on her. Carsie was moved deeply. His gaze seemed to respectfully appreciate Hannah's beauty and presence. She'd never witnessed such silent honest appraisal from a man without a trace of guile or underlying motive. Not that she'd ever experienced such emotion from a man, but she knew in her heart November Freed had fallen totally in love with Hannah Holmes. He was showering her with his affection from afar. And her dear friend Hannah was having difficulty just being herself and accepting it. Carsie smiled. Ah, what a beautiful picture.

Hannah turned suddenly toward Carsie. "Shall I walk with you to the *Post?*"

"Oh, I don't know that I'll go there today. I'm just not certain—"

"Nonsense," Harry interrupted, "of course you will. You stay right here, Hannah, and discuss with November how your new shop can be arranged."

"My new shop . . ." Hannah's mouth dropped slightly.

"We'll escort Carsie to Mr. Dimsdale's office, won't we, Libby?"

"Certainly. I'll see you this evening, Hannah, and I can't wait to hear all about your plans. Oh, this is so exciting. Just think, only a few weeks ago we were all pushing our way through mud and rain and snow to get here without any idea what we would do when we arrived. And now look at us. We all have something wonderful to do, and we've made wonderful new friends. It's like a dream."

"It is that," Harry concurred. "Now come along, ladies, time is wasting and the day will be gone before we know it. Carsie?" He lifted her shawl around her shoulders as she gathered her coat collar closer to her throat. "We're off to the *Post*. I'll stop in later, November. Thanks for the hospitality."

He ushered Carsie and Libby out of the store. Carsie took a last look over her shoulder and saw the dazed look on Hannah's face as November's approving gaze beamed over her.

"Now, Harry, you and Libby don't have to take me by the hand to go to the newspaper office."

"I think we do. And we want to." Harry kept one hand on her elbow while carefully guiding Libby through snow over the damaged boardwalk. Past the Fairweather Hotel he directed her to the door of *The Montana Post*. "Now just gather all that Carson Summers courage and go in there and ask for employment. You can do it."

"Tell me all about it tonight," Libby said. "I'll be at the Center Ring. Clint has asked me to play piano. Isn't that nice of him?"

"Nice," Carsie said. "Where is Clint this morning?" she ventured, unable to hold back the question any longer.

Harry opened the door to the newspaper office. "Don't dally. It's cold out here. We'll see you later." He urged her inside and closed the door behind her.

"Yes?" A man's voice came from behind a mountain of an oak desk covered with another mountain of papers and books.

For a fleet moment Carsie realized Harry hadn't answered her, and she had a vague feeling it was on purpose.

"I—I'm looking for Mr. Dimsdale." Her voice seemed to have lost all semblance of strength.

"You got him." The English accent was muffled.

Timidly she edged closer to the mountain.

"Want to place an advertisement? Milliner? Boarding-house?"

"No, sir."

Silence. "What then? Speak up. I don't have all day."

Carsie took a deep breath to steel herself against his cantankerousness, and let her words out with it. "I've come about work."

Silence again. "Don't need a housekeeper. Try that new circus saloon place. Or Goodnight's Good Times Emporium." His voice took on a derisive edge. "No doubt they could both use a good cleaning."

Carsie bristled. "Mr. Dimsdale, if you don't mind, I'm quite used to having gentlemen come out of hiding when they speak to me."

"Well, I do mind. I'm a busy man with important work to do. The *Post* is the only newspaper in the territory. That's an important burden, you know."

"And I'm here to help ease your burden. I'm a—a reporter."

There was an exasperated sigh, the sound of a pencil being slammed down on a stack of papers, and then a rustling of those papers and the scraping of a chair across a wood floor. Carsie backed up as if an ogre were about to emerge from the forest. Instead, a short man in suspendered striped woolen trousers, a ruffled shirt, and a bow tie emerged from behind the pile. He surprised her. The only time she'd ever been in the newspaper office she'd dealt with a young press boy.

"Fancy yourself a reporter, did you say?" His thick mustache twitched and the skin on his high forehead pleated as he tried to sound imperious.

"Yes, sir."

He observed her, hat to boots, and let out a scoffing breath through his nostrils. "Have a husband, do you?"

"No, sir."

"Children?"

"No, sir."

"Why not?"

"Wh-why not?"

"Why not?" he underscored. "You're old enough." He squinted. "You're past old enough. A woman needs a man to take care of her. She shouldn't attempt to do it herself unless, of course, she's of a different . . . sort."

"Sort?" Carsie understood his meaning in the next flash of a moment. She squared her shoulders and took in a breath that brought a strengthening edge. "Mr. Dimsdale, not every woman is married or a mother. Not every woman expects to be or I daresay wants to be. If it's your opinion to lump those women into some kind of 'sort,' then that's your right, even if it's wrong. I prefer to engage in my own life, and take care of myself. To do that I need employment. I can assure you I'm not afraid of hard work. The *Post* would be well served to have me working here."

Dimsdale pursed his lips and frowned. He turned his back on her and lifted a sheet of paper from his desk. "Perhaps you'd like to read today's front-page feature." He handed it to her.

Carsie accepted the paper. Next to an article on a newly established orphanage, she read a rather terse piece. With every word her blood bubbled.

As sisters, mothers, nurses, friends, sweethearts, and wives, women are the salt of the earth, the anchor of society, and the humanizing and purifying element in humanity. As such they cannot be too much respected, loved, and protected.

A bit too flowery, she thought, and rather out of touch with real women. No wonder Mrs. Dimsdale was so active in the ladies league. She finished the piece, the heat in her blood escalating with every word.

There is no need for them to step outside the protective confines of the home to do their purifying. It is deplorable enough when the occasional bold-spirited female oversteps conventional bounds to indulge in her own peculiar whim. It is unthinkable for crusading women, riot-inciting reformers, to enter public life and make spectacles of themselves in their attempt to change society's minds and accept the chaos they propose.

From Blue Stockings, Bloomers, and strong-minded she-males generally, GOOD LORD, DELIVER US.

Carsie folded the paper in half and tapped it against her open palm. "Mr. Dimsdale, I find your back-handed praise, as I suspect you want to call it, of women to be reprehensible for a member of the reporting press. An editorial opinion would be one thing, but to pass off this diatribe as a feature story is an insult to the public."

"And your mode of dress has been an insult to the public," he retorted through thin lips.

"What?" She looked down at the layers of skirts and petticoats that made her feel heavy and plodding. They were necessary in this cold wet weather. She'd wished she could put on men's woolen trousers over her thick stockings and tuck the pantlegs into boots. That arrangement would have kept out the cold wind that constantly found its way under her skirts and sent her to shivering. But it no doubt would have been too scandalous a mode of dress, even in this isolated city.

"I will admit that today you are dressed as a woman ought to be, but your arrival in those awful bloomers did not go unnoticed." Dimsdale sniffed and lifted his pointed chin in an air of superiority.

Carsie suppressed the urge to grab that chin and yank it down. "We dressed as we could most comfortably for such an arduous journey," she said, as calmly as she could.

"May I point out the others were not wearing bloomers?"

Curious, Carsie thought. The arrival of Miss Goodnight and her ladies decked out in the finery that bespoke their profession did not cause the kind of stir she had in her plain brown coat and bloomers. Perhaps it was not so curious after all. Her hackles went up again. Even in a wide-open place like Virginia City, certain women stayed in the house, whether it belonged to their husbands or was a place for men to visit to engage in more exotic pleasures. In either case, men were in control of the circumstances of women. Perhaps she'd become too complacent in her writings, too caught up in the raw romance of the New West.

"I can see there can be no discussion of the topic with you. And I will not stand here and suffer your dissertation on how women must be treated as possessions of men."

"As you will."

"Do not bother to offer me a reporting position with the *Post* because I have withdrawn my application."

"I wouldn't think you'd have the time as it is, what with the other inflammatory material you've been writing."

Carsie tilted her head. "You've read it?"

Dimsdale colored. "I wouldn't read such drivel. I simply noticed some of it when it was being printed on my press."

"Ah yes, your press. I do want to thank you for so graciously offering to print our last—and future—leaflets."

"Don't get any ideas. Mrs. Dimsdale was in a fit of hysteria, and it was the only way I could calm her. Typical female mental problems, of course. My wife is getting older. And keeping her calm is not helped by the likes of you." Dimsdale lifted his chin and settled his jowls in his stiff collar.

Carsie arched her back. "And isn't that a typical male idea, that any fervor a woman might have that wasn't for him could only be attributed to the insanity of a female past childbearing age." She suddenly went ramrod straight. She'd never said such a thing in the presence of a man. What was happening to her?

Dimsdale's mouth dropped open. His face turned deep red and he clenched his fists in futility. He adjusted his visor and cleared his throat. "Good day," he croaked.

Carsie sucked in a sharp breath. "Not at all for you, and

I mean that sincerely." She slammed the folded newspaper down on top of the mountain on the editor's desk. As she stormed out of Dimsdale's office, she heard the distinct sound of a paper mountain dissolving in an avalanche.

"Of all the temerity . . ." she muttered.

Trudging through the snow and muddy water on what was left of the boardwalk helped to diffuse her anger. In the past she'd found that emotion good for spurring her into action. Today it kept her blood warm as well as thawed her mind enough to set a plan forming. She wasn't suited for much in the way of salaried employment, but she could write. And she'd sold her writing before.

She stopped and looked back over her shoulder for a moment, then turned and trudged on. Snowflakes fell softly. All right, so the only establishment in Virginia City where her particular talents could be put to use had turned her down. What could she do next? She passed the last of the storefronts, taverns, and boardinghouses as she trudged toward the end of town. Snow fell more heavily now, but it was beautiful and she didn't mind it on her eyelashes and woolen mittens.

Hannah. The thought of Hannah popped into her mind. She wanted more than to continue to work at the Good Times Emporium. Once the seed had been planted in her mind about the possibility of operating a shop and selling women's apparel, Carsie easily saw the spark of excited possibility flare on Hannah's face. Up to now, Hannah wouldn't have considered such a venture. But here in Montana the idea was not preposterous. If you couldn't find employment that used your talents, work that you wanted to do, then you could devise your own scheme and put yourself to work.

"Why not?" Carsie mused, picking her feet up as the snow grew deeper. "I could write my own newspaper. For women. Why not?"

Excitement grew inside her as visions of a masthead and

columns of her carefully crafted articles materialized. She would write the whole thing. It would come out weekly. She could see to its distribution. She could . . . not print it. She had no printing press. It would be a monumental task to hand write every single copy of every single issue. Her spirits sank.

Where the road split in two directions, one heading toward open land and stretching east to west and the other circling toward a new construction and heading back into town, Carsie stopped. Someone had painted a sign and propped it up with a pile of rocks. She brushed the snow away and read it.

Fairweather Hotel, center of Virginia City. Dining Room.

She stood for a long time as a new idea took shape in her mind. That was it! She could write her newspaper and post it once a week in a storefront so women could read it. In the meantime she'd have to find a way to make some money so that she could go into production, buy her own printing press, sell her papers to make more money so that she could distribute them widely.

A gust of wind came up and she shivered. It was a great idea, she could feel it. Action, that's what it took to get closer to a dream.

She turned to go back toward town. She'd come farther than she'd thought. She wrapped her shawl closer around her neck and took a step. The ground gave way beneath her foot and she fell headlong into the snow. Her boots filled with frigid water and mud. She kicked her way out and stood, feeling the cold water soak through her stockings and chill her feet instantly. She'd never make it back to the Center Ring without seriously damaging her feet. Snow fell with dizzying speed. She whirled around.

Ahead lay the new construction she'd seen in the distance on the circling road. At least it would be shelter from the wind and snow if she could get inside. She had to get her boots and stockings off. She headed toward the building with determination. As she got closer, she saw two horses tethered under a shed near a small wagon covered with canvas. Someone had to be inside. She shivered as much in apprehension as from the cold. What if the wrong kind of people were inside? But what were her choices? Take a chance that the people inside were good, or freeze to death?

She pushed through the snow to the door, removed a mitten, and knocked.

No one came. She could hear the muffled sounds of voices inside, and then a spate of children's laughter. She relaxed. Children. The people inside couldn't be all bad. Shuddering in the cold, she knocked again. No one came. Probably they couldn't hear her.

She tried the latch. It was open. She lifted it and pushed on the door, knocking as she did so. She entered what appeared to be a small anteroom where boots were lined along the far wall and heavy coats hung on pegs. There was another door, beyond which she could hear a man's voice. It sounded as if he was reading aloud. Carefully she lifted the latch on that door and pushed it open. The aroma of simmering soup or stew floated out.

There was another spate of children's laughter. "Hello," she called and pushed the door wide open, stepping into the room.

No one could have prepared her for the scene in front of her. She lost all sense of freezing feet and numbing fingers.

There on the floor near a wood stove, a group of children sat cross-legged staring in rapt attention, their eyes fixed on the adult perched on a stool holding an open book.

Clint Bonner.

Seventeen

"Who's that?" A little boy's rasp cut through the soothing tone of Clint's reading voice.

"Hm?" Clint drew his concentration from the book.

"Right there. Who's that?" The boy pointed toward the door.

Clint followed the ragged-sleeved arm until his gaze fell on Carsie. She didn't move. The scene before her astonished her so completely that she could neither speak nor leave nor enter the room. Clint's face suddenly changed from the relaxed youthfulness she'd seen at first sight to the furrowed-brow concern of one who'd been caught in the act of doing something he'd hoped no one would ever discover.

"Who's that?" the boy insisted. "That your wife?"

Clint swallowed then and coughed. "Ah, no, this lady isn't my wife. She's . . . she's a friend."

"Your girlfriend?" a little girl's voice piped up.

"No." Clint said that fast.

A door at the back of the room kicked open then. "Soup's on!" Harry pushed in carrying a steaming tureen. He spotted Carsie. "Oh-oh." His eyes shifted to Clint before he labored over to the long table and set the hot tureen in the middle of it.

"Here's the bread!" Libby came into the room then, carrying a wooden tray heaped with bread and biscuits. Immediately she must have sensed the tense difference in the room for she stopped and the smile on her face froze. "What's the matter? Is everyone all right?"

Harry brushed his hands together then took the tray from Libby. "Everything is just fine. Carsie's come to visit."

Libby's face relaxed then and broke into a warm smile. "Carsie, oh how wonderful! I'm so pleased you came. What do you think? Isn't this place wonderful? Aren't the children wonderful?"

Carsie hugged herself against the shivers that had nothing to do with the cold. Her hands tingled as they warmed. She managed to close her mouth long enough to greet Libby. "Wonderful. Yes. Wonderful. Where did you get them?"

Libby laughed. "You mean the children? They're Clint's."

Carsie's jaw fell open again. Clint's children? So he wasn't *one of those,* as Miss Phoebe had assured her. This might explain the presence of dolls and other toys in his room. But what was he then? There must be at least eight or nine children in the room.

"Libby, now just a minute." Clint closed the book and stood. "They're not exactly my children . . ."

"Who . . . whose children are they then? Who are their parents?" Carsie forced out.

"They're Clint's," Harry said. "Aren't you, boys and girls?"

A chorus of youthful voices rose up in a cheer. One little girl crept over to Clint and wrapped her arms around his leg.

"Yes, they are," Clint said with quiet warmth, and he knew he meant it.

He looked down at the wide-eyed waif staring up at him with genuine love in her eyes and wrapped his arm around her thin shoulders. She and the other children were filling one of the empty places in his heart. They'd helped ease the hollowness he'd felt until Harry had brought him to this broken-down hovel where seven orphaned children were trying to hold life and limb together. Leave it to Harry to get him involved with lost humanity.

Harry had known what would happen when Clint saw those children. Clint had lived in such an arrangement himself once upon a time. And Harry had forgotten all about making his fortune in the gold fields; he'd traded it all for a blind girl, a baby boy, and seven lost children. The sight and knowledge of it sent Clint into his own hidden desires and he'd spent the last few days in a constant state of confusion and wonder.

He finally had what he wanted, a saloon of his own in a place he could settle down. Then why had something seemed missing? And why had it seemed even more was missing the morning after he and Carsie had made love? He didn't go back to the Good Times after that, and his physical prowess with women no longer seemed important to him. What in hell was the matter with him? Everybody who came in on the wagon train with him had something they wanted. Some of them had *somebody*. Maybe that was it. Or maybe it was just that he was weary from all the travel and now with the long days spent in the Center Ring.

And the discomfort he felt watching Carsie appear in his place every night, watching her pencil move over stacks of paper, recording, no doubt, every moment of what she was most likely describing as debauchery and female enslavement perpetuated by him and his establishment. She and her lunatic ladies society had distributed pamphlets attesting to just that. He'd thought she'd abandoned all that, but no, there she was publishing her crazy ideas. What she didn't know was that those pamphlets were the subject of ridicule and their distribution only made his business boom all the more. He felt kind of sorry for that.

He was glad she hadn't known about this place where the children lived. If she wrote about this, his reputation would be ruined as a lover of the ladies and owner of the best and busiest saloon in town. It was all Harry's fault.

He'd suckered Clint into this place with one sickly little girl with eyes like a scared rabbit's.

He'd started out by giving Harry money to build this new place and to provide food and clothing for the children. Now he was spending more than money. He was spending time with the children. *Time.* Hardly befitting the Clint Bonner he thought he'd known.

Carsie's gaze locked with Clint's. He saw a whirl of questions in her eyes. He owed her nothing in the way of explanation. Then why did he feel he wanted to explain something to her about his presence in this little orphanage? It wasn't that he wished to excuse his actions. It wasn't that he felt apologetic.

He wanted her to understand something about him, believe that the last thing he would ever do is trade something so low as money for human life of any kind. Money was a tool for him, a tool for doing what he wanted to do in his life. And it was also to use to help others when he could.

He found no words to express that to her.

He scooped up the little girl in his arms and with a wide grin walked toward Carsie. "This is Lily. Say hello to Carsie."

"Hello, Carsie," the child said shyly, then buried her face in Clint's neck.

Carsie swallowed a knot in her throat. "Hello, Lily." She rubbed the child's back.

Clint stared at her for a long moment. "The children had nobody," he said quietly at last, "and now they've got us."

She didn't move. The simple words drifted in the air between them.

"Come have supper with us, Carsie," Libby invited. "Georgie, bring the stool from the kitchen. We'll use it for an extra chair."

A little boy with scrubbed cheeks and slicked-down hair

banged through the kitchen door. He rumbled back through it toting a stool that was bigger than he was.

"Georgie never walks," Libby said, shaking her head. "Has to run wherever he goes."

"Makes him sleep better," Harry said. "Okay, everyone, are your hands clean?" At a chorus of yesses, Harry motioned for them all to sit down.

The children plopped in chairs all around the long table and immediately grasped hands. Clint offered Carsie a chair and took the stool at the end of the table. He looked huge perched up so high, like a great fatherly presence in the room. Lily took Carsie's hand on one side. When Carsie didn't lift her other hand, Lily let go and picked it up and put it in Clint's hand. Carsie felt heat rise up her throat and warm her face. She followed suit as the children, Harry, Libby, and Clint closed their eyes and bowed their heads.

She was shaken momentarily when Clint spoke.

"Thank you, Father, for bringing us all together," he said thickly, "and for this fine feast. Am——"

"Wait," Lily interrupted. "You forgot to put Carsie in."

"Oh, sorry." Clint bowed his head again. "And thank you for bringing Carsie to our table tonight." He waited.

Lily opened one eye. "Yep." She closed it.

"Amen," Clint said.

"Amen," came the chorus in unison.

Harry dished up the soup and Clint sliced bread and sent it around. The children chattered, all trying to tell Carsie at once about how Harry had found them and how Clint had helped Mr. Freed fix up their house, and how Libby brought a baby to them and cooked for them.

"And look," Georgie said, lifting his woolen shirtfront. "Clint sewed my shirt all back together just like brand new after it got all ripped up."

A slow ripple of amusement flowed through Carsie. A smile played at the corners of her mouth. She set down her spoon. "Really? Clint sewed your shirt?"

"Yep." Georgie nodded vigorously.

"And he made a coat for my dolly," a little girl with blond curls said without looking up. "She was cold."

"A doll's coat." She sent a curious look toward Clint. His return was quick and then focused on the soup. "I'd certainly like to see that."

"I'll show it to you." The little girl started to jump down from her chair.

"After supper," Libby reminded her.

"After supper," the girl said, settling back in her chair.

"Will wonders never cease?" Carsie said to no one in particular.

"You don't know the half of it," Harry responded.

"Do tell," Carsie rejoined.

"Don't bother," Clint put in, making it obvious he was changing the subject. "I think you'd rather like to know that I've located your friend Sophie."

Carsie snapped her head up. "Where? Where did you find her?"

"She and her man have a claim across the creek."

"A claim? You mean gold?"

"I mean gold."

"Oh my, Sophie's all right, then." Carsie suddenly wanted everything to be perfect, for her whole idea of Sophie allowing herself to be sold as a bride to an unsavory sort to be refuted. She longed to be wrong, as if it would somehow absolve all the terrible things she'd thought about Clint. "She must be living like the queen she always dreamed about," she rushed on. "I hope she won't mind a visit from me. I know I said I'd search for her until I could rescue her from what I believed would most certainly be a fate worse than death in the hands of a filthy miner with nothing on his mind but taking her whenever the whim struck him. But gold! I know now that she's made a fine choice and has made a success of it and is very happy." She paused, breathless.

"If I could stick a word in sideways in this conversation, such as it is," Clint said quickly, "there's something I think you should know."

"I'm sorry. I'm just so excited . . ." She saw the serious look on his face. "What?" She frowned.

"Sophie and her man have a gold claim, that's for certain. But I don't think they've managed to pan more than a teaspoon of color out of it. And I'd be careful going out there, if I were you. Cal Thornton's kind of a rough one."

All of Carsie's hope crumbled. She was sorrier than she could imagine. And not just for Sophie. "She needs me," she said absently. "I shall go there first thing in the morning and save her from what I knew would be her end if she went with those bride-sellers. I was right all along."

Clint sighed. "Have it your way. It's not my business." Carsie raised weary eyes and fixed her gaze on his face. "I meant that it was none of my business to poke my nose into the lives of other people."

"What you mean is you think I shouldn't either, am I right?"

"Now, don't go getting up on your high horse again and . . ." Clint suddenly noticed the silence around the table as seven pairs of wide eyes were fixed on him. He took a deep breath and let it out slowly. "What I meant was, I know you've been worried about your friend. But sometimes it's just better to . . . leave well enough alone, if you know what I mean."

Carsie wasn't sure she did know what he meant, but if he thought she could just blithely ignore the fact that Sophie had been located and she wouldn't go to see her and get her out of a bad situation if need be, then he was mistaken. She could no more do that than . . . well, she didn't know what, only that she couldn't do it.

"Don't worry," she said instead of everything else that rushed to her lips. "I won't cause her any trouble."

"We're going to have Thanksgiving dinner right here in

this room," Libby put in with a larger than ever air of lightness. "Will you join us, Carsie? Say you will."

"Yay!" came the children's voices, all begging her at once.

Carsie watched Clint, who vigorously scraped his soup plate. "Well, with that kind of warm invitation, how can I not join you? I would love to be here, but only if you let me help."

"All able hands welcome," Harry told her. "Especially with the dishes. Look at these hands. Shriveled up like prunes."

"Just like Clint," a little boy named James said. "He says he's wrinkled to the elbows from all the baths."

Clint colored. "And don't go thinking you can get out of yours tonight just to save my elbows from puckering."

"Aw, Clint."

"Aw, James."

Carsie smiled. She felt suddenly the way a moth might feel all warm and cozy in a cocoon, safely protected from the outside world.

"Let Carsie give us baths tonight," Lily said.

"Un-unh," Georgie said. "I'm not letting any girl give me a bath."

"Well, then," Libby said, rising. "Let Carsie bathe the girls and Clint bathe the boys." She picked up two bowls and started in the direction of the kitchen. Harry rose to guide her.

"Good idea. I'm very good at baths," Carsie said, smiling.

"Having had special practice and instruction out on an empty prairie," Clint said through tight lips, suppressing a grin.

"What?" Carsie's face burned.

"Oh yeah, remember that night?" Harry went around the table gathering up spoons and plates.

"Vividly," Clint said with a chuckle. "You remember it, don't you, Carsie?"

She stood up. "Barely."

Clint stood up. "Exactly."

Carsie stared at him, willing him to be quiet. "Lead me to the towels." Lily took her hand and fairly dragged her to a room in the back.

Twenty minutes later Carsie and Clint were side by side on their knees next to two large wooden tubs, sleeves rolled up above their elbows, damp hair falling in their faces, their clothes soaked through from splashing children in the throes of being bathed.

"Bet you never thought you'd be doing this tonight," Clint observed over his shoulder. He lunged for a bar of soap that had sailed out of the clutches of a little fist and skidded across the floor.

"And you'd win that bet." Carsie giggled as Lily lifted a cloud of soap bubbles and blew them into the air. They floated down like tiny iridescent Christmas balls. "And I bet you'd figure out how surprised I am about . . . all of this."

"And I bet you mean about my part in it, don't you?" He waited. She didn't answer. "And I'd win that bet."

She lifted Lily out of the tub and wrapped the wriggling child in a towel. "Yes, you would."

Keeping his back to Carsie and Lily, Clint lifted Georgie out of the tub, carefully protecting both children's nudity even though Georgie was most interested in Lily's. Clint was obliged to shift his shoulders one way and then the other to block the boy's curious eyes. No more bathing in the same room at the same time. The children were suddenly too old for that.

"I'm not what you think I am." Clint rose with a groan and packed Georgie through the curtains to the waiting Harry on the other side.

Carsie hefted Lily and took her to Libby. She turned back

and started to mop up the water. "What do you think I think you are?"

Clint worked with Carsie in tandem, mopping, dumping, hanging up towels as he pondered her question. "A flesh peddler."

"That seems a bit harsh, doesn't it?"

"Don't you? Didn't you think that?"

Carsie busied herself straightening towels so she wouldn't have to face him. "I confess I did . . . think those thoughts . . . in the beginning. But I don't think them anymore."

"Oh? What changed your mind?" He leaned his mop against the wall and started slowly toward her.

"Well, nothing in particular, I guess." She rolled her sleeves down carefully, keeping her eyes fixed on the task.

"What in general, then?" He was getting closer.

She felt the warmth of him as he drew near. "Oh, I don't know. I really haven't thought that much about it."

"I don't believe you."

She snapped her head up then. "What?"

"I said I don't believe you haven't thought much about it. I think you think much about everything. I think your mind moves as fast as your pencil, recording everything your eyes see and your heart feels."

He stood so close to her she was obliged to tip her head back to see into his face. He was doing it deliberately, intimidating her, and he took a certain pleasure in seeing her squirm, seeing her formidable exterior crumble just a bit. He reached to lift a long damp tendril of hair away from her cheek.

Carsie took in a shaky breath. "You . . . you don't know anything about my pencil, ah, recording my thoughts."

"Oh but I do. And I know how your heart feels."

"No . . ."

"Yes. And I certainly know how your body moves." He

flattened his hands against the wall on either side of her, successfully pinning her between his body and the wall.

"That was not gentlemanly of you."

"Nor was it ladylike of you. But we both enjoyed it, didn't we?"

"I mean what you said, not . . ." She swallowed. "Enjoyed . . . ?" Her voice squeaked.

"Yes, enjoyed," he whispered huskily. "I enjoyed making love to you, enjoyed the way your body responded to me."

"Oh." She sucked in a small breath and shivered.

"And you enjoyed it, too, didn't you?"

"I . . . that is, a woman doesn't . . ."

"A real woman does. And you are a real woman, Carsie, through and through. Admit it. You enjoyed making love with me. You enjoyed my body, enjoyed what your hands found out about me, as much as you enjoyed what my hands learned about you."

"Oh, but—"

"Admit it." He brought his mouth down to touch hers tenderly.

She let out a little shudder. Her knees buckled.

"Admit it," he commanded, kissing her more firmly.

Her eyelids fell heavily.

He took her shoulders in his hands. "Admit it, Carsie. Tell me."

She shuddered again. "Yes," came a feeble whisper.

He kissed her deeply then drew his mouth away. "I couldn't hear you."

"Yes," she said a little more loudly.

He kissed her sensuously, lingeringly. "Yes what?"

"Don't make me . . ." Her voice sounded pained.

"I will make you say it. Tell me. Tell me how much you enjoyed making love with me. Tell me, Carsie."

She shifted her eyes toward the curtained doorway. "Please don't," she whispered. "The children. Harry . . . Libby . . ."

He ran his lips along her throat and stopped at her ear. "They can't hear us. Harry and Libby are putting the children to bed. That's always a drawn-out event, what with the reading and prayers and scramble of whose nightshirt is whose. Nobody can hear you. So tell me. Tell me how much you enjoyed making love with me. Tell me how much you enjoyed this." He slid his hands firmly over her back, her waist, her hips, then cupped her buttocks and held her firmly, pressing himself against her thighs.

She moaned and dropped her head to his chest. "Clint, please don't . . . we shouldn't. That is, I shouldn't—"

"Yes, you should. Especially if you like it and want it. And you do want this, don't you?" He slid his hands up along her ribs and cupped her breasts, squeezing gently.

She pulled back, but he didn't let go. She pressed back into his hands and slid hers up his arms, along his shoulders and neck until she held his face. "Yes." The whisper was throaty. Giving another moan, she pulled his head down and kissed him deeply.

He crushed her to him and lost all sense of control, sweeping her emotions along with him. In the next few moments there was a flurry of clothing and boots and hands and kisses until they stood with her back pressed against the wall, her legs wrapped around his waist. Their lips clung, their tongues probed as he plunged deep inside her and held her heat around him. He lifted her away from the wall with his hands supporting her below her hips.

The exquisite tension of mutual desire held them both on the brink of a summit beyond which lay the open space of unknown emotion, untapped depths, frightening consequences. When they could take no more, they both gave in to the engulfing tide. She gave a little cry and released expression to every ounce of need she'd held back with her own incredible strength. In that moment of surrender her mind raced wildly. As she soared and then started her gradual descent, he rose to a shattering peak and stayed in the moments bringing her back up with him.

They clung in the shivering heat of their bodies against the crisp air in the room.

"I'd better get you covered before you freeze to death," he whispered huskily.

Shyly she dropped her head into the hollow of his neck. "I feel like I'm on fire."

"You'll be red as fire if Harry and Libby come back and find us like this."

She stiffened. *Harry and Libby. For a few blinding moments she'd forgotten they existed and where she was.*

He stepped back to retrieve her clothes. She stood leaning against the wall covering herself with her arms and hands. What an absurd thing to do, it suddenly occurred to her. She had just bared her soul and everything else to this man. And she'd done it in the bathing room of an orphanage with other people in another part of the house. And here she was trying to shield her nudity from his eyes. There was no understanding human thoughts.

She watched Clint in his nakedness picking up pieces of clothing they'd thrown in all directions in their haste to revel in one another's bodies. He was beautiful. The notion skittered along her nerves. The lamplight played among the curves and hollows of his waist and hips, and illuminated his long muscular legs. It deepened the golden color of his skin stretched over the muscles of his shoulders and arms, and brought out shining strands in his dark hair. He was a beautiful man—that's all there was to say about it. And she was wildly attracted to him, wanted him even now that they'd only moments before broken the seal of their bodies.

And Carsie understood those human thoughts completely.

They dressed in silence, hurrying while the numbness in their fingers returned as the heat dropped in the room. From the other room they could hear Harry and Libby descending the stairs, finished with the long session of putting the children to bed. Their voices neared the bathing room. Carsie grabbed a mop and hastened to the job of cleaning up. It was the only way to hide what she was certain was the flush of elation on her face.

"Would you two like some hot cocoa?" Harry came into the room. "What a mess."

Clint laughed. "It's pretty obvious, my friend, why you always make me give them baths."

A smile played over Harry's face as he paused a long moment. "Right. Funny, I never would have thought of giving children's baths in my bare feet in the middle of November. Interesting." He turned and left the room, a low chuckle coming from his throat.

Carsie blanched and looked down. She was indeed barefoot and hadn't even noticed. She looked over at Clint, who was also studying his feet. He lifted his head and looked at her. A rich laugh trickled out of him.

"This is not funny!" she rasped. "He knows . . . what we . . . he knows that—"

"We haven't been mopping the entire time?" Clint laughed again. "I'll bet you're right again."

"I'm mortified." She grabbed a towel and began to vigorously dry her feet.

"I wouldn't worry. Harry knows what naked women's feet look like." He paused, thinking. "That didn't come out right. I mean he knows what women's naked feet look like. Nothing to be embarrassed about."

"I'm mortified," she said again.

"Well, thanks a lot. Here I thought I'd given you something to remember me by, and all you can say is you're mortified."

She dropped down on a stool and grabbed her stocking. "You did . . . that is, I'll remember . . . I mean, I'm mortified that Harry knows what we—"

"I'm sure he's very happy for both of us."

"Oh! You are exasperating. How can I ever face them?

And you, you just stand there grinning like it's perfectly fine that other people know we've just—"

"Everybody knows people do this all the time. Just ask Phoebe." He laughed again.

She burned and wouldn't look at him. "We didn't do what they do at Phoebe's place."

He didn't say anything for a long time, just watched her pulling on thick stockings and her boots. "You're right." He walked to her and dropped down in front of her. "We made love. And I'm glad of it, proud of it. I wish you could be, too."

She stopped fussing with her boots and raised her eyes to his face. There was something in his eyes she hadn't seen before. What was it? Ardor? That was a word she'd read in a novel. Ardor. Could this be what it looked like?

"I am," she whispered. "I suppose in polite society that is a terrible admission. But I am glad."

"There was nothing polite in this. We are two people who wanted each other desperately, and we gave in to the moment. And it is made more exquisite by the knowledge that we are both happy about it."

A rustling came at the curtain. "Hey, cocoa's ready! You coming out here?" Harry stuck his head between the curtain panels. "Libby's getting tired. There's something we want to talk over with you. Come out before she goes to bed."

Clint rose. "Be right there." He took Carsie's hand and drew her to her feet. "You all right?"

She studied him for a long moment. She was not all right. She was moved beyond any emotion she'd ever felt. Moved by her feelings and moved by his action.

"Yes, of course," she whispered, and started to follow him out. Just before they reached the curtain, she touched his arm and stopped him. "Are you all right?"

Her question stopped Clint from more than just walking out of the room. His mind snapped to a brief moment of clarity before descending into a vortex of confusion. No, he was not all right. He was thunderstruck. He turned and saw in her guileless gaze a new depth in which his image was reflected. And he saw it clearly. He was in love with Miss Carson Rose Summers, suffragist from St. Joseph. He was in love with Carsie, a woman who'd insinuated herself under his skin and into his heart with her own brand of womanliness. He was definitely in love. And he was definitely not all right.

"Yes," he whispered. "I'm always all right, aren't I?"

She nodded and preceded him through the curtain.

"I guess the children made their usual bathing mess, didn't they?" Libby said when she heard them come into the room. "I'm sorry you received your baptism so soon, Carsie." She laughed lightly.

"I didn't mind at all," Carsie said, working to regain her composure. "The children are wonderful. How could anyone leave them behind?"

"I'll never understand that." Libby cradled little Harry in her arms.

"Some people find it easy." Clint dropped onto a stool in front of the fire.

Carsie watched him, knowing he was thinking of his own childhood at that moment. And she thought of her own and her heart ached for them both. "I'm still in a state of shock, over finding all of you here, I mean."

"Not as shocked as Clint was when he found himself right in the middle of it." Harry slapped his friend on the shoulder.

"You got that right," Clint responded. "Although, why I should be shocked at anything you sucker me into is beyond me."

"As if I've ever done that to you."

"Look how innocent he can act. And an act it is, my friends. He has put me in every kind of awkward position he possibly could since the moment I met him. How about the time you found that woman in Chicago and—"

"I don't think we'll talk about that now," Harry interrupted, his gaze darting to Libby's face. "Old news. We have great new news." He went to Libby's side. "My darling girl and I have an announcement."

Libby beamed with love. "Harry and I are getting married in June."

"Oh," Carsie breathed, "how wonderful. I'm so happy for you both."

"Married!" Clint rose quickly. "Wait a minute, old man. Didn't you and Jake and me always say we wouldn't weight ourselves down with the sandbags of marriage? Now why are you going to go and break up our act?"

"Sandbags? Clint Bonner, now I won't have you speaking that way in front of little Harry." Libby gave him a good-natured reprimand.

Carsie watched the three of them. They truly were connected to one another. She could see that clearly.

"Never thought it would happen to me," Harry said seriously. "That's why it was easy to make that pact. I never figured any woman as totally perfect as Libby would ever fall for a sawed-off jaded circus rat like me."

"Harry, dear," Libby said gently, "I won't have you talking like that in front of little Harry either."

"I'm sorry, love." Harry patted the sleeping baby's head. "This lovely lady came along and pulled the net out from under me and I landed like a sack of flour in the sawdust. When I came to, I was madly in love for the first time in my life."

"Now isn't that sickening?" Clint said with a twinkle in his eye. "I suppose we'll have to accept this marriage, won't we? I mean, this sounds incurable."

"Absolutely." Carsie joined in the bantering. "I mean, you know how I feel about marriage. But if my dear friend feels she must do it, I will support her completely."

"That's what we had in mind," Libby said. "Will you be my maid of honor, Carsie?"

Carsie sucked in her breath and tears flooded her eyes. "Oh, my, Libby. I've never been a maid of honor before. I'd be honored." She hugged Libby and the baby.

"And why I'm even going to say this, stuns me," Harry said, clamping a hand on Clint's shoulder, "but I want you and Jake to be my maids of honor, too."

Clint shook his head in wonder. "I've never been a maid of honor before, either."

"You mean best men, don't you?" Carsie's question was serious.

Harry laughed. "That's up for argument!"

The Journal of Carson Rose Summers

18 November 1866
Harry and Libby are to be married in the spring. I'm to be her maid of honor. I truly am honored by her invitation. They belong together. They are in love, of that there is no doubt. But they are considerate of each other, respect each other. I've never witnessed such a couple. I wonder if they have the private passion that I have learned is vital to feeling alive.

What made me construct myself the way I am? I know the answer. Protection of my life and limb. To be the warrior for other women. I do not regret that for a moment.

Yet why does it seem in opposition to be that warrior and still be the womanly person I feel whenever I am with Clint in an intimate way? I burn with the thought. I give over everything to him in those moments of passion. The passion knows no bounds because—because of love. I *love* him. Can't that passion be a different manifestation of the other passions of what is justice? Why must they be so opposed? Can't a woman be free, be her own self, and still be connected to a man? Must men and women be on opposite sides always—unless the women surrender completely? I don't think Harry believes he owns Libby. But they are clearly connected, one to the other, and each cannot live the life they want without the other. That seems to me to be the most wonderful situation.

Tomorrow I shall go to find Sophie. I have to see for myself how she is, if she needs me.

Eighteen

"Here we are." Clint's breath made white puffs of frosted mist. He dismounted and tied the reins to a broken hitching rail.

"Here we are where?" Atop a horse borrowed from November Freed, Carsie sat huddled under a long woolen shawl that had served as a blanket in another life.

"This is where your friend Sophie lives."

"Here? In *this?*" Carsie glanced around, her eyes watering from the biting cold. Through the frigid fog of a Montana winter morning loomed a ramshackle dwelling, if one could call such a structure a dwelling. She wondered what, if anything, stopped wind and snow from blowing through it.

Clint went to her side to help her down. She was so bundled and so cold and stiff she could barely move. The horse stomped and blew out twin columns of frosted breath. Clint reached up and she leaned into his arms gratefully and slid down into the snow. He held her steady and she absorbed the warmth he emanated. In a brief moment that filled her with yet another wave of acute feelings, everything about being engulfed in Clint's arms, imbued with the heat of his body and very essence, felt so very natural, so very right.

A low laugh bubbled from deep inside Clint.

"Just what is so funny?" she chattered.

"You, of course." He pulled the blanket closer around her shoulders and tucked it against her neck.

"I don't think freezing to death on the back of a horse in the middle of nowhere is at all amusing."

Clint laughed more. "You couldn't possibly freeze to death in that getup. The cold couldn't penetrate that pile of wool. You look like Georgie. Sometimes he puts on so many clothes he can't walk. And then he always has to . . . relieve himself the moment he puts the last piece on." He peered into her face. "You don't have to do that, do you?" He didn't even try to stifle a chuckle.

Carsie stared at him, her mouth clamped tightly shut. Her eyes watered.

"Ha!" The laugh burst out of him. "Just like Georgie. It'll take you an hour just to get out of those things, and we don't have all day."

"Just stop talking about it," Carsie gritted out.

Clint chuckled. "All right."

"And for heaven's sake, stop laughing!"

"You really are grumpy in the morning, aren't you? If I'd known that, I'd have sent Jake out here with you. He's pretty miserable himself until he gets a cup of that mud he brews into him. He—"

"Will you please be quiet?" Carsie trudged forward to the building. The snow was knee high and it took great effort to push through each step.

Clint trudged behind her. "You know, if I'd known you were going to treat me so impolitely," he chided, "I never would have come out here with you. I have my own work to do, you know. Least you could do is act civil."

She stopped and turned around with great effort. "You didn't have to come out here with me. I didn't beg you to come."

"Oh, and I suppose you think you could have found this place without me."

She twisted her head around. "I . . . I would have. I had directions."

"Did you now? Were they the ones that directed you to turn left at the snow-covered mound? Those directions? Who'd you get those from?"

"The man at the freight office gave them to me. He ought to know . . ."

"Are you going to tell me you didn't notice *everything* is a snow-covered mound? Everything is nothing but white with a few gray stumps sticking up?"

Carsie sent a darting glance around them. "I'd have managed."

"Can't give in, can you? Can't admit you're wrong for anything, can you? Can't admit you need help when you need it, either. You are the stubbornest woman I've ever met in my life, and—"

"Can we stop arguing out here? I don't want to stand here and listen to insults from you when I'm freezing to death." She turned back and headed for the building once again.

"Will you listen to them any better when we're standing next to a stove?"

Carsie turned back to him and let out a small growl of surrender. Clint let out a laugh that resounded around them. She couldn't help but smile.

Snowflakes fell silently between them and seemed to softly blanket their words. They stood, their gazes locked. Snowflakes attached themselves to her eyelashes. Clint reached out and took hold of her shoulders. He leaned down and licked the snowflakes away from her lashes.

She blinked in surprise but did not back away. "What . . . what did you do that for?"

"I wanted to taste snow that had touched you first."

His response surprised them both.

She shivered. "Was it . . . was it what you expected?"

He held his gaze steady. "I had no expectations. I just

enjoyed." His gaze fell to her mouth. He pulled her close, his arms enveloping her, and captured her lips with his own.

Carsie felt the breath in her lungs press out of her, felt herself melting into him, becoming a part of his phenomenal warmth. She slipped her hands up along his arms and shoulders until her arms crossed behind his neck. She felt right and natural standing in the haven of his arms, absorbing the warmth of him, gladly receiving his kiss and joyfully giving back. There was no pretense, and there was no question in her mind. At that moment everything faded away in the sheer completeness of the kiss.

Slowly he disengaged his lips from hers. She felt his chest rise and fall against hers. He was breathing hard. The thought stirred her. Their kiss had affected him as much as it had her. She knew it. She opened her eyes and found his open and staring down at her.

"And that?" she prompted in a whisper, surprised by her own boldness.

He swallowed. "Met all my expectations." His voice was husky.

She shivered and wrapped her arms more closely around his neck.

"Come on," he said, a small frown pleating between his eyes, "before I . . . we get carried away. We'd better see if anyone's home. You're getting cold."

"I'm not cold now," she said quietly, holding her gaze steady on his face.

He didn't, couldn't move while snowflakes floated around them. A sense of being suspended in time drifted around them with the snow. "I never knew snow could be so beautiful."

She said nothing. It was best he comprehend his new feelings in order to change those from the past. He gently took her arm and they pushed through the snow toward the house.

They stepped up onto the weak porch. At the door, Clint rapped loudly. All was silent. He banged harder.

"State your business." The harsh voice came from behind them.

Carsie jumped and turned around to face a leveled shotgun in the hands of a thin bearded man.

"Morning, Cal," Clint said slowly, and stepped off the porch.

"Talk." The bearded man punctuated his word with a jab of the shotgun into the air between them.

"I've brought a lady to visit your woman. Friend of hers from back East."

Carsie bristled and stepped off the porch to stand at Clint's side. "His woman. Just as I thought. She's nothing but his prisoner. She's—"

"Clamp it," Thornton commanded, pointing the gun at her. "Can't stand a woman goes on all the constant time."

Carsie jumped, then went still.

"Well, now," Clint chided, "would you look at that? Shut her up tighter than a spinster's—"

Carsie elbowed him, never taking her eyes off Cal Thornton and his shotgun.

"We don't take kindly to visitors, 'specially from the East." Thornton stood his ground, but Clint saw him shiver from the cold. He wore a thick threadbare coat and canvas trousers.

"Doesn't surprise me," Carsie let out from between tight lips.

"Will you let me handle this for once without your editorials?" Clint wrapped his arm around her shoulders and gave Thornton his direct address. "The lady here has taken sick."

"Don't sound sick to me," Thornton said. "Just loose at the mouth."

"That's only one of the things that ails her," Clint said, squeezing her face into his shoulder to keep her from spewing some epithet or other. "She was a good friend to Sophie. She just wants to say hello, be neighborly. We won't stay long. Won't disturb you. She just wants to know her friend's all right before, well . . . she hasn't much time left."

"What?" Carsie's voice was muffled in Clint's coat.

He squeezed her hard and muttered. "If you don't go along with this, neither of us is going to have much time left. You have noticed the shotgun in his cold hands, haven't you? One shiver and we're goners."

She nodded stiffly.

The creak of unyielding cold wood came from behind them. "Cal?" came a woman's voice.

Sophie! Carsie broke from Clint's grip. She turned toward the sound and saw a woman's face and a piece of clothing in the crack of the door.

"Sophie?" she breathed into the frigid air. "Sophie, it's me, Carsie. Are you all right?"

"Get back in there, woman, 'fore you freeze the place down," Cal called.

Carsie inched toward the door. "Sophie," she said gently. "It's Carsie."

"Carsie?" The door opened wide and the woman stepped out. "Carsie? Oh, my stars, how did you ever find me?"

"Shut the door, woman!" Cal started forward, the shotgun wobbling in his cold hands.

"Carsie! I've missed you!" Sophie ran into the snow and clasped Carsie. The two fell down, laughing, crying, looking into each other's face, hugging.

"She don't look too sickly," Cal observed.

Clint scratched his head. "Miraculous cure must be, seeing her friend. Must have been just melancholy."

Cal gave him a glance that said he knew he'd been lied to. "Here now," he called to the women, gesturing with the barrel of the shotgun, "get up out of there and get your reminiscin' over with." They ignored him and just kept chattering and hugging.

"Might as well give it up, Cal," Clint said, watching the two women roll around in the snow. "No chance of breaking those two up for the next five minutes, anyway. Got any coffee?"

Cal Thornton lowered his gun. "Yeah. Come on in. Place is probably gone to chill what with her leavin' the door open like that. Women. Beats me why I ever wanted one."

"Me, too." Clint followed Cal to the door.

"That talky one belong to you?"

Clint paused. Belong, Cal had said. Not a word he associated with a man and a woman, himself mostly. He realized something pretty stark right then. From the moment Carsie had joined the wagon train, she'd been in his charge. Sure, that was his job. At first. But the job was over the minute they reached Virginia City. Still he felt he had to look out for her. Even with all their bickering, her infernal opposition to everything he thought, they gravitated toward each other. Always.

"You might say that." He accepted a tin mug of coffee from Cal and looked around the cozy room. "But not where she can hear."

"Know just what you mean," Cal said. "Sophie, there, sure wasn't what I bargained for."

"Two peas in a pod, I guess, her and Carsie, right?"

"Well, she don't talk as much as she used to. Woman gets tired of prattin' on if she don't have somebody prattin' back."

"Hm, that's a thought."

"She's better'n I ever thought I deserved," Cal said thoughtfully.

"What?" Clint wondered how much Cal Thornton had changed. He was known to be mean and nasty to the core. Standing there huddled next to the stove, his cold hands clasped around a mug of coffee, his shoulders slumped forward from years of working over a sluice box or a tin pan, Cal looked tame, almost humble.

"Yep. Makes me a fine wife. Makes me a good home. Wish I could give her a better one. And she's about to make me a daddy."

Cal sounded proud and almost . . . Clint thought for a moment. Soft. Cal sounded almost soft.

"Say, Cal, are you saying you actually like being married?"

"Shore do." He colored deeper under his ruddy complexion. "Who'd a thunk it? Me. Ain't nothin' been so almighty sweet in my life as my Sophie. You? She your wife?"

Clint choked over a swallow of coffee. "Me? Naw, we're not married."

"How come? Not the marryin' kind?"

"That's right. She thinks marriage for a woman is some kind of slavery, and pure luxury for a man."

Cal eyed him from over his mug. "I meant ain't *you* the marryin' kind?"

Clint stopped the mug halfway to his lips. "Me? I—"

The door creaked open and the two women burst in, laughing and making shivering noises. They headed right for the stove, dropping wet shawls as they went. Carsie stripped off her gloves and held her hands out toward the heat. Cal scurried to get a chair for Sophie to sit next to the fire.

Carsie studied them both. Sophie looked worn, a bit pale, but she didn't look unhappy. Her hair had lightened, but she still wore it pulled back in a thick coil. She was excited about the baby coming. Cal hadn't provided much of a house for her, but it was clean with little touches of homeyness provided by Sophie's hand, and shelves placed in nooks created by his. Cal had a craggy face, weather-beaten skin, and rough hands. But there was something in his small gray eyes that told Carsie he truly cared about her friend.

Sophie had chosen marriage to a stranger and it had turned out the way she'd wanted. Carsie knew her friend was not there with Cal Thornton against her will. Her spirit had not been beaten out of her. She had a husband, a home, a baby coming. Sophie had a reason for her life, and that reason was hers alone and of her own choosing.

The four spent a companionable hour together. When it came time to leave, Carsie felt a sense of loss in the wake of the reunion with Sophie. Her quest to locate her friend and her determination to either rescue Sophie or avenge her untimely demise had melted like the snow from her boots at the feet of a wood stove in a homey miner's shack. It was a tepid ending to a heated quest, and the sense of quiet closure was not what Carsie had anticipated for months. It was better.

"Do you need anything?" Carsie asked Sophie as she looked around the room. "I'll bring whatever you need when I come back for a visit." Her gaze settled on Cal. "If it's all right with Cal, that is."

Sophie caught Carsie's scrutiny of her husband and her home. "It doesn't seem like much, I know, Carsie, but no, I don't need anything. I'm happy. I'm glad I came out here, even though I knew there was danger, even though you warned me about all the bad things that could happen. But they didn't. I'm so lucky. I wanted to come west. I wanted to find a husband. I believed I could find a good one and I have. It all turned out just fine."

"Yes, I can see that, Sophie. And I'm very happy for you." Carsie had no doubt that other women in Sophie's position had not made such a good bargain when they went west to marry. But she understood that Sophie had wanted this, chosen it, and was happy living here with her choice, even if she didn't live in comfort, let alone luxury.

"I know how you feel. God knows you have reason. Your own marriage was so terrible the way it ended." Sophie shook her head.

"Married?" Clint looked stunned. "You were married?"

Carsie swallowed hard and nodded faintly.

"You didn't know?" Sophie's expression turned to pain. "Oh, Carsie, I'm so sorry. I thought you two . . . I mean, I just assumed he knew."

"It's all right," Carsie assured her. "It just never seemed to be important enough to talk about."

"Oh, I get it now," Cal said. "She's the one killed her husband."

"Killed . . ." Shock replaced surprise on Clint's face.

"I know I probably should have told you about this. I guess I just wanted to keep it buried in the past. It ruined my life then. And I've been through a lot to start over."

"The past never stays buried, does it?" Clint snapped. "You ought to have learned that from me. And after . . . how could you keep such a thing from me? Don't you trust me?"

Panic flooded Carsie. "I don't know. I—"

"Are you a wanted criminal? Is that it?"

"No, I'm not wanted by the law," Carsie said quietly.

"Why did you—what happened?"

Carsie glanced at Sophie and Cal. "I don't want to talk about it now." She could see the anger in Clint's eyes. How could she ever explain this to him? She felt sick to her stomach and dizzy. How could she have been so naive as to think that time of her life would not be spoken of again?

"Why not?" Clint shouted.

"Listen here," Cal cut in, "I won't have yelling in my house. Not good for my wife in her condition."

Tears burned at the back of Carsie's eyes, but she willed them not to fall. "We should go now."

"He raped her."

"Sophie, no," Carsie said hoarsely.

Sophie ignored her. She pinned her gaze on Clint. "He was cruel and no good. Carsie's father took money from him for Carsie. She was just a girl. She didn't know what was happening."

The breath caught in Clint's chest. "Your husband raped you?" he rasped.

"All the time," Sophie went on. "Drunk or sober. I had gone to visit Carsie one day. I heard her crying hysterically inside the house. I had to break the door down to get in. I found her with him sprawled at her feet, a pair of scissors lodged in his throat.

"I calmed her down and she told me what happened. He'd been doing unspeakable things to her and she couldn't take it anymore. She just grabbed the scissors and stabbed him. He deserved it. She wanted to turn herself in to the local constable. I went with her. But I hid the scissors and swore on a Bible that the two of us had found him dead. No one seemed to care that he was dead. And Carsie and I left town and settled in St. Joseph."

"Oh God." Clint took Carsie into his arms. "I'm so sorry."

She went rigid. It was all back now, everything, back to haunt her life. She pushed out of his arms.

"What can I say?" Clint's face was wet with tears. "I feel helpless. You were always so strong. And Wheelock . . ." He touched her arm. "Why didn't you tell me? I guess I know that. I didn't trust you either, I guess. And then I told you about Mattie."

Carsie heard nothing more. She shrugged into her coat and went out into the snow.

They were quiet, deep in thought on the ride back to town. The memory of the moment she'd first taken up the reins of a team of oxen back in the wagon yard in St. Joseph floated in her mind. That seemed decades past. She felt decades older. And different. Finding Sophie brought everything into perspective. She sensed her purpose in life, everything she'd based her existence on, was gone.

What now? She could not let the old fears back into her life. She would lose herself completely if she did. She bit back tears. She knew what her new fears were now. She was afraid she would never experience what she sensed now was exquisite and complete surrender to love with a man. And a man—Clint, as long as truth glared in the setting sun ahead of her—would not surrender completely to loving her. They both had not learned that essential element of true love. Trust.

Winter fell heavily onto Virginia City, and the inhabitants spent their days and nights in the work of surviving the bitter cold. Carsie could not recall spending any winter months as harsh as these. She toiled at the children's home with Harry and Libby. The work kept her mind from thinking too much. She felt a real sense of purpose as she set up a classroom and began teaching simple reading and arithmetic skills.

Much as she loved being with the children and Harry and Libby, Carsie was still torn by her conviction to further the cause of women's rights. Yet sitting in an office and writing about what women should have as rights was unsatisfying. She felt useless in her work. She believed in it, but the actual work of it seemed ineffectual to her.

And then there was Clint. He acted distant since their visit with Sophie and Cal. Her emotions warred inside her. Every moment she was near him at the children's home, every hour she heard his laughter or his voice drift up to her room from the Center Ring, only made her ache with longing all the more. Longing for love, longing for connectedness to him. The longing deepened every day. She knew she had to move out of there.

On a frigid morning that started the way all the other winter days started, Carsie set out on her ride to the children's home in one of November's wagons filled with provisions. Out of the corner of her eye she caught a glimpse of something that looked like a blanket in the snow. Hauling the wagon to a stop, she jumped down and crept closer to investigate. Brushing snow away from the mound revealed a tattered blanket.

When she lifted the woolens she found a woman, her face swollen and covered with bruises. The woman groaned, and with great effort Carsie got her to stand and helped her up onto the wagon. She linked her arm through hers to keep her from falling then urged the horse on to the children's home.

Clint was already there gathering firewood when she pulled into the yard.

"Clint, help me!" she called through the wind.

He dropped the wood and ran to her. "What happened?"

Carsie gently helped the woman down into Clint's arms. "Found her in the snow back on the road. She's been beaten. That's all I can tell right now. Thought it best to just get her here."

Inside the house, Clint set the woman in a rocker near the stove and removed her shoes and thin gloves. "She's half frozen, poor thing. What in the world was she doing out here dressed like this?" He rubbed her fingers then helped her out of the wet outer coat. His eyes fell to her swollen abdomen. "She's pregnant, too."

Carsie sighed and knelt to pull on dry woolen stockings over the woman's chilled feet. "Looks like she was desperate to get away from someone, her husband no doubt," she said grimly.

"I'll never understand that. How can a man touch the woman he loves like that? And when she's carrying his child besides."

"Don't confuse love with this."

Clint instantly felt chagrined. "I'm sorry. I wasn't thinking."

Harry brought a mug of coffee laced with brandy and held it out to the woman. Clint helped her sip it. She trembled as much from fear as from the cold, he figured. Her eyes constantly darted toward the door as she drank.

"Don't worry," Clint said gently. "Whoever did this will not get to you here. We'll see to that."

"Th-thank you," she whispered through swollen lips.

Carsie came around to her side. "Your husband?"

The woman did not look up. She ignored the question it seemed and just drank the coffee.

Carsie rubbed the woman's hand tenderly. "If your husband beat you, he has to be punished just as if he were a stranger who broke into your house. You don't have to accept this. It's not a way of life for you or for any woman."

"Don't preach at her right now," Clint said quietly.

Carsie flared. "I'm not preaching. Look at her. If I hadn't found her, she and her baby would have frozen to death. Whoever did this is as low as Patch Wheelock. And if it was her husband, he's worse than any of them and deserves to be punished for this . . . crime. It's a crime, just as much as murder is a crime." She stared at him, wild-eyed.

"Carsie's right." Libby came up behind them. "Anyone who beats a woman or a child deserves fit treatment for it."

The children trooped into the room for breakfast in the next moments. The woman strained to see around Clint and Carsie, her eyes wide as a frightened deer. And then she sucked in her breath and let out a small cry.

"What is it?" Carsie studied her face then turned toward the children. "Do you know any of these children?"

The woman stared into her coffee mug and shook her head slowly, keeping her face hidden behind Clint.

A loud banging came to the door. Harry started toward it. He had his hand on the latch when the door flew open and slammed into him, knocking him to the floor. The woman's face went ashen as a man burst into the room. She tried to flee but was too weak even to push herself out of the chair. Carsie let out a yelp and took Libby's arm to get her to the table with the children. Dazed, Harry took a moment to focus. The children scrambled and several of them cried with terror. Clint was up and crossing the room in a flash. He grabbed the man by the arm and stopped him.

"What do you want, mister?" He used both hands to restrain the furious man.

"Get outside!" the man growled at the woman by the stove.

Slowly, her head hanging low, she started to rise.

Carsie stepped around her and stood between the woman and the angry man. "She's not going anywhere. She's sick."

The man struggled to get out of Clint's grasp. "I'm takin' her home and you ain't gonna stop me."

"I said she's sick and she's staying right here until we can help her get well. Now get out of here." Carsie planted her feet firmly in her spot.

One of the children scurried out from under the table and ran toward the sobbing woman. "Mama!" He threw himself into her lap then looked up at the man with tear-filled eyes. "Don't you touch her, you bastard. You touch her and I'll kill you!"

The man glared at the little boy. "So you managed to get away from the woodshed. You'll wish you died out there, boy, time I'm through with you." With a burst of strength he slammed both elbows into Clint's chest and sent him reeling backward. He landed some well-placed blows that knocked Clint to the floor. Then he lunged toward the woman.

"Don't!" she screamed. "I'll go! I'll go! Leave the boy here."

He grabbed her by the hair and sent a foot flying at the little boy. Harry was at him from behind. Frantically Carsie spun around looking for a weapon. The only thing she could find was a log for the stove. She grasped it with both hands and swung it out to slam the man across the knees. He let out a screech and fell. Harry pinned him to the floor. The man howled and hit Harry with force enough to lift him off the floor. Clint was up and across the room in the next instant. He grabbed the man by the shirtfront, lifted him, and landed a punch to his face that knocked him out cold.

The children cheered.

Clint staggered back against the wall and stood bent over, his breath coming in ragged gasps. Carsie ran to him and caught him just as he slumped toward the floor. Blood ran from a cut over his eye and his mouth swelled rapidly.

"You'll be fine, you'll be fine," Carsie whispered over and over. "You were wonderful, wonderful." She dabbed carefully at his cuts with a handkerchief, and cradled him in her arms.

He groaned and rubbed his forehead before looking up at her through one eye. "You were pretty wonderful yourself. Nice job with that log. We work well together."

Carsie warmed under his praise. "We do, don't we?"

She watched the woman and her son clinging together, crying and laughing at the same time. And she knew then where she and her convictions fit into life.

She lowered her gaze and, in the depth of Clint's eyes, saw the flames of the love of her life burning bright.

Nineteen

The harsh weeks of winter passed with a swift pace Carsie hadn't experienced in those dark months in the past. Up to now she'd abhorred the dark confines of winter, spending her days bundled in woolens and her nights longing for spring. But here in Virginia City with her friends and with the children, the time flew by filled with activity and gaiety, warmth and affection as she'd never known.

She threw herself into caring for the children, returning at the end of her day exhausted but happy at seeing them safely tucked away in their beds. Clint was a regular visitor most days, spending his nights at the Center Ring.

The holidays held lovely moments that Carsie recorded in her journal. When she reread her entries, she felt a new sense of inadequacy as a writer. No matter how much detail she set down on the page, the emotions she experienced never quite came through.

Thanksgiving day arrived with more than the usual anticipation of family gathering. There was an even greater sense of celebration than there had been upon the opening of the Center Ring.

And the day became one wherein Carsie could truly give thanks for the abundance they all experienced together. The long table in the children's home seemed to groan under the weight of the food that had been brought to them. And the warmth in the room enveloped them all with new life. Friends together. Harry and Libby, Miss Phoebe, Lola, Jake, and Hannah and November sitting next to each other exhibiting a shyness no one would have thought possible in those two people. Even Mr. and Mrs. Woo came to share the day.

Carsie sat among some of the children and watched Clint at the head of the table offer a poignant grace as they all held hands. Her own silent prayer gave thanks for the place in which she truly felt at home for the first time in her life.

At Christmas, no more joy could have been spread anywhere else on earth, Carsie was certain of that. Watching the children open their presents piled beneath a tree laden with paper chains and strung berries and topped with a special star fashioned by November gave her a sense of belonging to something she hadn't remembered ever feeling. And it also gave her an overwhelming sense of loneliness and emptiness.

The emptiness stemmed from something that had increasingly become clearer to her through the crisp days of winter. She wanted to belong to one person, wanted one person to belong to her. She hadn't felt that as a child, and she'd set her life as an adult so that there wasn't room for it. That had been a choice she'd made. Then why did she often feel a glimmer of hope that the circumstances could be different for her . . . if she let them?

She savored and held within her the feelings of love for Clint, which grew daily whether she was in his presence or alone in her room over the Center Ring. She seemed powerless to stop them, and then no longer even tried. She didn't even attempt to set down those emotions in her journal, for there were no words she knew that could possibly even touch upon the sensations that she experienced day to day.

She'd found a little house not far from the children's home. It was situated just at the edge of town and had been vacant for some time. When she'd inquired at the bank about it, she'd been informed that the owner had left and gone farther west. It would be possible to buy the house if the buyer had the right amount of cash as collateral or proof of monetary solidarity.

When she'd walked away from the bank that day, Carsie pondered this idea. What was she doing even thinking about buying a house? Buying a house signified an intention to settle in the community. And she hadn't made up her mind about leaving or staying. She'd never thought of what she would do after she found Sophie. Now the question loomed in her mind. She didn't have the money required to secure the place anyway. But she thought about that house constantly as the weeks stretched toward spring. The longer it stood vacant, the more significant it became to her.

"Good morning, November," Carsie called as she entered Freed's store on a sunny Saturday in April.

November stood near his stove lovingly gazing down into the beaming face of the comfortably seated Hannah Holmes. They each held a steaming mug, and Carsie could smell November's special spiced brew the moment she closed the door.

"Mornin' Carsie. Just in time for a cup of tea." November placed his mug on the counter and set to pouring one for her.

"Hello, Carsie," Hannah greeted her. "You're out and about early today."

Carsie peeled off her gloves and opened her coat. "Oh, it's such a glorious day. I just had to walk in the wonderful air. You can actually smell spring, smell the earth. I can feel things growing vigorously under the last blanket of snow. I love this time of year."

"Yes," Hannah said dreamily, "it is a glorious time of the year. Makes one think that a new life is coming and will always come. All one has to do is take it and begin anew."

Carsie accepted the mug November held out for her and sat down next to Hannah. She tilted her head in curiosity toward the woman who had become a dear friend. "My, you are poetic this morning." She caught the adoration in November's eyes as he gazed upon Hannah and her quick smile.

"I guess I am," Hannah said with a light laugh. "Comes from spending so much time with you, no doubt. I'm so happy I could burst."

"I have a feeling there's more to your happiness than spending time with me." Carsie sent a knowing glance toward November, who kept his gaze fastened on the object of his affections.

Hannah turned her excited face toward Carsie. "Today is the day I open my shop, my own shop. Can you believe it?"

"Yes, I absolutely can believe it," Carsie said, nodding her head to emphasize her words. "You are naturally gifted to handle your own business. You're going to make a lot of women in Virginia City, and I daresay a great many men, very happy."

"Carsie!" Hannah gave her a most surprised look. "Was it you who just uttered those words?"

"Indeed it was."

"Well, I guess it must truly be spring and a new time. I never thought I'd hear you say that, about the men I mean."

"Comes from spending a lot of wonderful time with you." Carsie gave Hannah's shoulders a warm hug. "I've learned a lot in the last few months." She stared down into her tea, then breathed in the spicy aroma.

"Oh, before I forget," November said, turning to the back of the counter, "I picked up this packet for you at the stage depot this morning. Looks important."

Carsie set down her mug and accepted the package November held out for her. "I can't imagine who could be sending me anything way out here in Montana." She slipped away the twine and paper. Her mouth dropped open as the contents were revealed.

"Four issues of *Harper's Weekly*. Wait, there's a letter."
She opened an envelope and took out a folded paper. A
bank draft fell into her lap. She read the letter slowly, read
it again to understand exactly what was being said. She
picked up the bank draft and stared at it. Her hands shook,
her voice breathless when she finally found it. "They published my articles, the ones I sent back as we traveled west.
They published them. They're paying me for the first in-
stallments. They're going to publish the rest and want me
to send them more. They'll pay me for them."

Hannah handed her mug to November and threw her arms
around her friend. "Oh, Carsie, that's wonderful! That's
what you wanted, isn't it? You're a writer! Oh, that's so
exciting! Isn't it exciting, November?"

"Indeed it is," November concurred. "Never knew a real
writer before. You're famous."

"Oh my," Carsie breathed. "Oh my. They published my
work. They want more. And they're paying me. Oh my."
The thought of the little house at the end of town focused
sharply in her mind. Surely this proof of her ability to pay
for it on a regular basis would convince the bank president
to sell it to her. And if she bought the house, that must
mean she meant to stay in Virginia City, and that meant . . .

"Well, of course they're paying you," Hannah's words
broke into Carsie's spinning thoughts. "You're good." Hannah took the letter and read it. "It's so official. Look, November, it says *Harper's Weekly* right at the top of the
letter."

"Mighty official," November concurred, leaning close to
Hannah.

"I'll tell them about the children," Carsie said in a faraway voice. "And I'll tell them about the women." Her face
became animated then. "And I'll write about you, Hannah,
and you, November. And Libby and Harry, and . . ."

"And Clint?" Hannah watched her face.

Carsie was silent for a moment. Then, "Everyone in Virginia City."

"If you write about Clint," November said with a knowing grin, "you'll have droves of females descending on Virginia City and there'll none of us have a moment's peace."

Hannah sent him what Carsie knew was most likely the first admonishing stare she'd ever given. November understood her meaning immediately and a look of contrition passed over his rugged features.

Carsie straightened and put on an unruffled air. "Well, then, that certainly ought to be good for your business, Hannah, for everyone's business."

The early days of June hummed with the flurry of wedding plans for Libby and Harry. Everyone seemed caught up in the excitement. Even Jake hummed as he worked alongside November building a wedding bower.

Other members of the community generously volunteered their services. The local baker offered the ingredients for the cake. Hannah had made the first order for her new shop and had sent for a bridal veil and a bolt of white satin for the bridal gown. A local seamstress traded her skills in fashioning the gown in exchange for Libby's piano instruction for her daughter. And Mother Nature promised an earlier spring than usual so the couple could be married with the wildflowers of Montana all around them.

Carsie enjoyed being part of all the wedding excitement. The diversion was something for her to be thankful for. It was spring. She'd vowed to herself she would make a decision about leaving Virginia City in the spring. But she'd been too busy to think about it, too busy to go and talk to the bank president about the house. At least that was what she told herself. The wedding was exactly what she needed to forestall the moment of her own decision.

Libby was as excited as a schoolgirl. Phoebe put her

sewing talents to work to fashion a lovely wedding cloak of lace and pearls, with not a brilliant feather anywhere or the trace of her usual flare for explicit costuming. Lola let her talent in the kitchen shine. Using the ingredients provided by the baker, she baked a magnificent four-tiered cake and set off the icing with multicolored wildflowers. Mrs. Woo appeared the day before the wedding bearing white paper fans she'd decorated with fanciful painted flowers and gold ribbons. Hannah provided a lovely trousseau from her shop.

Carsie and Clint transformed the Center Ring from a rowdy saloon to a wedding chapel complete with tall candle holders flanking the aisle formed by rows of chairs. They worked companionably side by side, and Carsie felt an overwhelming sense of comfort in their partnership in building something special for their friends. And she also felt an overwhelming sense of curiosity over the strange looks she received from Clint every now and then. She could not read them, but found herself looking for them often.

"I can barely believe this is happening," Clint said, handing up great white satin bows to Carsie.

Carsie stood at the top of a tall ladder at the bower November and Jake had made. She hadn't wanted to climb the ladder, but more than that, she hadn't wanted Clint to think she was afraid of being up high.

"What?" She questioned every word he uttered since those strange looks he'd been giving her the last few days.

"The wedding, of course. What did you think I meant?"

Carsie stuck long pins in her mouth and muttered something vague about how the bows didn't seem to want to stay anchored to the bower. She didn't want to consider if perhaps her shaking hands and lack of concentration might be at fault.

"Harry getting married," Clint said in an incredulous voice. "We always said, he, Jake, and I, that the circus would be our mistress forever. I guess forever was only temporary, at least for two of us. Jake stayed long after Harry and I were gone."

"Yes, but then he left the circus, too, back in St. Joseph." Carsie bit her lip. Her voice sounded entirely too hopeful; she knew that the moment the words came over her tongue.

"Does that mean there's no such thing as forever, no matter what is important to a man?"

He asked the question into the air, Carsie thought, didn't ask her directly. That must mean she shouldn't answer it, right? Or should she? He didn't really want her opinion on that. Did he?

"What do you think, Carsie?"

Oh Lord, he did want her opinion! He must. Why did he ask her if he didn't want to know her answer? She knew in that blinding moment that she believed completely in forever. She could stay here forever. She could be with him forever. Her own forever.

"I think," Carsie said, stepping carefully backward down one ladder rung, her hands perspiring, "that forever means different things to different people."

"What does forever mean to you?" he pressed.

She looked over her shoulder toward him, and in his eyes she saw the endless Montana sky. *Forever means you.* The words hung in front of her mind and behind her silent lips. She took another step back down and the ladder shook and slipped to the side. Then her foot slipped.

"Oh!" She gripped a rung tightly.

"Don't worry. I won't let you fall." Clint reached up to her. "Take my hand."

"I can't."

"Yes, you can. Just let go one hand and reach down."

"It's slipping. The ladder's slipping."

"I've got it. I won't let you fall. Come now, step down and give me your hand."

"No. I need to hang on with both hands."

Clint recognized in her a fright he hadn't seen before. Something must have frightened her once, something to do with being up high. He'd seen that panic in fright many times during his circus days. It was natural. Some people never got over it.

"All right," he said gently. "Steady yourself and take a deep breath. I will hold the ladder still."

She obeyed, keeping her eyes open and staring straight ahead through ladder rungs.

"Now, I want you to listen to me and to believe in your mind that you can simply lift one foot and set it down on the next rung, then lower the other foot, then one hand at a time. That's all you have to believe, that you can make it to one rung below your feet. You know it's not far, just a few inches."

"I can't," she said in a small voice.

"This is nothing," he continued smoothly, "compared to what you have accomplished already. You came clear across this wild country in a wagon. That's more than a mere few inches. You got out of a terrible ordeal with Patch Wheelock. You got through rain and snow and mud. You helped Libby have a baby out on the prairie. What is one step down a ladder compared to all of that?"

Carsie let out a shaky breath.

"You can believe you did all those things, can't you, Carsie?" He waited. "You did them without ever having done them before. You can do this."

"The ladder will tip over," she said weakly.

"I won't let it tip over. You can trust me to hold it for you so you can get down. You do trust me, don't you, Carsie?"

Carsie gripped the rung tighter and closed her eyes. Trust Clint. Slowly she descended one foot to one rung and then the other foot, and repeated it over until she felt Clint's hands around her arms, steadying her. She reached the floor, shaking all over. Clint lifted her hands from the rung. Slowly he turned her around.

"You did it. That was great." He rubbed her perspiring palms.

"I couldn't have . . . without you." She had difficulty steadying her breath.

"Yes, you could. You just forgot for a minute. If I hadn't been here, you'd have got down all by yourself." His eyes shone full of praise.

Carsie felt weak in the knees.

The door burst open and November rushed in. "Come and see what I've done," he called to them excitedly.

Carsie's shoulders jumped in relief. She turned toward November. "You sound like a child with a new drawing."

"It's better than that. Come see!" November pushed the door open and went back outside.

Carsie followed him. Clint waited a few minutes, then joined them in the street in front of the Center Ring.

"Oh," Carsie breathed. "How enchanting. Just like out of a fairy tale."

November had refurbished a small wagon into an elegant white conveyance for the wedding couple, decking it with bells and ribbons and shining the brass on a showy harness for Harry's white horses.

Clint stepped up next to Carsie and let out a long low whistle when he spied the wagon. "November—I'd say it looks to me like you've been pierced by the arrow of love yourself."

November grinned widely and sent a superior glance toward Clint. "Takes the hidden wounded to recognize the hidden wounded."

Clint stiffened. "Uh, time I spoke to Harry about arrangements."

Carsie watched him hurry back inside the Center Ring. She sent a questioning glance toward November.

"Can't nobody hide forever," November said, laughing. He led the horses down the street toward his store.

Carsie stood in the street basking in the fragrant spring breezes swirling around her. *Can't nobody hide forever.* A dawn of understanding broke over her. That November. He certainly was a brilliant philosopher.

The wedding day dawned golden bright. Carsie and Clint spent hours dressing the children in the best Sunday-go-to-meeting clothes they could gather, only to begin dressing them all over again later once they'd arrived at the Center Ring and gotten dirty stringing old shoes and harness pieces to the back of the wedding wagon. Miraculously they settled down into a small band of angels when the Reverend Richard Smith stood at the wedding bower and his wife Ada sat down at the gleaming piano and played an overture which heralded the arrival of the groom.

Harry came from the kitchen and stood at the bower, his gaze fixed on the door at the rear of the saloon through which his beloved Libby would emerge. Jake and Clint stood proudly behind him, Jake tugging at his collar and Clint settling his broad shoulders under his new black coat.

Reverend Smith nodded his head and Ada switched her music sheets and started into a wedding march. The door opened and the bridesmaids started down the aisle between chairs decorated with Mrs. Woo's white fans. Clint watched the ladies of Goodnight's Good Times Emporium float toward him in uncustomary demure gowns of blue silk. Lola beamed and Hannah had a tear in her eye. He smiled at them.

And then Carsie appeared and his breath caught in his throat. The high neck of her russet silk gown set off her skin and tinted it softly with peach, making her brown eyes flash with golden specks. Her softly coiled hair shone in the candlelight and appeared gilded with more gold. She carried little Harry dressed in a white satin suit and clutching a flower between his fists.

Clint watched her glide toward him. She was a woman of uncommon beauty. He couldn't take his eyes from her. She took her place opposite him as Libby's attendant of honor. When she settled her gaze on him briefly before turning toward the back of the room, Clint felt the last vestiges of his resistance dissolve inside him. *So much for forever.*

Ada pounded the keys harder and the gathered guests stood. Through the door came Libby, gowned in white satin and pearls. Her arm was linked through that of Miss Phoebe, who was dressed in a deep green skirt with a matching fitted jacket, looking completely like the mother of the bride. Perhaps she'd become the mother of them all, Clint thought, and smiled with pleasure.

Libby fairly beamed as Phoebe whispered in her ear. Clint surmised Phoebe was describing the look of pure joy that lit Harry's face at the sight of his lovely bride walking toward him.

As Libby and Harry repeated their vows, on either side of them Carsie and Clint exchanged furtive glances. It took supreme strength for Carsie to will her gaze from fastening on him and remaining there throughout the ceremony. Every word exchanged by the reverend and the wedding couple seemed to penetrate her mind and imbed themselves in her soul. She, the only woman she'd ever known who believed marriage an unnatural state, stood in the midst of a marriage ceremony feeling overwhelmed by what she recognized as the courage it took for two people to commit to love and to cherish one another through happiness and adversity forever. Forever was just that, forever. She went through the rest of the ceremony in a numb daze.

The bride and groom kissed to seal their union. They turned toward the guests, who stood, many wiping tears.

Harry reached to Carsie for little Harry. He set the boy down between Libby and himself. Each took a hand and little Harry showed off his new walking prowess by taking a few faltered steps down the aisle. The guests applauded. Grinning with happiness, Harry scooped up the boy in one arm, linked his other through Libby's, and the new family walked the rest of the way down the aisle together.

The celebration following was one the likes of which Virginia City residents had never seen. Clint, with Jake, Harry, and November, had constructed a circus ring in back of the building, complete with a tightrope, trapeze, and the bank president dressed as a clown. Food was everywhere. The Virginia City Town Band played rousing music. Dancing, drinking, eating became the order of the day, and Libby and Harry and little Harry basked at the center of the celebration.

Clint and Jake gathered everyone to chairs set up along both sides of the circus ring. Clint grabbed Jake's battered stovepipe hat and planted it firmly on his own head.

"Lay-dees and gentlemen," he called, "and children of all ages. Welcome to Virginia City's first circus!"

A cheer went up from the crowd.

Carsie edged her way to Libby. She leaned over and spoke to her. "I didn't know you were planning a circus performance for your wedding. How wonderful."

"Harry and Clint have been planning it for a long time," Libby replied. "It's going to be wonderful. Lots of surprises. The children will be thrilled."

The children weren't the only thrilled members of the audience. The rapt attention of young and old alike was fastened on Clint and Mr. Woo, who juggled colorfully painted wooden tenpins amid kitchen utensils and blacksmith tools. Harry, barefoot and in his wedding suit, walked the tightrope high above their heads while spouting Shakespearean sonnets of love to Libby. The supreme quiet of the crowd as he balanced a long bamboo rod across his

chest was broken only by nervous gasps as he faked tripping
and almost falling.

Jake climbed the ladder to the trapeze and, with a tightly
wrapped cloth around his middle to brace the small of his
back, took one brave child at a time to the top with him.
He settled himself on the bar, held a child on his lap, and
swung out over a wide net. Mothers bit their knuckles or
covered their eyes as they watched their children sail overhead in the arms of an old man whose silver hair flew out
behind him in the wind. Soon every child wanted a ride,
and the mixture of their excited laughter and thrilled shouts
rose above the applause of the crowd.

The bank president did a fair act as a clown, squeaking
a horn and handing out candy. November, dressed in a lion
tamer's outfit that showed to best advantage every muscle
and sinew of his powerful body, put Harry's horses through
some intricate paces. Carsie was as fascinated as everyone
else by the turns and bows of one, and the counting up to
ten with a front hoof by the other. Her fascination spilled
over to Hannah, who seemed mesmerized with November's
every move.

And then Libby handed little Harry back to Carsie. She
slipped her hand into her groom's and they walked to the
ladder that led up to the tightrope platform. Without a moment of obvious trepidation, Libby preceded him up the
ladder. Carsie's breath caught in her chest. What was happening? Harry came up behind his new wife and stood on
the platform.

"Lay-dees and gentlemen!" Clint called. "Making her
circus debut for you today, Mrs. Libby Allen Hardin on the
high wire!"

The crowd gasped. Carsie's gasp was the loudest as she
held little Harry.

Libby slid one slippered foot out onto the wire. Harry
slipped his arms around her and held the bamboo pole in
front of her. She grasped the pole loosely with both hands.

Harry grasped the pole and placed his own hands closely on either side of hers. He slipped one bare foot out behind hers and touched the back of her heel. She slid her other foot out in front on the wire. He slid his along to touch hers. And then as one, Libby's chin high and a beatific smile on her face, the new husband and wife smoothly began their journey across the length of the wire. Now and then a tentative stop, a teetering step caused momentary faltering. But they persevered and moved forward together, trust between them so apparent, not even the most hardened man in the crowd could have missed.

"That's your mama and daddy," Carsie whispered in little Harry's ear. "You're the luckiest boy in the world for you'll grow up to be just as brave as they are."

Little Harry giggled and patted his hands together.

Libby and Harry reached the opposite platform. The crowd that had seemed to have held its collective breath for the few moments, their heads tipped back and their eyes fixed upon the bride and groom high above them, rose to their feet amid wild applause. Carsie saw the sheer pride and pleasure reflected on Clint's face as he beamed at his two friends, who were locked in an embrace on the platform.

Carsie knew then he'd been right all those months ago when he'd told her the circus was the greatest show on earth. Even this one, put together by a few friends for a wedding celebration, was far and away better than anything Carsie had ever witnessed. She'd been thrilled to tears as she'd absorbed it all and took in all the meaning behind the wedding couple's performance.

Thrilled. Clint had been right about that, too. The circus offered thrills. And when she thought back to the nights when she and Clint had made love over the Center Ring, she'd learned in a blinding flash exactly what it meant to be thrilled.

She watched Clint in his own center ring, one arm around

Libby's waist and the other around Harry's shoulders, surrounded by chattering children and townspeople. This was his element. He was perfectly natural in the center of it with excitement swirling around him. She could offer him nothing quite so exciting and satisfying as these moments.

Miss Phoebe came up beside Carsie. "Life is a circus every day of the week if one learns how to juggle and to walk a tightrope."

Carsie turned toward her with emerging understanding. "You've done that, haven't you? You've juggled things in your life and had to follow precarious paths at times."

Phoebe smiled. "Only I didn't call it a circus. I called it survival."

"You're a very courageous woman, Phoebe."

"Takes courage to be a woman. You know that."

Carsie looked down at her feet. "I always thought so. I think the fight has gone out of me, or something."

"Never thought I'd hear you say that."

"Neither did I. I thought I could go on the way I was going forever." Forever. That word again.

"You can."

"I don't think so. Others can carry on without me. Others who now feel compelled to take up the cause."

"Because of you. Perhaps you need to test your own courage again. Perhaps you need to find inside yourself the mettle you think you've lost. Not everything is a cause, my dear, but that doesn't mean it doesn't take courage to live." Phoebe's gaze traveled toward Clint and the children. "Sometimes it takes courage just to say what we think. You've demonstrated that. Sometimes it takes courage to know what we think. And you've shown that as well. But it takes the most courage to know what we truly want and need and to have the strength to get it, no matter what or how long it takes."

Carsie turned toward her, wondering what she meant by her last words. Phoebe wasn't looking at her. Carsie followed her gaze to the object of her scrutiny. Clint. She looked back again at Phoebe, whose mouth tipped in an enigmatic smile.

"Pick up Harry's and Libby's bamboo pole," Phoebe said. "You'll understand everything then."

Twenty

After the wedding celebration, Clint left the circus apparatus intact. The circus ground became a place where the children gathered to stare longingly through the fence and dream of walking the high wire, taming tigers, flying through the air, or standing up on the back of a galloping horse.

On a particularly warm late spring morning Carsie stood among them watching Harry juggle some old oranges November had found in his storeroom. Emily, the shyest of the children at the home, leaned against Carsie's hip, clutching her skirt. She let out a long wistful sigh. Carsie knew exactly what the child was thinking.

"You wish you could juggle, too, don't you, Emily?"

The little girl's answer was to burrow her face into the folds of Carsie's skirt. Carsie's heart ached for the child. Her mother had died in childbirth, and her father had all but abandoned her after years of berating her for causing her mother's death. Emily didn't have one ounce of love for herself, one moment of believing she was worth anything. She barely talked and never laughed. Carsie understood just how starved for affection and attention the child had been. She was the most downtrodden of all the children. Over the months Carsie had spent a great deal of time with the frail little girl, and had managed to bring her out of some of her darkness by teaching her to read. Now the child was a voracious reader.

She stroked the child's golden silky hair and looked down at her. Emily's head was tipped back and she was staring up, a look of awe transforming her pinched features. Carsie turned toward the direction of Emily's rapt gaze. The tightrope. It stretched taut from one rigid pole to another, cutting across the sun like a well-shot arrow.

Carsie understood. Walking the tightrope was Emily's heart's desire. Walking the tightrope would take an ultimate act of courage the child knew she couldn't demonstrate. Carsie ached for her. As the sun's brilliance turned the tightrope to a string of white diamonds, in her mind she saw Emily in a ballerina costume, strong and sure, climbing the ladder to the platform, opening a lacy white parasol and sliding a first confident step out onto the tightrope. And she saw herself standing on the platform behind her, willing the child with every ounce of her own courage to make it to the other platform. Emily turned on the opposite platform and waved to the cheering crowd, a smile of pure joy lighting her face.

Applause from the children broke into Carsie's dream.

Harry bowed with élan. "All right," he called loudly. "Who wants to juggle oranges?"

Several boys and girls clambered up the fence with choruses of "I do! I do!"

Harry instructed them to go through the gate and he would give them lessons. Emily hung back, still clinging to Carsie's skirt.

"What do you say, Emily? Would you like to learn to juggle?" Carsie stroked the girl's thin shoulder.

Emily shook her head, but studied closely as Harry lined up the children and took more oranges from a wooden box, tossing out the rotten ones as he selected. Carsie sighed. She longed for a way to help Emily break through this protective wall she kept around herself. A child should simply be without all the heavy cares that plagued Emily. She should feel free, to run, to play, to laugh, to take all the childhood risks that petrify mothers, but are necessary for learning how to cope with the living in a hard world.

Her eyes drifted to the tightrope. That was it! If Emily could walk that tightrope from one platform to the other, Carsie believed that would open the gates to a whole new life for the child, a life filled with courage to try new things.

And this revelation was like a sunlit beam of purpose for Carsie.

"What do you think?" she asked Clint an hour later as they worked side by side in the garden behind the children's home. "Can you teach Emily to walk the tightrope?"

"I can teach Eskimoes how to build igloos." Clint stripped off his shirt and wiped his brow with it before tossing it on a fence post.

Carsie's face burned several degrees more that had nothing to do with the sun. For a moment she was fascinated by the undulation of his muscles beneath glistening bronzed skin as he moved with the rhythm of his hoe. She sucked in her bottom lip before speaking and gave him a good-natured barb to cover her nervousness.

"I see these last few months haven't altered your usual modest appraisal of yourself."

"Just being accurate." Clint gave her a wide teasing smile that seemed to go right through her.

Ever since the wedding, Carsie had had no strength to keep her own defenses intact where Clint was concerned. And every now and then she wondered why she even tried to reconstruct them. It was hopeless. She loved him beyond all reason, but there was nothing to be done about it. He was constantly surrounded by women, beautiful women, fun-loving women who felt not the slightest twinge of holding back anything.

"So you think it's possible?" she said at last.

"Anything is possible," he responded quickly.

Carsie wiped her brow with her sleeve. It was growing beastly hot. She'd forgone her stockings and shoes, had raised her bloomers up to hug around her knees, and stood barefoot in the garden soil. The idea that any polite woman wouldn't do such a thing did not matter to her.

"I wouldn't say that," she said without looking up.

"I would. Here I stand with you in the sun, me without a shirt and you without a skirt for all the world to see. Most people would think our display rather shocking, don't you think?"

Carsie burned. "I don't care if they do," she retorted. "That's their worry." She dropped down and shored up the soil around a droopy tomato plant. She pinched off some yellowed leaves.

Clint stared down at her. The sun glinted off her hair, giving her a coppery halo. She wiped perspiration from her cheek, leaving a dark streak of garden soil. She'd opened the neck of her white shirt and he could see the gentle swell of her moist breast. He watched her capable hands lovingly rescue the tomato plant. Suddenly he wanted those loving hands to rescue the ache inside him.

"It's too hot to be here right now," he said, dropping the hoe.

"Well, we have to get this done. And you never really answered my question about Emily." Carsie didn't look up.

Clint wiped the sweat from his eyes. He was beside her in two long steps. "Come on." He took her hand, pulled her to her feet, and hurried her toward a grove of trees.

"What are you doing?" Carsie tried to wrench from his grip.

He held on tightly. "Getting us out of the glare of the sun."

"But we have to——"

"We don't have to do anything we don't want to do," he said breathlessly. "And we should do everything we want to do."

"I want to . . . to garden," she said more breathlessly than he. "Right now."

He kept pulling her along. They reached the cool shade of the trees but still he kept walking. On the other side of the trees lay a narrow stream that rushed from a rocky hillside. He tugged her along until they were both knee-deep in the cold water. Then he stopped.

"What did you do this for?"

"I need a drink." He stared into her eyes. "And your feet needed washing."

"Godawmighty," Carsie muttered. Her heart thumped wildly. From the exertion, that had to be why.

"Your face is dirty, too." Clint bent and filled his cupped palm with water. He wet the fingertips of his other hand, and wiped the dirt from her cheek. Then he ran his wet fingers over her lips. "There, that's much better. Isn't it?"

Carsie felt her throat close. "Yes," she squeaked.

He cupped more water and trickled it over her lips, gently parting them to give her a taste of the cool purity from the stream. He sipped the water from his own hand, and Carsie's nerves grew alive with sheer energy when the water glistened on his mouth. She'd have melted into the ground at that moment, she knew, if it hadn't been for the cold water swirling around her legs.

"I . . ." she breathed, swaying toward him.

He clutched her shoulders. "So do I." His voice came from deep in his throat.

And then they were together, pressing lips and bodies with the intense immediacy of their mutual need. They splashed out of the stream and up onto the grassy bank where they fell, locked in each other's arms, and released the power of their shared energies with abandon.

Some exquisite moments later they lay naked in the grass that was moist from the stream and their bodies.

Clint breathed heavily as if he'd just sailed down from the best trapeze act he'd ever performed. "I . . . don't know . . . what to say," he whispered hoarsely.

Carsie was very still. It took her a long time to speak. "There is nothing to say."

"I won't apologize. I wanted to make love to you. I wanted to feel your hands all over me. I wanted my mouth all over you."

Carsie rolled her head toward him. "There is no need to apologize. I wanted the same thing."

Clint rolled toward her and braced himself on one elbow. "You are the most honest woman I have ever known."

"You mean the most wanton, don't you?" Her voice was serious.

"If you think you have to call it that. I call it sensual, more giving than any experience in my life. Honest."

Carsie sat up. "What does that all mean?"

Clint sat up and grasped his knees. He cleared his throat. "It means we should get married."

Carsie snapped her head around. "What?"

He grinned. "Yes! That's what it means. It means we should get married."

Carsie scrambled up and grabbed her clothes, yanking them on with a force that strained their seams. "Well, that's the worst thing you've ever said to me!" She stomped off.

Stunned, Clint got to his feet. "What the hell does that mean?" he shouted.

"You know exactly what it means!" she shouted into the trees.

"What is the matter with you? Don't you realize I've just asked you to marry me? Any other woman in her right mind would be shouting yes in the middle of the town!"

"I'm not any woman!"

"You think I don't know that? Godawmighty, I've been living with you long enough to know that."

"Don't say Godawmighty."

"Why not?" He ran a frustrated hand through his hair.

"Because that's mine!"

"You don't own it!"

"And you don't own me!" She turned and stomped out of the woods.

"I never said I did! I don't want to own . . ." Clint realized his shouting wasn't doing anything except disturbing the peace of the grove full of birds. "Damn it to hell," he muttered, and fell down trying to shove his leg into his pants.

If it hadn't been for Harry's and Libby's willingness to coach Carsie walking the wire, she believed she'd never have attempted it. And if it hadn't been for the encouragement of the children cheering her on to take the first step on the taut wire strung in back of their home, she believed she couldn't have taken the second step. And if it hadn't been for the total adoration on Emily's face as she peeked out from behind Hannah's skirts, she wouldn't have made it to the other side.

She felt enormously proud of herself for overcoming her fears, even more so when Harry secretly began to teach her how to fly the trapeze. Jake stood below them near a wide strung net of cargo rope shouting up praise or criticism. Emily took to standing by him, one little hand clutching his stovepipe hat as she gazed in awe at Carsie flying overhead.

Carsie had begun to soar inside her heart. And it was as much for Emily as for herself.

Excitement was palpable in Virginia City the late summer day the freight wagon arrived bearing the huge circus tent. A cheer went up from all the members of Bonner's original freight passengers who'd traveled the long road from St. Joseph with him when they saw Martha jump down from the wagon box. She'd brought the circus tent herself all the way from California.

And it was a noisy and even more excited crowd that pressed into the tent and took bench seats the opening night of the circus. The event opened with the singing of "The Star-Spangled Banner" by all the children from the orphanage under the direction and piano playing of Libby.

Clint, master of the entertainments, stood in the center and opened his arms wide. "Lay-dees and gentlemen and children of all ages!" he shouted. "Welcome! Welcome to the new, the marvelous, the gigantic, the stupendous, the most completely splendiferous circus ever to appear in the world! The Virginia City New Western Circus!" The crowd cheered and stomped their feet.

Carsie thought she'd never seen Clint look so handsome as he was that night in his black swallow-tailed suit and highly shined black boots. She fell in love with him all over again in that moment.

And then the town band struck up lively music, and the circus ground filled with activity. Jake replayed his famous clown act. Harry juggled everything in sight, and performed feats of acrobatics that had the crowd on their feet applauding. Then he brought out the children, who went into the juggling and tumbling acts he'd taught them, including little Harry. Mothers were crying, fathers were poking each other saying, "That's my Bobby! There's my Amelia, she's so graceful!"

Clint thrilled them all as he swung through the air on the trapeze, sometimes hanging by his knees, other times standing up without holding on, his hair flying out behind his head.

Libby treated the audience with a walk along the high wire. Carsie marveled at her courage and total trust and faith in Harry's guidance. She made it all look so easy, so simple.

Georgie showed his trained dog act for the first time and beamed at the thunderous applause. Hannah led out Harry's great white horses dressed in fabulous regalia fashioned by

Phoebe. November put the horses through tricks that astounded the audience. Lola sold sweet treats she'd baked herself and fresh lemonade and popcorn she made fresh over a special stove the local stone mason had made for her. Carsie suspected a budding romance there.

Mr. Woo sold souvenirs he'd ordered from California. Mrs. Woo performed with flaming wands to the sounds of "Oh my!"

And then Carsie, Libby at her side encouraging her, made the decision to debut her own recent circus skills. Carsie took a deep breath. Libby squeezed her hand. Dressed in a white satin camisole and matching knickers designed by Hannah, and white stockings and slippers, she climbed to the tightrope platform and waved to the crowd. Her copper hair was loosely dressed in ribbons and coiled down her back. Stunned at her appearance, they could only stare at her.

She took up a bright red parasol and slid one foot out onto the wire. She stepped back, perspiration beading on her forehead, her heart thundering wildly. She looked across to the opposite platform. Clint stood there in the close-fitting black trapeze shirt and pants he'd worn earlier. The surprise on his face quickly changed. He held out his arms.

"Look straight at me, Carsie, nowhere else. Just let your feet follow your eyes."

"I . . . can't." Her voice quavered.

"Yes, you can. You've done it before."

She shook her head, then caught a glimpse of Emily, her hand locked in Libby's, her eyes wide and fastened on Carsie.

"Come here, Carsie," Clint called above the hushed crowd. "Believe you can do it and you will. And believe I'm here to welcome you with my arms open."

Carsie stared first at Clint, then back at Emily. She raised her eyes and locked her gaze with Clint's. Letting out a shaky breath and taking in a strong strengthening one, she started across the tightrope. Arms out for balance, the parasol wavered in her hand. Her foot slipped once, the crowd gasped, but she regained her balance, never taking her eyes from Clint's outstretched arms.

She reached him and he drew her onto the platform. Loud cheering, whistling, and applause from the audience swelled up to embrace her. Clint stepped back as tears fell from her eyes. She waved to Emily, who jumped up and down still clutching Libby's hand.

Carsie, basking in her new accomplishment and the accolades it brought her, was taken completely unaware when she was suddenly lifted up and found her back pressed against Clint's chest, her legs slipping out from under her. He swung her around. A second later she realized they were sitting on a trapeze swing and sailing out over the net as her parasol floated down.

"Godawmighty!" she let out on a whoosh of air.

"Clintawmighty you mean, right?" he said into her ear.

"What are . . . you doing?" She gripped the swing ropes with all her strength.

"Taking you flying, of course. I thought you'd figured that out by now."

The crowd applauded below them.

"I . . . can't fly . . . be flying . . . with you," Carsie managed.

"But you are, you see. Isn't it a marvelous freedom to be way up here flying like a bird over the world?"

"Freedom! I'm petrified. I'm clinging to these ropes for dear life! You are crazy!"

"So I've learned, finally. I'm crazy, all right, crazy in love with you. Crazy, because I know I can't live my life without you. I must be crazy to want you never to leave me. Look at all I'm going to have to contend with." Clint swung them harder.

Carsie felt the wind in her ears. She became breathless,

not only from the fear. "Contend with . . . what sort of contention do you mean? What are you talking about?"

"Marriage of course. You really are rather dense, aren't you. Are your bloomers too tight? Are they cutting off air to your brain?"

"What?"

"Hm, and your hearing, too. Well, there's only one thing that can help that."

Carsie was filled with more trepidation over those words than almost any she'd ever heard before. "What . . . what do you intend to do?"

"Drop you!"

She screamed when he eased her off his lap. How he ever managed it, she would never be able to explain, but she quite suddenly found her arms in his strong grip as he hung from his knees on the swing and she dangled below him.

The crowd let out a collective gasp, broken only by loud laughing from Jake and Harry.

They were flying all right, upside down.

"Will you marry me?"

"You are crazy!" Carsie's heart fluttered wildly. She could not determine if it had more to do with his proposal than the flying.

"We've established that. Will you marry me?"

"No!"

"Why not? What are you afraid of?"

"I just don't believe in marriage. Can we talk about this later?"

"No. Up here. I know you can't get away. And I know you've changed your mind about marriage."

"What makes you say that?"

"I saw you crying at Harry and Libby's wedding."

"Women always cry at weddings and funerals." The moment the words came from her mouth, she regretted saying them. She hated lumping women together in some form of emotional display. It was exactly what men always accused them of.

"Not you. You're not like all women. You know it and I know it. I want you to marry me. Will you?"

"No!"

"Fine. Looks like I'll have to drop you, then." He let her arms slip. She squeaked a stifled scream. Another gasp came from the audience.

Suddenly a big grin crossed her face. Clint looked down at her, puzzled.

"You won't drop me," she said confidently.

"What makes you so sure?"

"Because you never have. You picked me up in St. Joe and carried me out here where I needed to be. You've been picking me up ever since. And now I'm flying."

"Aha! I was right?"

"Oh no. I hate when you aha. What do you think you're right about this time?"

"You just said you're flying. But more, you know you can trust me, don't you?"

Carsie swallowed. She could admit that now. "Yes, I do trust you. Now, aside from the fact that my arms are getting a few inches longer, what else are you trying to say?"

"That I can fly, too, but it's better with you floating through the air with me. And you have a lot of heart. Look at you. Dangling in the air in your . . . what does Hannah call it? Ah, your lingerie. That's it. You're dangling in your lingerie over the population of Virginia City, and you're not even bothered."

"This is not lingerie! This is a circus costume!"

"Oh really. Fine. Even in your lingerie you can fly on your own. But you know you will fly higher and longer with me flying with you. And you can trust me to always be there to break your fall."

Carsie became speechless.

"Say something. You always do." Clint grinned.

Carsie closed her eyes. "I can't. You've got to let me down now."

"Not until you say yes."

She snapped her eyes open. "To what?"

The crowd was growing restless.

"To my proposal of marriage. We can fly together for the rest of our lives." Clint swung her harder. He called out to the tense crowd. "Lay-dees and gentlemen! I have just asked Miss Carson Rose Summers to marry me!"

"Godawmighty." Carsie gripped his upper arms tightly.

Applause.

"She hasn't given me her answer!"

Collective "aww" from the crowd.

"What do you think she should say?"

"Yes!" came the collective shout.

"Hear that?" Clint asked her.

"Time you dropped me, Major Bonner."

"Not a chance." He turned his head and shouted, "Will you marry me, Carson Rose Summers?"

"No!" she shouted back. "I don't need marriage."

"You need me," he shouted for all to hear. "And I need you. I promise to love you and love your freedom and love your bloomers or lingerie or whatever you want to wear . . . or don't wear which sounds better to me . . . for the rest of our lives!"

Carsie gasped and stared up at him. The passing tent roof overhead as they swung slowly back and forth made her dizzy. "Let me go, please."

"Never, thank you. All right. I give up. You can wear your bloomers even to bed."

The crowd cheered.

"You! You haven't changed one bit. You're"—she breathed hard—"exasperating."

"I know. But I have changed. I want us to get married and make a life of excitement and good work . . . together."

He turned back and shouted again, "Now, then, Carson Rose Summers, will you marry me?"

Carsie couldn't say anything. A smile of surrender started to spread over her face. Her lips parted.

With a powerful show of strength Clint pulled her up and caught her mouth in a deep kiss as they swung back and forth through the air.

Below them Harry and Jake chanted, "Yes, yes." Phoebe, Lola, Hannah, and November joined in. "Yes, yes, yes." The children got out of their seats along with a mother or two. "Yes, yes, yes, yes," they chanted. And then the entire crowd of Virginia City residents were on their feet, clapping and yelling, "Yes, yes, yes, yes, *yes!!*"

Carsie broke her lips free. She panted. "All right, you win. Yes."

Stunned, Clint tipped his head. "What did you say?"

"Yes," she said again.

"What did you say?" he shouted.

"Yes!" she shouted back.

"Louder!"

"Yes! Yes, I'll marry you, Clint Bonner!" And then she started to laugh.

The crowd yelled "Yes!" and cheered wildly.

Clint slipped his legs from the trapeze and they sailed down to the net. They rolled into each other's arms kissing and laughing as the cheering crowd gathered around them.

Emily ran toward them and jumped on top of them. "Now can I be your daughter, hunh, can I? Can I fly, too? Can I be a circus girl?"

Clint and Carsie gathered the beaming child into their arms.

"Yes, you can be our daughter," he told her.

"You can be anything you want to be," Carsie said, hugging her closely.

Jake slapped his old friend on the shoulder and shifted his pipe to the other side of his mouth. "Well, I can see you made your last barter, son, your free bachelor days for years of husband and father chains." He lifted his stovepipe hat and plunked it on Emily's head.

"Guess I did," Clint said, gazing lovingly at his future wife and daughter. "We both did. And it's our last and best barter ever."

"I'm going to be a wife," Carsie said with stunned expression. "Me, a wife. I said I would never be. Godawmighty."

Clint wrapped his arms tighter around his new family. "Aha!" Before Carsie could spout a rebuttal, he closed her lips with his own while a cheer from their friends echoed around them.

The Journal of Carson Rose Summers

Christmas 1867

I have been reborn. What few people have known me would not believe this. Sophie was especially stunned. Carson Rose Summers, married to a man who could only have existed in a dream until Clint Bonner came to earth. And to be blessed with a beautiful daughter. Emily is a joy to behold as she grows into young womanhood. She is confident, she is smart. Already she has taught three new children at the home how to read. And she is a willing pupil in the circus arts, learning everything she can from Jake and Harry and from Clint, her father.

All of us who set out in Clint's wagon train so many months ago in St. Joseph, are still here in Virginia City. I've learned how surprising that is. People have died along the way or given up and turned around. But not us, not a one. That shows what we're made of, the men as well as the women.

Jake and Martha have built a cabin together near

Sophie and her husband and son. They seem to have become grandparents to all the children. Harry and Libby have taken in even more children, and Little Harry now has a baby sister, Phoebe Hannah Lola Carson Rose Hardin, who has the fanciest layette in all of Montana, I'll wager. I know she has the proudest godmothers in all the territory.

Hannah and November are as happy as ever. Phoebe and Lola let the new troupe of professional women who'd arrived in Virginia City take over their business. The Good Times Emporium is now a thriving hotel and dining room.

It's all a miracle. But the greatest miracle of all is the one I will share with them at dinner tonight. The doctor has told me that I will have a baby in the spring. That is a true miracle. I thought I would never bear a child.

I feel as if I could embrace the world and let women know it is their right to be the best of themselves with or without marriage. Only they know the best road to take.

And here in Virginia City I have never felt freer in my life.

About the Author

GARDA PARKER has been writing historical and contemporary fiction since 1992. She is a national and regional writers' conference workshop leader and speaker, and continuing education teacher of romance fiction writing. She and her partner, Bob Milner, live in central New York. Her daughter Tamara and son-in-law Chas Plummer made her the proud grandmother of Amelia May in 1994.

JANE KIDDER'S EXCITING
WELLESLEY BROTHERS SERIES

THE FIERY PASSION, EARTHY SENSUALITY, AND THRILLING ADVENTURES OF THE McLOUGHLIN CLAN

Book I, CARESS OF FIRE   (3718, $4.50/$5.50)
by Martha Hix
Lisette Keller wanted out of Texas. The stubborn beauty was willing to work her way north, but first she needed a job. Why not hire on as trail cook with the McLoughlin outfit? To virile rancher Gil McLoughlin, a cattle drive was no place for a lady. Soon, he not only hired her, he also vowed to find out if her lips were as sweet as her cooking . . .

Book II, LONE STAR LOVING   (4029, $4.50/$5.50)
by Martha Hix
The law at her heels, smuggler Charity McLoughlin had enough trouble without getting abducted by a black-haired savage called Hawk. When he fired her passion, were her fortunes looking up or down? But she wouldn't try to get away just yet, even though he would deliver her to a fate worse than death. For one night, she'd surrender to those dark eyes and his every desire . . .

Book III, WILD SIERRA ROGUE   (4256, $4.50/$5.50)
by Martha Hix
Sparks flew when Rafe Delgado teamed with starchy and absolutely desperate Margaret McLoughlin on a rescue mission to save her mother. It irked Margaret, depending on the very rogue who'd wronged the family to lead her to the legendary Copper Canyon of Chihuahua. She condemned the rake's lack of redeeming values, while he meant to take the starch out of her drawers. They didn't count on falling in love . . .

Available wherever paperbacks are sold, or order direct from the Publisher. Send cover price plus 50¢ per copy for mailing and handling to Penguin USA, P.O. Box 999, c/o Dept. 17109, Bergenfield, NJ 07621. Residents of New York and Tennessee must include sales tax. DO NOT SEND CASH.

Taylor-made Romance from Zebra Books

WHISPERED KISSES   (0-8217-3830-5, $4.99/$5.99)
Beautiful Texas heiress Laura Leigh Webster never imagined
that her biggest worry on her African safari would be the handsome Jace Elliot, her tour guide. Laura's guardian, Lord Chad-
wick Hamilton, warns her of Jace's dangerous past; she simply
cannot resist the lure of his strong arms and the passion of his
Whispered Kisses.

KISS OF THE NIGHT WIND   (0-8217-5279-0, $5.99/$6.99)
Carrie Sue Strover thought she was leaving trouble behind her
when she deserted her brother's outlaw gang to live her life as
schoolmarm Carolyn Starns. On her journey, her stagecoach
was attacked and she was rescued by handsome T.J. Rogue. T.J.
plots to have Carrie lead him to her brother's cohorts who mur-
dered his family. T.J., however, soon succumbs to the beautiful
runaway's charms and loving caresses.

FORTUNE'S FLAMES   (0-8217-3825-9, $4.99/$5.99)
Impatient to begin her journey back home to New Orleans,
beautiful Maren James was furious when Captain Hawk delayed
the voyage by searching for stowaways. Impatience gave way
to uncontrollable desire once the handsome captain searched
her cabin. He was looking for illegal passengers; what he found
was wild passion with a woman he knew was unlike all those
he had known before!

PASSIONS WILD AND FREE   (0-8217-5275-8, $5.99/$6.99)
After seeing her family and home destroyed by the cruel and
hateful Epson gang, Randee Hollis swore revenge. She knew
she found the perfect man to help her—gunslinger Marsh
Logan. Not only strong and brave, Marsh had the ebony hair
and light blue eyes to make Randee forget her hate and seek
the love and passion that only he could give her.

*Available wherever paperbacks are sold, or order direct from the
Publisher. Send cover price plus 50¢ per copy for mailing and
handling to Penguin USA, P.O. Box 999, c/o Dept. 17109,
Bergenfield, NJ 07621. Residents of New York and Tennessee
must include sales tax. DO NOT SEND CASH.*

TODAY'S HOTTEST READS
ARE TOMORROW'S SUPERSTARS

VICTORY'S WOMAN   (4484, $4.50)
by Gretchen Genet
Andrew—the carefree soldier who sought glory on the battlefield, and
returned a shattered man . . . Niall—the legandary frontiersman and
a former Shawnee captive, tormented by his past . . . Roger—the trou-
bled youth, who would rise up to claim a shocking legacy . . . and
Clarice—the passionate beauty bound by one man, and hopelessly in
love with another. Set against the backdrop of the American revolution,
three men fight for their heritage—and one woman is destined to
change all their lives forever!

FORBIDDEN   (4488, $4.99)
by Jo Beverley
While fleeing from her brothers, who are attempting to sell her into a
loveless marriage, Serena Riverton accepts a carriage ride from a
stranger—who is the handsomest man she has ever seen. Lord Mid-
dlethorpe, himself, is actually contemplating marriage to a dull daughter of the aristocracy, when he encounters the breathtaking Serena. She
arouses him as no woman ever has. And after a night of thrilling in-
timacy—a forbidden liaison—Serena must choose between a lady's
place and a woman's passion!

WINDS OF DESTINY   (4489, $4.99)
by Victoria Thompson
Becky Tate is a half-breed outcast—branded by her Comanche heritage. Then she meets a rugged stranger who awakens her heart to the
magic and mystery of passion. Hiding a desperate past, Texas Ranger
Clint Masterson has ridden into cattle country to bring peace to a
divided land. But a greater battle rages inside him when he dares to
desire the beautiful Becky!

WILDEST HEART   (4456, $4.99)
by Virginia Brown
Maggie Malone had come to cattle country to forge her future as a
healer. Now she was faced by Devon Conrad, an outlaw wounded body
and soul by his shadowy past . . . whose eyes blazed with fury even
as his burning caress sent her spiraling with desire. They came together
in a Texas town about to explode in sin and scandal. Danger was their
destiny—and there was nothing they wouldn't dare for love!

*Available wherever paperbacks are sold, or order direct from the
Publisher. Send cover price plus 50¢ per copy for mailing and
handling to Penguin USA, P.O. Box 999, c/o Dept. 17109,
Bergenfield, NJ 07621. Residents of New York and Tennessee
must include sales tax. DO NOT SEND CASH.*